The Chanterelle Chronicles

A Myth

5th Edition

By: Sylvain de Ville-Amois

sylvaindevilleamois@gmail.com

The cover art of Volume I is based on an image taken by the author in his backyard.

Hardcover ISBN: 978-1-7751602-0-5

epub ISBN: 978-1-7751602-1-2

Paperback ISBN: 978-1-7751602-2-9

Kindle ISBN: 978-1-7751602-3-6

Table of Contents

One moment, please.

Past

- Oh the Giants.
- In addition to Passillé, Ville-Amois, Lislèle and Ville-Perdue are all on the gift list. The extent of the count's generosity, not to mention the specific choice of villages now under the Abbey's control definitely indicates he has been on to us for some time now.

- Conan has his own special way of getting his message across to those concerned. After 990 years of Judeo-Christian rule, discretion can only go so far. Our ancestors have successfully transgressed the Enochian, Celtic and Roman empires before us. We will succeed to transgress this empire as well. Time and space have always been our most important allies. They are propelling our transgression now as they have done so in the past.
- Should we return to Vinland?

- Yes. But not now. We will have to wait till our modern day instigators have at least begun to domesticate the natives.
- They have barely started to explore. That will take multiple generations!

- If you factor in synchrony and a century or so of on-site preparation, I figure a millennium will suffice.
- Well. We better hunker down. It's going to be a bumpy ride.

- At least the view from atop Mont Saint-Michel is a beautiful one.
- If for nothing else, this will be a May Day to remember.

☥☘CMXXIII☥

- *Maman! Ohh non. Maman! Maman!!*

- shhhhlaaaaAACK.

Victor-Laurent's alpha male demeanor was nowhere near the one stereotypically depicted by the French historians partial to the ideologies of the Arras lawyer Maximilien Robespierre. Ironically at the time, M. Robespierre firmly seated on the far left side of the First French Republic's assembly chamber, would have fit the dandified stereotype far better than would have Victor-Laurent.

Born of a Brythonic father and an Austro-Teutonic mother, Victor-Laurent's head would have stood well over six feet above the soles of his horsemen's boots. Unfortunately, for what used to be Victor-Laurent, his head was now ceremoniously at the bottom of a wicker skull bucket placed just ahead of a falling "National Razor". One which was installed on an elevated stage temporarily built at the center of Renne's public square.

To the delight of the *sans-culottes* and the *Jacobien* peasantry alike, the executioner pulled Victor-Laurent's head by the scruff of his blond beard at placed it on the back of his Teutonic-sized carcass, which in turn was unstrapped from the poplar-beamed stretcher. The duo of body parts were stuffed in a hastily conceived wooden box having the look and finish of a cheap shipping crate. The top of the crate was nailed shut and placed at the rear of the stage for further processing.

Those processing papers accompanying this latest carcass-filled shipping crate revealed the official reason for the presumptive end to Victor-Laurent's adventure on this blue-tinged marble. Dated June 12th, this latest revolutionary lopping was due to Victor-Laurent's classification as an emigrant returning to France from outside the Republic. Taking into consideration the combined realities of his parental legacy, his recent documented stay inside the Realm of the Habsburg Monarchy, his close ties to the Mont Saint-Michel clergy, and his status as the former noble head of Ville-Perdue, the assumption that Victor-Laurent could be an Austrian spy more than satisfied his timely engagement with the guillotine.

An engagement forcibly undertaken one fortnight to the day before the Battle of Fleurus. Bad luck comes in threes... times two!

In hindsight, thirteen hundred fortnights on the marble is not such a bad stint for a former French nobleman in the year of his adoptive Lord 1794.

- *Maman! Ohh non. Maman! Maman!!*

Today the shoreline of *Lac Rond* includes some of the most sought after real estate properties in Upper Chanticleer. Though barely more than a mile in circumference, it is the heart and centerpiece of this small four-season resort community. In the summer of 1912 however, it was still in its pristine natural state, untouched by the axes, saws, and earth movers commanded by a developer's will.

- *Ma... haah...mamaan.*

The lake is a volcanic formation, with no rivers or streams feeding it. The only sources of water are rainfall and a series of springs situated nearly 200 feet underneath the surface.

- *S'il-vous-plait, non...*

The boreal forest that lines the shoreline is populated mainly with maple, birch and poplar trees. After years of having their roots flooded by the spring runoff flowing into the lake from the south facing hill next to the marsh, the pine trees near the marshland on the northwest shore of the lake tend to present themselves as standing dead timber. With no rivers feeding the lake sediment formations are limited, and as such the cutoff between the shallow bottom of the shore and the deeper reaches towards the center of the lake is relatively abrupt. Even on a hot cloudless July day, the noontime sun fails to illuminate the murky bottom of this small but deep liquid body.

- ...

In keeping with a New World theme, Laurent chose to travel light when moving himself and his three companions to the Dominion. This included a thick leather satchel filled with gold coins from the sale of Château de Ville-Amois and its legacy heirlooms. Vestiges from a noble time before the French Revolution. New World inevitably meant New Beginning.

Two large travel trunks were the only pieces of luggage brought over for this transatlantic voyage: one for himself and one for his wife Josée-Anne and his daughter Claudette. The trunks were filled mainly with finely tailored clothing from France, Germany, Switzerland and Norway. Items one would not easily find in Canada a baker's dozen years after the turn of the 20th century.

Items of personal value were kept to a minimum. For Josée-Anne this was a small wooden box filled with gold jewelery, half of which were legged to her from her mother's estate and the other half composed of items given to her by her husband on their wedding anniversary. One item for each year they were married. For Laurent the only item of sentimental value he wished to keep in his possession was a fine gold pocket watch legged to him from his father's estate. The white porcelain face was chipped and cracked but it still kept good time. He would keep it on his person every day. Keeping track of the fleeting moments of time was as important to him as it was to his father.

Their eyes betrayed them.
Okay, and so did their noses.

At first glance, one would admit they made an odd couple. At six feet, six inches tall and 290 pounds, Otto dwarfed his traveling companion. Vincent's comparatively diminutive 62 year old physique was only accentuated by the fact that he was nearly 34 years Otto's elder.

At second glance the duo was just as odd. Vincent was a fervent monarchist and equally fervent anti-Semite. Born of a Jewish mother, Otto was an irreducible Marxist.

Despite their diverging political and social views, several factors defined the two as a minimalist consort, not the least of which was their love of classical music, particularly the works of Richard Wagner.

- Monsieur du Cinqcent?
- Yes?

- Hello Monsieur du Cinqcent. We last met nearly twenty years ago. I was not yet a teenager, so please let me reintroduce myself. My name is Laurent. Laurent de Ville-Amois. I am Edouard's son.
- Oh My! At the risk of sounding like everyone's Aunt Joséphine during a Christmas family gathering... My you have grown!

- May I ask what brings you on this transatlantic voyage? A musical engagement? Or maybe an educational one.
- Actually, a bit of both. Please let me introduce you to Herr Otto Klempner. Otto is a very promising conductor from Germany. He has agreed to accompany me as a guest conductor and stage master for the summertime production of Richard Wagner's Lohengrin in Montreal. The production is being put on by the first graduating class of Marguerite-Bourgeoys College's faculty of music. The rector of the college has invited both of us to help the students in their ambitious endeavor.

- A pleasure to meet you Herr Klempner. Is this your first voyage to Montreal?
- Yes. This is my first voyage to the continent. So this is a bit of an adventure for me. Vincent is a persuasive man and teacher. It was his recommendation to the college's rector that made it possible for me to join Vincent on this trip. I am still not sure who is going to learn more from this operatic production: the students or me!

- And where is this production going to take place Herr Klempner?
- The production and rehearsals will take place in the concert hall of the Windsor Hotel. This is where Vincent's persuasive nature really came into play. I will let him fill in the details!
- Okay, if you insist, Otto. The students are naturally on a tight budget and Otto is on a tight schedule due to a short-lived summertime reprieve from his conducting duties in Barmen. We needed to find a venue that would not only be affordable for the students but also close to the Windsor Hotel, where we will both reside during our stay in Montreal. When I explained our situation to the hotel manager while making our reservations for the summer, it was he who came up with a practical solution for all involved including himself. The manager had yet to book the concert hall for the last three weeks of August. The concert pianist that is presently booked up until the first week of August only rehearses during the afternoon hours leaving the concert hall empty during the morning hours. This will make it possible for Otto and myself to engage in rehearsals and practice sessions with the students every morning until the start of their public presentations at the end of the summer.

- And don't forget your barter, Vincent!
- Oh yes, I almost forgot. As all involved will be present in the Windsor Hotel at noontime, six days a week, I have agreed to perform a series of my own compositions including a piano sonata I have recently completed. A selection of my string quartets will also be performed by some of the students. These concerts will be performed during the lunchtime hour every Monday, Wednesday and Friday up until the run of the opera. The same will be done for a series of Otto's own compositions every Tuesday, Thursday and Saturday. In lieu of remuneration for these lunchtime concerts, the Windsor's management has waived our hotel bill and has graciously offered a late lunch for all the students involved in these concerts.

- You could say you are all singing for your supper. I jest.
- Yes. You could say that Laurent. As a music teacher for nearly twenty years now, I have seen my fair share of college attending and self-taught starving artists. That said, I too am partial to the occasional jest. So feel free to do so. It brings spice to the conversation.

- Life without laughter is like a praline-filled *crêpe Bretonne* without ice cream.
- And blueberries on top!

- Or schnitzel without sauerkraut.
- And a Berliner Lager in a chilled mug!

- Or *rôti-au-jus* without the *jus.*
- And summer harvest baby potatœs with freshly churned butter on top!

Now that our Breton, German, and French explorers had all chimed in on their own version of the traditional laughter-as-food correlation, all three agreed to head out to the main dining room and continue this conversation over lunch and a bottle of jest inducing Bordeaux.

From the port's vantage, Laurent and his small family were greeted by two points of reference. An imposing yellow brick clock tower could be seen east of the ship's dock. To the north, looking more like a dark green giant sleeping in the center of the island rather than an actual mountain, the characteristic outline of Mont Royal dominated the skyline. Despite its tectonic plate smashing origins, this mountain has a smooth low and elongated profile. The result of having been whittled away by millenniums of wind, snow, rain and ice storms ravaging this island in the center of the Saint-Laurence River.

The porter set the tone, having introduced both Laurent and Josée-Anne to Curé Lacloche in English rather than French.

- Welcome to the Dominion, Mr. de Ville-Amois, I hope your trip from Saint-Malo was not strewn with too many unpleasant adventures.
- Thank-you for the kind words, *Curé* Lacloche. And thank-you for the pleasant surprise of greeting us at the Port of Montreal. The voyage across the Atlantic was speckled with several unfortunate encounters with rough seas. Once we reached Tadoussac, the trip was much less adventurous. Though I will admit the view of the New World from the upper deck of the ship was quite spectacular.

- I mentioned to *Mère* Joséphine that your scheduled transatlantic ship would be docking in Rimouski sometime during the last week of June and asked her if she could help you find lodging during your stopover. However my last visit to Rimouski was over six months ago. Was your short stay in this small port of call a pleasant one?
- Yes. We docked for two days in Rimouski, and were graciously housed and generously fed by the nuns of the *Couvent des Urselines. Mère* Joséphine had only kind words to say about you when she unexpectedly

greeted us at the port, and was truly excited to have us as guests. We weren't expecting such a comforting surprise.

- Rimouski is quite beautiful, but it is primarily a shipping port. As such, it can be a little rowdy for a young family newly arrived from Brittany and with a delicate young daughter in tow.
- Not to mention a second child on the way!

- Congratulations to the both of you!
- Though this will be only our second child, we hope to have several more once we settle into our new home in the Dominion.

- Have you decided on a name yet?
- Yes. If it is a girl, Josée-Anne would like to call her Suzanne. And if it's a boy, my preference would be to call him Louis.

- Wonderful choices. May God guide you in your pursuit of an ever growing family.
- Thank-you for the kind thoughts, Monsignor Lacloche.

To make sure all of the de Ville-Amois's essential supplies were purchased before heading out to the small rural village of Chanticleer, where such purchases are more difficult if not impossible to complete, Monsignor Lacloche had reserved a two day stay in the Metropolis for himself and his new European guests.

With only a short stroll to make from the bridge of the transatlantic ship they had just disembarked, Bonsecours Market was the first order of business for these new emigrants to the New World.

With its gray stoned, low profile, oblong box construction and customary Renaissance inspired dome dividing the market into two equal parts, Montreal's principal central market looks like a cross between an oversized rural train station and a Vatican cathedral. This seemingly contradictory architectural amalgamation would be the result of the equally contradictory cultural legacies of the original British architect and Irish-born colleague who penned the subsequent alterations to the market thirteen years after it originally opened.

The similarly domed city hall across the street and the Sulpician Notre-Dame-de-Bon-Secours chapel next door make the market an oddity not totally out-of-place in the immediate vicinity.

Entering from the west side of the market, your sense of smell is the first to be aroused, compliments of a bakery on the north side of this entrance and a local cheese shop to the south. Though food is not on top of their shopping list at this time and place, a quick snack of sourdough baguettes and extra-old cheddar cheese is an excellent way to start the first of several shopping sprees before eventually heading out to the Laurentian mountains.

On this Wednesday morning, the market is packed with local customers and more importantly farmers and regional craftsmen from as far east as Quebec City and as far west as Berlin, Ontario. And it is those craftsmen from Berlin that caught Laurent's eye.

Once in the spring, once in the summer, and once in the fall, several of these Berliners, all Mennonites and each experts in their own domain, fill their hackney coaches with the wares they have made by hand months earlier. They head off on the old colonial roads of Southern Ontario, and make the 700 kilometer journey from Berlin to Montreal. During their week long stay at Bonsecours Market, these men, their wives and at least one each of their children, rent out the central banquet room on the main floor. The wives set up shop on the south wall of the banquet room, and the men do the same on the north wall.

When our quintet of potential customers entered the banquet's main hall, it was instinctively agreed upon to split up according to established gender. *Curé* Lacloche and Laurent would head to the left. Josée-Anne, and Claudette headed to the right. They would all meet again at this same spot by two-thirty in the afternoon, just in time for tea.

Contrary to his father, Laurent chose a commoner to marry and raise a family. As the daughter of a pork farmer, Josée-Anne felt like a kid in a candy store as she walked amongst the stalls and counters displaying the traditional wares made by these Germanic Mennonite farmers.

So as not to return to Berlin with empty coaches at the end of their week long stay in Montreal, these Mennonite entrepreneurs complete two different types of business transactions before setting up shop in the banquet hall. First, they pick up the unique imported goods from Europe and beyond that they cannot find either in Toronto or Montreal. These goods have been ordered and paid for, months earlier, and are sent out from different points of call to make the transatlantic and trans-Caribbean trips to the Port of Montreal, where they are kept in storage, a few blocks away from Bonsecours Market.

These farmers and their wives also make a point of purchasing a selection of the best primary materials offered by the local farmers who are regulars at the Bonsecours Market. As we enter the second week of May, one such primary material is freshly sheared wool from a reputable sheep farmer whose ancestors settled in the Eastern Townships of Quebec at around the same time the Mennonites settled in southwestern Ontario.

Four of the farmer's daughters are seated near the southeast corner of the banquet hall and are busily spinning raw wool. Several balls of this naturally colored artisan yarn was the first purchase Josée-Anne would make that day. The second were a few balls of wool dyed chocolate-brown, and an equal number of dark blue yarn, each dyed a year earlier.

One of the items worn by the majority of the Mennonite women but curiously not offered for sale in any of the displays and tables on the wives' side of the banquet hall, were the multilayer burnt wool and heavy cotton ankle length dresses which have become iconic work wear for the Mennonite and Amish women of the central regions of North America. Warm in the winter and cool in the summer, this virtually indestructible attire makes for a comfortable and practical dress that can be worn throughout the year. Their conservative design and free-flowing drape, make the women who wear them adequately prepared as much for an early morning goat milking, as they would be for a late afternoon tea-break with unexpected neighborly guests.

- Thank-you for your purchase, Madame. May I be so bold as to ask you what you plan on knitting with all the yarn you have just acquired?
- I think I will start by making an over-sized sweater as a Christmas gift for my husband and a pair comfy slippers for myself. I am expecting my second child this winter, so I would like to knit a warm crib blanket in a neutral color. That will be an easy project to complete during the autumn months. This is why I purchased so much yarn that hasn't been wool-dyed.

- Well that is wonderful news! Your adorable little daughter will soon have an excellent companion.
- Thank-you for the kind compliments. Claudette is my first child, and I want her to have a brother or sister as close to her age as possible. It is my turn to be a bit bold. Not only dœs the dress you are wearing look beautiful, but it also looks quite comfortable. Do you offer similar dresses for sale?

- Your question is not so bold. These are traditional Mennonite work dresses. and most of us wear these on a regular basis. We don't sell such dresses at Bonsecours Market because we didn't think them fancy enough for the urban clientèle of Montreal.
- An unfortunate turn of events for us both. I am literally fresh off the boat from Brittany. Our luggage is still on board. Though it may not look like it now, we are moving to a small rural town north of here, so I won't be concerned about being fashion conscious once I settle into my new home.

- Though my great grandparents emigrated from the Old World, I have never had the chance to visit Europe. I hope I will get a chance to visit at least once before I get old. I appreciate your adventurous nature. You are right. If you are starting anew in a rural region of the Dominion, choosing to wear attire like I am wearing now is a smart choice. Let me see what I can do for you. Please be patient. I will be back in a moment.

Claudia exited by the main entrance and headed to her husband's hackney-less coach parked in a lot 100 meters to the east. She unlocked the rear doors of the coach and entered. Moments later she exited with a brand new work dress she had made for herself before heading out to Montreal. Being of about the same size and height as Josée-Anne, she figured this extra dress she brought, in case of emergencies, should fit her potential client. Rolling-up the dress and placing it in a small burlap bag, she quickly locked-up the coach and headed back to the market's entrance.

- My apologies for making you wait so long.
- That's okay. I had a look at the canning supplies with your marketplace neighbor Mary-Jane. She explained to me that many people here use modern canning equipment and have abandoned the traditional European canning supplies years ago. The German-made glass lids, jars and accessories she has for sale here are the same type I am used to using back home in Brittany. Mary-Jane suggested I visit the local canning equipment supplier. He has a kiosk at the far northwest corner of the main marketplace, where I can view this modern equipment. I will then be able to decide if I should purchase the more expensive German supplies or try my luck with the less expensive equipment offered by the local retailer.

- Yes, Mary-Jane Is also my neighbor back in Berlin. Her homestead is just east of mine. Our front doorsteps are less than 300 meters apart. Her husband is a goat farmer but she is the canning guru of the local Mennonite community. When it became next to impossible to acquire traditional European canning supplies, she started her own small business and began importing wide and small mouth canning and juice jars from a specialty glass-blower in Nuremberg.
- We are only staying in Montreal for two days and I can tell that tomorrow will be a busy day for me. I considered the formal attire I chose to wear this morning would be appropriate for my first visit to the Metropolis of Lower Canada. Tomorrow I think I will wear something more comfortable and practical for what will be a long day of shopping and exploration.

- What an excellent segue!

As she spoke, Claudia removed the dress from the burlap bag, to the delight of Josée-Anne's enlightened mien.

- I think I have found just what you are looking for. I too am expecting in the early spring. I recently made myself a new work dress with a more generous waist adjustment for when I begin showing. I brought this dress along for our journey to Montreal, as supplemental attire in case of emergencies. I think this may just be right for you. Come with me, I will show you to the ladies' room.

Keeping the Claudette-filled baby carriage in the experienced and prudish hands of her homestead and marketplace neighbor, Claudia and her Old World client headed to the southwest corner of the banquet hall. When Josée-Anne exited the ladies' room, the transformation was nearly complete. All that was missing was a pair of springtime ready boots with a sensible heel and a calico Amish sunbonnet, and you would have a hard time telling her apart from most any Mennonite woman on a Saturday afternoon outing to Berlin's farmer's market. Of course, her strong French-Breton accent would be a dead giveaway, betraying her real origins.

Conveniently set up in the northwest corner of the hall, the productively mobile Mennonite cobbler was in the process of lasting a pair of work boots. To his right was a display of hand made, man sized boots and to his left, a display of lady sized boots. One beautiful pair caught her eye, constructed with calf length, deerskin uppers and finished with a pig suede lining. The vulcanized sole was made of one uniform piece and was as thick at the tœ as it was at the heel. It was welted to the mid-sole using heavyweight corded thread, insuring the latter would outlast the former. Exactly what she was looking for.

Josée-Anne excused herself and asked the cobbler if her chosen boots were offered in European size 32. The cobbler taking his turn to do the same, headed to the northwest wall of the hall and came back with the same pair of boots in Josée-Anne's desired size. Placing her Polonaise and shawl on the bench next to the display, she proceeded to sit down and try on her new boots. The shœmaker having helped her lace up the 8 holes of each boot, she stood up and took a few steps back and forth along the northern corridor of the hall. She was amazed at how comfy she felt in this sturdy foot gear.

Josée-Anne purchased her new boots on the spot. Seeing that she had no intention of removing her newly acquired footwear, the cobbler graciously offered Josée-Anne an over-sized burlap bag for her discarded attire. He then placed her dress shœs at the bottom, followed by her Polonaise and shawl that were each uncharacteristically rolled up in military fashion and placed inside Josée-Anne's new makeshift duffel bag. He finished sealing the package by rolling up the top flap of the burlap bag onto itself and tied everything up with two equal lengths of waxed twine.

- Though your formal dress is quite beautiful, this attire also suits you very well.
- Um, thank-you...
- ...

Realizing that Claudia's compliment to her client was being pronounced as the former was looking at Josée-Anne's, crepe styled, formal hairdo, a light pink blush began covering her cheeks and forehead.

- Oh my! It's the hairdo, isn't it.

A healthy and honest Mennonite smile ran across Claudia's face as quickly as the blushing appeared on Josée-Anne's face. Removing the half dozen hairpins strategically placed on the top and back of her head, the silky smooth dark brown locks tumbled down her shoulders; the ends settling just above her lower back.

- I will weave it into a pigtail when I have the time.
- Let's get back to my kiosk. I will help you with that.

After thanking Mary-Jane for tending to Claudette and paying for her new work dress, Josée-Anne sat down next to the front counter of Claudia's kiosk and had the latter expertly weave her hair into a perfect pigtail, tied in place with a short length of dark brown leather lacing generously provided by the shœmaker, the latter having had entertainingly witnessed Josée-Anne's unceremonious dismantling of her bourgeois coiffure moments earlier.

Untying her new makeshift duffel bag, she grabbed the yarn she had purchased, placed it on top of her shawl, folded and tied everything in the same way she had been shown by her shœ making teacher and placed the package back underneath Claudette's carriage.

- It is nearly noon. If possible, I would very much appreciate if I could invite both of you to a small lunch as a token of my appreciation for all your help and service since meeting you this morning. There is a *café* next to a cheese shop near the eastern entrance of the main market. If their lunchtime fare is half as good as the cheddar cheese I tasted earlier today, I am sure we should be able to have an excellent bite-to-eat.
- That is truly not necessary, but the Lord dœs say that it is more important to give as it is to receive. For that to work you sometimes have to be on the receiving end! My two daughters will be able to tend to the kiosk for the few extra moments I am away.
- I concur, and graciously accept your invitation. My three daughters are more than able to tend to my little kiosk for the length of a short noontime bite.

What was meant to be a simple noontime chat between three rural farm girls ended up being far more informative than Josée-Anne could have possibly expected. Her knack for asking a few simple questions at the right time combined to her natural inclination for being an excellent listener, made it possible for Josée-Anne to learn a lot about these profoundly spiritual people who have been able to preserve their German legacy and values even several generations after having emigrated to the New World.

More importantly, the parallels between the German Mennonites and the French Trappists' are striking to say the least. Josée-Anne's close ties to the Trappist monks and nuns of her French homeland has made her first encounter with the Mennonites of Upper Canada an unexpectedly pleasant experience. First impressions are always lasting ones.

The same could be said of Laurent's introductory shopping adventure on the north side of the Bonsecours Market's banquet hall.

By the time the lunch hour rolled around, Laurent had nearly filled a two cubic meter poplar wood crate with several of the specialty tools necessary to build his first home on his yet to be acquired acreage in Chanticleer.

From a hand made hickory bucksaw imported from an Amish community in Ohio, to a safe and practical frœ that places your hand above the cutting edge instead of below it, the Mennonites and Amish of North America have been refining and improving traditional woodworking tools originally brought over by their German, Dutch, and Russian ancestors generations ago. If they can't find exactly what they are looking for from their American or European contemporaries, they will build it themselves.

Some tools need no improving and Laurent was able to purchase an excellent crosscut saw, a carpenters' adze and a straight drawknife imported directly from a craftsman in Germany. He was even able to find a practical set of steel gimlets manufactured by the same French manufacturer as those Laurent used back home in Ville-Perdue. And what woodworkers' toolkit be without a fine English made hardwood carvers' mallet.

The last three woodworking tools Laurent bought that morning were from the same British tool maker and were those that took the most space in his shipping crate: a peavey, a two-man timber carrier and an ingenious log jack that doubled as a cant-hook, all made with fine rock maple handles and malleable iron hooks.

- I am new to the Dominion, and as such, I am not accustomed to this new type of canning jars. How exactly do they work?
- The canning lids are in two parts: a metal lid which includes an integral rubber gasket and a hollow metal band that screws the glass jar and locks the metal and rubber lid to the top of the jar. Once the jar has been heated with water or steam, the contents are sealed inside the jar.

- I see. Since the lid is made of metal and not glass, is it reusable?
- Um. No. Both the thin rubber gasket and the metal lid it is bonded to, often begins deteriorating after being opened following the first canning. The rubber gasket will not survive several sterilizations.

- I see. I notice that you have several canning jars on display. You have a choice of several sizes, but all the jars are of the same shape and their construction seems quite delicate. The walls of these glass jars are quite thin. Do yo have jars with thicker walls? And what about different shapes. Do you have jars of a variety of shapes such as those suitable for preserving homemade juices? And what about presentation. Do you have jars that don't have the manufacturer's logo and trademarks boldly and permanently molded on its side?

- Um... No, no, and no.

- I see. Well thank-you for your help and time.
- Um... You are welcome. Good day.
- Yes. Good day.

Knowledge is power. Be it by personal observation or second hand discovery, knowledge may be a means of obtaining power. When obtained surreptitiously, knowledge can also be a means of exerting power.

Time is money. Though no money was exchanged between Josée-Anne and the owner of the local marketplace kitchenware supplier, a surreptitious exchange of knowledge was completed between the two parties. All to Josée-Anne's advantage. As much as a consummated purchase can be a means of exerting power over a customer, an unconsummated purchase can be a means of exerting power over a merchant.

A purchase can be something obtained for a price in fiat currency or its equivalent. When viewed in a temporal context, two purchases were defined and completed during Josée-Anne's most recent exchange. One obtained by avoiding the investment in substandard equipment. The other in the form of an introduction to North American Post-Republican capitalism.

Glancing at her gold, French *Haut-Jura* movement wristwatch, Josée-Anne realized it was already ten-to-two. Time for her rendezvous with Laurent and Monsignor Lacloche.

Once Josée-Anne reached the eastern third of Bonsecours Market, she was able to locate her husband, not by his appearance, but by his laughter. From the top of his wide brimmed, black banded, Sunset-Straw hat, to the heels of his new hand made, dark burgundy, work boots, Laurent's outwardly transformation into a Mennonite pig farmer was as complete as Josée-Anne's. With his freshly purchased midnight blue burnt wool German work trousers of thick weight, held-up by a pair of heavy duty buttoned suspenders in the same color and his nearly as thick, natural white, Swiss cotton, tapered work shirt complementing Laurent's athletic V shaped torso, he looked all the part. Though Josée-Anne was laughing almost as loudly as her husband, she couldn't help but think to herself how much more handsome and attractive Laurent looked in his new, Mennonite inspired work clothes compared to the Sunday Best he was wearing when they debarked from their transatlantic ship earlier that morning.

- At this rate, you are both going to get baptized a second time and will have converted to Protestantism before we reach Chanticleer!
- Agronomy, not apostasy is what I had in mind Monsignor Lacloche!
- I concur. After all I was born a farmer's daughter. And this new clothing is as wonderfully functional as it is comfortable. Now take off your hat, Laurent. We're not outside, on the farm... yet.

Realizing his ethical indiscretion, Laurent smiled, and blushed at the same time, as he removed his hat, and stored it inside his new daysack.

As Josée-Anne gave him a *snog* on the left cheek, his smile grew wider, and the blushing disappeared.

- With a man sized shipping crate's worth of logging and woodworking tools, Laurent is just about set to clear the land for himself and his newly found farmer's wife.
- You are right, *Curé* Lacloche. Though I am not finished getting organized, having met these Mennonite farmers and craftsmen has been an excellent start to my homestead building project. And what about you Josée-Anne, are your new work clothes the only purchase you have made so far today?
- No, not at all. Though I did get sidetracked by the purchase of my new attire, I did purchase some nice wool yarn from Claudia; the lady who not only sold me this dress but also had sewn it herself. By the way Laurent, is there still room inside that shipping crate?

- Yes. It's only about half full.
- It won't be once I'm finished with it.

- Maximilien be damned!
- That's the spirit, Laurent. I'll introduce you to Mary-Jane and Claudia.

Desperately trying to avoid any references to peas and pods and with her now trademark Amish grin, Claudia welcomed Josée-Anne and her consorts.

- You successfully tracked down your better half. You are much more successful at such endeavors than my husband Murphy and I. Whenever we go on a shopping trip to the big city, both of us spend most of the day going about our business alone. Once the time comes for us to meet at a predetermined place, one of the following happens. One of us ends-up lost, someone forgets where the meeting place is, or either one or both of us have lost the track of time. The Lord works in mysterious ways. Like my husband would say, be it good or bad, if something can happen, it will.
- He might be on to something, Claudia. And here are two eventful people that were also meant to be. Please welcome my husband Laurent and Monsignor Lacloche. *Curé* Lacloche is a Sulpician priest who has been guiding us logistically and spiritually ever since we decided to embark on this transatlantic adventure. I don't think we would ever have reached this point without his invaluable help.

- It is a pleasure to meet both of you. No matter what the denomination, and be it big or small, spiritual guidance is always a necessity whenever we take on an important journey.
- Words of wisdom, Claudia. If you have no objections, I will quote you during my next sermon.

Claudia blushed during a moment of bashful acknowledgment.

- And it is a pleasure to meet you too, Mary-Jane.
- Equally so, Mr de Ville-Amois. I had the wonderful opportunity to keep an eye on your daughter Claudette while Josée-Anne and Claudia took a moment to tryout out her new outfit. Claudette is just adorable. So Josée-Anne, did you get a chance to check out the jars?

Mary-Jane's abrupt change of subject and interlocutor, exposed the greed drowning her intentions.

- Yes, I did. It was enlightening. Not to cause prejudice, let me just say I will be purchasing as many jars from you as I can fit in Laurent's shipping crate holding the logging equipment he just acquired.
- Excellent! Thomas is a very good packer. If you still need more supplies for the upcoming harvest season, we all will return to Bonsecours Market on the eve of the summer solstice.

Contrary to the Mennonites' frugal decision to sleep next to their coaches in the makeshift campsite set up behind the market, the Laurentian bound quintet would spend their stay-over in the metropolis inside the rather stately accommodations of the Viger Hotel.

Two factors motivated Monsignor Lacloche to make reservations at the Viger. The first was a practical one with the Viger only a short easterly walk from both the port and Bonsecours Market. The hotel complex also houses CPR's east side train station. Canadian Pacific being the owner of the Laurentian bound rail line between Montreal and Mont-Laurier, the task of hauling the de Ville-Amois's new and old belongings will be a simple question of properly tipping the CPR rail clerks responsible for the heavy lifting.

The second was more historical in nature.

The Plains of Abraham was a theater of war where multitudes of worms were unearthed, processed and lidded. Cans subsequently opened and unleashing generations worth of, at best, failed draconian measures and at worst, good intention paved laxity on the part of the victors. Cans refilled with Hirudinea, lidded and opened once more leeching dogma driven religious, culture driven social, and language driven tribal guerrilla warfare on the part of the Lower Canada losers.

Dogma driven by Greed. Cultures driven by Sex. Dialects driven by Fundamentalism.

Caught in the middle of this interminably lingering war zone, are a litany of corporate upper management executives forced to take redundant business decisions so as to satisfy identical service requirements of the linguistically segregated waring factions who have set-up camp on either side of the north-south buffer zone officially christened St-Laurence Boulevard by the city's topography department.

Canadian Pacific Railway could easily be chosen as the corporate poster child of this redundancy. In 1913, CPR was not only one side of the Canadian railway duopoly, it was also a major real estate developer of this island metropolis. CPR was the creator of Dominion Square to the west and its mirror-imaged Viger Square to the east of the city's principle buffer-zone boulevard, the latter affectionately known by both linguistic factions as the Main.

Two of CPR's real estate holdings to the west of the buffer zone were Dominion Square and Windsor Station. As the centerpiece of Montreal's upper class WASP ghetto, Dominion Square bordered Windsor Street, the main north-south artery on the British side of the island. Windsor Station appropriately bordering the west side of Windsor Street, faced the southern half of the square.

In a feat of irony only the CPR treasurer's barber could explain, the architectural design responsibilities of Windsor Station, which also housed CPR's new corporate headquarters, were handed over to an American. I guess a century of post war cooperation and collusion between the traditional British and fledgling American empires would make it possible to envision the choice of an American architect over the logical choice of a British subject, the latter being more in touch with the tastes of the Windsor Station's loyalist clientèle. In an attempt to counter this irony, Mr. Price chose to drape the station in a Romanesque styled exterior, borrowed from one of his American consorts. Henry Hobson Richardson would approve, and it seems, so did the loyalists. To this day, the Windsor Station is still one of the most beautiful public buildings on the island.

Viger Hotel, on the commercially underdeveloped east side of the main buffer zone, also housed a CPR train terminal, uselessly duplicating the services of the west side Windsor Station, the two located a relatively short coach ride apart from each other.

CPR's treasurer was so pleased with Mr. Price's fourth and successful attempt at designing the Windsor Station that he entrusted the latter with the design of the Viger complex.

Unfortunately for history, train and architecture buffs alike, Mr. Price's response to the daunting task of satisfying the look-at-me tastes of the east side's n*ouveaux-riches* clientèle, resulted in a less-than-enduring centerpiece and anchor for this French, *beau-monde* ghetto.

Mr. Price's decision to garner inspiration for his latest architectural endeavor from a previous Quebec-City creation was hampered by several factors.

His first design obstacle to overcome was the dual nature of Château Viger's vocation, compared to the single minded focus of Quebec City's Château Frontenac.

With the hotel built directly over the train station, the guests of the former are forced to share the same entry and exit points as the general public using the latter. Though the sharing of these public and private spaces may be of interest to the see-and-be-seen portion of this upper class clientèle, the older and more reserved traveler choosing to spend a fortnight at the Viger, will likely find such social accommodations taxing after his first night's stay in Montreal.

The second constraint facing Mr. Price was more economic than social. Due to the inherent redundancy of the Viger Station, this terminal was relegated to being a regional hub serving the Laurentian and eastern north-shore of the Dominion's St-Laurence River. Realizing the relative uselessness of this dual purpose complex, other than a corporate contribution to the segregation of Montreal's two solitudes, CPR's upper management chose to limit the budget envelop of this development project. As a result, Château Viger would inevitably become an underwhelming architectural dwarf, hiding in the virtual shadow of its Quebec City counterpart.

The third constraint of importance Mr. Price had to take into consideration, finds its origin in the timeless concept of location-location-location. Perched atop the natural escarpment on the eastern edge of Quebec City, it is Château Frontenac's location as much as its size and grandiose architectural style that has come to define its skyline. A skyline of historical significance once one acknowledges Quebec City as this British Dominion's original capital city.

In contrast, by placing Château Viger as far south from the foot of Mount Royal and as close as possible to the Port of Montreal as the CPR rail line could permit, the Viger ended-up at the center of what has traditionally been recognized in almost all port cities the world over, as the neighborhood of questionable moral and judicial activity.

Taken as a whole, these design obstacles resulted in a feeble imitation of a Loire Valley château. Using cut rate 20th century construction materials and methods, this multipurpose complex looked impressive from afar, but was far from impressive. The accompanying Viger Square, bordering a glorified train yard, disappointingly tried to look like a French royal garden, replete with imported vegetation and trees totally alien to the natural ecology of the river's shoreline.

If this privately-financed urban development project had been built a hundred years after its original construction date, it would have been better suited as a Vegas-Strip casino parking lot tourist attraction, rather than the neighborhood centerpiece of Montreal's upper-class French elite.

Ironically, had the undefined presence of the original planners' blinded vision been exploited by their unsuspecting late 20th century consorts, the present day Montreal Casino would have been set-up in a recommissioned Viger Hotel and

Station rather than in the former French Pavilion of Expo '67. Facing the epicenter of Montreal's red-light district to the North and the epicenter of the Italian-Canadian-mafia-controlled-heroine-drug-smuggling Port of Montreal to the south, Saint-Antoine Street could have been a northern Vegas Strip rivaling the financial and money laundering success of its Nevada counterpart.

Just think. Céline Dion's principle fan base would just need to take a short stroll down Amherst Street and turn right on Saint-Antoine for a couple of city blocks. And voila! They would be at the doorstep of her casino concert hall extravaganza.

C'est Céline!! performing six days a week only a handful of blocks away from the heart of Montreal's gay ghetto. What a concept!

Okay, I jest and digress. Sometimes plausible truisms can be more enthralling than fiction.

Which brings me back to Monsignor Lacloche's secondary motivation in choosing the east-side Viger over the more upscale and better serviced west side Windsor Hotel.

As one of the Dominion's leading and most influential Roman Catholic missionaries of the early twentieth century, Curé Lacloche was responsible for the near single-handed colonization of this northern gateway between St-Eustache and Ste-Jovite; right down to the founding of the Vatican approved, saintly named, villages following CPR's northbound rail line.

Though his European guests would have left Montreal before the start of Sunday mass, the thought of having them surrounded by Presbyterian, Anglican and vanilla-flavored Protestant churches on the west side of Montreal's demilitarized buffer zone was out of the question. When you're a French, Roman Catholic priest, linguistic politics and religion always takes precedence over comfort, class, and privacy, no matter how noble and reserved your travel worn companions are.

Granted, having their transatlantic and freshly purchased Bonsecours Market belongings a short carriage ride away from the Laurentian bound Viger complex was logistically to their advantage. Being several blocks away from the heart of Montreal's retail and commercial district was not.

The de Ville-Amois's second and final day of shopping in the metropolis would be a long and tedious one.

©©

To shorten the duration of the day's schedule, this Josée-Anne-centric shopping spree was limited to the three major department stores, at the center of the anglophone downtown core; from east to west: Morgan's, Timothy Eaton's and Ogilvy's.

In 1913, Henry Morgan and Company was the oldest department store chain in the Dominion. Though not the first Morgan's to open in the city, the Sainte-Catherine Street location was the most ambitious business endeavor of Henry's storied career. Inspired by the first department store built in the French Republic, his was a smaller but none-the-less modern and innovative interpretation of Paris' Au Bon Marché.

Several of Josée-Anne's before-and-after gestational needs were satisfied following her multilevel stroll through Morgan's vast array of departments. But it was Morgan's impressive selection of sewing fabrics and equipment, that made it possible for her to convince Laurent to invest in their first treadle-activated Singer sewing machine. Yes, *theirs.* Laurent had a knack for sewing much of his own work wear and informal attire. Not to mention an uncanny ability to design, grade and cut his own patterns. A hobby discretely passed on to him by his mother using her first Pfaff sewing machine, legged to him following the gifting of new more expensive model by her husband years earlier.

A bit of assembly would be required, but the machine base, treadle mechanism, and head were all ingeniously packaged inside a crate of manageable size. They would pick-up their new acquisition as they headed back to Château Viger at the end of the day.

Next up. Timothy Eaton's. By now Laurent was beginning to loose patience. Intuitively sensing her husband's temporal discomfort, she gladly accepted Laurent's offer to take Claudette for a mid-morning stroll, both promising to be in front of Eaton's main entrance by one o'clock.

- I will stay with Josée-Anne during your absence.
- Excellent Monsignor Lacloche. I have a lot of village gossip to catch-up on!
- You couldn't have made a better choice of companion for such a conversation. You can both fill me in on the juiciest details when I get back.

...

- Pardon me sir. Would you be kind enough to tell me the quickest way to reach the main entrance of the Windsor Hotel?
- Yes, that's easy. You are nearly there. Go west here on Ste-Catherine's, a couple of blocks till you reach Mansfield Street. Turn left on Mansfield and head three blocks south until you reach Dorchester Boulevard. You will be able to see the Windsor from that corner. Turn right on Dorchester and walk one block west till you reach the northeast corn of Dominion Square. Walk towards the central water fountain, then west towards Windsor Street. The Windsor's main entrance is just across the street, in the center of the Windsor's eastern facade.

- Thank-you for your time and help, sir.
- You are welcome. Oh. And be careful when crossing Windsor Street as you won't be at a main intersection. Those newfangled electric trams are way faster than the horse-drawn ones and they don't stop as quickly. Good Day!

- Good Day!

Bifurcating onto Dominion Square's western pathway, Laurent had just enough time to close his eyes and toss a 10 centimes coin towards the square's center.

By the time he entered the Windsor's rotunda it was precisely 11 o'clock in the morning. Though infused with a heavy Breton accent, Laurent's near-perfect Old World English made it evident to the hotel clerk that he was dealing with a man of proper education and refined origins. With a cursory glance over the lobby's main desk towards Laurent's stroller, complete with an over-sized copy of the Eaton's spring and summer catalog predominantly exposed over a pile of clean cotton diapers underneath the stroller's cradle, the clerk concluded that Laurent's story stood up to the smell test.

Following a short discussion with the hotel manager, the latter gladly escorted Laurent and Claudette to the Windsor's concert hall.

Escorting Laurent to the concert hall was not a question of security but rather of direction. Built in the French Second Empire style, the hotel emulated a four-walled fortress with a series of buildings and extensions in the center, intricately interconnected by a number of hallways, doors and external landscaped pathways.

A sleeping Claudette, with Laurent closely behind, followed the manager back towards the main entrance and turned left on a long northbound hallway. Passing in front of the hotel's own barbershop, haberdasher's shop and chemist's shop to their right and the main entrance to the Windsor's pub to their left, the trio finally reached the end of the hallway before turning left once more, and faced the entrance of the billiards room.

A short walk past the latter and Laurent had reached the main lobby of the concert hall just underneath the organ balcony. Passing the ticket office to the right, Laurent was presented with one last obstacle before reaching his destination. Two sunken plateaus separated each by four extra wide marble stairs. The manager holding the lower front section of Claudette's carriage and Laurent holding the handle bar over his head, the two men gingerly negotiated the two sets of stairs before reaching one final locked doorway. Opening one side of an over-sized redwood French door, the manager graciously offered his guests entrance to the eastern, rear section of the concert hall.

With this east facing door locked behind them, the trio were presented with the rear of a spectacular 30 foot high, oblong box, concert hall, running nearly the whole length of the fortress exterior's north-facing wall. On both sides of the box's length, hung five, equally-spaced, 15 foot high, round top, French windows, running between the organ balcony and the main concert stage.

On this early-summer morning, the sun entering the windows to their right and left was strong enough to render the hall's three massive wrought-iron chandeliers virtually useless. Ceiling ornaments of intricate construction and finish. By the time Laurent had reached the pair of central window panes, he was but sightly startled by the resounding guffaws of Otto's trademark Teutonic laughter.

- You sneaky devil! But I must admit offering to babysit your daughter to escape your downtown department store shopping duties is a win-win proposition for both you and your wife.
- Ha! Your intuitive reasoning abilities are nothing short of amazing, Otto. To be honest, my Machiavellian escape was not as planned as it may first appear. My wife has become accustomed to my last-minute adventurous decisions. It puts a bit of spice in our relationship.

- Your timing is amazing, Laurent! Our rehearsal began at the break of dawn this morning and I have had the privilege of sampling the musical and theatrical abilities of each of these students for the past few hours. It is now the teachers' turn to do the same. Vincent and I have agreed to play each a short excerpt from our own bodies of works.
- Since you had the misfortune of breaking your one and only conductor's baton while transporting your luggage from the ship to the hotel, and I had an equally unfortunate bout of forgetfulness resulting in my trusty metronome still being perched atop my grand piano back home in France, ending our first day of rehearsals on a musical note is the least we can do for all those having to endure our disorganized state of affairs.

- As a consequence, we're giving the students the day off tomorrow so that we both can complete a few last minute errands, as we get properly organized for our first official day of production rehearsals, bright and early on Monday morning. By the way Mr. Ferguson, would you have a suggestion for a good music shop near the Windsor that would be open on Saturday morning?
- It is a bit of a stroll, but the biggest music store I know of is Archibald's Music, about two dozen blocks east of Windsor Street on the corner of Ste-Catherine's and Berri streets. I figure your best strategy would be to head west on Dorchester, then north on Berri to Archibald's as your first destination tomorrow morning, then back west on Ste-Catherine's where you will cross most of the downtown's largest department and specialty stores.

- Thank-you Mr. Ferguson. After ten days on ship, a bit of exercise will do Vincent and me a world of good. But enough chit-chat now. It is time to tickle the ivories!

Comfortably installing themselves next to each other on the front-center row of hardwood chairs, the hotel manager and Laurent were treated to a long-tempo selection of piano pieces masterfully composed and played by Otto on the hall's Steinway. Followed by an equally masterful execution of Vincent's own piano Sonata in E minor, performed by the composer himself.

...

- Oh! Bravo Vincent. That was spectacular. A real treat for my ears and my soul. Your students have found true mentors in both you and Otto. Now you have given Josée-Anne and I reason to come back to Montreal at least twice before the end of the summer. One extended visit to listen to you and Otto in a formal concert and one overnight visit to experience you and your students' production of Lohengrin. Mr. Ferguson, your kind help and understanding has resulted in two new guests for the Windsor. Before leaving I hope to be able to take a few more minutes of your time to make reservations for later this summer.

- Absolutely, Mr. de Ville-Amois. But please, don't forget Claudette. We have four nannies at our service 24 hours a day. They will be more than willing to take proper care of you quiet daughter while you and your wife are out and about during your stay at the Windsor.
- And Fetus makes four, Laurent!

- Yes. You are right, Otto. I keep forgetting. It will be easier to remember when Josée-Anne begins to show. And speaking of Josée-Anne, I must be going. I promised to meet her in front of Timothy Eaton's at one o'clock.
- Don't worry Mr. de Ville-Amois. I will summon the coachman. This will give us time to complete your reservations with time to spare to meet your rendezvous.
- I look forward to seeing you again Laurent.
- I concur! Okay students, it is lunchtime. We all have our own rendezvous with the grand dinning room's waiters.

- And though you are more than welcome to return here with your wife for lunch at the Windsor, may I suggest, for purposes of convenience and time, the ninth floor of Timothy Eaton's. They have one of the most beautiful and elegant dining rooms in Montreal. Their lunchtime menu is excellent. Still one of the best kept secrets in the metropolis.
- That sounds like an excellent idea, Mr. Ferguson. I am sure my wife will agree.

Gingerly placing a blanket-wrapped Claudette on the back seat of the coach, Laurent took out a freshly-minted dollar bill from his wallet and quickly exited the right rear door onto the Catherine's eastbound sidewalk.

- This is for you. Thank-you very much for the prompt and excellent service.
- Oh my! That's not a tip, that's my day's salary. You need not be so generous Master de Ville-Amois.

- I am yet to be officially a client of the Windsor Hotel. It is the least I can do. If you feel generous in return, offer to pay a round of draft to Mr. Ferguson and your immediate colleagues if ever the occasion arises.
- Monday's are staff night at the Windsor's bar and Mr. Ferguson always makes a point of attending. I will make sure to offer the first round of stout in your honor.

- Ah. Stout! My favorite. I hope Timothy Eaton's dinning hall offers Guinness on tap.
- Absolutely and may I suggest their bangers and mash. The best in town. I will help you now with the carriage.

Jumping down from the elevated driver's seat, the unmistakably Irish coachman went directly to the rear of his vehicle and offhandedly removed the oversized baby carriage from the coach's travel trunk compartment. Without even breaking a sweat.

Putting Claudette back in her cradle as carefully as he placed her on the back seat of the coach, Laurent proceeded to give a delicate *snog* on the forehead of his sleeping daughter. Walking east towards University, Laurent crossed Ste-Catherine's and then headed back west towards Eatons's main entrance. Like clockwork, *Curé* Lacloche and Josée-Anne having exited there, moments earlier.

- Well, that was a pretty spectacular return from your morning's last minute adventure. I figure you will have, at the very least, an interesting tale to tell the Monsignor and myself over lunch.
- You are beginning to read me like a book my darling wife! All will be revealed over bangers and mash and a pint of stout. But first we must reenter Timothy Eaton's and head for the ninth floor, where lunch awaits.

...

- May I be so bold to ask what bangers, mash and stout are?
- If you liked the modern day *tourterelle*-less *tourtière* we had for lunch at Bonsecours Market yesterday, you should like bangers and mash. As for stout, it is a bit like Westvleteren 12, a Belgian ale brewed by the Trappist monks of St. Sixtus' Abbey; however, Westvleteren 12 has a much higher alcohol content making stout more suitable as a lunchtime beverage. By the end of the day, I will have made you an honorary Irishman, Monsignor.

- Oh my, not from Ulster, I hope!

♔♕♱

As much as the first two shopping venues catered to Josée-Anne and Laurent's practical, day to day needs, Ogilvy's catered more to their sense of refinement. Specifically Laurent's. Offering local interpretations of European attire, designed and crafted in the sweatshops of Chabanel Avenue's fashion district.

Suits for gents, *tailleurs* for ladies, tweed jackets, polos, sweaters, and dresses amongst other vestments, cut from fabrics thicker and warmer than similar offerings from London and Paris. Suitable attire for both the professorial and student bodies of nearby McGill and Concordia Universities. Clothing too formal for daily use on Josée-Anne and Laurent's homestead, but just right for a rural night out in one of Upper Chanticleer's finer dining establishments.

Speaking of gastronomic nights on the town, Laurent's enlightened outing to the Windsor would induce him to take the one planned for Château Viger in honor of Monsignor Lacloche's patience and help during the last two days, and move it to the grand dining room of the Windsor Hotel. Hopefully including Vincent and Otto as equally honored table mates. The Monsignor's new found appreciation for traditional British fare, would make the transfer of the last of this day's events, from the east to the west side of the buffer zone, an easily convincing one for all concerned.

...

Berri street being one of two axises slicing Viger Square into roughly three equal parts, a quick stroll to Archibald's Music would not be much of an excursion for Laurent, once Cludette, Josée-Anne Monsignor Lacloche, and the day's purchases were dropped off at Château Viger by the coachman hailed as the foursome exited Ogilvy's.

♔♕♱♔♖

- Otto, this is the finest handcrafted conductor's baton they had at Archibald's, and Vincent this is the best German metronome the clerk could find in stock. Please accept these as small tokens of my appreciation, for not only the pleasure of your company these past two days, but also for the privilege of having attended such a beautiful concert given by both of you earlier today.

- Why thank-you Laurent. That's fantastic. But now I won't get my exercise tomorrow. I think there are a few extra secondary items I can purchase at Archi...
- Don't mention it, Vincent! Laurent's generosity will kick in to high gear again and we will no longer have any reason to go shopping. I jest.

- *Touché,* Otto. You have the timing and recollection of a Vaudevillian actor.
- That's why I chose him as a conductor.

- And for you, Monsignor, I saw you eying that cashmere sweater while we were in Ogilvy's, so I had one of the clerks choose one for you, as I was having my new tweed dinner jacket adjusted by the store's tailor. I hope it will fit...
- Oh my. It fits like a glove. Christmas six months early. Thank-you, Laurent.

Copious amounts of Guinness, roast beef, Yorkshire pudding, in-season wild strawberry shortcake and quadruple chocolate almond torte (to satisfy Otto's sweet tooth) ensued, as the linguistic-barriers set-up on both sides of Montreal's two solitudes were temporarily ignored by both the Old and New World guests of the Windsor's grand dining room.

...

- Well, that backfired.
- For who?

- For Antoine and the Vatican.
- Xenophobia can only go so far. Once you extricate your nose from the recesses of your navel and stick the former over the Wall, it starts falling apart.

- The Wall?
- Exactly.

- The Wall started crumbling apart the moment Laurent got off the ship. I don't think he spoke one word of French. At least not in the presence of Antoine.
- And to think that Antoine was counting on Laurent to help put up linguistic barriers inside the significantly protestant confines of Upper Chanticleer. Now he has to deal with his unforeseen penchant for British fare.

- A way to man's heart is through his stomach.
- And an audaciously copious one at that.

- You are such a diplomat.

Consequently, *Curé* Lacloche's newly acquired appreciation for and understanding of the finer things in life on the British side of the Island of Montreal, would have the equally unforeseen effect of accelerating the economic and social fortunes of the small rural villages dotting the mountainous northbound route of *Le Petit Train du Nord.*

It is on this train, that the final stage of our Brythonic immigrants' journey from Château de Ville-Amois was completed, as they departed from Viger Station on Saturday morning.

- With all the purchases you both have made in the last few days, you will undoubtedly have delighted several members of Montreal's retail community!
- I figure I would kill two birds with one stone by purchasing most of the essential supplies we needed for the summer while we were in the big city.

- A wise decision. Speaking of killing birds; are you a hunter Laurent?
- I would hunt pheasant back home in Ville-Perdue.

- I don't think you will find too many pheasants in Chanticleer, but partridge are abundant everywhere in the region. They are smaller than pheasants but their meat is delicious. A real delicacy.
- I very much like cooking wild game. It is more challenging than cooking butcher-prepared meats but the results are often more satisfying. I will have to ask the local women for recipes.
- You shouldn't have any problem doing that, Josée-Anne. The Chanticleer are very friendly people and with your knowledge of French and Breton

cuisine I am sure you will be creating your own variations of traditional local dishes before you know it.

- I smell a cook book in the making, Josée-Anne.
- Now that's an idea Laurent. I hadn't thought of that. You will have to purchase a new rifle before the partridge season begins. I figure it must start in autumn. Is that correct Monsignor?
- Yes, I concur.

- Oh, I just remembered. We will be entering Ste-Thérèse in about twenty minutes. There is a stopover lasting about a half an hour while the train waits for the passengers coming in from Lachute and Hawkesbury. I know of an excellent hunting supplies retailer less than a block away from the train station. If we make a run for it, we should have enough time for you to look at what they have on offer.
- I am a big fan of last minute adventures. I know exactly what I need and I have heard that Winchester is an American manufacturer that's makes an excellent small game rifle. Is that okay with you, Josée-Anne? I promise to make it back before the train leaves the station.
- I am getting used to your spur of the moment decisions. It's one of the things I like the most about your character. Just don't break your promise because that will mean both of you will miss the train home!
- Promise!

Lesage Guns, Rifles and Outdoorsman Supplies was appropriately named, being situated on Lesage Street and as stated by Monsignor Lacloche, only four buildings north of the station.

The nondescript, two story, red brick building was dominated by two large, plate glass display windows flanking the entrance, the latter being embedded six feet into the front of the store. A two piece, French styled, wrought iron, security gate, hinged on both sides of the entrance would open onto the outside face of the building during regular business hours, and would transform the entrance into a locked cubicle during off hours.

Four windows – twice as high as wide and framed in red cedar– were equally spaced across the front facade of the second floor, the latter housing the owner of the store below. Mr Lesage, his Irish physique defying his French Canadian family name, was topped with a tightly cropped, flame red *recon* worn two meters above the heels of his spit shone 10 hole Rangers. His mother's Irish accent only served to accentuate the reality of her having been smitten by the deceiving charm of a *Quebecois* resident.

- Hello their preacher. How are you this fine morning?
- The priest is doing very well this morning! And by the look of your contagious smile, I deduct the same must be true of yourself.

- Absolutely their, preacher. How can I help you?
- Albert, meet Laurent de Ville-Amois. He is a newcomer from Brittany. Mr. de Ville-Amois is moving to Chanticleer and I am accompanying him on the Little Northern Train. As a consequence, he only has a few minutes to shop during the train's stopover in Ste-Thérèse.

- Hello, Laurent! And welcome to the colonies. What purchases are you looking to make this morning?
- Good day, Albert. A pleasure to meet you. I am looking for a small game hunting rifle – preferably a Winchester. A 12 gauge would be nice.

- Single or double barrel?
- I have never hunted partridge before. A double barrel would be preferable.

Albert excused himself, and went to the back store. A few moments later, he came back to the front counter with the most expensive Winchester side-by-side, double barrel, 12 gauge hunting rifle he had in stock.

- There you go Laurent. This model comes with a carry bag of good quality.
- Perfect. Sold. And six cartons of small lead munitions.

Albert removed a carry bag from the display case behind the counter and six boxes of munitions from under the latter. Laurent quickly examined the rifle, carefully placed it in the transport bag, and proceeded to take out his wallet from his left hand back pocket.

- An important sale in less than 10 minutes. It's not a record, but almost. Thank-you, Laurent.
- I promise to return, and have a longer discussion with you when I have more time. Thank-you, Albert.

After the proper salutations, Laurent exited Lesage Guns, Rifles and Outdoorsman Supplies with *Curé* Lacloche in tow. Outside the entrance, Laurent caught the sweet smell of freshly baked bread coming from across the street. He quickly made a b-line for the bakery, and came out five minutes later with a kraft paper bag containing three cherry turnovers (Josée-Anne's favorite), three *mille-feuilles* (his favorite), a carton of whole milk and a half dozen picnic cups and plates.

...

- I see you made your purchase, and you both got back to the train with five minutes to spare. You are getting good at these last minute adventures, Laurent.
- I even had time to bring you some treats from the bakery across the street. Turnovers. Cherry. I hope they are good. Would you like a pastry and some milk, Monsignor?
- I admit I do have a sweet tooth. I will have a *mille-feuilles*, Thank-you.

- No need to show me inside the train, but I am interested in knowing what rifle you bought. Is it made by that American company you mentioned earlier?
- Yes, it's a Winchester double-barrel 12 gauge. The fit and finish are not of the same level as the Schmidt-Rubin rifles I had back home, but it dœs look like a well made, good quality firearm. The Swiss tend to be sticklers for detailed craftsmanship. The Americans tend to favor simplicity.

- An interesting observation, Mr. de Ville-Amois. I tend to agree.
- Now, I am looking forward to partridge season to test and see if simplicity equals reliability. But first I need to purchase some land to hunt on, and more importantly to build a home before the first snowfall which, if I am not mistaken would be around the beginning of November. Is that right?

- That is about right, Laurent. I have seen snow in August, but most of it is gone by morning. As for land, there is a veritable abundance of prime land to acquire in Upper Chanticleer.
- As explained to me by the Vatican emissaries to Brittany, you are an ecclesiastic pioneer of this northern region, and as such your knowledge and understanding of the Laurentian Mountains is undoubtedly unparalleled. I have no doubt that the land you have in mind for us will have been chosen with the best of intentions.

- A statement from man of noble origins such as yourself, is truly a compliment. Your decision to leave your homeland, and build a new life in this uncharted and adventurous land was definitely not taken lightly. Your presence as a new resident is not only appreciated but a privilege. I will admit that I have narrowed down several potential choices to a few ideal locations.
- Please elaborate.

- Chanticleer is delimited by two series of mountains stretching roughly north to south. The river that flows through the valley separating these two mountain chains has been appropriately named *La Rivière du Nord.* To the east of the river, you will find the neighborhood christened Ste-Marguerite Station. To the west, two neighborhoods. Chanticleer Valley is at the foot of these mountains. About halfway up the mountain range to the west of the valley, is a plateau. That plateau forms the neighborhood of Upper Chanticleer. Route 11, the main road that passes through Chanticleer, also links most Laurentian towns from Montreal to Mont-Laurier. Saint-Hyacinthe Street runs east to west and links Route 11 to Upper Chanticleer. It is along this street, on the plateau, that I would suggest you acquire an estate.
- This sounds interesting. As long as the acreage fronts a main road and not a dangerous stretch of water such as a rapids strewn river or a deep lake. I do not want to build my home next to water as I fear for the safety of my children, and do not want them readily accessing a dangerous waterfront.

- Hmm, what a coincidence. I was about to offer you a tract of land that links Saint-Hyacinthe Street to *Lac Rond*, on the plateau. However last summer a tragic event occurred. A young Chanticleer of six years old, Lorette Michauld, bless her soul, is suspected to have drowned in *Lac Rond.* Her clothing and a small knapsack were found on the lake's shore, but Lorette was nowhere to be found.
- I wish to have at least one stretch of land separating my future property to that of the waterfront. Is that possible?

- Absolutely. There is a 140 acre property just west of the one I was offering you. It is on higher ground than the land bordering the lake so there is less chance of flooding during the spring runoff.
- That sounds just right. Sold! I will share the last *mille-feuilles* with you, and toast this real-estate transaction with a cup of milk.

I wouldn't celebrate too much if I were you, Laurent. The *Quebecois* lawyer that owns the land you're planning to purchase, is about to make a ten thousand percent profit off of you.

Even by today's standards, calling the lawyer a shark in the same sentence, would be a redundant expression. No wonder *les Independantistes* north of *le Plateau Mont Royal,* have christened him *un patriot...*

- Excellent idea!
- Cheers!

By now, the quintet had reached Piedmont, and Laurent took a few quiet moments to admire the landscape of his new homeland. The panoramic views offered by the train car's generous accommodations only emphasized the subtle beauty of this weather worn Laurentian mountain range passing in front of his eyes.

Taking out the first of the last few purchases he was able to make before leaving Montreal, Laurent went into the dark confines of the car's loo, and proceeded to put the first exposure plate in his new Voigtländer Bijou 4.5×6 cm *Miniatur-Reflex Kamera* fitted with a standard focal-length Heliar F4.5 lens and integrated Compur shutter. As early 20th century folding plate cameras go, this Bijou deservedly wore its *Miniatur* designation. At least when its bellow and lens were folded back into its film box, the latter which doubled as a sturdy metal carrying case.

Fortunately for him, this last minute purchase was made possible due the convenient location of the L. R. Violo Camera Shop, but a few blocks north of Château Viger on de Maisonneuve Boulevard, not far from the corner of St-André Street which doubles as the eastern border of Viger Square.

Unfortunately for him, the premium he had to pay for the purchase of a new-old-stock camera, originally introduced in Germany five years earlier, made him regret having sold his own example of this particular camera before leaving Brittany.

Alas, the trials and tribulations of choosing to emigrate light.

In 1913, Laurent was was still decades away from the politically correct obligation of calling it a *starter home*. For the time being, the small 1½ story, steeped roof cottage *Curé* Lacloche had reserved for his Brythonic newcomers, would have to suffice. Laurent's ambitions for a larger family would dictate an equally larger homestead be built on the new land he had just acquired.

Three kilometers west of Laurent's Upper Chanticleer acreage, the cottage was conveniently situated on the corner of Saint-Hyacinthe Street and the one fronting the local bakery and the Chanticleer Valley Post Office. Saint-Hyacinthe Street was not only the main link between Chanticleer Valley and the outer reaches of Upper Chanticleer but was also the main link between the latter and the village of Thomson Heights. Acquiring a large parcel of land off one of Chanticleer's main arteries would insure efficient access to the latter's commerce and services while still being adequately isolated from the rural *oi-poloi* of Chanticleer Valley.

Situated in the heart of Chanticleer Valley's commercial district, his freshly acquired, transitional abode was understandably a less than discrete location; forcing Laurent to graciously endure the zealous xenophilia of the local population. *Noblesse oblige.*

Noble origins were one of several common denominators shared by Laurent and Herr Meier. Contrary to Laurent, Herr Meier chose to change his family name when he hastily emigrated to the Dominion five years earlier.

Herr Meier's love of horses and equestrian breeding came from his Prussian upbringing. For reasons of discretion, the breeding of competition class jumping horses was now but a hobby for the Austrian national; a hobby bounded by the realm encompassing his personal satisfaction. His business would focus on raising quality hackneys and in the manufacture of custom utility carriages, the latter being the responsibility of his eldest son Victor-Louis.

- Good Afternoon, Herr Meier. My Name is Laurent de Ville-Amois. I have recently moved myself and my family from Brittany. I am in the preliminary stages of building a home on my new acreage west of *Lac Rond* and will be in need of a Hackney and an accompanying carriage. According to much of the local population I have spoken to, your enterprise comes highly recommended as a turnkey supplier.
- Word of mouth is the best of compliments. But first, please call me Victor-Louis. The enterprise belongs to my father and I am still too young for such formal greetings.

- As I suspect we are about of the same age, I will call you Victor-Louis if you call me Laurent.
- Agreed. How would you like to begin, Laurent, with the hackney or the carriage?

- As the pun gœs, I don't want to place the carriage before the horse. So let's begin with the hackney.
- My expertise is in the design and building of your carriage, so I will introduce you first to my father. I believe he is in the stables.

- Papa! Papa? There is a guest here for you.
- I'm in the back office! I will be right out.

With his trademark, full muttonchops beard, partially hidden behind his beauteously wide mustache and a hairline receding halfway up the top of his skull, Herr Meier was a near spitting image of the Prussian royal monarch Wilhelm I. With a head start of about one and a half generations, his Austro-Hungarian features were nearly identical to those of his facial hair challenged son Victor-Louis.

Combined with his stout yet muscular body, Herr Meier's physical presence exuded an imposing aura, in an I'm-the-boss sort of way. Informal greetings like those agreed upon with Victor Louis were definitely out of the question in this case.

- Papa, please welcome Laurent de Ville-Amois. He and his family have just arrived from Brittany and he is about to build a home not far from *Lac Rond.* He wishes to acquire a hackney and utility carriage.
- Welcome, Monsieur de Ville-Amois. If I am not mistaken Ville-Perdue is a *Lieu-dit* a few kilometers, as the raven flies, from the Mont Saint-Michel Abbey. Have you atrophied your family name?
- You are correct, Herr Meier. I atrophy my last name for reasons of simplicity. My lineage is from the Boullevraye family. My full last name is therefore Boullevraye de Ville-Amois. Have you ever been to Mont Saint-Michel?

- Only once, for a christening. I remember the Abbey's Monsignor mentioning that one of the four villages donated to the Abbey in 990 by Conan II, that is Conan-le-Tort, the Count of Rennes, was named Villam Perdutit, which if I am not mistaken is today a *Lieu-dit* inside the village limits of Saint-Pierre-des-Nids. Unfortunately, I didn't have the time to visit the surrounding area. From what I got to see during my trip to the Abbey, your homeland is quite beautiful.
- Yes. The rural countryside north of Rennes is one of the nicer regions of Brittany. The mountain range that passes through Ville-Perdue is the oldest in Europe making the topography similar to that of the Laurentian mountains, minus the Atlantic Ocean. Such ancient mountains are not as spectacular as the Austrian alps, but they do have their charm.

Herr Meier's photographic memory for details of past events was not left unnoticed by Laurent. At such an early stage of his relationship with the former, he knew by experience that expressing his realization of such a personal aptitude would be unwise to say the least. For the time being, he would keep such an observation to himself.

- I guess choosing Chanticleer as a similar environment to move was an easy decision for you. As you have stated, all that is missing is the ocean.
- Though Saint-Malo is only a few kilometers from Ville-Perdue, I would rarely visit. I tend to fear such waterfront destinations. To this day Saint-Malo still has a reputation for piracy, making it an undesirable port-city to visit for a fortnight. Chanticleer is several days travel to the Atlantic oceanfront. And that suits me fine.

- Yes. I remember being warned of such dangers when frequenting the local population of Saint-Malo. Especially when you are visiting from as far away as I was. I guess such reputations are difficult to overcome.
- The hallmark of an honorable man is trust. The hallmark of a criminal mind is suspicion. If you are an alien, attempting to befriend a local resident of Saint-Malo is like befriending a wild fox. You never know when it will turn on you. Trust me, I speak from experience. So be it. Saint-Malo is now an ocean away. It is now time to start anew, and what better way than by acquiring a new horse and buggy.

- Well you definitely came to the right place for such an endeavor. Let me show you the horses I have to offer you.

Victor-Louis leading the way, both Meiers accompanied Laurent to the western-facing stable doors. The coral on this side of the stable is reserved for hackneys, ponies and donkeys, and forms a rectangle nearly five acres in size. The western fence of the coral is a little over 300 feet in length and the same distance from the eastern shore of *La Rivière du Nord*. As the last of the trio exited the stable doors, a duo of donkeys immediately approached the former and proceeded to introduce themselves to their new guest.

- Eiee-aahh! Eiee-aahh!
- Well. Hello you two. And What are your names?
- The brown one is Albert. The spotted one is Horus. They are the four-legged ambassadors of Meier Breeding and Carriage.

- There is no better gauge of a good breeder than the sociability of the resident asses he raises. You have chosen an excellent duo of ambassadors.
- Thank-you, Mr. de Ville-Amois. That is an original and astute observation. Have you ever raised your own?

- Yes, I raised two stallions, two hackneys and two asses on my small hobby farm back in Ville-Perdue. Of all the animals I had to leave behind when I sold my property, it was the two asses that were the hardest to say good-bye to. The only animals on my farm that had more character than my asses were my four pigs.
- Another interesting observation. Pigs are the most sociable and intelligent animals on a farm in my opinion.

- And also the cleanest, contrary to popular belief. If ever they cover themselves in mud, it is only to protect themselves from the harmful rays of the summertime sun, and whenever they're in their enclosure, all four always did their business in the same corner. Such behavior comes naturally to them. They need no training from us to do so. But alas, pigs, donkeys, chickens, and cattle will have to wait until I build my first home on my new acreage. A hobby farm will come next, after I have completed this first construction project.
- For a project such as the one you are undertaking, a hackney of good stature and strength is best. I have two colts that should be satisfactory for such a purpose. They are both grazing at the far end of the coral, near the river. Come with me. I will present them to you.

To say the two colts were exceptional specimens would be an understatement. Each a near mirror image of the other. Borne of two separate mares, each of near identical genetic lineage, and each inseminated at the same time with the sperm of a common stud. Chestnut in color, with white pasterns and a diamond shaped patch running the length of their faces, from their black forelocks tapering to a point between their nostrils.

Though not yet three years old, nearly six feet separate the tip of their ears and the base of their front hoofs. With a wide and muscular stance, these two colts were both strong and sure-footed.

- These two are an extraordinary pair. Though I was looking for a simple single-horse carriage, this pair is ideal for a hackney coach. If you can build me a modified multipurpose coach with a strong open-air flatbed, I would be interested in acquiring both colts.
- It would be dishonest of me, if I didn't tell you that this was my first intent. Both horses have been raised and trained to be sold as a pair. These two have been purpose bred to pull a hackney coach. It is comforting and important for me to find a client like yourself, that appreciates the work and effort involved in raising a pair of colts for such a purpose.

Victor-Louis interjected:

- I have already begun building the coach for these two horses, but have yet to design and construct the passenger cubicle. I have learned from experience that each client has their own particular needs and demands. Building a flatbed instead of passenger compartment will result in a simple design and make an excellent purpose-built carriage for your construction project.
- So if I am not mistaken, I will end up with the front end of a coach and the rear end of a dray.

- Exactly. I think I will christen my new creation a dray-coach.
- That makes sense, and it sounds better than a coach-dray.

- I agree!

With no barn to call his own yet, Laurent not only bought a new coach and two colts from Meier Breeding and Carriage, but also rented out two stalls in Meier's main stable and a small parking space to the east of the latter. The stable was as far south of his cottage as the latter was from his acreage. Laurent's workday would therefore include two healthy forty minute walks to and from his temporary home.

Visiting their home and place of work on a nearly daily basis, transformed Laurent's business relationship with the Meiers into a mutually respected friendship.

One of the offshoots of this developing friendship, was the generous and accepted offer by Victor-Louis to assist Laurent in clearing his acreage and building his new homestead in exchange for a symbolic and rudimentary remuneration.

There are two explanations for making Victor-Louis' offer a viable reality: one logistical and one pathological in nature.

Logistically speaking, it is important to note that many of the parts going into the assembly of Victor-Louis' coaches are sourced from third-party suppliers, making his contribution to Meier Breeding and Carriage's business model less labor-and-time intensive than his father's.

Pathologically speaking, his ability to help his father in the breeding and raising of his stable of horses is hindered by his allergic reactions to the latter. Though no longer as much a hindrance as it was when he was a younger lad, his presence in the horse stable is limited to half-hour stints. Spending the morning cleaning the stalls is out of the question. Which in turn explains his motivation in pursuing the self-taught career of building carriages, placing himself at a safe distance from the quadrupedal motorization of said carriages.

Ironically, he had no such allergic reaction to the asses. Even the doctors couldn't figure it out. He never did find out why.

Having the opportunity to spend a few hours a day away from the equine-intensive environment of his father's horse farm while still being exposed to a limited number of horses in a safe outdoor setting is just what the doctor ordered to help Victor-Louis develop a natural resistance to the allergens produced by his four-legged companions.

Laurent knew the size and basic outline of the home he wished to build on his newly acquired property. He just wasn't set yet on the style, methods and materials used in its final construction. The extent of a Laurentian winter's wrath would determine the details of such a decision.

He knew he could not depend on the local population for an accurate and objective description of winters past as each would be tinged by the bias of the storyteller's perspective. He would have to live through such a winter himself.

So, first things first; starting with the location of the main homestead's raising: a clearing, at least a half acre in size with adequate drainage, a safe distance from the shores of *Lac Rond* and a relatively short stroll from the shoulder of Saint-Hyacinthe Street, would suffice.

Saint-Hyacinthe Street sliced Laurent's acreage into two unequal parts: three quarters are to the north and one quarter is to the south of the blade's path. With Victor-Louis' knowledge and experience of the local topography, flora, and fauna serving as a guide, together both men scouted the entirety of the property's expanse, before jointly agreeing on the southern quarter as the best location for Laurent's initial construction project.

The first order of business would be to make way for a clearing linking Saint-Hyacinthe Street from the north face of Laurent's new home. The winding pathway, 150 meters from the street's shoulder, would offer a sufficient visual barrier and lesser acoustical barrier between the home's front yard and those newfangled, fire-and-brimstone powered contraptions manufactured by Henry Ford.

- GRRrrrr...
- CLANG, CLANG, KLING, KLING, KLING, CLANG, CLANG, FORT!, HINWEG!, CLANG, CLANG, CLANG, FOOOORT!, HINWEG!
- KLING, KLING, KLING, BARBOTEUSE!, BARBOTEUSE!!, CLANG, CLANG, CLANG, CLANG...

- Ouuaaaa... Ouuaaaa...

- Vaaaat?... *Barboteuse*?
- Screaming, "GO AWAY" in French is far less aggressively forthcoming than when it is screamed in German. I would sound like a spoiled child whining about his porridge that's too cold. Under the circumstances, *Barboteuse* was the best I could come up with as an alternative. We were successful.

- You are right about that. And you are very good at tin cup clanging. A real team effort! That was definitely an adult. At least two years old. Probably a female, but I am not sure. If so, there is a good chance her offspring are nearby. I figure it is best to keep a watchful eye for a little while.
- Back in Brittany, the biggest wild animal I crossed in my back yard is a fox. Nothing this big.

- If you think bears are big, wait till you start spotting moose: less dangerous; three times the size. It is impressive to watch them negotiate thick underbrush. Moose are very elegant beasts despite their size. In the Austrian Alps, the closest related species is the mountain goat. Mountain goats are a hoot to watch cross even the most treacherous of mountain passes. That is one beast which has no concept of the term vertigo!
- I will have to purchase a telephoto lens when I return to Montreal later this summer and a close-up filter lens for the wonderful wild plants and flowers I have observed in the forest In a way, the flora is as impressive as the fauna.

- Often, both are edible! Though I enjoy small game hunting in the autumn and fishing during the summer, backyard foraging is probably the most satisfying of all my pastimes I have undertaken since emigrating to the Dominion.
- Adapting your wild harvest to traditional Austrian fare must be quite a creative challenge.

- That is where my mother comes in. She is a very good cook and was responsible for getting me hooked on foraging as well. She is also a very good teacher. The only thing more fun than discovering a new plant to eat, is learning new ways of eating it.
- I too enjoy foraging, but it is not my mother that got me interested. It was the pigs back home on my hobby farm. One in particular was a true character. I named him Henry. He became a quadrupedal friend. We would both go out hunting for truffles, but it was not only truffles that Henry discovered as delicacies to sample. If it is good for a pig, it is probably good for a human. I made a point of trying out all the species he had previously eaten. Some were not all that tasty, but I never got sick. Many of the plants, flowers and fungi Henry taught me to eat, ended up as the most delicious additions to my favorite dishes. The process of preparation is often one of trial and error, but after a while you get the hang of it.

- You speak of Henry in the past tense. Did you end up eating him too?
- Yes, but only after he had died of natural causes!

With the help of Victor-Louis' skillful and strong hands and Laurent's stubborn and patient perseverance, both men were able to clear an initial pathway to the base of the projected foundation where Laurent's first structure would lay. The first stage of this project included the removal of the underbrush and the felling, quartering, and stacking of timber for use once the latter had dried.

This first step took just under three week's time to complete.

The second would have taken much longer than the first had it not been for one of Victor-Louis' numerous creative sparks of Germanic innovative thinking.

With Laurent's insistence on keeping all the mature maple trees in preparation for his first sugaring season in the Dominion and his desire to preserve as many cedar and pine trees for reasons of four-season privacy, the pathway's final trajectory was decided as much by nature as it was by the human interventions of grading, drainage, and surfacing. This meant that the remaining species slated for felling were principally limited to poplar and birch.

As Murphy would dictate, these species are precisely the ones that tend to aggregate into closely intertwined clumps of competing, widowhood instigating, birch and poplar trees. The overbearingly invasive nature of these species make the resultant groupings far larger and challenging to fell, and the remaining stumps even more of a challenge to remove. It is the daunting task of removing these over-sized, deep-rooted tree stumps in an effective and timely manner, without disturbing the far-reaching root systems of the neighboring sugar maples, that got Victor-Louis thinking of a horse-drawn, cart-based solution to the problem at hand.

His eureka moment came after finishing the final assembly of a one-horse trap and a two-horse dray in the same afternoon, two weeks after having started to help Laurent clear the latter's prospective front yard pathway.

A dray is definitely too big: too many wheels. A trap is too small: too few wheels. Building the front-end half of a dray and placing one trap wheel, four feet to the rear and centered between the two dray wheels should keep everything balanced, compact, with little chance of the puller toppling over while the two horses are applying the forward thrust to the triple-bladed grape hœ mechanism digging underneath the tree stump to be removed.

Hinging the other end of the puller just rear of the three-wheeled dray's center of gravity and just over the row of five equally spaced half furrow shovels welded to the undercarriage of the modified dray, should assure that the latter progressively stays in place as the tree stump gets progressively extricated upwards and forward.

...

- Done! Sort of. Now the hard part begins. I guess we better call it a morning and start again bright and early tomorrow. We better sharpen our pickaxes. Even the strongest of hackneys will have a hard go of removing the larger clumps of tree stumps even if we cut all the roots on the periphery beforehand. I have no intention of making life difficult for either of the horses. They are as much four-legged companions as they are working partners. They are so well-behaved and have been so well-raised by your father that I would not have the heart to force them into becoming beasts of burden.
- I had a Eureka moment. I have been working on it every day for two weeks now. I just finished yesterday.

- Hm... What is it?
- It is a surprise; I hope a pleasant one. If it works, neither horse will have a hard time of even the biggest of tree stumps. However, if it is okay with you, we will have to do two trips to the work site. One regular trip for our gear, and one for the surprise. Everything should fit on the rear deck of your dray-coach.

- Now you really have me intrigued. I won't sleep a wink tonight.
- You need not worry, but if I say anymore, it will no longer be a surprise!

- Okay. okay. I'm not a lawyer. Cross-examination should only be conducted by imbeciles.
- I agree on both counts! Now that I have teased you like this, the least I can do is pay you lunch. Dœs Hymir's Cauldron sound okay?

- Mm... Sheppard's pie. The best of comfort foods. It will help me sleep. At least I'll get a nap during the afternoon.
- Lets pack up. I'm hungry!

The duo rounded up their gear onto the rear deck of Laurent's dray-coach. Seeing their companions were preparing to leave, the two hackneys headed towards the front of the dray-coach where Laurent and Victor-Louis proceeded to reattach the vehicle to the respective harnesses of each horse.

Once the foursome had reached the corner of Saint-Hyacinthe and Route 11, they turned right on the latter and traveled less than a block before reaching a hardened dirt parking lot where stood a sturdily built pinewood shack, a field stone chimney rising noticeably and functionally high above its center. The shack had but one wall in the shape of a circle. It had the look of a Mongolian yurt where the leather hides used to cover the roof were replaced with a thick layer of lush green sod. Atop the roof, a billy goat and his female companion were tending to the roof's dual function.

Hymir would be proud.

Contrary to what Laurent had predicted, it was not he who had a restless night but rather Victor-Louis; both men filling their thoughts with anticipation.

On the one hand, Victor-Louis' night was filled with what ifs. What if the there weren't enough furrow shovels to hold the dray-trap in place while the horses pulled on the unforgiving tree stump. What if the grape hœ blades were not long enough to properly reach underneath the stump as it was being pulled out and forward from its original resting place. What if the horses pull too much to one side, breaking the multiple grape-hœ main shaft at its pivot point, toppling over the horses in a horizontal plane, circular trajectory, while the hœ shaft is thrust in the opposite direction. Yikes, what a mess.

On the other, Laurent's night was filled with nostalgic dreams of Yuletides past where he would await the unwrapping of gifted surprises on the fifth morning following the winter solstice.

...

- Yesterday, I had a dream of the childhood gifts I hoped to receive during Yule's celebrations. Tree stump remover wasn't on my wish list. Today, I can say without hesitation, I have long entered adulthood. Giving me the opportunity to try out your new prototype is the absolute, number one most desired gift I could have ever hoped for when you told me you had a surprise for me this morning.
- My night was filled with sleepless nightmares of what might go wrong. As you will be the first to try my new dray-trap, we will both have to be extra careful for not only our safety but also that of the horses.

- May I suggest, at least to begin with, that we proceed slowly. If I base myself on experience, we should not let arrogance take over our actions after the first tree stump is successfully removed.
- You are wise beyond your years, Laurent! I promise to proceed as you have suggested until all tree stumps are removed from your new property.

You got to give Victor-Louis credit. More than a century before the advent of proprietary mainframe powered, finite element analysis software and three-quarters of a century before the introduction of Linux based, open source alternatives, Victor-Louis' estimation of this dray-trap's center of gravity, the grape-hœ's lever-arm torque and the latter's cam movement under load were just about right on the money.

Having chosen for the prototype's first task, a birch and poplar tree stump clump somewhere near the median between the worst case scenario and the smallest tree stump to clear, both men severed the main roots around the surface of the stump while digging a trench having a depth of no more than two feet.

With Laurent at the helm and Victor-Louis a safe but observant distance behind the grape hœs' initial position, Laurent proceeded to slowly and kindly direct his two hackneys. Gradually, the duo thrust forward in a controlled and synchronized fashion. With the furrow shovels progressively tunneling into the ground with near linear momentum, 45 degrees off quilter to the ground surface plane, the three grape hœs slowly wrapped themselves around the underbelly of the tree stump in, at first, a rotational motion that progressively transferred to a primarily reward linear thrust once all the grape hœ blades were parallel to the horses' trajectory.

The hœ blades reaching, once again, the front periphery of the trench, the former dug into the latter forcing the grape hœ cam mechanism to rotate in reverse and releasing the newly extricated tree stump clump at the same time as the furrow shovels removed themselves from the soil's embrace.

- Victor-Louis, you were supposed to tell me when to stop. It's okay, the horses and I figured it out once they both began to lurch forward a bit. Victor-Louis?... If you don't lift your jaw up a bit, you are going drop it on the ground, and you will end up swallowing the flies around the underbrush. Victor-Louis?
- *Entschuldigen Sie, Bitte...* I don't believe it... Neither will he. He was convinced it wouldn't work. I should have had a camera. He won't believe me when I tell him it worked on the first try. I don't believe it.

- Don't move. I will get my camera. It's in my daysack. I'll be back in a moment...

A Kodak moment.

Removing the second of the last purchases he made before leaving Montreal, Laurent retrieved a still unused Brownie from the daysack he had placed inside the storage compartment underneath the dray-coach's driver seat. Though the image quality and size of the photographs captured by the Brownie would be far inferior to those obtained with his Bijou, the convenience of not having to change plates after each exposure would make it possible for him to take a series of several photos in a relatively short span of time.

His first picture was from the perspective of the dray-coach's rear deck. Having yet to install a culvert between the street and the pathway, Laurent was forced to park the dray-coach at about the same place the entrance to Laurent's driveway would eventually be on the street's eastbound shoulder. Standing up on the deck, he was able to capture not only Victor-Louis' backside but also the freshly removed tree stump, the gaping hole left by said tree stump, the dray-trap and the two hackneys, the latter being the furthest away from the photographer's point of reference.

Jumping off the dray-coach, Laurent proceeded to take four more shots. One side view spanning from Victor-Louis to the noses of the two horses, one detailed shot of the stump and its hole, and finally, two shots sitting atop the croup and facing the dock of the most obliging of his two hackneys. Zone focusing and placing the camera next to his stomach so as to steady the former, he was able to catch the details of Victor-Louis' facial expression which had recently morphed from an astonishment filled dropped jaw to what was now a grin filled with accomplishment and joy.

- Now who's not going to believe you?
- My father. When I showed him the finished prototype, he thought I had lost my senses. I think he was convinced I was possessed by a demon of sorts!

- A demon of creativity?
- Or mischief!

As both teams of horses and men got accustomed to working with Victor-Louis' prototype, all became better aware of the potential and limitations of his newly designed tool.

Once the sun had reached its highest point over the horizon, they confidently chose to accelerate the stump removal process by reducing the number of roots to sever to only the largest and most unyielding of those around each of the remaining tree stumps blocking Laurent's future driveway.

As the bipedal duo grew ever more enthused by the progression of the task at hand, their enthusiasm seemed to have rubbed off on their quadrupedal counterparts. You could almost say that for the horses, their participation in this team effort had become a form of sporting challenge rather than an actual chore. As a result, Laurent's coaxing would be limited to the realms of direction and timing.

- It's past noon, Victor-Louis. You have your carriage building work to get back to.
- Oh, please no. My other obligations can be placed on the back-burner for today. Let's give the horses a rest from pulling the dray-coach, and bareback to the Chanterelle for lunch. My treat. It's only a short trot away. My allergies should be able to handle it on a beautiful day like today. I would really appreciate if we could continue this afternoon, and clear a few more tree stumps as long as the horses don't get too tired.

Compared to the massive blight on the Laurentian landscape it has unfortunately morphed into today, in 1913, the Chanterelle Hotel was a far less imposing and intimidating site. Its original Y-shaped, oblong box construction was built halfway up the same hill shared by *Lac Rond* to the south, and the northern half of Laurent's property to the west. Volcanic stones of different shapes and sizes, salvaged from the surrounding Laurentian Highlands, were used to clad the hand-sown beam skeleton of the structure. The rustic, château style architecture of this young building infused a sense of strength and timeless durability that insured the original construction would age gracefully even a hundred years after the laying of its initial foundations.

Having yet to clear a hiking path from Saint-Hyacinthe Street to the border of the Chanterelle's estate, a detour to the latter's dining room was in order. Following the village's main roads bordering the lake, both men and horses reached the hotel's main entrance in less than half an hour.

Though far less formal in its interior design and dress code than that of the Windsor's main dining room, the Chanterelle's hall was none-the-less several notches above what could be expected from an *oi-poloi* frequented establishment such as Hymir's Cauldron. Covered in mud, dirt, and wood chips, and smelling like a cross between a horse stable and a drainage ditch, neither man was prepared for a luncheon where several courses would be served on fine English china using Sunday-best silverware.

As a relatively unknown newcomer to the village, Laurent was obliged to rely on the well established reputation and status of the Meier family, to gain unfettered access to a lake-front table for two, courtesy of an obliging and understanding head waiter that doubled for one of Victor-Louis' good friends.

- Yes or No?!
- Yes. I win. You lose!
- Hmm. I'm a little confused. Could someone be kind enough to elaborate?

- Please accept my apologies, Monsieur de Ville-Amois. I can only deduct by Victor-Louis' smile, that not only did I lose my bet with him, but he has yet to explain to you that I am very good friend of his. Let me introduce myself. My name is Nari Stevenson, and I am the grand dining room's head waiter at the Chanterelle Hotel. Though this is the first time that we meet, it is though I have known you for some time now. Victor-Louis has had only good things to say about you.
- I too must apologize, Laurent. I have been so overwhelmed by having succeeded in my challenge to design and build a functioning tree stump removing dray-trap, I have omitted to explain the details of the bet I have undertaken with my friend Nari. To be fair, the omission was a bit intentional. As for the bet, it is more of an incentive to succeed in completing this latest challenge rather than any diversion of opinion resulting in the undertaking of a traditional bet.

- Oh Please, Victor-Louis, your omission being a bit intentional is like a woman being a bit pregnant.
- Pregnancy and intentional omissions are like syphilis infections: the longer you try to hide from them, the worst they get.
- That's the most convoluted apology I have ever received from two people at the same time: a bit icky but enlightening none-the-less.

- Yikes. We're definitely going to get along. You see, Laurent, I am even more convinced than Victor-Louis in the eventual success of his latest challenge. So it is I who initiated this so called bet. Simply put, I have agreed to reserve a table in the main dining room every day Victor-Louis would test a new version of his dray-trap. If the prototype is successful, I lose and will not only personally waiter your table but will also pick up the tab for both of you. If I win and the current prototype dœsn't work,

Laurent picks up the tab for lunch at Hymir's Cauldron while finding a creative way of convincing you to accept the invitation. He agrees to continue the challenge until a functioning prototype is completed and successfully tested.

- So, if I understand correctly, you initiated a bet that would only end when you lose!

- Exactly! I lose. Victor-Louis wins, and so do you. Now, I better get to work. I will show you to your table.

Though all three men were about the same age, only Laurent sported a gold band on his ring finger, placing the remaining two comfortably in the realm of established bachelorhood. Though a Parisian would call them *Vieux Garçons*, neither of the two could be called old maids. Their positive outlook to life and to the obstacles presented to them during their passage through the same negated any possibility to refer to them in such a derogatory fashion.

The resultant noontime feast, consisting of an irresistible onslaught of course after course of French and German fare only served to emphasize how seriously the losing party of this bet was determined to fulfill his debt obligations, and how happy and joyful he was to do so. If not for his penchant for low alcoholic content, German lager, Victor-Louis would have never been able to get back on his horse to finish the day's newly scheduled work, and neither would have Laurent.

By the time the two had wobbled out the hotel's main entrance, it became clear to both men that they weren't the only ones to have been pampered in the last two hours.

- What happened to the horses?
- You don't think I would feed both of you while neglecting your two most important companions, did you? Follow me. They are just up the way in the stables.

- The hackneys are quite friendly and accommodating but not that accommodating. How did you get to have them follow you all the way into the hotel stables?
- That's how I first met Victor-Louis. When I was a younger man, his father offered me a job as a stable hand. I worked there, four days a week, until last year, when I was promoted to head waiter, and where my part-time job at the hotel became a full time job. And that's why your horses are well accustomed to my pampering them. I helped raise them since they were newborn colts.

- And that must be why you were always out of breath every time you came to serve us another course during lunch.
- Exactly! It's the uphill dash to the stables that is hard on the metabolism. I did get to feed them, clean the mud off their shanks, and brush their manes. Edward, the stable hand, took care of the rest.

- Now I know why they are so well behaved. In less than two hours you have given me three reasons to be grateful, Nari. The food, the horses, and their raising.
- You need not feel obliged, Laurent. If it wasn't your willingness to let Victor-Louis test his new prototype, he wouldn't have been able to demonstrate its worthiness. Trust is the hallmark of a noble man.
- And Laurent even took pictures to prove it!
- Now that I am looking forward to see.

By the time the sun had reached its supper time position in the sky, the four stump removing workers had pulled all the overgrown vegetative obstacles along Laurent's initial pathway. One month ahead of schedule.

...

- Eiee-aahh! Eiee-aahh!
- I know. I know, Horus. I was gone all day and I didn't give you any warning. I apologize cuddle-kins.
- And I was worried about you too. I was sure your diabolical contraption had gotten the better of both of you.

- You need not worry, Papa. My "contraption" was a success. We completed a month's worth of work in one day.
- You have to see this Herr Meier. The hackneys are tired and it is time for them to rest. So I invite you to visit my property tomorrow morning. The results of this day's work are simply amazing.
- Your horses are not the only ones that looked tired. My wife and I have already had supper, but there is more than enough leftover for both of you. Please, come inside, wash up and have a bite to eat. I will set up my coach and we can all go and witness your day's accomplishment before the sun sets.

- Agreed! You are more than kind Herr Meier.
- Agreed! Thank-you, Papa.

Having visited Laurent's property a few days before the pathway had begun being cleared, and now eying the huge mound of discarded tree stumps nearby, Herr Meier quickly realized that a significant amount of work had been completed in a relatively short span of time. His stubborn determination to prove his son wrong became blatantly clear to Laurent's ears, as he and more importantly Victor-Louis, suffered through Herr Meier's token, and comically terse, congratulatory comments. The pathway clearing duo sustained less damage to their eyes as they observed the older man's body language and facial expressions betray his true sense of amazement.

Sometimes, little truths are the most cherished and enduring.

The remainder of the week was spent building a traditional Roman style culvert spanning the ditch between Saint-Hyacinthe Street and the start of Laurent's pathway. Now with a more efficient access to the property, the following week's task of grading the pathway was, though labor intensive, a simpler one to complete.

One month after having received title to his acreage, and having finished clearing and grading his initial work site, Laurent was ready to prepare the footing of his new home. Three months ahead of schedule.

- Now what?
- I haven't decided yet if I want to build a timber frame, a *pièce-sur-pièce*, or a traditional Scandinavian compression saddle-notch and scribed Log home. I was hoping to live through my first Laurentian winter before making a decision. The type of foundation and the species of trees that will be felled during the wintertime will depend on my final choice. I hadn't factored in the possibility of being so ahead of schedule.

- Another serving of *pâté chinois* M. de Ville-Amois?
- Yes please, Lorette. And what about you Victor-Louis?

- Yes, please... this shepherds' pie is as good as the one Nari makes. That's no mean feat, but don't tell him that. I think I may be able to help you make a decision, but first you will have to visit Nari's newly built home. Let me explain. As you have more than likely deducted by his family name, his physique, and his accent, Nari is of Swedish descent. How he got to learn to bake a really good traditional Irish shepherd's pie will take me the better part of week to explain! But I digress. Nari's father is a construction worker. He helped to build Montreal's Windsor Hotel. It was built nearly entirely using a new construction material called reinforced concrete. Have you heard about this new method?

- No. But I have visited the Windsor. It is an impressive building. Inside and out. Please, continue.

- Fantastic. Since, you have been inside I deduct you have been in the main lobby. But did you visit the concert hall?
- Yes. In its own way, it is almost as nice as the interior of the Vienna Opera house and the acoustics are better. But what dœs this have to do with Nari's new home? ...Thank-you, Lorette.

- I concur ... Thanks Lorette... Where was I. Oh, yes. Nari's new home. Though they vary in intensity, Laurentian winters can get pretty cold. At least as cold as those he recalled, during his early childhood years, back home in Sweden. For that reason, and for sentimental ones as well, he chose to build a Scandinavian log home instead of a more conventional French Canadian styled timber frame home. With the help of his father and the latter's workmates, Nari was ready to start building the foundation of his new home well before the summer solstice. He faced however a twofold dilemma. Not only did he have to wait till the sap ran dry in the trees he was going to fell for construction logs, he was starting to feel the pinch of an ever-expanding construction budget. The services rendered by his father's workmates were inexpensive but not free. Another year of rent for the home he was living in next to the Chanterelle, did nothing to help his financial situation.
- So, what did he do?

- He killed two birds with one stone. Following his father's advice and newfound knowledge of reinforced concrete construction methods, Nari built a basement with reinforced concrete walls, a concrete slab basement floor, and a reinforced concrete ceiling aka first floor, that would be able to double as a flat roof during his first year in his basement level, concrete home. He was not only able to save a year's rent, but he could now build his log home on an extended schedule. Even if that meant finishing the construction in two to three years instead of one. And that's exactly what he did. He took one season to close the house and another two to cut out and finish the openings, and to complete the interior.
- What a smart, ingenious, and frugal solution. All at the same time. Sold!

- That was easy!
- Now I just have to convince my wife to live in a basement for a year. Or two. Or three. I am sure I can convince her during the first year. I'm not too sure about the other two. However, I don't think I have the same

financial concerns that Nari faced while building his first home. Building a log home means I am going to have to find more people to help out with the construction.

- You just did. You convince your wife, and I'll convince Nari. As the head waiter of a major hotel, his days off are Tuesdays and Wednesdays. That means we can prepare ourselves on Mondays, get the heavy lifting done on Tuesdays and Wednesdays, and finish what we started on Thursdays, Fridays, and Saturdays if necessary.
- I have an idea. First off, are you a fan of classical music?

- I'm a big fan of baroque, less of opera.
- That's what I figured. Baroque is widely acclaimed and appreciated. My father warned me that opera is an acquired taste, that I would come to better enjoy with age. Though I am yet to be considered an old man, my burgeoning enthusiasm for opera can only be explained by my mother's gentle coaching. My wife and I have planed to attend a couple of relatively short, lunchtime concerts by two composers we had the opportunity to meet during our most recent transatlantic trip. As a thank-you for Nari's delicious lunch and care of my horses, I was hoping to invite both of you as well. If we take the last train on a Monday, we will have reached the Windsor just before 3 o'clock on Tuesday morning. We can attend the concert after brunch. Following Wednesday's concert, we'll head back to Chanticleer on the evening train. This would give all concerned nearly two days to do other activities of their choice before heading back home. This will also place both of us in the proper social environment to better convince Josée-Anne and Nari of your inspired housing and construction plans.

- Sold! A two day holiday at the Windsor, courtesy of your generosity definitely is an offer I can't refuse. And I am sure Nari will come to the same conclusion. I can't wait to tell him!
- Fantastic. Now let's finish this *pâté chinois* before it gets cold.

With his work week finishing at 11:00 pm and the last Monday night train leaving for Montreal at 11:30 pm, the only way Nari was going to get to the station on time was by swapping his not-so-Influential corporate position at the hotel in favor of leveraging his team spirit demeanor and intrinsic love of horses.

Having kept his promise to clean out the stables on the prior Friday, and Saturday mornings, in return, so did Edward.

Like clockwork, and with Nari's luggage already neatly set on the rear bench, Edward had barely reined in his two horses, when his coworker-client burst out from the main entrance, and entered the rear cabin of the hotel's coach. Uncharacteristically donning his carriage driver's uniform and heading out to greet the last southbound milk run train on a night when the chances of picking-up or dropping-off an authentic hotel client are next to nil, were two reasons for Nari completing two mornings worth of Edward's early-dawn chores.

Taking a back-road shortcut towards the Hills 40/80's side-street, down and around Rolland Street which melded into Archambault, the duo turned left at the end of the latter to eventually reach Chanticleer's main intersection in record time.

Nari had reached the entrance to the train station's parking lot with five minutes to spare. With his luggage in hand, he thanked Edward for honoring his side of the oath they had taken a week earlier. Crossing the main entrance, Nari headed inside the train station where Laurent, Victor-Louis, Josée-Anne, and Claudette were waiting for him.

At the turn of the 20th century the transnational, poster child of the Canadian Dream was naturally its newly built coast-to-coast rail network. A century later that dream had morphed into a nightmare. And its poster child had starved itself into an anorexic white elephant.

In the summer of 1913, the privately-held half of this national rail network was anything but a white elephant. And even less so, a starving one. Fortunately for a hungry and tired Nari, he had boarded a rail car where he knew the level of service and dining would be a notch above the norm. Not wanting to take too much advantage of Laurent's generosity, he gratefully accepted the latter's offer to join him for a late night snack and a pint of stout, the other two members of the quintet having already taken a b-line for their respective sleeper cars for a few hours of Zs before reaching Montreal.

- Cheers! And yes, I can't wait to start. I know, I know, Victor-Louis told me to wait till we got to Montreal but it's been a week now and I can no longer hold back my enthusiasm. Of all the hobbies I have undertaken in my short life, building my own log home has been the most satisfying and enjoyable to date. I'm sure Nari will understand.
- He told you a week ago? I only told him a week ago.

- I have known Victor-Louis for several years now, and just like his mom, he can't keep a secret if his life depended on it! When he told me the good news that you had offered us to join Josée-Anne and yourself on a trip to the Windsor, it was evident just by observing his body language that he wasn't giving me the whole story. It didn't take much prodding to have him spill the remainder of the beans!
- Just like his mom?! No wonder Josée-Anne has been sporting a Machiavellian grin for the last few days. Well at least now I know she has already agreed to living in a basement for a year or two. Or three. We can now all concentrate on the business of enjoying ourselves for the next few days. Cheers!

Laurent, now sporting his own Machiavellian rising-left-eyebrow and grin, entered his sleeper compartment by making just enough noise to intentionally startle Josée-Anne out of her slumber.

- Now you know that the only member of the Meier family you can rely on to be discreet is Klaus-Otto.
- And what about his four daughters? I should not have asked.
- Oh My! Last week was my first girls' night out at Angelika's invitation. The Meier's entire female contingent were present. The only ones that had more gossip to unveil than Angelika were her daughters. It was almost like a dueling challenge, where one daughter would try to out-gossip the other. Even Katherine, the Anglican pastor's wife, didn't come close to the Meiers! Though to be fair, Katherine's stories were the most erotically entertaining of the night.
- I knew I should have been more inquisitive once you had returned from your outing. I didn't want to intrude.

- You tend to forget, Laurent that I grew up on a farm. I have seen my fair share of rough winters. And lean times following mediocre harvests. Angelika had the opportunity to visit Nari's basement dwelling several times while he was building the upper floors. His flat was filled with sunlit, warm and cozy in the winter and surprisingly cool in the summer.
- Now you are the one convincing me that this is a good idea!... Cuddles?

- Cuddles.

♡☞♡

With all forms of machinations behind them, the quintet entered Viger Station. Except for a sleeping Claudette, all were in a decidedly celebratory mood. Having telegraphed reservations for two extra rooms a week earlier, in addition to the suite he had already reserved for himself and Josée-Anne when they first visited Montreal, Laurent was only mildly surprised to see a Windsor Hotel shuttle coach waiting for them, despite the fact it was already past 3 o'clock on a Tuesday morning.

Waking up to cuddles and with a baby in the oven, who needs brunch. Aware of his natural propensity to being an early riser, and equally inclined to being curious by nature, Laurent figured this would be good time to try out an innovative new gadget recently installed in several of the more luxurious suites of the Windsor. Following the instructions posted above the dresser, Laurent picked up the receiver and waited.

- Click, click, click... click, click ... Front Desk, Good Morning how may I help you?
- Oh, that's incredible. Apologies, first time trying this out. Since I can't see you and you me, I figure I better introduce myself. This is Laurent de Ville-Amois in room 245. Good Morning Sir. I was planning to have brunch in the Grand Dining Room but having checked in only a few hours ago I have had a change of heart. I wish to order breakfast in bed for me, my wife and daughter. I wish to offer the same to Mr. Stevenson and Mr. Meir in room 238. I would also like to make post-concert lunch reservations for all four guests, please.

- Consider it done, Mr. de Ville-Amois. Would you like a Continental Breakfast or something more substantial?
- We have relatively good appetites, so scrambled eggs, bacon and sourdough bread would be appreciated. And a small bowl of Irish oats, a cup of blueberry yoghurt, and a glass of orange juice for Claudette, please.

- I will give a ring to Mr. Stevenson and Mr. Meir to advise them. And congratulations on your first telephone conversation! I hope you have enjoyed the convenience of this modern age innovation.
- Yes, thank-you Sir. I must admit, I look forward to the day this new invention reaches all of Chanticleer.

- Bon appetit, Mr. de Ville-Amois. And enjoy the concert. Good day.
- Thank-you Sir. Good day. Click.

☏

- When I telegraphed Mr. Ferguson from the train station last week, I didn't expect him to get all five of us front row tickets.
- When Mr. Ferguson mentioned it to us during staff night at the bar last week, Otto and I insisted on it. Are you going to have lunch at the Grand Dining Room after the concert?

- That was really kind of both of you, thanks. And yes, we reserved a table for lunch after the concert.
- Good. I would really appreciate if all four of you could join us. After the morning rehearsals, we have made it a routine to have lunch with all the students around a single table. There is always room for a few more people, so it would be a pleasure to have you as *gemettæ*.

- That would be an honor. And a lot of fun to boot!
- You will excuse me now. We both take turns introducing the other to the audience before each concert. I will be back in a minute.

Claudette having been serenaded into a quiet sleep by the soothing sounds of classical music, Josée-Anne found it wise to make a quick detour in the direction of the hotel's nursery, where her daughter could catch up on the previous night's slumber; one constantly disturbed by her trip from Chanticleer to Montreal.

♫☕

Entering the dining room, one is welcomed into a ballroom sized hall, with twenty-foot high ceilings and nine, ten-foot high southern facing windows, the latter bringing in more than enough sunlight to brighten the dark mahogany paneling surrounding the interior walls of the hall.

Creating an innovative and sociopolitical fusion of architectural styles, the Americans who designed the Windsor chose to meld a French inspired exterior with decidedly Victorian interiors. The latter to satisfy the equally Victorian protocol of the hotel's clientèle, and the former as a nod to the New France origins of the inhabitants on the east side of the city's buffer zone. Today, over a century after the first laying of the Windsor's foundations, the Old World colonists north of the 49th parallel still have a lot to learn from the progressive melting pot frame-of-mind expounded by our New World revolutionary neighbors to the south.

With nearly thirty members of the student body actively participating in the production of Lohengrin, Mr. Ferguson set up a semi-permanent, 36 seat Kazaz-shaped[1] table in the northeast corner of the grand dining room. Though the majority of those in the production team were of the male persuasion, the half dozen unwed female participants were more than welcome in the grand dining room and did not have to eat lunch in the ladies' ordinary.

As strongly suggested by the management, all members attending the rehearsals were encouraged to wear their Sunday Best. You never know when one or several of the late-Victoria's consorts or, better yet, one of her family members may be having lunch at the same time.

Some of the students did find, at first, the rigidity of such vestmental protocol, a little stuffy to say the least. At the end of the second week of rehearsals, all agreed that having the opportunity to attend a formal sit-down lunch at the Windsor, six days a week, was an enjoyable privilege. And the food was always excellent.

The only deviance one could find to this protocol, was the wearing by several members of the production team, including Vincent and Otto, of a discretely shaded but none-the-less noticeable red bow tie. Interestingly enough, when Nari and Victor-Louis entered the dining room, they were sporting the same.

- Vincent, Otto, Please let me introduce you to Victor-Louis Meier and Nari Stevenson. Victor-Louis is the carriage making half of the prestigious and innovative Meier Breeding and Carriage Company of Chanticleer and Nari is the head waiter of the equally prestigious Chanterelle Hotel.
- Teutons and Meier go together like Bratwurst and sauerkraut. And just by looking at you Nari, if you are not of Scandinavian descent, I'll eat my bow tie!
- You are right on both counts Otto. I emigrated from Austria as a young child, and Nari did the same from Sweden. But the qualities of my family's company pale in comparison to the prestige and innovation of your musical compositions. It is a rare treat to hear such beautiful works of music performed by the composer himself.
- And lest we forget the angelic voice of Miss Lafontaine, who sang the exquisite lieder you composed and accompanied during the concert. A true delight to the ears. It is a pleasure to be in your presence, Miss Lafontaine.

---

1 Kazaz is the sixth rune of the elder futhark. It is the rune of creativity. Its phonetic equivalent is that of the letter k. Kazaz is most commonly drawn in the shape of a stylized arrow tip, pointing to the left of the reading surface.

- Please, call me Lise. And thank you for the kind words, Mr. Stevenson. Having Otto as a guide and Vincent as a tutor have made the rehearsal of these songs a delightfully demanding one, and the performance an equally successful one.
- Speaking of truly successful delights for the ears, It is now time for some truly successful delights of the pallet. As the French Canadians would say, *À La Soupe*!

The appropriate and traditional placement of the two heads of this operatic production team were at the left most corner of the Kazaz: Otto facing south and Vincent facing east. Nari and Victor-Louis to Otto's right; Laurent, Josée-Anne and Lise to Vincent's right.

With the ever increasing popularity of these lunchtime concerts, Vincent and Otto made a point of always reserving the two settings next to them for last minute, post concert, lunch guests. This would ensure that the student body would sit at their habitual position on the borders of the rune.

Though Laurent had planned this Montreal-bound excursion well in advance, so as to coincide with the return of the Mennonites to Bonsecours Market, an outing at the Main Market was on the minds of all four visiting Chanticleers. Using this coincidence as a conversation starter, it soon became apparent to Josée-Anne that she and her southern dining companion had more in common than just their love of classical music, both being farmer's daughters.

Just because Lise had traded in her parent's vocation as dairy farmers for one of operatic singing, didn't mean she had foregone her penchant for all things down to earth and practical. As a result, a trip to Bonsecours Market would be the third commonality both women would share that afternoon.

The remaining three quarters of the foursome all shared a common reason to visit the market, though each to varying degrees of expenditure. Being Laurent's first attempt at building a Scandinavian log home, he had the most equipment, tools and knowledge to acquire. Then came Victor-Louis, who had grown tired of sharing several of Nari's tools while helping build the latter's first permanent Laurentian residence. Finally Nari had a number of tools to upgrade and looked forward to finding better performing redundancies with the level of functionality and craftsmanship, that are the hallmarks of nearly everything the Mennonites build with their hands.

Having yet to visit the market since they arrived in the Dominion, their guests' common topic of conversation peeked Vincent's and Otto's curiosity resulting in both men choosing to tag along before heading out, later that afternoon, to the Stanley Tearoom on the street of the same name.

☘♋☞

- That didn't take long, Nari. Your efficiency in finding the proper tools for Laurent's upcoming construction project borders on the Teutonic!
- When I know what I want and I know what I need, I don't waste any time getting it, Otto.
- I'll keep that in mind, Nari.

- Ahem...And with the help of the Mennonites, all that is left to do is to pick up our crated purchases, on our way to Viger Station tomorrow.
- Yes Laurent. And speaking of being organized, I almost forgot. Nari's father spends his weekdays on the construction site of the Sunlife Building project, and only spends his weekends back home in Piedmont during the construction season. Last weekend Nari told him we would both be in Montreal today and we agreed to all meet at the Windsor's pub after diner this evening. I'm sure Nari will agree that your presence at the pub would be an excellent opportunity to get your basement home project started on a proper footing. Pardon the pun!

- That's a great idea. I'll be there.
- And Vincent, Otto, you are both more than welcome to have a pint or two or three with us if you wish.
- The more the merrier. Will you be there too Otto?
- Count me in! But first things first. Otto and I have a rendezvous at the Stanley Tearoom in an hour or so. Many members of the local artistic community are regulars there. It's less than a block away from the hotel so we will be back to the Windsor for diner with no need for a coach ride. Would anyone like to join us?
- I've done enough shopping for today. I will share a coach with you. What about you Victor-Louis?
- I'll come along. This should be fun. And Laurent?
- Oh, I still have some errands to do before the stores close. I wish to purchase some lenses at a photography store nearby. Thank-you for the offer, Vincent, none-the-less.

Laurent removed his pocket watch from his vest. It was five to four. As agreed upon nearly two hours earlier, all would meet in front of the bakery shop by four pm. From the southwest corridor of the market Laurent could just make out the feminine silhouettes of the two remaining members of the Windsor's shopping expedition.

- You are like clockwork Josée-Anne. Thank-you. I am heading out to L.R. Violo. Would you like to accompany me?
- Yes I would. With all the beautiful fauna, flora and scenery offered to us by the Laurentian mountains, I too would like to purchase a camera. Would you like to join us Lise?
- What a wonderful idea. I have never dabbled in photography. I have seen several advertisements in National Geographic Magazine for an inexpensive camera called the Brownie made by Eastman Kodak Company and that peeked my interest. If I have enough money left in my purse I may just take the plunge.

CPR's decision to build Place Viger at the turn of the 20th century was motivated by both geopolitical and practical reasoning. Alas, the excellent logic of the British decision makers lacked an essential subjective motivator. One that should have been infused with an awareness and understanding of the vision shared by the New France upper classes, who were the targeted clientèle of this dual purpose hotel terminal complex. And this lack of vision was the harbinger of its ørlög[2].

By 1913, the slow and steady creep of the French speaking downtown core, northward along St-Hubert street, had reached the East-West axis of De Maisonneuve Boulevard. Consequently, the densely constructed, multilevel, brown brick flats, with their signature, three story, wrote-iron exterior staircases, stretching to the sidewalks of De Maisonneuve were having their large, street level apartments transformed into commercial and retail service boutiques.

It is precisely in one of those street-level flats that Mr Violo set up shop. Entering his establishment is like entering someone's kitchen, where the counters, cabinets, table, appliances and wash basin were removed and replaced by two opposing all-glass presentation counters running southward all the way to the kitchen's rear wall. All the latest and most desirable cameras are placed in these

2 The Old Norse concept of ørlög can roughly be defined by its Post-Norman Era, Anglo-Saxon counterpart of *doom.*

counters with their accompanying accessories inside glass cabinets just above eye level and to the rear of the salesman's principle working environment.

To the west of the kitchen, in what used to be the former apartment dwellers' dining room, a similar retail space to the first is set up, but where the main counter follows an east-west axis filled with inexpensive domestically manufactured consumer-oriented point and shoot equipment destined to be acquired by the budding photographer on a budget. This is where one can admire and fondle iconic gems, pumped-out yearly in the hundreds of thousands by Rochester's Eastman Kodak Corporation. A few of Kodak's better folding plate cameras could also be found in the dining room's main display case.

In front and to the north of this counter are a series of presentation counters and cabinets reserved for used, discounted and discontinued equipment of all sorts and vintages.

Laurent was eying a series of close-up filter lenses, and a Petzval portrait and a Tele-Dynar f/6.3 lens. As beginners, Josée-Anne and Lise both had less ambitious and onerous objectives in mind.

Prior to the trio's arrival, the only people inside the shop were Mr. Violo and his son/salesman Luigi Jr. Mr. Violo took care of the gentleman and the two ladies were introduced to the interior of the dining room by Luigj Jr.

When it comes to photography, an important truism that Josée-Anne gleaned from her husband's established hobby, was that the best camera is the one with you at all times. Having seen the extraordinary results obtained from her better half's traditional, semiprofessional equipment, and understanding the most important feature of any camera is the quality of the lens in front of the plate box, Josée-Anne decided to splurge a bit on a relatively inexpensive Kodak folding camera with a metal lens mount. The latter fitted with a more expensive, Voigtländer, wide angle lens. The camera used 116 size film rather than plates and was small enough to easily fit in a purse, if not a small knapsack. The lens optimized for her preferred subject matter of landscape photography.

To state that an aspiring opera singer from a tiny Eastern Townships farming community was on a tight budget, would obviously be an understatement. Thank the gods for Mr. Eastman's belief in functionally practical, industrial designs and Mr. Ford's innovative production line manufacturing techniques for making the-simple-to-use, simple-to-make Kodak Brownie a reality. Even with a nearly nonexistent disposable income, the economies of scale resulting from the Brownie's overwhelming success, made Lise's two dollar purchase a viable one.

☀

With a fresh roll of film in each of the ladies' cameras and an unexposed plate in Laurent's, our trio of street photographers headed west on De Maisonneuve to get a handle on their new and upgraded tools of the trade. The two rows of virtually equidistant staircases dotting each side of the boulevard made for an excellent first exercise *focused* on the primary concepts of composition and perspective. With Laurent having just installed his newly acquired Tele-Dynar telephoto lens on the Bijou, each camera would offer a different angle of view which in turn would influence the photographer's final decision on both composition and perspective at the same time.

Ironically, it was the simplest and least expensive of the three cameras that would be the most challenging to use. With no shutter adjustment other than a rudimentary time exposure lever mechanism and no aperture adjustment for the camera's lens, Lise would have to rely on relatively strong ambient light when taking hand-held shots.

Luckily for this novice snapper, her tool of choice is equipped with a lens permanently focused at infinity, and the inclusion of both portrait and landscape oriented viewfinders, optimized for use with the Brownie's fixed focal length lens, the latter with a field of view roughly equivalent to that of the human eye, made Lise free to concentrate on successfully manipulating the two concepts of her first photographic tutorial.

- The shutter speed range of your Brownie spans the not terribly fast, to the terribly slow. The lens is not all that fast either. Consequently, if you don't want to have blurry photos, you will have to hold your camera as steady as possible. The best way to hold it will be close to your belly, with your hands cradling each side of the camera.
- I will have to look at the world through the eyes of Claudette, Laurent!

- A child's eyes are the most inquisitive we use in our lifetime. They are the cradle of our creative soul. Applying a childhood perspective to the moment you are about to capture with your camera will make you a better photographer.
- That makes sense. So my physical perspective should always be the one I used when I first discovered the world around me.

- Almost. Without a close-up lens screwed to the front of the camera's fixed lens you will have to be 3 yards away from your subject if you want everything to be in focus; about the distance it takes to make three large steps. Much further away than your average child's inquisitive eyes. Look inside the bag Mr. Violo placed purchase in...
- Kodak Portrait Attachment. How did that get there?

- When I saw you were about ready to make your purchase, I asked Luigi Sr to slip this little accessory in your bag. An essential one if you are going to view the world though the eyes of your past childhood. This will make it possible for you to have subjects close to you in focus, while the subjects further away, at infinity, will be a little blurry. If you follow these principles, your actual results will soon begin to look more and more like your imagined ones. After a few rolls of film, it will become second nature.
- How thoughtful of you Mr de Ville-Amois. A very useful gift. So when I don't use this lens the subjects close to me will be blurry and those at infinity will be in focus.

- Exactly. A good way to start is to take two photos from the same point of reference. One with the close-up lens and one without.
- How about this row of staircases.

- An excellent idea Lise... And now it's your turn Josée-Anne. Your choice of equipment captures a wide angle of view which is ideal for capturing landscapes when outside and versatile enough to shoot group photos when inside the cramped quarters of a small living room.
- Yes. That's right Laurent. The lens is similar to the model we were looking at in the photography store back in Rennes. This lens is slower than your standard lens but with a wide angle lens, everything tends to be in focus even at maximum aperture, making zooming with your feet a less challenging endeavor. I wanted something small and simple enough that I could carry with me when we are out foraging in the forest. And I didn't want to bring several lenses at the same time. I will leave that up to you!

To better help out Lise understand the concepts being explained to her, each photographer would take a snapshot of predetermined composition, at the same point of reference. A half dozen photos would be taken with each camera. Once Laurent and Josée-Anne, returned to Montreal, latter in the summer, to attend Lohengrin, Lise would be able to compare the results from the three different types of equipment.

The last of these six photographic exercises would be the trickiest one for Lise to complete, as she had yet to equip her Brownie with a flash strobe. The trio was now just behind the rearmost pew inside Christ's Church Cathedral. The noontime sun streaming through the stained glass windows was strong that day, but not strong enough to adequately enlighten the cathedral's nave. Fortunately, the pastor had kept the lights on directly over the pulpit.

- I'm not totally sure of the results you will obtain with your camera, Lise. You should be able to capture the pulpit, but the rest will be darker. Comparing Josée-Anne's and my photos to the one you are about to take will be most revealing about the limitations of your camera's lens rather than an exercise in composition. What dœs your camera manual say about timed exposures?
- It says to lift the time exposure slide on top of the camera and to place the camera on a sturdy surface. Pull the shutter lever down for between ½ and 5 seconds. And then lift the shutter lever back up ... Simple enough. Now I just need to find a sturdy surface to take a picture of the pulpit.

- I'm one step ahead of you. I borrowed a few bibles from the rear pews and placed them on the church pamphlet table.
- That should do it. So how long should the exposure be?

- I would say halfway between the two extremes, so about three seconds. Ready? Go!
- ... Sliip! ... Sliip! Good. The manual says not to forget to push the time exposure slide back into its slot before taking another snapshot. okay.

- And I'll put the bibles back where I found them.
- I figure photography is a bit like performing music. Both are artistic endeavors. The most interesting results are not always obtained from the best instruments. Sometimes, the most original and entertaining outcomes can be obtained from using the most unlikely tools. A few weeks ago, I attended a concert given by a quartet of friends of mine. They are all professional members of the same chamber music orchestra. Instead of using their own instruments, ones designed and constructed for adult hands, the whole concert was performed using toy instruments. The performance was not only whimsical, but also quite enlightening. The musicians chose not to work around the instruments limitations, but rather they embraced those same limitations by learning and in some cases, relearning to use these childhood toys. Their original adaptation of

traditional classical music gave a whole new life to works that were composed for the most part over two hundred years ago.

- With such an original and positive attitude, I'm learning not only from Laurent today but from you as well Lise!

- That makes two of us. I have been so preoccupied by using the best equipment I can afford, I have neglected to take the time to learn how to use the tools I already have to the best of their capabilities. Thank-you Lise. You have brought me down to earth. We have both become teachers today!
- I believe this new hobby will be more fun than I first imagined.

- This teacher turned student would now like to graciously invite both my female companions to the ninth floor of the establishment just west of us.
- High tea at Eaton's; now that's a treat! I accept your invitation, Mr. de Ville-Amois!

- Excellent timing, my dear!

Other than sharing Victorian influences in their interior designs, the Stanley Tea Room offered quite a different social experience compared to the one on the ninth floor of Timothy Eaton's department store. Taking an unconscious cue from Mr. Violo, the tearoom was established on the first floor of a renovated Lower Westmount townhouse. The wall separating the original dining room and study was knocked down to make room for the ladies' ordinary, with a view onto Stanley Street. The wall separating the living and drawing rooms was also removed to make way for the male only, grand tea room, with view and access to a private inner garden at the rear of the townhouse.

When the four Windsor Hotel guests crossed the front stained glass and mahogany doors of the tea room entrance, they were greeted by a small but well lit, redwood paneled lobby. To the right were a pair of French doors accented with a mosaic of delicate floral patterns etched into the frosted glass of each of the door's windows. These doors gave access to the ladies' ordinary. To the left was a black marble floored corridor, ending with a set of French doors similar in style to those of the ladies' ordinary. However instead of a floral mosaic, each door had an intricately detailed imposing and anatomically correct, wild boar etched into the frosted glass. The two were facing each other, their snouts only separated by the redwood frame of each door. These gave access to the grand tea room.

The right wall of the corridor and the perpendicular, adjoining rear wall of the front lobby, served to hide the back-of-the-house common kitchen, shared by both the grand tea room and the ladies' ordinary. The lobby side of the rear wall was adorned with a duo of richly sculpted mahogany counters. The sculpting found on the rightmost counter mirrored the floral patterns found on the doors to the ladies' ordinary. The sculpting on the leftmost counter mirrored the Celtic inspired etching on the access doors to the grand tea room.

The greeter standing behind the left side lobby desk was as tall, ripped, handsome and Irish as the greeter standing behind the right side lobby desk was petite, delicate, beauteous, and French. Both were attired in such a way that would have made Alexandrina proud to be a guest in such an establishment.

- Good Afternoon Otto! Good afternoon Vincent. I see both of you are accompanied by two new and distinguished guests. Welcome all to Stanley's. Will a table for six be sufficient?
- Yes, that will be more than sufficient, Ernest. Oh. I almost forgot. Our two distinguished guests are also friends of Laurent de Ville-Amois, the kind and generous Breton who accompanied both of us on our voyage to the Dominion.

- Yes. I remember both of you speaking fondly of Monsieur de Ville-Amois during your first visit to Stanley's.
- Good afternoon Ernest. My name is Victor-Louis Meier. Me and my friend Nari, are in the process of helping to build Monsieur de Ville-Amois's new log home in Chanticleer. As a token of his appreciation for our assistance, he has invited us to attend two concerts by Otto and Vincent.
- Monsieur de Ville-Amois's generosity is equaled by his class. I hope to meet Laurent before you all return from your expedition to Montreal!

As Ernest spoke, he guided his four guests to the entrance of the grand tea room. Holding the right side door open for his clients, he escorted them to a six foot diameter table in the southeast corner of the room. To be honest, the tabletop wasn't exactly round, as just under a quarter of its outer circumference was straightened out, resulting in a four foot long straight edge, which in turn was butted up to the lower ledge of a bay window with a view onto Stanley's private courtyard.

Access to the latter was restricted ever since the early days of spring to make way for a major construction and landscaping project encompassing the entirety of the nearly one quarter acre surface of the inner courtyard.

The first phase of this project consisted of building a subterranean extension to the former townhouse. When completed, this basement addition would take up nearly half the total area of the courtyard. All six sides of this oblong box shaped structure would be made of reinforced concrete. The flat roof of this box would be 3 feet above the courtyard's surface and the floor would be eighteen feet below.

A 21 foot high, visual and acoustic barrier, similarly constructed of reinforced-concrete, was erected. It enveloped the three-sided perimeter of the courtyard that, as of a year prior, still had open access to the latter's immediate neighbors. The outer walls were finished in brownstone brick, sourced from the same supplier as those used to construct the original townhouse. Several lengths of the structure's reinforcing iron rod were bent inwards at a ninety degree angle, resulting in a grid pattern of two inch protrusions on the surface of each wall. The distance separating each protrusion was four feet, both in the horizontal and vertical directions. These protrusions covered the majority of the three inner walls of the barrier. A series of wrote iron, sun-star-shaped lanterns would be spot welded to the protrusions during the fourth and final stage of this construction and landscaping project. The tips of the sun stars were finished in such a way to double as attachment points for a variety of wall vines, which in turn would creep in a controlled fashion throughout the entirety of the inner walls' surface. When filled with lemon-scented oil, the lanterns would serve several functions including – but not limited to – ambiance lighting during the evening hours and as a natural repellent to the mosquitœs that otherwise would tend to congregate in and around the leaf system of the vines.

The north facing wall of this barrier would include a 10 foot high by twelve foot wide opening. All four sides of the latter finished with an eight inch deep wrote iron frame used to support two six by ten foot solid cedar gates, each crafted from lengths of 6×6's whose joinery was at a forty-five degree angle to the horizon.

Comfortably seated at their dinning table, the foursome were able to observe the final stages of Stanley's renovation project from an ideal vantage point. The eastern half of this private garden was manned by several landscapers who were busy transplanting trees and several varieties of wall vines, while others were building a series of flat rock walkways that would snake amongst the newly-planted and old growth specimens populating the courtyard.

The western half of the courtyard was manned by a series of joiners, carpenters, and iron smiths in the advanced stages of completing an elaborate outer deck. Most having finished the brunt of the interior design work encompassing the spaces below them, a fortnight earlier. Once built, this cedar and wrote iron deck would completely cover the roof of Stanley's new concrete, oblong box extension.

As our four teetotalers watched the renovators straining against their tools of choice, the two skilled laborers closest to the opposite side of the window pane had one thing in common... Um, let me rephrase that. They had everything in common.

- If they're not identical twins, I'll eat my napkin.
- Don't do that Victor-Louis. You won't have anything left to wipe the droo... oh, never mind.
- They're too short to be German.
- And they're too tall to be French.

- The color of their hair and eyes gives them native overtones.
- They're too muscular to be Indians.
- Their close-cropped hairstyles and clean-shaven, distinguished facial features almost make them look like Prussian noblemen.
- Or Russian Czars.

- I think you're on to something, Vincent. They do have a Nordic look to them though.
- They're not Swedish. Finnish.
- That's It! With a name like Stevenson, you should know.
- Now, we just need to find someone with the negotiating skills and courage to find a way to go outside and ask one of them to confirm our suspicions.

- I nominate Nari. He's a waiter so that makes him a talented negotiator. And he's the one who came closest to a general consensus.
- Well, I guess I will have to volunteer. If Vincent was the first to suggest the idea, it's more than likely that he is the least willing to be the one to get the job done.
- If you're as good a negotiator as you are a psychoanalyst, we are going to have to start calling you Sigmund!
- Ha, ha! I think you are right on both counts Otto.

- I'll be back in a few minutes. The rest of you can watch in the relative security of this inner sanctum.

Once Nari had convinced the grand tea room's head waiter to grant him access to the work site, both gastronomic consorts headed outside to greet the two mirror-imaged tradesmen. From inside the tea room, one could observe that the conversation was dominated by a discussion between Nari and one of the two identical twins, the latter's placental consort remaining silent throughout the just over three minute exchange. It was only a handful of moments away from the two hundred second mark since the start of the conversation, that the silent twin, cocking his head to the left, followed by a thirty degree rotation to the right, gazed straight through the bay window and with a Nordic smile capable of melting the coldest of Siberian snow drifts, looked straight into the eyes of Victor-Louis.

- Are you okay, Victor-Louis? Your face is almost as red as your bow tie.
- Oh...um. Here comes Nari. I think he's finished talking to the two Nordic Go... um tradesmen. So Nari, were you right? Are they Finnish?
- Victor-Louis and I were right on both proposals. The one I was talking to is the eldest of the two twins. They grew up in Imatra; a three-hour journey by foot from the border town of Svetogorsk, the latter barely 150 km northeast of Saint-Petersburg.
- I admit having been the furthest off the mark. Being only a morning's carriage ride from Saint-Petersburg, your conclusion was far more plausible than mine, Vincent.

- With age, advanced as it may be, comes knowledge and wisdom, Otto!
- Don't be so hard on yourself, Monsieur du Cinqcent. Though you are at least a generation my elder, I have come to learn in my short life that with age also comes distinction.
- Victor-Louis is not the only one who finds you distinguished. As I was speaking to the elder Thomas, I explained to him that my French colleague thought the pair were Russian, and that my German colleague thought they were Prussian. He responded by stating that he and his younger twin brother Ulrich were Finnish, and followed by asking if the distinguished gentleman to the far left was my French colleague and if the handsome young giant next to him was my German colleague.
- Well, at least he found me handsome!

- And Ulrich seems to have the same opinion of Nari as his brother has of Otto!
- Oh please! If I start blushing again, I am going to hide underneath the table for the rest of the afternoon.
- You're too tall to hide under the table, Victor-Louis. You need not be so bashful. We are not in Chanticleer. Montreal is far more cosmopolitan.
- And most probably more so than your hometown of Spittal an der Drau. I have visited the latter a few times, and though a truly beautiful small town, to call this community conservative would be an understatement.

- You are right Otto. That conservatism has definitely rubbed off on my father, and in return on me. When my immediate family emigrated to the Dominion over a decade ago, it was a bit of a culture shock for all of us. Even more so than if we had moved to the British motherland. Chanticleer is far more laid back than Spittal an der Drau. None-the-less, the former still has very much a small town mindset, making discretion and reservation personal qualities that are just as important to hone and preserve in Chanticleer as they are in Spittal an der Drau.

- Please accept my apologies for being so tardy. Are we all ready to order?
- *Meine Rede! Gerade noch einmal davonkommen.* Yes. I will begin. I saw a blue stripe, stoneware pitcher filled with fresh cut flowers in the lobby. Fill mine with hot chocolate. And a double serving of triple-chocolate-fudge cheesecake... please.
- Now that is a hearty serving of comfort food! I will have the same as Victor-Louis... please.
- Me too! *Danke schön...* please.
- As the smallest of the four, I too will have the same, but only fill a large mug with hot chocolate... please.

- Well, that was quick. You are all making my job a simple one to complete. I will be back in a few moments.

At twenty-eight years old, Otto was at the doorstep of middle age and Vincent was a year shy of his fortieth wedding anniversary, placing both men at a particular, but temporally different turning point in their social, and biological lives. Their wives having chosen to stay close to their homes and children during their husbands' stay in Montreal, each man was now free to explore the intricacies and consequences of facing an equally important crossroad in their respective life journeys.

As all four men drowned their early twentieth-century, social etiquette obligations in copious amounts of cocoa-laden afternoon delights, the conscious and instinctive jousting between Nari's progressive-liberal and Victor-Louis' feudal-conservative mindsets served as a catalyst for the evolving exploration of Vincent and Otto's decades-old latent desires.

Prior to this afternoon, both classically trained minstrels had adopted a strict look-but-don't-provoke attitude during their regular outings to the Stanley Tea Room. With the help of Nari's Viking-inspired brashness and Victor-Louis' natural curiosity, the two musical travelers decided that it was high time to extricate themselves from the still waters filling the undefined presence of their virtual desires and intentions, and plunge into the active rapids propelling the defined presence of the plausible probabilities inhabiting the adventures of their immediate futures. In other words, Vincent and Otto finally decided to mutate from being composer-posers into being inspired instigators[3].

- As you are all aware, Monsieur de Ville-Amois's plan to build a new scribed-notch log home on his Laurentian homestead is one of the reasons for Victor-Louis and myself being in Montreal today. When Thomas asked me what brought me to Stanley's this afternoon, I took the opportunity to explain my construction building intentions to him. I could hardly believe my luck when he explained that the two twins were hired by one of the contractors also responsible for building the Sunlife Building.
- Oh no. You didn't.
- Yes I did. I replied by asking if he could be kind enough to tell me the name of the contractor. It is the same contractor my father is working for at the present time.
- Oh no. You didn't.
- Yes I did. I invited both twins to the Windsor Hotel's pub this evening to discuss the possibility of them working on Monsieur de Ville-Amois's new home.
- And that's when Victor-Louis got struck by an ocular cupid arrow from Ulrich's iceberg melting gaze?
- Exactly, Vincent.
- I am sure I am small enough to hide underneath this table now.
- Figuratively, maybe. Physically, probably not.
- Touché, Otto.

3 With thanks to Instigator Magazine's founding editor.

☕☕☕☕☕☕

At twelve feet high, the Windsor Hotel pub's ceiling was far lower than the one sheltering its concert hall, giving a relatively intimate atmosphere to the pub's interior. All the while permitting the patron's cigar and cigarette smoke to waffle upwards, out-of-the-way of the establishment's non-smoking minority.

The brass tubing bordering the pub's main counter, its low-hanging Victorian styled chandeliers, each sporting a half dozen large porcelain lampshades, and the equally Victorian dark mahogany wood paneling strategically covering most of the white-stucco concrete walls, helped to transport several members of the clientèle back to Liverpool, where they would have taken their last pint of stout or lager before heading out to the colonies on the Empress of Ireland.

When Nari's father crossed the pub's entrance, he was flanked by two Scottish hulks that even dwarfed their compatriot. The Stanley six-pack were comfortably sharing two brass-accented mahogany tables at the far northwest corner of the pub. Once the customary introductions were completed, the nine men settled in to their respective seats and a round of draft was ordered on Nari's tab.

Only one future patron had yet to join this group of revelers. Laurent was on his way to the pub when he crossed Mr. Ferguson in the hotel lobby. Asking him if he knew of any photo shops nearby willing to let him develop his own exposures, Mr. Ferguson explained that the hotel had recently set up their own small darkroom specifically for that purpose and promptly offered Laurent a tour of the Windsor's latest technological installation. An offer Laurent could hardly refuse.

- The only one missing now is... ah. Speaking of which, here he comes now.
- Terribly sorry. I figuratively and literally got sideswiped by an unforeseen opportunity. My apologies. My name is Laurent de Ville-Amois. Thank-you all for joining me here on such short notice.

- You need not apologize, Laurent. We have all just arrived a few moments ago. Please have a seat and a pint of draft as you catch your breath.
- Cheers!
- Cheers, Mr. de Ville-Amois! I am Asmund, Nari's father. When Nari explained your construction project to me, he immediately peaked my interest. The two people that would be most interested in this project easily came to mind. Please let me introduce you to Henry Morganthau...
- Just call me Henry.
- ... and Samuel Housman.

- Just call me Sam.

- Now it's my turn. Here are the two tradesmen I told you about Laurent, during dinner this evening. Please welcome Thomas Wulfila...
- Just call me Tom.
- ... and his brother Ulrich...
- Just call me Uli.

- Nari told me you are both not only skilled laborers when it comes to building reinforced concrete structures but your chosen professions are in the woodworking industry. May I ask if you had ever worked on the construction and raising of a traditional log home?
- Last year, we both finished the construction of a *pièce-sur-pièce* log home on land we purchased together in Thomson Heights. We were going to build a notch-and-scribe but for reasons of frugality, we chose to build in a style that would not need extra laborers, horses and winches. At the present, we only go there on the weekends, as most of our work is conducted in Montreal. You should come and visit when you have a chance.

- On what road is your home situated?
- Saint-Hyacinthe Street.

- That can't be more than a few miles from my homestead.
- Asmund will correct me if I am wrong, Mr. de Ville-Amois, but you will need at least a half dozen workers to complete the first phase of your project. If you choose to hire me and my brother in addition to Asmund, Sam and Henry, we will be more than enough if you factor in Nari, Victor-Louis and yourself as active participants. And since our home is not far from the work site, Sam and Henry are more than welcome to share our retreat, during the few weekends it will take to complete your basement home. Is that okay with you, Uli?
- That sounds like a wonderful idea big brother! What do you think Mr. de Ville-Amois?

- It's a go, if Tom's offer sounds okay with Sam and Henry.
- I'm in, as long as Sam dœs the dishes.
- I'm in, as long as Henry dœs the windows!

It had been a long day for the ten seated at those two intimately-spaced Windsor Pub tables. So after two final rounds of stout, courtesy of Laurent's generosity, and new-found fondness for Saint-James Gate's famous roasted malt ale, it was time for goodbyes, *au-revoirs*, and *tschüsses* all around.

Okay. At least for four of them. The night was still as young for Nari, Victor-Louis and the Wulfila twins as it was for Otto & Vincent. And all six had promised Ernest they would attend the unofficial opening celebrations.

☾ ☽

- Are you sure you are up for it, Vincent?
- In France we call it a *nuit blanche.* The trick to such events, is not to go back to sleep for an extended period until you have reached your normal bedtime hour. Ideally a short, afternoon nap at around 3 o'clock will suffice to tie me over till then. However it would be kind of you to take a leadership role during the rehearsals, this morning.

- Consider it done. Luckily you planned to only perform your own compositions during today's lunchtime concert. You literally know these like the back of your hand.
- Yes, I could play them in my sleep!

- Don't tempt the mischievous one. He may grant you a wish you didn't expect to come true.
- He already did that last night. That will be enough for this week.

- Despite your age, you're being more mischievous than he!
- I will take that as a compliment.

♬☕

Laurent's concrete basement home was completed faster than the ten had anticipated when they first met at the Windsor's Pub, nearly a month earlier. With the continued help of Nari, Victor-Louis, Tom and Uli, Laurent could now take the time to properly and extensively finish the interior of his subterranean lodging; thus making it possible to prolong the construction of the upper floors.

- Oh, come on. Where am I?
- In the kitchen. Facing the open-air dining room. Okay, I will take your blindfold off now. Ready?

- Oh, my! The ceilings are even higher than those back home at the château.
- Now follow me. I will show you the living room.

- What an intelligent idea. The wall on the far side of the dining room, separating the living room has no doors. Only two opposite and equally-spaced openings that reach to the ceiling. All the light coming from the kitchen, the dining and living rooms are shared by all three spaces. And there is enough room for... oh, my. We only had a stand-up back in Britany. I never thought I would... How did you afford it?
- It's not a grand. A baby grand. When Asmund reserved a boxcar to haul the specialized steel and wooden forms used to mold and set the cement walls, the steel girders for the ceiling, the reinforcing steel rods, and the steel grating for the cement roof, there still was enough room for the baby grand. It was an opportunity I couldn't pass up.

- It's in such good condition, it must be new. And a Steinway to boot. Where did you get it?
- Almost new. And you can thank Vincent. And Tom. When I mentioned I was looking for a baby grand to Vincent, he promised he would get back to me as soon as possible. Two weeks before Asmund was ready to lock-up the boxcar headed north on the CP rail line, Tom mentioned to me that Vincent had come upon an opportunity I could hardly refuse. We were working on finishing the footing that would support the walls of our new home. One of Vincent's summertime students is a promising pianist who emigrated from Austria a few years earlier. When a talent scout from the London Opera heard his virtuoso renditions during rehearsals for Lohengrin, he hired him for next summer's season in London. As his newly purchased baby grand was out of the question as stored baggage on the Empress of Ireland, he chose to sell it as soon as he could. The Steinway was a timely bargain, and Tom, Uli, and Asmund took care of the cumbersome logistics.

- And the furniture. They seem to have been custom tailored to fit the enlightened and modern interior decor. The delicate white stucco finish of the massive and minimalistic walls. The warmth of the lightly-colored varnish on the maple hardwood floors. They all complement the simple beauty of this furniture. Who were the designers? Who crafted these unique pieces?
- Tom's favorite hobby is carpentry. Uli's is graphic art and design. Uli applies his creative spark to paper. Tom transfers his brother's creations to wood, hides, and iron.

- His inspiration must have come from his childhood neighbors.
- You are right, Josée-Anne. I remember how you raved about the local creations you dined and sat on, during our last Nordic holiday. When I took the time to visit the interior of Tom and Uli's weekend retreat, I was struck by the beauty and originality of their own hand-made furniture. I knew then, they would be the ones to design and build the furniture for our new home in Chanticleer.

- Did Uli also help you with the interior design of our new home?
- Absolutely. He is the one who designed the floor plan and chose the finish and colors of the walls and floors. He spent several hours sitting in the middle of each room, just so he could see how the light traveling through the windows, would hit each surface. It was only after completing this enlightened exercise, was he ready to complete the final designs of both the interior and of the custom-made furniture that would inhabit each room.

- He is quite the innovator.
- Yes. He's even given a name to the results of his design work. He calls it art deco.

- So now I know why I have yet to be invited to Tom and Uli's.
- That would have ruined the surprise!

- It's time to make some thank-you gifts. I have two extra special heavy-wool sweaters to knit before the coming equinox.
- At least they both will be the same size! And as for our Finnish neighbors' intentionally ignored invitations, that was the hardest part about keeping the surprise intact. With all the love you put into making the hearty lunches for everyone working on this construction project, Tom and Uli both made an oath to me, promising they would do the same as they applied their artistic and woodworking skills to the design and creation of the furniture we will be using for years to come.

- I can sense there was a lot of love put into all aspects of building this new home. And not just from Tom and Uli. Thank-you, Laurent. This is the finest gift you have ever given me.

That coming equinox would also bring an autumn wind to the Gulf of Saint-Laurence. One that would soon descend on the waters of the Louise Basin at the foot of Quebec City's Château Frontenac.

An unpredictable wind.

As unpredictable as the winds of the coming spring.

Bringing with them the sun of day and the starlight of night, one moment, and indiscernible fog, sleet, rain, and gale, the next.

The autumn winds from the Adriatic Sea, are just as unpredictable but of far less influence once they have reached the eastern Serbian city of Sarajevo.

For the moment, the unpredictable nature of the winds wafting over this mountain enclave, are not being defined by the laws of nature, but of man.

As part of an Austro-Hungarian dominated kingdom of Serbs, Slovenes and Croats – not to mention the ethnic Albanians, Macedonians, Bulgarians, Romanians and traveling gypsies (did I forget anyone? I'm sure I forgot someone) – all vowing for their piece of the royal pie, these figurative winds can be virtually xenophilous one moment, insular and psychotic, the next.

Sarajevo's winds are not of the changing seasons, but of instigation.

...

The chronicles of the past, be they our own or those of another, are the directors who guide our perception of what is and is not a present moment in time.

Procedure

- Oh the Gods!
- And the Giants.

Otto, Vincent, Nari, Victor-Louis, Tom and Uli were all present on the opening night of Stanley's underground lair.

The the inner surface of the wooden casings used to form the four inside walls of this underground establishment, were sculpted in such a manner that once the concrete poured and set, and the casings removed, a concrete fresco on each of the four walls would be exposed to the lair's occupants.

Each wall had its own theme and inspiration: to the north, the story of Ragnarok; to the south, a Gregorian inspired depiction of cloaked monks chanting inside the ruins of a Welsh cathedral; to the east, a Celtic moment of observation capturing wild boars, bears, wolves and horses in the throws of heated fornication and to the west, leather hooded christian hulks in a heated exchange with heretic warlocks, the latter strapped to a series of Spanish inquisitor's racks.

The concrete frescœs were, for the most part, kept in the same state as they were found when the casings were removed. The only finishing touches were the sanding of sharp edges that could risk injuring unsuspecting clients and the installation of rot-iron lamp shades in the shape of medieval torches, bolted to supports previously welded to the reinforcing iron bars of the concrete walls.

For the newcomer, the sombre surroundings of the lair made, at best, the deciphering of what had been etched into the walls of the latter, a difficult undertaking. Giving incentive for one to return in a pursuit to uncover the secrets these walls were hiding.

Tom and Uli were responsible for the creative etching on the inner surface of each casing, and intricately aware of the secrets they held.

¿♈?

- Hoof!, Hoof!!, Hoof!!!...Are we in Shawbridge yet?
- No. We've left Shawbridge.

- Hoof!, Hoof!!, Hoof!!!...Are we in Prévost?
- No. We've past both Lesage and Prévost.

- AHHGGHGGOOooouuff... So where did I have Louis?
- Somewhere inside...

- Echo Lake?
- Far away inside...

- Echo Lake.
- I was told the lake has a beautiful natural beachfront.

- We will have to visit this summer.
- With Louis.

✝¿✝

- *Youville ou Hôtel-Dieu?*

- *Le plus proche s'il-vous-plait.*
  The closest please.

The coach headed west on du Palais and turned left on Saint-Georges, past the Jérômeville Cathedral to their left, the hackney gingerly trotting a dozen blocks to the south. The latter seemingly well aware of the delicate passenger, wrapped in a hastily packed cotton bed sheet and a heavy wool blanket, knitted by Josée-Anne a month earlier.

Turning right onto the main entrance of Hôtel-Dieu Hospital, the hackney and its burden slowed as they reached the roundabout and came to a standing stop at the front doorstep of the institution.

✝♨✝

Crossing one of the janitors scrubbing the nursery's main corridor, Laurent figured the latter would be far a better choice as a last minute lodging adviser, than the prudish head nurse or the elitist pediatrician.

- *Pardonez-moi, Monsieur.*
  Excuse- me, Sir.
- Ouan?

The mop wielding sweeper was of a certain age and gave life to his cleaning implement with the same theatrical creativity as would a slightly older Fred Astaire dancing with a wooden chair.

- *Seriez-vous assez obligeant pour me suggérer un hôtelier qui pourrais m'offrir unr chambre pour la nuit?*
  Would you be kind enough to suggest an innkeeper who could lodge me for the night?
- *Ma fille travail à une auberge sur le coin de La Rolland et Saint-Georges. Les déjeuners sont pas fantastiques, mais les chambres sont propres, confortables et biens chauffées.*
  My daughter works at an inn on the corner of La Rolland and Saint-Georges. The breakfasts aren't fantastic but the rooms are clean, comfortable, and well heated.

- *Merci! Et les déjeuners?*
  Thanks. And the breakfasts?
- *Le frère du tenacier a ouvert une brasserie juste au nord de l'auberge. Les meilleurs déjeuners en ville.*
  The master's brother opened a beer-house just to the north of the inn. The best breakfasts in town.

- *Un vrai travail d'équipe! Vendu. Encore, merci.*
  Now that's teamwork! Sold. Again, thanks.

Calling the innkeeper *"un tenacier"* rather than *"un hôtelier"* became a far more relevant question of definition, after Laurent had spent a night at the inn. By the early hours of the morning, it became abundantly clear to Laurent that it would be wise to keep the answer to this question for himself.

By seven o'clock in the morning, Laurent had finished bathing and had donned his soiled work clothing, having slept less than three hours due to his attempted slumber constantly having been perturbed by the moans, groans and occasional cries of ecstasy, emanating from the neighboring rooms inside the inn.

By seven twenty he had crossed the doorstep of the beer-house's main entrance. The cafeteria sized interior was virtually standing room only. Most of the maple wood benches occupied by the graveyard shift workmen from the Rolland Paper Mill, located on its redundantly named road, half a mile west of the inn.

⚒☕⚚

- To say you look frazzled, Laurent, would be an understatement. Did you not find adequate lodging last night?
- The room at the local whor... *auberge* was OK but I had a hard time falling asleep. Maybe it was the "unfamiliar" surroundings.

- Oh, come on. You could daydream through a tornado.

Laurent cracked an equally beautiful and mischievous smile.

- Maybe I was thinking of Louis. May I hold him?

- Of course. Here.
- Baby cuddle love-kins snuggle... boup cuddle-kins... boup.

Louis cracked his father's smile. And returned to sleep in his father's arms.

♆♈♂

Laurent, Josée-Anne and Louis decide to pay a visit to Antoine Lacloche and ask if Curé Lacloche could baptize Louis before they head back to Chanticleer. As Antoine was Jérômeville's parish priest, their first stop following Louis' and Josée-Anne's discharge from Hôtel-Dieu, would be to Jérômeville's presbytery next door to the parish's main cathedral.

To their confused dismay they find out that Curé Lacloche died, on January 4th, 1891 of complications following a hernia operation conducted at Hôtel-Dieu Hospital... in Quebec City.

The same year the CPR train finally reached Chanticleer for the first time.

Following a private baptism presided by Curé Lacloche's immediate successor, Laurent's and Josée-Anne's curiosity got the better of them, giving the trio just enough time to catch the southbound train to Viger Station.

Less than half an hour later, they debarked well before reaching Montreal, at the Ste-Thérèse Station, for a quick shopping spree at Armurier Lesage, giving Laurent a second opportunity to speak with the owner. The latter is the only defined entity that immediately recognized Curé Lacloche. And Antoine was the only one to introduce either Laurent or Josée-Anne to his acquaintance.

Though pleasantly surprised to meet Louis for the first time, Mr. Lesage's enthusiasm at the sight of the trio entering his establishment, clearly suggested Mr. Lesage was impatiently waiting for Laurent's promised return.

Mr. Lesage's response to Laurent's recent acknowledgment of Antoine's passing, a generation earlier, was as enlightening as it was dark.

- My last name is actually not Lesage. It is Brosseau. I died for the first time in 1876. They found my carcass floating near the northwest shore of Chanticleer's Lac Rond. The village doctor penned in "Death by drowning" on my morbid certificate. I knew better and so did...
- How old were you when you first died?

- Eleven. The Giant Thiazi has given me the tools necessary to pursue my stay in the Realm of Midgard. But only as a ghost.
- You have aged as if you were still one of the living.

- A gift from The Giant of Time.
- A gift not bestowed onto the ghost of Antoine Lacloche.

- You are beginning to understand, Laurent.
- Under the circumstances, I assume Antoine also knows you are a ghost.

- Yes. But he is not aware of my true identity.
- Under the circumstances, I assume you wish for Antoine's ignorance to be kept intact.

- In more ways than one. At least until the true reason for my first death is understood by the living.
- Those of Midgard.

- Those of all the realms including Midgard.
- Consider my promise, an oath.

Josée-Anne interjected:

- One I too pronounce to you, M. Brosseau.

- Though it has stopped beating for some time now, a heartfelt thanks to both of you. And to Louis.
- A secret easy for Louis to keep. At least for now.

☜☝☞☟☠

Laurent's first winter in the Laurentians was not only one of inward contemplation but also of outward exploration. Both offering a more than adequate environment for enlightened learning and evolution.

The sap has run dry. The pine trees are ready for harvesting.
Nari and Victor-Louis help Laurent with the selective felling. The hackneys haul the logs next to the concrete home for air drying.

Decades before Eleuthère Irénée du Pont de Nemours' successors helped coin the now common expression of *composite materials*, Laurent was using the latter both in the construction of his reinforced concrete basement and in the upper floors of his notched and scribed pine log home.

Though it could be argued the rot iron mesh used to stabilize and strengthen the concrete matrix of Laurent's underground dwelling was a recent addition to the pantheon of composite materials, the unidirectional fibers running the length of the massive pine trees on Laurent's acreage, were not.

They were almost as old as time itself. And though the former was engineered by man, the latter was engineered by evolution. Millions of years of evolutionary refinement that would insure that the upper floors of Laurent's new homestead would outlast by centuries, its lower foundations.

Nari's penchant for the esthetic made sure the chosen trees were as straight as possible, and Victor-Louis' penchant for engineering principles made sure the pines' longitudinal fibers had minimal twist through the length of their trunks.

☝☕☼

Nari wasn't the only one with an eye for the esthetic. Mr. Story was after all an accomplished painter. And an accomplished table-hopper at that. Making his regular outings to The Chanterelle's main dining room, a logical prelude to a his platonic friendship with the hotel's head waiter.

- Don't let Alexander get the best of you, Laurent! I jest. Mr Story's passion for table-hopping is at worst, harmless and at best will result in a contagious friendship.
- You should know Nari. And thank you for the excellent segue!
- Well Mr Story, Nari's friendship is already one thing we have in common. Please, entertain me!

- Now that our introductions are nearly complete, I will surely indulge your request by completing mine. I am a painter. My canvases are filled with still life and watercolors. Though most of my adult life was part of London's urban landscape, my first visit to the savage beauty of the Dominion's North, was my last. I have lived here ever since.
- We already have three commonalities, Mr Story. My wife Josée-Anne and our two children are also immigrants, though we are from Brittany. I too have been smitten by the beauty of this savage landscape. If you are curious of my family origins, my last name is Boullevraye de Ville-Amois.

- That is a name filled with a noble heritage. One which an English commoner would have difficulty pronouncing. At least on a first try! I will need to practice first. In the meantime please call me Alexander and I will call you Laurent.
- An excellent barter, Alexander. You need not worry about such phonetic details. Even *Curé Lacloche's* Chanticleers have trouble pronouncing my name. However, I appreciate your offer to make a concerted effort. My wife and I capture these landscapes on media of silver, glass and cellulose. You capture them on landscape. May I suggest we explore our newly adopted homeland together. This will give the chance to practice your French and me my English in an environment free of social prejudice.

- An excellent barter, Laurent. I look forward to start such explorations. And would you be joining us Lady Josée-Anne?
- Only when I can find an obliging babysitter!

- If I was only a painter, I would also be a popper. My main remuneration is thankfully due to my employment at The Shawbridge High School. As an English teacher I direct classrooms filled with potential babysitting candidates. Several commute with me by train and live nearby.
- Put in a good word for me, Alexander. I can only ask Mrs Meier to babysit so often. Finding affordable alternatives would be best for both of us. On occasion, indulging in a more extended outing, one filled with discovery, will be good for the soul.

✍☉☀

The vast expanses of virtually undeveloped forest to the west of Laurent's homestead was an excellent realm for Alexander and Laurent's first mutual endeavor of exploration and discovery; one accompanied by Alexander's long *standing* companion.

- Laurent, please meet Henry. Henry Morgan.
- Pleasure to meet you Henry. Any relation to Henry Morgan and Company of Montreal?

- The one and only.

Laurent raised an un-frazzled eyebrow as he silently recalled reading the memorial plaque at the entrance of Morgan's flagship location, earlier that month.

- Now that we have that indiscretion out of the way, I am sure all three of you will have a lot to talk about, once Josée-Anne joins us for dinner this evening.
- Roast beef at The Chanterelle?
- With Yorkshire pudding, I hope.

- Absolutely... Their pudding is the best in the region. A recipe the head waiter received with the help of Herbert Thomson, while on a trip to Toronto a few years ago. Herbert, the resident barber where Nari spent his fortnight, introduced the head waiter of The Chanterelle to the head chef of The Grosvenor Hotel, and the rest is history.
- As is yourself, Mr Morgan. I jest.
- Touché, Laurent!

- Last year, I purchased a new sewing machine from you at very reasonable price. Why is the large selection of sewing supplies in your department store such a focus of your business model?
- Yes. I recall. I was there when you purchased it.

- Hm... Bizarre. I didn't notice.
- With someone of your acumen, I try to make an effort to be discrete, as well as discreet. But we are getting ahead of ourselves. The best advice I ever got from my father was to only start a business in a domain you understand. I started my retail career in the sewing industry. The rest is history.

- Oooouh! Ooouh, ouh.
- There he is.

- Oooouh! Ooouh, ouh.
- By the sound of it, about forty paces to the northwest.

- Oooouh! Ooouh, ouh.

Laurent cocked his Winchester and headed off the trail towards the sound of the fowl beast. He could see him now. Thirty feet above the roots of an old maple tree, the latter's branches having replaced its autumn foliage with an icing of freshly deposited snow.

- Oooouh! Ooouh, Bang!! Bang!!

Laurent headed back towards the trail, his emptied rifle in one hand, the carcass of a beautiful gray owl in the other. A trail of blood dripping from its obliterated heart.

- Shlick!

It was Alexander's turn to shoot. The shutter of Laurent's Bijou closing effortlessly despite the cold dry snow falling in front of the camera's optics.

The threesome headed back to the relative warmth and security of the de Ville-Amois's new concrete homestead. The sculpted and scribed pine logs of the latter's upper floors having yet to be hoisted in place. A task that would wait until the upcoming construction season.

...

The foursome had yet to finish their respective bowl of Cointreau-spiked hot chocolate, when a knock was heard at the kitchen door. It was the babysitter. Her cheeks almost as red as her Irish locks.

Once the informal niceties completed and Josée-Anne had recited the suggested duties bestowed upon the newly arrived parental contractor, the two couples began to prepare themselves to head out for dinner at The Chanterelle. Reservations made earlier that day with the help of Mr. Morgan's uncharacteristic generosity. The living obliviously conscious to the ghostly nature of their Scottish host.

✢☕♘

The snow had stopped. Laurent's hackneys comfortably installed in The Chanterelle's stables. The dray-coach parked outside.

A ring of snow-covered ice had begun to form around the shore of *Lac Rond*, the center still blackened by the lake's deep bottom. The heat from the deceased summer slowly rising from the water's surface, like a vaporous ghost escaping oblivion.

Alexander opened his sketchbook and propped it halfway up the edge of the dinner table. Taking out a sliver of charcoal from a pocket where his handkerchief should have been, he began to draw a shoulder high portrait of his subject across the table. The warm glow emanating from the stone fireplace, in the center of the dinning room, accentuating his facial features.

- You can join in the conversation Laurent, but just stay still while I capture the details of your grin.
- That shouldn't be difficult Alexander. He hasn't stopped smiling since capturing that owl this afternoon.
- Owls are difficult targets. They are faster and far more intelligent than partridge.

- You can almost step on a partridge if you're not careful. They are almost as simpleminded as free-range chickens.
- With their head cut off.
- They sure taste good. Especially wrapped in bacon!
- Not to change the subject, but how should I prepare the owl?

- They taste a bit like chicken but the meat is darker, tougher and more gamey.
- I had the opportunity years ago to visit the Kingdom of China. One of the finest meals I had while there was not at a fancy restaurant, but rather at the home of one my business associates. We went hunting for owls one weekend. He shot two. His wife plucked & cleaned them faster than you can say Woo! Quite impressive. We all pitched in and made Moo Goo Gai Pan, replacing chicken with owl. I still remember the recipe. I'll write it down for you.

Mr Story tore off a blank page from his sketch pad, folded it twice and handed it over to Mr Morgan. Still wearing his trademark frugal Scottish smile, Mr Morgan silently removed a sliver of charcoal from Alexander's handkerchief pocket.

- I haven't had owl in years. In Brittany, they have become a rare bird indeed. The last time I ate some, it was prepared like Chicken à la Philistine.
- Let me see. We have garlic, rosemary, veal stock, thyme, bay leaves... Dried parsley would have to do. Celery is out of season, but we have plenty of apples, carrots, and onions. We are out of Riesling. Maybe we will have better luck with Henry's recipe.

Henry handed over the folded sheet of sketch vellum to Josée-Anne.

- Hm... We can replace the button mushrooms with the dried porchinos I foraged during the summer and early autumn. We can use the pickled ramps Laurent foraged this spring, in lieu of the bamboo shoots, water chestnuts and minced garlic. Ginger, owl stock, sugar, cornstarch, and sesame seed oil are not a problem...
- ... And now you can use the oyster sauce, rice wine and soy sauce my nephew added to your wok purchase when you visited my store last month.

- Your nephew is a very convincing salesman, and you a very discrete ghost, Mr Morgan.
- He takes after his uncle. At least in the realm of the living.

Sequence

Be you from a small rural village in Northern France, or have been raised in a large cosmopolitan Parisian burrow, if one can find a single common truism between the two it would be the lifelong pleasure of food.

The only integral pleasure more enjoyable than eating food, is the derived pleasure of making it.

When two like-minded people get together to prepare a series of freshly-made dishes, the time spent often can morph into an intimate social experience. When a gaggle of the same gets together, a culinary event can be seen on the ensuing horizon.

Having completed the last of her eleven successful gestation cycles nearly two years prior, Josée-Anne's offspring now gather every Saturday afternoon for what has become a traditional culinary event. Pasta Night.

With a baker's dozen worth of mouths to feed, six days a week, Pasta Night gives Josée-Anne and Laurent a much deserved breather. Three times a month, that breather takes the form of a social and gastronomic rendezvous. This gathering's sextet including Josée-Anne, Laurent and Nari on one side and Herr Meier, his wife and his eldest son, Victor-Louis on the other.

On the week of the full moon's occurrence, Josée-Anne's breather takes a hopelessly romantic tack with the Meier and de Ville-Amois duos going their separate ways, each creating their own interpretation of a romantic night out.

Not to mention Nari and Victor-Louis.

Laurent's interpretation of hopeless romanticism takes on a slightly mischievous aura. At times, resulting from several months of advance preparation.

Escorting his long-term sweetheart to a different secret location every month, an eventful meeting filled with music and gastronomic delights are almost always on the agenda. Depending on how far the location is from the family homestead, their agenda often extends well into Sunday morning.

Or afternoon.

Or evening.

Herr Meier's interpretation favors tradition over mischief but is none-the-less as hopelessly romantic an endeavor as Laurent's, once cultural differences between the two couples are taken into account.

...

- What do you think Claudette. You have successfully managed to hand out each of the preparatory chores to your brothers and sisters ever since we started Pasta Night. Consequently I thought it would be appropriate to find an official-sounding title to your essential responsibilities. I have two choices. I will let you decide which of the two you prefer.
- Oh Pleease, Louis. That's ridiculous! But since you have taken the time to think-up, not one but two titles, I will take the time to listen. After all you have peeked my curiosity. Go ahead. Entertain me!

- All right, all right. Ever since you began your own small business with Madeleine's help, you have demonstrated a truly enterprising streak in your character. Your talent in making pottery combined to Madeleine's artistic talents in hand-painting your creations, have really showed off your business acumen. You even built your own masonry oven. You are an inspiration! So naturally my first attempt was to find you a business title. Since you "manage" to find work for everyone, even the youngest of family members, Manager should be part of this business-inspired title. As a Pasta Night Manager, what do you manage? Well, in your case that's your brothers and sisters. But when you think about it, "Brother and Sister Manager" sounds a bit too parental for my taste. So how do your brothers and sisters contribute to Pasta Night? Well, for the most part they are definitely resourceful, so I thought to myself, what about "Resource Manager"? Too inhuman. Then it donned on me. "Human Resource Manager" Well...well? What do you think?
- Hold-on. Let me check my Webster's... That's what I thought. A resource is a thing. Your brothers and sisters are people. That makes "Human Resource" an oxymoron! I hope your second choice is better than your first.

- Let me see... Your right. "Human Resource" ends up being an oxymoron no matter how you interpret the definition of "Resource". You would have to be an imbecile to call yourself a "Human Resource Manager". Okay, okay, let me see what you think of my second choice.
- If it's no better than your first attempt you will have to go back to the drawing board and start all over again!

- Your hobby is pottery. However, mine is the violin. Consequently my second choice for your title is musically inspired. If one embodies Papa and Mama's undefined presence, Pasta Night is a team effort that involves all members of the same family. Sort of like an orchestra. Of course, the one in charge of deciding who-dœs-what in an orchestra, is the conductor. That would make you the conductor of a gastronomic orchestra rather than a musical orchestra. Consequently, your title would be "Gastronomic Conductor".
- Now that makes sense! And no opposing definitions.

- Feouuff. I had already whittled down the best six attempts to these two choices. Last week I had over a dozen possible titles following a brainstorming event. Granted my brain was the only one present while the storm was underway, but still.
- Well Louis. Don't forget Papa's favorite patois.

- If you want to do something right, do it yourself?
- Exactly. We are already influenced enough by other people's ideas, even when they are not present in the same room. If you want to be truly creative, I believe that it is best to at least start by thinking things out for yourself.

- You are right about that. But you do have to admit that if it wasn't for you, I would have overlooked my *faux-pas.*
- Yes, but my input was limited to verification and confirmation. It had nothing to do with creativity. Whenever I am brainstorming with friends at school, what could be a really good idea is almost always shot down by someone's own perspective and personal agenda. What's important when you are trying to brainstorm with several people at the same time, is to extricate those personal perspectives from the agendas hidden underneath the latter. If you don't succeed, you end up with compromise instead of creativity.

- Yikes! With all this talk about creative processes, the Ravioli Stuffer and Sealer aka me has fallen behind the Pasta Sheet Maker and Cutter aka the newly titled Gastronomic Conductor...
- Luckily the Pasta-Dough Mixer aka you, and the Pasta Dough Ball Maker and Kneader aka me have gotten into the habit of cutting up the large balls I make into smaller portions that will fit into my new pasta cutter I purchased last week while on our semi-annual trip to Bonsecours Market.

- Well, since we always make the dough the night before, spending a little extra time cutting and kneading smaller balls before having everything cold and ready for Pasta Night, is time well spent.
- And I have to admit this new pasta cutter really speeds things up!

- And talking about speeding things up, I wonder how François is doing.
- While you catch up on your ravioli stuffing and sealing, I will take a look.

When Claudette entered the dining room, she was expecting to see the Pastry-Dough Maker aka Josette busily preparing pastry shells and tops and the Fruit-filling Processor aka François peeling, coring, and slicing apples for the dozen or so deep dish apple pies that will be baked and eaten not only for tonight's first course of desserts but also for tomorrow's Sunday night supper.

Alas, François and Josette were nowhere to be found. Instead, on the dinning table was a baker's dozen of nearly identical uncooked apple pies, each covered with a chilled dish cloth and ready for egg-basting and baking in the kitchen's over-sized wood-fired cooking stove. To the left and front of the pies was François's new Reading 78, purchased at the same time and place as Claudette's pasta cutter. In a similarly enterprising fashion to his older sister, François's productivity enhancing apple peeler and corer was acquired with some of the funds received from the local farmers in exchange for scything their lawns during the summer holidays.

She finally found the first member of the lost duo, in the backyard next to the hobby barn, feeding Henry II the apple peelings her brother had prepared moments earlier. Based on the melodically muffled grunts and snorts emanating from this latest porcine member of the de Ville-Amois family, Henry was clearly in sweet apple-peeling bliss.

- Now that is one happy pig, Josette!
- He deserves it. He's the fastest growing piglet I have ever seen. At this rate he will be as big as his father by this time next year.

- He is also very well-behaved. Papa says he will make an excellent breeding pig.
- I hope Papa keeps him for that purpose. He is a gentle and intelligent beast.

- Talking about gentle and intelligent beasts. Did you see François? You both have finished making your apple pies in record time. François' new peeler must be a very effective tool!
- In anticipation of his increased performance, I took a cue from you and Louis. I prepared two batches of pastry dough before going to bed last night. But even that wasn't enough of a head start. This afternoon, I had barely finished preparing my second batch of pastry dough. François had already finished peeling, coring and slicing all the apples for the thirteen extra large apple pies! So I got to show François how to properly prepare a pastry shell. After few pies, he's gotten quite good at it. He will make an excellent cook.

- Ha! That will make him a *Bon-à-Marier....* or not. With that in mind, I was hoping you both could help out with the second course of desserts. I was thinking we could make a second dessert with some of the apples that are ready to be picked out back.
- François is one step ahead of you! He is picking some more apples and we were both going to make a gallon of apple sauce.

- Mm. Cinnamon shortbread cookies dunked in freshly made hot apple sauce. I Will leave you two with your delicious apple preserve making initiative and see if Madeleine and Jean are up to making a batch or three of shortbread cookies.
- This Pasta Night is going to be a gourmand's delight!

- Honrrronhonk! Honrronk!
- You got that right, Jr!

✝☕✝

This was the first Pasta Night where the de Ville-Amois parental authority had permitted the two eldest members of the offspring detachment to indulge in an adult, gastronomic tasting. A tasting consisting of no more than half a bottle of mead from Laurent's latest *cuvé* of homemade *Hydromel Nouveau.*

This added up to one wine glass each during the main course and one glass each to be taken with dessert. Having mead with dessert was made possible for two reasons. The distillation process and subsequent bottling having been been completed but a week ago, the resultant beverage was still relatively sweet to the pallet. Secondly, Laurent's mead recipes were always spiced with Earl Gray tea, making such a beverage ideal not only for the main course but also for the closing cheese course of homemade goat milk and walnut cheese served with hot-from-the-oven sourdough bread.

As a consequence of their recent exit from the shackles of puberty and their limited experience with the mindful effects of such distilled beverages, both Claudette and Louis were just slightly tipsy as they proceeded with their final chore of washing the dishes. The rest of the siblings were outside, completing their chores of herding in the farm animals for the night.

Claudette, being a little bit more just-slightly-tipsy than Laurent, her bout of *in vino veritas* was tinged with more emotion.

- What's the matter Claudette? Pasta-Night was the best ever.
- … Do you think they have Pasta-Night at the Monastery?

- At Oka? If they don't, they should. And with Oka cheese after dessert!
- Lots of Oka Cheese.

- You bet... Why do you ask?
- I have dreams. My sheets are wet in the morning.

- When I have a nightmare, my sheets are drenched with sweat when I awake.
- It's not sweat. Neither is it urine... Nor is it bloo...

- Oh... Wet dreams. I thought only men had wet dreams. Silly me.
- You mean... I can too?

- Papa explained it to me a few weeks ago, but didn't go into the details.
- Mama explained it to me two years ago, but didn't go into the details.

- I should have been more curious. It was a bit embarrassing.
- For both of us. Times two.

- Well at least your whimpers are subsiding. I think I see a smile.
- It's the stories inside the dreams that scare me.

- What kind of stories?
- Erotic stories.

- Oh... Do you see hippopotamuses in your stories? I always see hippopotamuses in my erotic dreams. I don't know why.
- No silly. Women. I always see women.

- What are the women doing?
- They're with me. Close to me... Very close.

- I often have men close to me. But only in my daydreams. The hippopotamuses are gone by then. I don't know why.
- Are your daydreams wet?

- … Sometimes.
- Mine. Always. They scare me.

- The women? Or the stories.
- Both. I'm scared of liking them.

- The women? Or the stories.
- Both.

- Oh... What dœs this have to do with Oka? Never mind. Silly me.
- I think you're beginning to understand. I think I'm beginning to understand.

- You don't want to join the cloistered nuns... Do you?
- Yes. That's what scares me the most.

- You should only join the cloistered nuns because of a sense of devotion, not from one of fear.
- And why are you thinking of joining the priesthood? Is it because of devotion?... Or fear?

- …
- ...

¿†¿

"At News-Talk 99.9 FM and on your smart-phone at newstalk999.com here is a 99 second news update for Tuesday January 21st, 2014...

Pope Francis addressed the thorny subject of pedophilia in the priesthood by giving his opinion the possible root cause for what seems a widespread phenomenon. Speaking in Italian during the Feast of Saint Agnes, after having blessed the pallia of the new metropolitan archbishops gathered on the Solemnity of Saints Peter and Paul, Holy Apostles, His Holy Father commented that the traditional social structure adopted by the vast majority of seminaries throughout the world have a tendency to create "little monsters" out of a large subset of students preparing for a life in the priesthood. Though not mentioning pedophilia by name, he suggested the cloistered gender-segregated educational environment combined with the strict disciplinary attitudes prevalent in the professorial body, whose members are more often than not several generations the elders of the members of the student body make for priests ill-prepared for the realities of modern urban life... "

©

Louis' choice of career path was influenced by his parents conservative religious leanings and by his close relationship to his sister Claudette, the latter being less than two years his elder.

To insure an appropriate psychiatric profile replete with behavioral mechanisms of prudish abstinence and longings for a life of celibacy, the subtle encouragements and disciplined breeding of his parents resulted in Louis choosing a path towards a life of ecclesiastical devotion years before the beginning of his puberty.

In the autumn of 1933, they both succumbed to their fears.

Claudette chose not to listen to her younger brother's advice. She convinced herself, the meditative process of isolation would help her tame the closeted monsters haunting her erotic dreams.

Louis was still undecided between becoming a Trappist monk at Oka or completing his classical studies at Montreal's Grand Seminary.

He chose to compromise. And entered the Oka Agricultural Institute to give himself time to reflect and take a final decision once he had finished his pedestrian studies.

†

With the help of the University of Montreal, and the priests of the Grand Seminary of the Sulpician Order, the Oka Agricultural Institute, was set up inside the confines of Oka's Trappist Monastery.

Though conservative by today's standards, the Trappists and their female counterparts, the Trappistines have setup monasteries throughout the world in order to spread their relatively modern Cistercian interpretation of the gospel.

As is the case for the Trappist monks and the Trappistine nuns, the male and female Agricultural Institute students live in separate quarters and are educated in gender segregated classrooms. Both the male and female students, however, share the same and only library. They also share in the duties of farming, production, processing and distribution of the Seminary's Norman inspired cheese, chocolates and butcher's delicacies.

One of the first year courses was titled "The History of the Cistercian Order: 1098 to 1664". Despite their social and work ethics being steeped in tradition, studying the social, theological, and political histories of the Cistercian Order prior to the Reform would be a test of austerity for even the most introspective of Trappist monks.

On Monday, Wednesday and Friday mornings, starting at 8 o'clock, the female version of this three hour long history class was given by a well-versed Sulpician nun. With the help of an equally well-versed Sulpician priest, the male version of this class was given on the same days, right after lunch.

Despite her virtually androgynous name, Marie-Pierre was by far the most delicate and feminine looking of all the students in her first year history class. During the hour before lunchtime, she and several of her classmates made a point to complete their history-class homework in the staid and austere silence of the main library.

At 5'6"and 112 lbs wet, she was neither too tall, nor too small to compliment a strictly hypothetical French-Canadian male partner's equally hypothetical presence. Her ballet-dancer physique and finely chiseled Parisian face defied the near-obese, mud-wrestler carcasses, typically found on women in her pig-farming hometown of Sainte-Marie-de-Beauce.

To indulge in their stereotypical procrastination, the male history students would also make it a point to attend the library at the same time as their female counterparts, as the latter were always one history-class homework assignment ahead of the former.

At 5'8" and 150 lbs wet, Louis was neither too tall, nor too small to compliment a strictly hypothetical French-Canadian female partner's equally hypothetical presence. His rural Laurentian upbringing and sporting acquaintance to Lepus Hohannsen gave Louis a slim, well-toned and athletic *coureur-des-bois* physique.

At 5'10" and 180 lbs wet, Luc's athletic physique came courtesy of extensive snow-shœing jaunts during the winter and equally extensive swimming sessions in the summer in his appropriately named hometown of Saint-Aimé-des-Lacs.

At 5'10" and 275 lbs wet, the seminary's head librarian had the eagle-eyed authoritativeness of a *Schutzstaffel* interrogator and the physical characteristics of Rosanne Barr.

Louis' and Luc's first constructive encounter with the interior of the main library was on the Monday morning of their second week at the Institute, having been given their first history assignment the prior Friday. Louis had quickly made friends with Luc who took to sitting next to Louis in most of the classes common to both students. Louis and Luc were curious by nature and shared a common interest in exploring the forests in their respective homes of the Laurentian and Charlevoix mountains.

This common interest included the hunting of small and large beasts in the forest, and fishing the aquatic beasts of the surrounding lakes and rivers. Both men subscribed to the motto of "waste not, want not" and became quite apt in preparing the wild meat which they would share with the other members of their families come supper time. Their subscription to this motto also resulted in them learning how to tan the hides of the animals they hunted.

This commonality resulted in Louis and his new found friend spending most of their first weekend at the seminary exploring the forests surrounding the Trappist farm, and fishing on the shores of Lake of Two Mountains. Fortunately, as agreed upon by the academic body, the first year student's initial weekend was meant for acquainting themselves to their new surroundings rather than for studying. The only academicians not clear on the concept were the Cistercian history teachers.

By 11 o'clock, Marie-Pierre and three of her classmates were comfortably seated at a large table, standing next to several tall and slender windows with a view of the seminary's dairy farm. Louis and Luc were installed at a neighboring table, Louis two seats to the right of Marie-Pierre and Luc facing him across the table.

With his testosterone-infused cerebellum taking precedence over both his logical and draconian auricles, Louis was still able to muster enough cognitive energy to formulate the following three self-answered questions under his breath:

- What am I doing here? ... What is she doing here?... What are we doing here?

Alas, the sinking reality of the surrounding Benedictine-ruling Trappist library environment, made the answers to the preceding three questions all the more sexually and emotively moot. His strait-leaning exploratory endeavors would have to wait for another space and time. He understood the wisdom of completing his homework assignments with at best, the platonic help of Marie-Pierre and her classmates.

Though the student contingent of Louis' history class were all ideal candidates for his not-so-strait-leaning exploratory endeavors, all such forward-thinking forms of social interaction would also be out of the question. The reason for making these interactions taboo, had nothing to do with the nature of this class' subject matter. It had everything to do with the nature of the history teacher in front of the class.

The true reason for Father Caissie's hastened return from his missionary work at the Sulpicians' all-male Colombian orphanage in Cúcuta, was in turn, the Oka Seminary's worst kept secret.

Father Caissie's below average body-mass index for a priest over half a century old, hid decades of opiate addiction and long nights spent "bush cruising" in and around the nearby Public Beach. Hence, both digressions added at least two decades to his facial characteristics.

His obsessive-compulsive, sexually-charged harassment towards any male student that showed even the most platonic and conservative of social courtesies towards him, earned Farther Caissie the appropriately termed French Canadian nickname of *La Vielle Sacoche*, loosely translated to "the Old Purse". Under the circumstances, calling the Old Purse a sleaze-bag would be considered an expression of restraint.

The Old Purse's eagle eye for all things homœrotic insured that Louis' exploratory foreplay would also have to wait for another space and time. Father Caissie's latent tendencies, combined with his cringe-inducing social deficiencies and expiry-dated physical characteristics, made any form of erotic innuendo totally out of the question. By consequence history class was an all-business, all-the-time endeavor.

©

Be it choosing to become a Trappist monk or a Sulpician priest, both vocations are primordially philosophical endeavors. One of the side effects of having the aptitudes and mindset to pursue such a path, is a propensity for one to get lost in deep thought. Regardless of Louis' final decision, as a potential candidate, he did have the chops for either one of these gigs. As such, Louis was no stranger to getting lost in deep thought. His friends would jokingly comment that daydreaming was Louis' favorite hobby.

Though well established as an off-limits cruising environment, what better space-time continuum to daydream than a seminary library during the starting weeks of an undergraduate's first year semester.

With all the players in their equally well-established seating positions, Louis propped open his history textbook and placed it in its standard daydreaming position: the upper-third peaking above the edge of the table and the lower two-thirds held in place with the help of his lap. Though their friendship was still in its initial stages, Luc had already grown accustomed to his new found companion's daydreaming incursions. He knew that Louis' latest virtual adventure would end after a short nap-induced REM cycle...

The dark chestnut horsehide covering the cushions on the armrests and seat of his study chair, had been seared by the strong early-fall sun seeping through the seminary window, and was soft and warm to the touch. More than the touch, the aroma from this leather brought back memories of his father's horse-drawn carriage. Louis wasn't too sure what turned him on more: the touch, smell and feel of these hides or the horses these hides were tanned from. He figured it was a bit of both.

Louis' muscular v-shaped back, encased in his thick bison-wool sweater was also getting warmer and warmer, courtesy of this midday sun.

Marie-Pierre's standard Sulpician uniform was an unsuccessful vestmental attempt at masking her delicate yet athletic physique...

- Louis... Louis!
- Shh, I'm daydreaming.

- We're going to be late for class. You know how *La Vielle Sacoche* gets his K.O...
- ... all tied up in a knot?

- He is um... a cock of the walk.
- Careful Luc. The library's Sparrow Hawk will have both of us washing our mouths out with soap.

- And then, we will really be late for class!

®

If Louis had anything to do with it, Pasta Night always had one ingredient included in the main course's preparation. Mushrooms. Wild mushrooms.

Because several species of edible mushrooms are similar in appearance to their toxic counterparts, positive identification is essential when foraging for such delicacies, be it in the forest, or the ungulate-grazing pastures of the nearest available farmer's homestead.

Laurent would kill two partridges with one double barrel shotgun, by not only teaching his son the intricacies of mushroom identification, but also by introducing a young Louis to his first practical application of Latin outside the strict confines of a Sunday-morning Eucharist.

Now was the time for Louis to strap on his hunting boots and pass on this delicious tradition to someone outside the immediate family circle.

- Let's get going, Luc, before the farm animals step on all of them. Lest they only be good for the slugs.
- Slugs?

- The first rule of mushroom picking. If it's good for the slug, it's good for you!
- That makes sense. They're always around when I'm picking berries. So they must like eating mushrooms too.

- It has been raining for two days. The sun only started coming out yesterday evening. The fields and forest will be bursting with fungi by now.
- I'm ready. Let's go!

Though it was already 6:00 AM, the fog covering the grazing fields had yet to dissipate. Fortunately clocks had recently been turned back to standard time, giving an extra hour of sunlight during the morning hours, precipitating the day's accelerating dusk.

- This is a good start. Agaricus arvensis. The family is Agaricaceæ. The genus, Agaricus. The species, A.arvensis.
- Arvensis means "of the field".

- A field of horses. They're also found in meadows. They call them horse mushrooms.
- And if you found them in meadows, would you call them moose mushrooms?

- That's an idea. I wouldn't see why not. You could start a trend.
- Like *Ail-des-bois*. Forest garlic. The Americans call them ramps. I've heard them called wood leeks or wild garlic. Or wild leeks. Or spring onions.

- Yes. My father called them ramson. But for the reasons you just described, he preferred to call that springtime vegetable by its generic name, Allium tricoccum.
- Less confusing. We'll stick to the Latin names. Good practice.

- And here. Agaricus campestris. Same family. Same genus. Different species. Both have caps that flatten-out with age. More so with campestris. The gills, underneath, start-off light-pink on the arvensis. They start-off gray on the campestris. The gills on both turn dark brown with age. Campestris is derived from the Latin campus.
- Campus. So they must call them field mushrooms.

- Exactly. I've also heard them called meadow mushrooms.
- I'll stick with Agaricus campestris...

- Good... Actually bad. This is Agaricus xanthodermus. When you bruise the surface, the flesh turns yellow. Xanthodermus will give you stomach aches. When you bruise campestris it turns red. That's okay.
- Yellow is bad. Red is good. Got it.

After barely an hour of field picking, the duo had already filled two ten-pound burlap potato sacs with enough horse and meadow mushrooms to compliment the feasting aspirations of an army. Okay, at least a small contingent.

- They call them white-outs. With all the horses, asses, cows, pigs, and goats around here, I'm not surprised it only took us an hour.
- The more p...,

- ... the merrier.
- That's the spirit. Sort of.

- Sister Christine! Are you headed to the seminary?
- Yes. I just finished milking the cows with Sister Augustine, and I'm heading back to the cafeteria kitchen. Why?

- Luc and I have foraged enough mushrooms to augment today's lunchtime meal. Would you be kind enough to give these two bags to the chef. He has to use them today or they will go bad.
- Oh. That's wonderful. The chef is serving trout as a special meal, before the start of the long Thanksgiving weekend.

- Mmm. Trout in a cream, wine and mushroom sauce. Lots of cream and mushrooms. Just a little wine.
- White or Red?

- White. Dry.
- I'll explain your suggestion to the chef. That's a delicious idea. Thank-you.

- You are welcome. Now it's time to find some woodland mushrooms.
- Let's go. We have two potato bags left to fill before classes start.

Filling two more bags full of wild fungi would be no more difficult than filling the first two. The pine, maple, and birch grove behind the seminary's barn was filled with just the varieties Louis was looking for.

- We're know looking for two separate types of fungi. You'll understand once we find them.
- Can you at least give me a hint?

- Oh. Yes. One has a white stem and a brown cap. And the other is a beautiful bright-fire yellow in color.
- Like the little brown and white mushroom I almost stepped on a minute ago?

- Where?
- There.

- That's it! Boletus Edulis. Family Boletaceæ. Genus Boletus. Species B.edulis... Porcino!

- They have porcino festivals back in Europe. The Little Pierre Bulliard knew a good mushroom when he saw one. The porcino is his claim to fame.
- Bull-is-ard?

- No Bull-i-ard.
- Oh... okay. You know what they say. Small packages can hold the biggest surprises.

- I think we're getting off-topic. Sort of.
- So how do you eat the little guy?

- The porcino? Um, of course, the porcino. I guess it depends on the country. The French, Germans and Italians all have there own way of eating the little guy.
- Of course they do.

- The Germans eat them in soups. The Italians, with pasta or rice. And the French in *cèpes.*
- If they are all this small it will take us more than an hour to fill our sacks.

- Oh, they vary greatly in size. The small ones are best. If they are too large and old, they end-up being slimy, soft, and caustic... I can't believe I said that.
- So age... and size, matters?

- Did I mention if they're too old they end up full of maggots?
- Like an old, discarded handbag that's been left at the bottom of a dumpster for too long?

- You mean a *Vielle-Sacoche*? I think we're getting off-topic.
- Again.

- Oh. Look!
- Where?

- There. Cantharellus cibarius. Family Cantharellaceæ. Genus Cantharellus. Species C.cibarius. Chanterelles! Better than truffles. A noble delicacy. These are good for drying. I'll show you how when we get back to the seminary. We can dry them in our rooms while we are away for the long weekend. We will have the porcini for Pasta-Night.
- I'll go for the little guys, you go for the nobles.

Louis' homestead was about forty kilometers away from Oka. Luc's was over four hundred. When Louis invited him to spend the Thanksgiving weekend with his family in Chanticleer, Luc graciously accepted. Avoiding in one breath, twelve hours of train travel to Charlevoix and back, on an overcrowded holiday-bound rail car.

A pasta and apple pie feast on Saturday. A Thanksgiving one on Sunday. They would both be wobbling back to their dormitory rooms once the holiday had ended.

That weekend in Chanticleer cemented Luc and Louis' friendship. A relationship that grew stronger with the passing of each semester shared at the Institute. A platonic relationship. One filled with vivid daydreams shared by both men. At different times and different spaces.

Daydreams they both chose to keep to themselves.

By the end of the last semester, Luc's exploration had come to an end. And so did his fear. For now.

Louis' exploration had just begun. And his fear was far from over. That much he knew.

Luc's career would take him on a laical path.
Louis', a clerical one.

Two paths that were unlikely to intersect.
For now.

®®

Louis had completed the journey through his teenage years and was firmly into his twenty-somethings when he entered the Grand Seminary as a resident student, and began his studies towards a degree in Theology. The Great Depression had matured into a chronic social-economic phenomenon and was nearly two generations away from the post-Woodstock sexual revolution of the disco era. Donna Summers was but a twinkling crystal dance ball in her mother's eye.

Four years of rural agricultural studies under the uncomfortably watchful eyes of the Sulpician priests and Trappist monks, combined with an equally uncomfortable prudish family environment, only served to delay the defined presence of Louis' sexual and gender identity. Consequently, his acceptance to the Grand Seminary coincided with the temporal booting of that defined presence from the Roaring Twenties to the Dirty Thirties.

That roaring party had come to a pretentious end.

As pretentious as the logic behind the naming of the war-to-end-all-wars. The end of the latter having precipitated the party to begin with.

A great hangover lasting a dirty decade was almost halfway over.

Four subsequent decades, each as pretentious and dirty as the one before it, would pass before the real party began.

Louis didn't have the time, nor the foresight to wait. It was time for him to get his hands dirty.

As dirty as his time away from both Montreal's Grand Seminary and Chanticleer's rural hometown environments would let him.

Environments cleansed by the hypocrisy of their prudish facades.

...

A present moment in time, is defined by the observation of our actions, as much as it is undefined by the intent of our inaction.

Freedom

Skeletons in one's closet are perceived as events of our past we desperately want to have buried in the deepest recesses of our forgotten memory. More often than not, these skeletons are the virtual remains of people that long have passed away from our physical lives. Unfortunately for most of us, that closet is locked and our instinct has grabbed the key from our hands, unlocking the door to that closet only when it sees fit to do so. Worst still, it has taken the trouble to hide the door from our conscious sight exposing the skeletal remains only to its own instinctive eyes. The results are often unforeseen and undesirable.

Monsters in one's closet are, on the other hand, not only unwanted events of our past but also of our present and even of our probable future. None the less, our instinct's modus operandi hasn't changed just because the monster has yet to die and fossilize. The door to the closet is still a hidden entity.

¿☣?

Once you have entered *L'Annonciation*, you have also reached the northern reaches of Route 11. The one eastbound road out of town is more of a bush trail than a road. We are, after all, in the summer of 1864. Sunday, June 5th to be exact. To say the least, it's a bumpy ride. Though less than ten kilometers separate *L'Annociation* to the shores of *Lac Nominigue*, this last stretch of dirt road will take all of an hour to complete by coach.

- *Oh, mon Dieu.*

Lac Nominigue is as big as Chanticleer's *Lac Rond* is small. The former's shores are nowhere near as deep as the latter's. The density and size of the horseflies are as large as its expanse. They don't call it the bush for nothing.

- *Non, mon Dieu.*

The volcanic pebbles covering the shore's bottom are as soft to the touch as they are hard to the durometer. Even fifteen meters from the lake's edge that bottom is only one meter deep. For a young adult like Lucy, it is difficult to get into any trouble unless you have no knowledge of water safety whatsœver. Possible, but difficult.

- *Non, Monseigneur.*

Thirty years to the day had passed. A coincidence?

Maybe not.

Twins. Identical twins. An unexpected blessing?

Probably not.

Roy would stay in Toronto, with Herbert and Alice, his biological parents. Gabriel would be shipped to Mariastern Abbey, in Banja Luka, a short, 100 kilometer train ride northwest of Sarajevo. A decision of economic misfortune?

Definitely not.

Gabriel would be *raised* by The Trappist monks. And only the monks. Sealing his fate. If not his faith.

The fog had begun to dissipate off The Saint-Lawrence's shores of *Pointe-au-Père*. It had been nearly an hour since the sun had started to shine above the *Rivière-du Nord's* shores of Chanticleer. Without a trace of fog in site. On this last Friday of the month of May, the snow banks had finally melted away on the borders of Josée-Anne and Laurent's entrance. The last remnants of their first winter in the Dominion.

- I had the most beautiful of dreams last night. I was dressed in my Gabrielle of Paris polonaise.
- Gabrielle?

- Coco.
- Oh, OK.

- I'm comfortably seated in the living room, listening to a virtuosic performance of a Chopin piano concerto.
- How did you know it was a Chopin concerto? It was a dream.

- I could hear it.
- So could I. *Coincidentally,* I was wearing my Otto of Braunschweig Tux and Tales during *my* dream, last night.

- Otto?
- Otto Jeschke.

- Oh, OK.
- Who was playing?

- He was a handsome young man that vaguely resembled the Austrian pianist who performed during our outing to Montreal, last year, for the representation of Lohengrin.
- Jr?

- Jr?
- Gustav's son. Sr died three years ago. Jr 's the one I bought the piano from. Vincent introduced us to him after the performance.

- Yes, Jr. Didn't he sell you the piano because he was going to London?
- This spring.

- We're going to have to have a word with M. Brosseau.
- I concur.

Breakfast had just finished. The morning dishes were cleaned and placed in their appropriate cabinets.

When Jose-Anne entered the living room to settle into her daily piano scales regimen. she found a red silk bow tie on the opened keyboard: an uncustomary position for this time of day.

If they could share the same placenta for nine months, it wasn't a stretch for Tom and Uli to share the same room during their work week in the metropolis. On Fridays, they would take CPR's overnight milk run to L'Annociation; reaching the Chanticleer Station by three AM on Saturday.

- Oh no...
- Oh no...

She started listing severely from her starboard side; her bow was a mess.

- Hurry Lucy, we have to get to the port side.
- I can't see anything. Give me your hand Laurence.

Henry wasn't so lucky. An unforeseen consequence of his innate frugality and his explorer's nature. When he awoke from the steel-ripping ruckus, it was already too late: his third-class cabin, chest high in water, rushing in from the lower air vent of the cabin's door; the latter forced shut by the rising water on both sides of the wall separating the cabin's interior from the central corridor outside.

By now, she had just lurched onto her starboard side.

- The only way out is through the porthole. It's now or never, Lucy.
- I can't believe you said that. You go first, and pull me out once your ready.

- The show's not over till the fat lady sings! I can't believe I said that.
- You are such a drama queen, Laurence. Go!

Henry's cabin door was on the starboard side. And with no port hole he was now trapped inside his cabin with only an air pocket left for breathing and the port-side wall now serving as the ceiling of his makeshift cell. All that was left was to wait... And panic.

The less than airtight and longitudinal bulkheads on her starboard side were quickly filling up with water, suddenly jerking her stern skyward and her hull further into The Saint Lawrence.

- Laurence!

Lucy lost her grip on his right hand as she was jerked into the freezing spring waters with hundreds of other passengers who had also found their way onto her port side. Laurence was able to hold on as his left arm was still wrapped around the porthole window.

Lucy couldn't swim. Laurence could. So into the water he went.

Laurence was a good swimmer, but he was no lifeguard. By now, Lucy was in an aggressive state of panic.

So was Henry...

- Thump!
- Thump!

- Did you have the same dream I had?
- Maybe. You go first.

- I was drowning. Alone. In the dark. It felt like I was caught in a prison cell.
- I was drowning. With a hysterical lesbian around my neck. It was dark, but I could see the moon.

Tom and Uli simultaneously picked themselves up from their shared woolen rug in the center of the bedroom. Both taking the time to reorganize their severely displaced bedspreads, sheets, and pillows before preparing to head out to start Friday's construction work shift.

◴⚒◷

For Stanley's masters, it was a foregone conclusion. After all, the Wulfila twins having contributed to the design, construction, and initial notoriety of Stanley's new underground enterprise, calling the latter "Tom and Uli's" was an instinctive decision.

- Is it a role-playing theme night? We should have come in our construction gear instead of our breeches.
- I don't understand. What do you mean?

- Look. Over in the far corner. The big, fat fifty-something. He's all dressed up in a Roman Catholic parish priest tunic. All black, with a large red silk sash around his even larger belly. Granted, there are several priests of all denominations here tonight, but they are the most discrete of clientèle. The last thing they want to do is stand out from the crowd.
- And who's the scrawny little Englishman next to him? All decked out in his slim-fit dark-blue tailored suit, and smoking a cigarette at the end of a six-inch stem. He looks like a gay pimp from London's Lower East Side.

- Maybe they are just play acting.
- The little guy looks familiar, but I can't put my finger on it. He's kind of cute though. In a mischievous sort of way. I think I will go strike a conversation.

By the time Tom was less than ten paces from the odd couple, the priest was nowhere to be found... anywhere.

Now it was Uli's turn. His gaze instinctively focusing on the opposite corner of the lair. The couple he was eying was also a bit odd, but not for the same reasons as the first.

Their beauteous mustaches defied their standard issue English barrister hair cuts and clean shaven cheeks. The two could have been twins were it not for the thirty years separating them in the realm of time: the youngest barely having started his journey as a thirty-something.

The elder's English prep school demeanor patently clashed with the attire he wore that night. His cowboy boots, slim fit indigo blue jeans, buckskin hunter's vest, and thick cotton work shirt, made him look like a weekend cattle rancher from Wyoming on his way home to Oxford, after a week long hunting expedition out west... with his son.

Curiosity got the better of him; not to mention his unexpected and yet to be explained attraction to the rugged yet distinguished appearance of the younger Harrow School graduate turned Rocky Mountain explorer.

By the time Uli had transgressed the younger part-time explorer's comfort zone, the elder had conveniently disappeared. Nowhere to be found... anywhere.

♛♋♣

They made it just in time. A consequence of their short detour by their temporary abode, a second story lair located on the corner of Dorchester and Montcalm. Each grabbing their respective duffel bag filled with a work week's worth of dirty laundry.

Tom and Uli completed this pedestrian journey from their namesake's Stanley Street underground liar and caught Viger Station's last train to Chanticleer, with but a few seconds to spare.

Their new found escorts in tœ.

As regulars on this CPR line, and to take advantage of discounted fares, Tom and Uli always had at least a month's worth of return tickets on their person at any given time.

As the foursome settled into the opposing seat cubicle at the rear of the car closest to the caboose, Tom handed a pair to Laurence, and Uli did the same for George Bernard.

Not a trace of fog could be seen over the relative calm surface of the Saint-Lawrence: a deceiving calm; the raging current underneath still deadly and imposing, 600 kilometers upstream of the village of *Pointe-au-Père*.

...

As the locomotive came to a prolonged stop at the rear of the Ste-Thérèse Station, its platform glowed a pale gray, courtesy of a full moon above.

As glowing as the baldish head of the rifle-wielding graybeard racing through the cars of the freshly stationed train.

- Isn't that the fat priest you were with at the lair?
  Laurence responded in silence to Tom's inquisition.

- And isn't that the tall out-of-place ranch man you were playing pool with?
  George Bernard responded in silence to Uli's inquisition?

- As long as the Irishman dœsn't start...
- Bang! Bang! Bang!
- ... inside the train.

- That got the Roman Catholic priest and the urban redneck running faster than a moment ago.
- At least the three of them are off the train now. Good thing or someone...
- Bang! Bang! Bang!

- ... might of got hurt.

The gray-haired muckraker and his two targets disappeared into the night. No shell casings to be found. No apparent damage to the rail cars. Only the foursome at the rear of the train seemingly aware of the disturbance that had run amok.

The graybeard fighting to stem the cancer growing around him. A ghostly cancer spreading with every newly found psychopath joining Antoine's deadly flock.

- He has the temper of an Irishman, but he looks more like a Scot.
- With the demeanor of a rural redneck.
- A frustrated one.
- Probably a sexually frustrated one at that.

- Emasculation?
- With a temper like that, I would say partial.
- Heads, it was the left one...
- Tails! It was the right one.

- He was screaming something in what sounded like an aboriginal tongue.
- It wasn't Cree nor Algonquin.
- I heard him say, "Christian whore", under his breath as he passed by. He spoke English with a southern drawl.
- It was probably Cherokee.

- That would make him from the Confederate States.
- Several Scot-Irish emigrated to Virginia, at the end of the eighteenth century. Some moved on, and settled in the Indian and Mexican territories to the south and west.
- Amazing how he used his rifle as a walking stick without it going off before he chose to take aim.
- Despite his limping gate, I would call it a running stick rather than a walking one.

Laurence was a true performer. Bringing lovemaking to heights of theatrical and comical ecstasy.

- For a ghost you are quite an entertainer. I believe the English would call you a hoot.
- I was a dramatist, and a novelist, during my stint in the realm of the living. Enlightened improvisation comes naturally.

- Who was the hysterical lesbian around my -um your- neck during my dream I had yesterday?
- My wife. She too was an actress. Our relationship began as one of discretion and convenience. Through the years it has grown into one of platonic love.

- True love; one without the love making.
- I never thought of it that way. Until I sacrificed my own life to attempt to save hers.

- You are taming the monster inside your closet.
- Ironically, my death and my wife's has permitted me to begin just such a journey. Unfortunately, the priest you saw me with at the lair still hasn't found the door to the lair where his own monsters are hiding.

- And he has become a monster himself.
- He began in the realm of the living, and has become an even more formidable monster in the realm of the dead.

- How did you get to know the priest so well?
- Albert. Albert Brosseau. I met him during a performance of Typhoon in Montreal last year. I was on stage. Albert was in the first row. He wore a red bow tie for the occasion. We made eye contact. The rest is ...

- Is he good in bed?
- He is aggressively passionate. A consequence of his violent death.

- How did he die?.. Oh... The priest... Yikes.
- Albert is prone to aggressive events. Ironically, he is not a jealous man.

- Is that why the graybeard muckraker ended up shooting at the priest instead of Albert?
- The graybeard is Scot-Irish and resided in Texas for much of his life. He has a short fuse but not as short as Albert's. He was a politician and a lawyer.

- Making him prone to modulated aggression rather than emotional outbursts.
- Exactly.

- Dœs the priest know of your relationship with Albert?
- No, not yet.

- And how dœs your recent death affect your relationship?
- It gives relevance to permanence.

Contrary to his Irish counterpart, George Bernard's aggressive passion was internalized...

- You were a real cuddle-kins last night, Georgie.
- I hoped you didn't mind the vanilla. I am aware you may have preferred more than snogs and snuggles.

- That's OK. I had a hard week at work. Lots of heavy lifting. You are like a big warm, toy bear. Not at all what I was expecting from a ghost. I slept like a baby.
- It is a stereotype I have come to expect. I figure this is your first experience.

- With a ghost? Yes; I believe for Tom too. We tend to do things in synchrony. Even when we don't consciously plan on it.
- You must be identical twins. Have you always lived together?

- Yes. You could say we are inseparable. Despite the fact we are not Siamese.
- Ha! If had to start my life over again, I hope it would be as a twin. If ever the opportunity arises, any words of wisdom?

- Don't confuse brotherly love with lust. Though we do most everything together, even cruising, we draw the line at the foot of our respective beds: no hanky-panky and definitely no threesomes.
- Makes sense. I deduct, neither of you have lacked parental affection.

- An astute observation... OK. I will take the bait. Now it's your turn. Was that your father I saw you with at the lair last night?
- An astute observation. And thank-you for accepting the bait. I hope it won't leave a sour taste in your mouth. He died yesterday. At the break of dawn. He haunted me when I was alive. He couldn't wait to haunt me in his death.

- And he is the one who caused yours?
- Last night, I came to grips with my father's psychosis. The trauma of his own death has been more enlightening to me than it has been for him. As I spoke to him, his denial became more evident... And intrenched. In life, he refused to find and confront the monsters hidden inside the deepest realms of his soul. I fear that denial will only become permanent as he travels through time on the edge of Midgard and oblivion.

- You are finding, and taming, the monsters, and skeletons in your own soul. You are healing. Understanding your father's downfall will shield you from further harm.
- I rather be a bear than a cat. He can't kill me twice.

- That's the spirit! Pardon the pun.

¿☨?

Ironically, Louis' childhood was plastered with layer upon layer of parental sexual repression. The irony coming from the number and frequency of pockmarks eventually punching holes in his otherwise prudish shell.

His first memorable pockmark was more virtual than physical. Fodder for his vivid imagination. It took the form of Jon's first encounter with a member of the de Ville-Amois family.

Louis was hunting partridge, about two kilometers due north of The Chanterelle's main entrance He was given permission to do so by the hotel's owner, Mr. Thompson, on condition he stay a safe distance away from the clientèle. Though it was the afternoon of the winter solstice, there was already two feet of snow in the forest. He was making his way through the snow covered underbrush with a new pair of bear-gut and maple wood snowshœs he was using for the first time. A gift from his father, who had recently returned from a trip to Hudson's Bay's Oskelaneo Trading Post in the region.

- TRAAACK!!!

Louis almost jumped out of his sealskin moccasins. It was snowing. He had just enough time to turn his head towards the sound of the forceful command before coming face to face with a spry 55 year old Norwegian Viking on a pair of touring skis. Jon came to a silent but equally forceful stop. The tip of skis inches away from the tail ends of Louis' snowshœs.

- Now I understand what this makeshift trail is for. Pardon my ignorance.
- Apologies excepted. Now it's my turn. I shouldn't startle someone holding a loaded rifle. Specially one as young as you. How old are you?

- 16. My name is Louis. I have never met a touring skier before. I have only seen pictures in The Gazette. You glide through the snow like an owl diving for his prey. Quick and quiet. I understand your motivation behind such an effective warning cry.
- You would be a more successful hunter on these than on snowshœs. My name is Jon. Nice to meet you Louis.

- Nice to meet you sir. My parents always buy me clothing at least one size larger than necessary. I think my moccasins should fit you. Would you be willing to trade your skis for my snowshœs: the time it takes to show me how to glide?
- Wise parents. And yes, I would be more than willing to show you how to "glide".

¿♋?

Jon's second encounter with the de Ville-Amois family was not a sporting one, but rather a foraging one with Louis and his younger brother François.

By now Hare-Hop, a name Jon was more affectionately known by, had permanently moved his family from the shark infested waters of Lake Placid to the literally more placid environment of Piedmont.

For reasons that will only become clear in subsequent installments of this literary endeavor, Hare-Hop had amputated the first half of his hyphenated name and was legally referred to as Jon Hohannsen. The same descriptive amputation was conducted on the other members of his immediate family including his wife Aline.

Two weeks had passed since spring equinox of 1932. The grasslands on the south face of the 40/80 mountain range had lost most of its snow cover, bringing to an end Louis' second season of Telemark skiing.

Louis had invited Jon to forage for ramps on the family homestead. For Louis and François the short expedition was a gastronomic one. For Jon it was one of survival.

For Louis and his sibling, their developing friendship with Jon was their first with an adult outside their apparent family circle. A relationship made plausible by the viking's demeanor, characterized by an emotional maturity well over a generation behind his physical maturity. To be fair, though well over a half century old, he could run circles around his two younger companions in all manner of physical and sporting activities. An undefined consequence of Jon having yet to reach his own rendition of middle age.

Socially speaking, such outings were made possible by the tempered accompaniment of Bob, Jon's first son. Tempered by the prying eyes of those around them, Bob being nearly exactly the same age as François.

Little did they know; including the foursome. Louis' attraction to Jon and François' to Bob was first instinctive in nature. An undefined presence yet to be consummated.

¿☕?

Comfortably installed in one of the library's overstuffed, leather-clad easy chairs, Louis was in a daydreaming mood. Instigated after reading a letter from Luc. The letter was inside a package delivered to him by the Grand Séminaire's gofer.

The gofer is the resident closet boy toy. A homeless street prostitute turned born again christian, "mercifully" taken in by the Seminary staff in an attempt to save the sinner's soul from the fires of damnation... right.

The letter includes a picture of Luc on the latest gift from his father, one offered in celebration of graduating from the Oka Agricultural Institute. The picture is of Luc straddling a spectacular dark chestnut hackney. Luc is wearing a pair of saddle tan deerskin riding breeches he designed and tailored himself with deer hides he and Louis had tanned and dyed after last year's deer hunting expedition.

The package contains another surprise. A pair of similar riding breeches to the pair in the photo, custom tailored by Luc, using Louis' personal measurements taken by the latter last year...

...The forest is aflame in seasonal colors. Poplar yellows mix with the browning sheen of the fading birch leaves. The late afternoon sun still strong enough to turn that sheen a bright gold in the eyes of the casual observer. The maples have started to turn. Each painted the same uniform color they had adopted the year before. The most spectacular are the red ones. A deep blood red turned bright by that same autumn sun on the verge of setting over the Laurentian hills.

And valleys.

The two wolves are chasing a male white-tailed deer through one whose foot has been cleared with a path just wide enough for pair of touring skis. A decision taken during a moment of instinctive panic. One that will seal his ørlög.

Both wolves finally catch-up to the exhausted deer. Luc strikes his throatlatch, Louis, his hind leg at the height of his stifle...

- You should try them on to see if they fit... Louis... LOUIS!!
- Shhh!
- Hmm?

- I said you should try on your new breeches. They are beautiful. I bet you look quite handsome in them.
- Hm.. Yes, Gofer. Thank you for the compliment and the delivery. I will pass on your approval of these breeches to Luc.

- Luc?
- Luc was a classmate at Oka. We became good friends. Look. Here. He's on his new companion.

Holding the picture in his left hand, Gofer blushed as his already tight fitting indigo bluejeans became progressively tighter around upper inseam.

- Ouff... I could see him at Tom and Uli's.
- Tom and Uli's?

- It's a club.
- A horseman's club?

As Gofer's blushing cheeks faded, they were pushed towards the back of his jaw to make room for a mischievous grin.

- No... It's a night club. Though more than one Italian Stallion are known to frequent its halls on a regular basis.
- Oh... That type of club. I am beginning to understand.

Gofer's eyes widened as to say a silent "Finally!".

- I'll go try on my new breeches.
- I'll wait.

Louis returned from the library's loo, the bottoms of his new gift tucked into his well worn and equally well maintained twelve-inch black leather logger's boots.

The sight of Louis walking towards him, did nothing to make room inside Gofer's momentarily uncomfortable work wear.

- Would you see *me* at Tom and Uli's?
- With Luc in tœ!

ϟ⚔ϟ

It was Friday afternoon. Seminary classes finished at noon, to give the students and their masters time to prepare for their weekend endeavors. Gofer would escort Louis to the ghetto. Dinner at Stanely's Tearoom. A socially acceptable introduction to the latter. Followed by a discreet introduction to Tom and Uli's. Louis would take the last train Up North.

How convenient.

Ørlög not withstanding.

It didn't take much coaxing on Louis' part. Nor on Gofer's. It was after all the weekend of Tom and Uli's twenty-fifth anniversary.

How convenient.

Synchrony not withstanding.

Gofer knew the alleyways, parks, dead-end streets and shortcuts of ill repute that made up this ghetto. A consequence of his checkered and recent past. A ghetto filled with hidden doors, both virtual and real. One sandwiched between two others: Westmount, one populated by the wealthy and legally influential, to the west, and McGill's student ghetto, one populated by the cognitive and influential-to-be, to the east.

He guided Louis to destination, avoiding the prying eyes of both the Gray Nuns, tending to their estate gardens, and the well-to-do, tending to their weekend business on Mountain Street, just west of The Ritz Carlton.

They reached Stanley's entrance as the sun was setting over the sleeping green giant's forested profile: Mount Royal Park. The giant may be asleep, but the mountain was about to awaken: filling its cemetery with the ghosts of the city's past; the observation deck, with the eyes of the romantic, and the park's walking paths, with the souls hiding from their monsters within.

...

As the duo headed towards the left hand side of the tearoom's front desk, Ernest took over Gofer's duties and found the guests a table in the sunken center-back of the grand tearoom, giving the young regular and the older newcomer a gladiator's view of both the courtyard deck and the tearoom's occupants, and the latter, a bird's eye view of the former.

Though clearly distinct compared to the standard issue, black-leather clad consorts having dinner that evening, the unpretentious earth tones of the newcomer's saddle tan deerskin attire, blended in seamlessly with the discerning warmth of the Mahogany clad walls of Stanley's grand tearoom, now having temporally morphed into the establishment's Grand Dining Room.

Making Louis' presence even more discreet than it was discrete.

Go figure.

...

- Luc is going to have to tailor you a pair of breeches too. You are one of the only patrons without a pair here.
- Thank the Gods you mentioned it.

- The Gods?
- I'll explain in due time. Of importance is the present moment. Uniform Night always starts with dinner at The Grand, at least for the regulars.

- I guess that's why we ended up the focus of attention.
- You got that right sist... um Sir!

Oskar, The Grand's head waiter had celebrated his twenty-fifth anniversary at Stanley's service three years earlier, and was now well into the later half of his fifth decade of travel through The Realm of *Midhgardhr.* His graying flattop giving him an air of Romanian distinction. In turn, complementing his trademark vest, finely tailored of Midnight Blue crushed velvet, and worn underneath an equally tailored Scottish-wool dinner jacket of the same color.

- Are we ready to order?
- I see you have venison on the menu.

- Yes. We are supplied by the Iroquois of the South Shore. The steak is grilled to order and topped with a wild mushroom and pickled ramp sauce.
- I will have mine medium-rare.

- With wild rice and mashed potatœs?
- Yes, please.

- And what about you Gofer?
- I'll have the same, but well-done.

- And what will we begin with?
- What is today's soup?

- Green Pea and Onions.
- That will be excellent.
- That's my favorite. I will have a large bowl.

- Gofer the gourmand. I will be back in a few minutes. The sommelier will greet you while you wait.

Louis exchanged the menu for the wine list, and opened the latter to peruse the Bordeaux section of the list.

- They call you Gofer here too?
- Yes, but not *officially* for the same reasons.

- *Officially?*
- *Hypocrisy oblige!* Let me explain. As you can tell I've become sort of "part-of-the-furniture" around here. They nicknamed me Gofer because I was game to offer *nearly* any service to anyone... for a fee.

- *Nearly?*
- We all have our limits... and *scruples.*

- *Scruples?*
- I try to uphold most of *your* Ten Commandments.

- *Mine?*
- I'm not just a sinner, I'm also a heathen.

- I'm starting to understand where the hypocrisy fits in.
- Where I'm from, the future is an uncertainty. Vœs are not meant to be kept. We must see them as oaths to the future. If the future is uncertain, we have to be able to accept the failure of such an undertaking. And that is where lies the hypocrisy of your theocracy.

- In the nature of its future determinacy?
- Exactly. We are human animals. Our atrophied instinct will not permit us to accept such a determinacy. Sooner or later it will catch up with you.

- Why have you accepted to expand your reach to that of the Seminary?
- There is a time and a place for everything. I am approaching true adulthood. And though with time comes experience, that same time will bring beauty to a fleeting end. It was time for me to move on...

- ... To a more captive audience?
- Exactly! You are not like the others, Louis. You are not part of that captive audience.

- My exploration has only recently begun.
- When did it begin?

- Two years ago. It was the third Thanksgiving I spent with Luc. It was Indian Summer. We were foraging on my father's homestead We had stopped under a fire-red silver maple, and began contemplating aloud about the decisions we would have to make the following year, the last one of our extended fortnight at the Oka Agricultural Institute. It was then that he had chosen to confide in me. His exploration had ended. It was time for mine to begin. Beauty is in the eye of the beholder. He offered me to become at ease with the beauty of my own body. For a moment, the mirror image of Luc's. He felt right. He smelt right. His touch was, just right. He could have gone further, but he didn't. It wasn't the time. It may never be.

- Dœs Luc have a companion now?

- I don't have the courage to ask him.
- We have work to do.

- That why I'm here.
- Exactly!

...

- Have we chosen a bottle to our liking?
- Yes. We are eating venison. So we will have a red: a Château Mauleon Caramany.

- A particular vintage?
- Your most recent.

- I will be back in a moment.
- Thank-you...

- ...Why do you suppose that woman is at the table on the far side of the room? Wouldn't it be more appropriate for her to be seated in the ladies' ordinary?
- I don't suppose. That, Louis, is a transvestite. And yes, she's being a bitch.

- My father would call them Robespierres.
- Now THAT's a historic truism.

- My father told me all Robespierres are bitches. It's part of their persona.
- Your father is a wise and observant man. And how did that conversation start?

- We were outside, on a park bench, in front of Holt and Renfrew's. It was a beautifully hot summer day. We were each eating an ice cream cone while we waited for my mother to finish her shopping.
- That would be a long conversation.

- A heavyset lady passed in front of us. She wasn't obese. Rather, one would say she had large bones. I didn't make eye contact, but as she passed I swear I saw a three o'clock shadow under her foundation. That's when the conversation turned from double chocolate fudge, cherry swirl ice cream to a more adult oriented discussion on the birds and the bees. One cleverly disguised as an innocent dissertation on the finer details of female interpretation.
- And the rest is history.

...

It was well past dusk, as the diners slowly began to disappear into the darkness of Stanley's walled courtyard. Only a few table-hoppers were left.

And Louis. Gofer having abstained from such activities: up until now.

As Conrad approached their table, Gofer cringed a smile. If Gofer was "part-of-the-furniture", Conrad was "part-of-the-fixtures". The latter was as rotund as he was stocky. Like a compressed Ronald Mac Donald. So was his demeanor. A distorted Ronald, in constant denial of his acting gig's mediocrity. One forced upon him by the social limits of his past: a mother who raised dairy cows in Black Lake, and a father who raised pigs in East Hereford, a small village straddling the border between the Eastern Townships and New Hampshire.

He wore his leathers as awkwardly as his demeanor. Vestments that looked as if they had been purchased from a discount vendor inside The Grands Magasins Dufayel, in the northern part of Paris. Their cut-rate finish equaled by their questionable tailoring; both having aged disgracefully.

He spoke with an accent; a hybrid of Loyalist English tinged with undertones of a Beauçeron dialect of French-Canadian *Joual.*

- In the context of this evening's event, your dining companion seems far more clear-on-the concept than you Gofer.
- I'm working on it. I'm working on it.

- We have yet to be introduced, Sir. My name is Conrad. I am a founding member of The Rumpus Rousers.
- Mine is Louis. A pleas....

Before Louis could finish his etiquette-filled complimentary response, he had received a swift and well-defined kick in the right shin, compliments of Gofer's left boot; morphing Louis' amputated response into a silent, cringed smile, vaguely reminiscent of the one produced by his dining companion, moments earlier.

- It's Uniform Night. The latter is young. I'm off to Tom and Uli's. I hope, Louis, you will be able to convince Gofer to get as properly into gear as you are now.

Still smiling, Louis nodded in agreement. Conrad disappeared behind the door separating The Grand and the courtyard's deck.

- Sorry about that Louis. The first unwritten rule of survival to cruising at Tom and Uli's. Never show an outwardly interest in Conrad. Especially in his presence. Mark my words. If you do so, you will regret it.
- May I ask why?

- Conrad is not a bad person. Even less a bad ass. Your universe is limited by the stars you observe on a clear summer night, as you lie in the wild grass atop Chanticleer's Hills 40/80. Conrad's is limited to the sculpted walls inside Tom and Uli's.
- I will remember that. I feel your words will resonate well beyond the walls beneath us.

- Time will tell Louis... It's time to go. At least *you* will be fashionably late.
- We'll work on it. We'll work on it!

...

And they did. Gofer supplying his personal measurements. Louis taking them. From the top of Gofer's head to the heals of his feet. And Luc agreeing to tailor a pair of black deertan breeches. For a fee...

Sort of.

Gofer would barter his hustling skills for a complimentary pair of breeches. And compliment they did. Their drape and near perfect fit serving to emphasize his just slightly diminutive and near perfect athletic build. He need not speak first. Letting his piercing cobalt blue eyes and Adonis smile do the introductions for him. More often than not, his potential client and potentially Luc's, would begin the conversation with a...

- Where did you get the pants there ~~sailor, cuddle-kins, snuggle-muffin,~~ Sir?
- Oh... From a tailor in Charlevoix.

- Charlevoix? That's at least 500 kilometers away.
- Not a problem. Louis will take your measurements and wire them to Luc.

- Louis? Luc?
- Luc is the tailor from Charlevoix. Louis, his friend. He is studying Theology at the Grand Séminaire. Louis will take your measurements here, if he is available, or in the storeroom upstairs during the tearoom's business hours. He will wire them to Charlevoix. Once completed, Luc will send the vestment to Stanley's Tearoom. You can pick it up at the front desk or here, at the coat-check. Your convenience. A deposit is customary, but not required.

- Is Louis here tonight?
- Actually, yes. He is the dapper gentleman over there, in the saddle-tan breeches. I will introduce you to him...

Friedrich, Luc's new client, and Louis' latest exploratory endeavor, was himself a sailor. On leave from a German merchant ship, one hailing from the Port of Hamburg. Freiderick's build was as Teutonic as Gofer's was diminutive. He was imposing but not overwhelming so. Muscular but not to the point of restricting the gracefulness of his movements.

The center of the lair was dominated by a four-sided island. Three of those sides served as the perimeter of the main bar. The fourth separating the public space of the lair from the private space of the back room inside the island.

The island was covered by a massive steel-beamed mezzanine. its floor constructed of tightly-spaced grading, fashioned of the same metal as the joists it lay upon; the grading doubling for the island's first-floor open-aired ceiling. The lair's spacious and multifunctional public loo was one of the mezzanine's two main attractions and aloft the back room's perimeter. The other, was a makeshift stage, and covered most of the island's main bar.

That night, in between two sets of Gregorian chants, performed by a large contingent of male students from Marguerite-Bourgeoys College's faculty of music, the empty stage offered the space and time for Louis to take Friederick's measurements; to the delight of the observers around and below the two men.

By the time Friederick had stripped to his balbriggans, you could here a pin drop. His scent and the beauty of his hard-laborer's physique, overwhelming Louis' instinct with thoughts of Thanksgiving, and fire-red silver maples.

☎♞☩

By the time Luc had tailored a dozen pairs of breeches, he had graduated from his mom's Singer Flatbed, to a Pfaff 195: an industrial, walking-foot, vertical post sewing machine, purchased from the German manufacturer's Quebec-City distributor. With a removable Tilt Base and Work Support, the 195 was easily transformed from a vertical post into a flatbed machine when needed. Doubling its usage and the efficiency of Luc's investment.

He was now able to tailor coats as well as breeches. His first project would be a German Military styled wraparound, bartered by Friederick, in exchange for the breeches he ordered a few weeks prior. He made two prototypes: one in saddle tan leather, the other in black; to the delight of Louis and Gofer respectively.

One must observe that Louis and Gofer were not only respectively student and employee of The Grand Séminaire, they were also residents. Albeit on a transitory basis for Louis and a permanent one for Gofer.

Having Gofer, on occasion, exit the seminary in full gear, may have turned heads inside the student and professorial bodies alike, no accompanying noses were dislocated because of the momentary spectacle. After, all, Gofer's past and his laical status inside the seminary's administration, were well understood by all concerned. You can take the trick out of the ghetto, but you can't take the ghetto out of the trick.

It was another story all together for Louis. Having yet to take an oath of celibacy, Louis' occasional exit towards Tom and Uli's darkened entrance, was one cloaked more in discretion than hypocrisy.

Having been shown all the necessary shortcuts and detours between the two institutions, Louis would now make a point of exiting the first, either well before or shortly after Gofer had entered the second.

Louis would do the same as several of Stanley's patrons who were in similar predicaments as he. Renting out a locker inside the shower room adjoining Tom and Uli's equally infamous back room. A locker where he would leave his tailored gifts: most of the time.

...

He remembered the date. Monday, July 1st, 1935. The first official day of his summer holidays following his first year at the Grand Séminaire. They all chose to place their Luc-tailored leather gear in their duffel bags, rather than their respective lockers. Tom, Uli, Gofer, Louis and Friederick. Gofer not foreign to the occasional threesome from time to time. He would be paid in fine Laurentian gastronomy, handcrafted art deco surroundings, and Finnish affection.

Louis would be paid with the sent of a Hamburg sailor and the touch of Luc's undefined presence.

They would take the first train to Chanticleer. Following a short stopover at Tom and Uli's, on the corner of Dorchester and Montcalm. The quintet having showered and changed into cotton gear, at Tom and Uli's, on the corner of Stanley and Cypress. They had an early breakfast: a very early breakfast; at Dunn's; on Ste-Catherine facing Christ Church Cathedral.

They were all on holidays: Tom and Uli in between two construction jobs. Friederick was on leave, halfway through his second transatlantic loop in a little over two months. It was on the first, returning to Hamburg, that he met Luc at the Port of Baie-Saint-Paul. There, he bartered his German-made wraparound, and had his lower measurements double-checked. Intimately.

On his second loop, returning from Hamburg, Friederick picked-up his new breeches, and had Luc double check his upper measurements. Intimately.

The first train up, on this Monday morning, was a quiet one. One filled with contemplation and equally quiet conversation.

- Do you sense any, Uli?
- No, Tom. Not at the moment. What about you, Louis?

- No. Bizarre.
- Neither do I. Granted, it's the first time I take a trip on this train.

- It's not for lack of trying. Tom and I have been inviting you for the past five years.
- I wasn't ready. Our common interests were more metaphysical than they were physical. I wanted it to stay that way. I needed it stay that way.

- What triggered your acceptance today?
- Adulthood. I turned 25 a few months ago. My birthday is the same as Louis'. Same day. Different year.

- How do you know my birth date, Gofer? I don't recall ever telling you.
- Albert told me.

- Albert? Albert Brosseau?
- Yes.

- I don't recall ever seeing you in his presence.
- You weren't ready. He wanted it to stay that way. He needed it to stay that way.

- Up until now.
- Up until now.

They flipped for it.
Anna Maria was heads.
Alexandra Mary was tails.

Tails won.

The adoptive parents weren't even meant to be parents. Military Intelligence operatives tend to have a knack for keeping a secret.

And what a secret.
Ironically Anna Maria was the first out the womb.

He was from Wales.
And gay.

She was from the Newfoundland Protectorate.
And a dyke.

They fudged the birth certificate by flipping the last digit of her birth date upside down.

Making Anna Maria three years younger than her twin sister.

...

The Dirty Thirties was coming to a close and so was Louis' stint at Montreal's Grand Seminary.

Louis' preferred destination for his first mission, would have been to head for the relative tranquility of the Belgian Colony of Congo's Monastère Notre-Dame des Mokoto, on the lakefront community of Goma. This would be a far more quite environment than the bustling cacophony of the colony's other Trappist monastery built on the outskirts of Kinshasa, the largest and most populous urban center in the protectorate.

Neither was it Laurent's. At least to begin with.

- Hmm...
- Well. What did they decide?

- No cells left in Goma and a malaria outbreak in Kinshasa.
- That leaves your third choice.

- And your first.
- The Priory in Birine is one of the most beautiful in all of Northern Africa, Louis.

- The Algerians are almost as snobbish, and arrogant as the Parisians. That is why it was my last choice. I better start learning to keep these comments to myself. The letter says I am free to start my mission as soon as I am ready.
- Louis, your decision to complete a monastical mission with the Trappists rather than a pastoral one with the Sulpicians, was to find the time and space in isolation, as you decide between a life of a Trappist monk or a Sulpician priest.

- You are right about that, Papa. But the Algerians?
- You will be in prayer and meditation most of the time, and the vast majority of the Trappists living in the monastery are from outside the African continent. The little contact you do have with the local population will be a good workout of your already excellent diplomatic skills. Such skills will be essential whichever path you choose for your Eucharistic career.

- Their should always be a silver lining somewhere. At least there are no Trappist monasteries in Lebanon.
- *Oh Mon Dieu!* Now that would really tax your diplomatic aptitudes. I wouldn't wish that on my worst enemy.

Birine is a beautiful place. In a sub-Saharan sort of way. Under 100 kilometers south of Algiers' city limits, the abbey is built just inside the border between the Sahara's semi-arid and arid regions.

Though not as spectacular as the massifs on the Moroccan side of the Atlas Mountain Range, the acreage acquired by the Trappists on the Algerian side of the latter, was well adapted to the production of cash crops. In accordance to the Rule of St. Benedict, such productive use of the member's hands was a duty. And as a graduate of the Oka Agricultural Institute, as well as Le Grand Séminaire de Montréal, Louis would be a near perfect fit for the Algerian Trappists' Strict Cistercian agenda.

And his father's.

♛⚄♕

In her adopted home of Newton-Center, Mass., the Dirty Thirties started off on a depressing note for Anna Maria. On the other side of the Pond, they were rolling along in royal fashion, for Alexandra Mary.

The twins were but toddlers by now. Too young to fully understand. Old enough to remember.

George, would be the sixth. But Edward was the first in line. Death and abdication would have to wait. Death is like taxes. Abdication is like the future: only a probability.

To pass the time, George started a new hobby. One similar to Laurent and Louis'. George's pictures were moving. Laurent and Louis' stood still.

All were frozen in time.

Louis would keep his in boxes. Neatly stored in the basement of his Chanticleer homestead. Far away from his former château in Brittany.

George would keep his in a tower. One integral to his current chateau. Not so far away from Brittany.

♳♴♵♶♷

Under functional circumstances, the higher up the food chain a particular species is situated, the less it reproduces in order to conserve balance inside the ecosystem it belongs to.

Under those same circumstances, most humans, as a defined species, acknowledge being at or near the top of the food chain.

As social animals, humans are naturally inclined to reproduce only if and when they are fit and apt to do so. Their social inclinations are based on the mutual observations and analysis of their peers and their personal inclinations are based on their introspective observations and analysis. Consequently a functional, sexually active human will only become consciously and instinctively fit to reproduce, once they are personally and socially aware of, and at ease with, their own psyches and bodies.

Even with all the technological advancements in the field of virtual reality, the best and only way of properly understanding one's own body is by taking the opportunity of intimately exploring the mirror image of oneself.

Here we must make the distinction between one's sexual orientation and one's sexual exploration. No matter what the eventual awareness and subsequent acceptance of one's sexual orientation will take, you must first be physically aware of your own body. This physical exploration can only be properly realized by having at least one post-pubescent same-gender encounter.

By finding a short-term partner of the same age and with the same physical, and if possible, the same psychiatric profile as yourself, you are basically setting-up an exploratory "one-night-stand". Though not necessary in all circumstances, it is best that both partners have the same exploratory mindset going into this one-night-stand.

This exploratory mindset should be present in all physically and psychically functional humans, regardless of their sexual orientation or gender. The resultant conscious expression of this mindset, is dependent on one's capacity and aptitude to be in touch with our innermost instincts.

Not-to-mention one's ability to maneuver amongst the social and ethical obstacles inside the space-time continuum used to attempt this exploratory journey.

As we age, our body-and-soul gœs through significant physical and mental changes. As you reach the end of your post-pubescent life-cycle, your body-and-soul will be significantly different to the one encountered and observed at the end of your adult, middle-age or autumn-age stage of life. As you reach this transformational moment of instigation, you will instinctively trigger this exploratory mindset as you transfer from one stage to the next.

Under normal circumstances, and for each stage of our active lives, one or two of these exploratory encounters will suffice as we come to understand and accept the state and condition of our body-and-soul at a given time.

For the near totality of all humans, a half-dozen of these same-gender encounters should be anticipated during one's life.

...

My last motorcycle was a memorable one. Not as much for what it was, but rather for where it took me.

The Queen Elizabeth Way would merge into the Gardener. Moments after passing the late night lights of the CN Tower and the Skydome, I would find myself on Eastern Ave.

Even on a Friday, the expressways were virtually deserted. Even more so on Eastern Ave. In the early 90's, the Queen City had as prudish an exterior as its namesake.

The brown brick townhouse on the northwest corner of Eastern, would have been built once Louis had graduated from the Grand Séminaire. The saplings that were planted in front at the time, were now mature maples, the latter hiding a spatter of motorcycles parked in front of its facade, and the occupants discretely entering its equally discrete side door.

The tree-lined neighbors to the north were as quiet and residential as those to the south were nondescript and industrial.

As close to perfect a location one could ask for, under the circumstances. The original owners of Tom and Uli's Stanley Street lair would concur.

The original owners of the Eastern Avenue counterpart called their lair the Toolbox.

Ymir

He remembered the date: June 28th, 1914.
He'll remember the date.
His monsters won't let him forget.

- Slaash-hack, slaash-hack, slaash-hack!

His eyes betrayed his violent past.
A past filled with submission.

Eyes filled with a psychotic rage.
A passive rage.

- Slaash-hack, slaash-hack... CRAACK!!... CRAACK!!!

Distant eyes.
At the edge of emotion's oblivion.

A voided emotion, handled by a master puppeteer.
The same hands who have crafted the eyes.

⚔⚑☠⚔⚔⚔

"You are listening to the Bosnian Broadcasting Cooperative at 106.9 FM and on your smart-phone at 1069bbc.com. At the sound of the tone, following ten seconds of silence it will be precisely one o'clock, Saturday, June 28th, 2014. Blip, blip, blip, blip, blip, blip, blip, blip, blip, beeeeeeeeeeep...

... Outrage mixed with sadness filled the otherwise stately halls of the parliament building, after yesterday's terrorist attacks in Ottawa, The Dominion of Canada's Federal Capital.

The first of two attacks was conducted at the site of the National War Monument, where a nineteen year old exchange student shot and killed the ceremonial soldier standing guard at the memorial.

The assassin, still grasping his semi-automatic rifle and dressed in full battle fatigues, then entered the main parliament building, and instigated a gun battle between himself and several Parliament Hill security guards.

Kevin Dullpound, the RCMP Sargent in Arms of The Dominion's Parliament Buildings, cornered and shot dead the attacker, steps away from the caucus meeting room where the conservative government ministers, including Prime Minister Stephanie Herumtreiber, were discussing strategy before Friday's session of question period..."

...

The ~~Kaiser~~ Prime Minister was handed a blank check. The sounds of gunshots still ringing in the memories of the four leaders seated to the right of parliament hill's speaker of the lower chamber.

"At News-Talk 99.9 FM and on your smart-phone at newstalk999.com here is a 99 second news update for Monday, July 5th, 2014...

... The Prime Minister circled the Dominion's historic peace dove, and in a blink of an eye swooped down to grab the doomed prey in her hawkish claws. The Hon. Stephanie Herumtreiber took to the floor of the House of Commons to announce Her Majesty's Royal Canadian Air Force would enter Iraq's theater of war, and conduct air strikes against the expanding Sunni Caliphate inside this cradle of modern civilization..."

...

- What a difference a century makes...
- Is that a statement of fact or a question?

- A question in the form of a statement of fact.
- Cynical but fair.

- The last time he attacked, it was a declaration of war.
- This time it's a divergence.

- The wonders of fanaticism.
- It makes great press copy.

- The war promotions department is working over time.
- On both sides.

- What's amazing is that neither have changed a single line from the protocol manual.
- They just dusted off the cover, and continued from where they left off.

- What a difference a century makes...
- The players are the same. Only the borders have changed.

- And the size of the strategic weapons...
- Look! Monseigneur finally ran over one with his new Citrœn.

- First one down gets the giblets!

¿☜☝☞☟?

Be it by feudalism, fascism, or federalism, war is almost always instigated by an artisan who can effectively balance public relations with hidden intent.

You need a public for public relations. In an information age, that public is connected to the global village via the magical web-net. In the waning moments of 1914's autumn, the magic had just begun. The Scottish-born warlock responsible for these magical enterprises was still alive and well, wielding his craft in a burgeoning Ontario.

The French and Russians collude to face the Germans, Austrians and Hungarians. The British enter the war to cover their asses, colluding with the former.

The Dominion is by definition, a colony. Recruitment is voluntary: of interest to the urban, and of little to the rural.

- DLING-DLING-DLING!!!
- What's that?

- It's our new telephone. Quick. Answer it!

Imitating the burly Scotsman from the Bell Telephone Company, who had installed the heathen contraption a day earlier, Josée-Anne removed the black cone from its cradle, and holding it in her right hand, placed the free end to her right ear. She picked up the body of the telephone in her left hand, and brought the microphone close to her mouth.

- Hello. This is Josée-Anne Boullevraye de Ville-Amois from Chanticleer.
- This is the operator from The Bell Telephone Company. I have a reverse long distance call from Uli Wulfila. Do you accept the charges?

- One Question. Dœs the operator have a name?
- Yes. Pardon me. My name is Geraldine.

- Thank-you, Geraldine. Yes. I accept the charges.
- Thank-you. I will put you through now, Mrs. Boullevraye de Ville-Amois.
- Hello, Josée-Anne?

- Hello, Uli. You sound like a ghost speaking from the ether.
- Speaking of the ether, Tom and me were about to board the last train up north, when we crossed Mr. Morgan.

- I wasn't aware you were aware.
- As identical twins, we often communicate with each other at a distance... Without the help of a telephone. Often interference occurs during such conversations. Mr. Morgan's presence is but a partially physical occurrence of this virtual interference.

- We will have a lot to talk about next time we meet.
- That should be sooner than you may expect. Henry told me about Laurent's successful owl hunt. He told me you were planning on preparing a Chinese feast but were missing a few ingredients. We decided to skip the train, and go shopping in Chinatown the next day. That's where I am now.

- How kind of you.
- We wouldn't miss it for the world.

- That will make six of us for dinner. Adding bamboo shoots and water chestnuts to the mix will make an excellent main course.
- You know what they say about Chinese food. We will bring you some fresh Spring rolls to complement the feast. Dœs shrimp and pork sound good to you?

- That would be excellent. Could you find some chicken dumplings? I would like to make some wonton soup with chanterelle mushrooms.
- Absolutely. Anything else? How about some wine?

- With owl, we will need a coarse Bordeaux.
- I will bring two bottles... OK, three to make sure!

- Fantastic! We look forward to seeing you this evening.
- We will try to get there for the early evening; to help you with the cooking.

- The owl will be ready for the wok by then. Speak to you later. Bye, bye.
- Bye, bye Josée-Anne.
- Click!

- You did the talking, I'll do the carrying.

As both men exchanged the same, silent smile, Uli handed over the freshly purchased provisions to Tom's free hand, the other holding a week's worth of dirty laundry inside the well-used Russian army issue duffel bag strapped over his left shoulder.

Grasping the equally well-used rot iron handle of the Chinese market's entrance door, Tom exited onto the bustle of a snow covered Craig Street, closely followed by his identical sibling.

Still holding the handle as he closed the door, Uli had just the time to hear an old teenager who, in perfect Russian, mumbling under his breath, "Get out of my way.", as Tom tumbled off his feet.

Regaining his stance, and wiping the snow off his pea-coat, Tom turned towards Uli, the latter watching the improvised rugby player disappearing north on Saint-Urbain Street.

- He dœsn't look Russian: too scrawny.
- I think I detected a slight Bosnian accent in his comment.

- That would explain the latent frustrations.
- And his narcissistic tendencies.

...

Maison de Buillion was only a few blocks east, on the street of the same name. Mr de Ville-Amois, the owner, had chosen an excellent location. A stone's throw away from city hall and but a short dray ride from King Edward's Dock, Mr de Ville-Amois's wine shop was at the center of Montreal's administrative district and close enough to the heart of the metropolis' international logistics network, for him to restock his shelves with a minimum of manpower.

That manpower took the form of a young dapper Jersey boy from Saint-Helier. Straight off the boat from a Norman Dukedom, Sederick was naturally apt at spanning the two solitudes of Montreal's linguistic divide, just as his forefathers had done for centuries in his native homeland. The son of a sheep farmer, he was both agile and strong. Sporting a blond mop-top and piercing blue eyes, Sederick was a svelte and compact version of the Nordic Vikings, who would had invaded the island protectorate, nearly a millennium earlier.

- Dliiing, Dliing, Dling, Dling, dling, dling, dling, dling, dling.

The door jinglier reverberated throughout the cavernous gray stone and hardwood interior of the dimly lit shop; bringing back childhood memories of Tom and Uli's only yuletide observance of the Eucharist, inside the small, millennium-old chapel of Avenches, an ancient Roman village on the outskirts of Fribourg.

- Good day Sir... and Sir.

It was hard to tell, by Sederick's tone of voice and the docile Machiavellian expression on his face, if his double take was simply an acknowledgment of his clients' genetic symmetry or just a discreet solicitation. Maybe, it was a bit of both.

Tom did the talking. Uli just smiled.

- Hello. We are looking for a wine that will accompany a unique and original dish. The wine will be served with a dish of Gai Pan where chicken will be replaced with wild owl. The dish will be both spicy and gamey to the taste. The cook suggested a coarse Bordeaux.
- Gai... Pan? Definitely a red. One as far north of the Spanish and Andorran borders as possible.

- Yes. Gai... Pan will definitely go well with a red... Like your bow-tie...
- Yes. Like my red bow-tie! Now back to the Gai.. Pan.

- Yes, back to the Gai... Pan.

By now, Tom and Uli were also smiling in mischievous synchrony. Sederick excused himself, and headed towards the rear of the shop. With the help of a hefty maple wood stepladder, he extricated a bottle from the top left shelf of the rearmost display case. His mid section now at eye level to the clients below.

- This one has been aging since the turn of the century. A good year. And from a *vignoble* on the northern border of Bordeaux.

- Excellent! We will take three bottles.

Sederick returned to the back of the store, and as he stretched his well toned body to remove two more bottles, so did the clients' silent grins.

...

- Isn't life Gai...
- Pan! OK, enough already.

- That reminds me... We forgot the oil.
- What dœs a cute little wine shop clerk have to do with oil? Rendered lard, maybe...oil?

- Not the clerk, silly, the spring rolls.
- You're right. My mind's in the gutter. A pretty gutter, but a gutter none-the-less.

- We bought the uncooked ones. Only the meat inside was seared so they won't go bad before we fry them. We don't have any peanut oil left, and it will be next to impossible to find any in Chanticleer.
- We're facing Bonsecours Market. Sort of. We'll just cut through the carriage lot next to city hall, and before you know it we will be facing the market's central dome. We'll buy some there. We still have half an hour before the train leaves.

- Let's get going. We don't want to be late!

The spice and condiment importer was to the left of the dome, on the ladies' side of the market. Tom chose a one quart bottle. The label read "Grown and refined by Carter Farms of Georgia State." Go figure. For good measure, he also purchased a small bottle of soy sauce. The label read, "Fermented in Beijing by Shipeng and Wong Ltd."

Tom inserted the two bottles inside the opened duffel bag deposited at Uli's feet, atop the three bottles of Bordeaux that Uli, moments earlier, individually wrapped using his dirty work shirts as packing material.

Heading towards the eastern exit of the market, on the gentleman's side of the main corridor, the wood workers passed in front of a blacksmith stand. A chopping ax caught Tom's eye. The inscription engraved on the side of the hickory handle read "Fiskars OY, AB, Billhäs, Finland."

Still holding the ax in his left hand, Tom turned towards Uli, and suddenly froze in horror. Two paces in front of him, the carcass of a man was spread across the market's floor. His vestments would have been fit for a king -or at the very least a count- had they not been torn to shreds, or more appropriately, hacked to shreds. His remaining eye was still open. The other, lost among the remnants of his open skull. His left leg, hastily amputated just above his fractured hipbone.

What was the lady next to him, lay in a similar state of affairs.

There was blood everywhere. Almost everywhere. Including the ax tightly grasped in Tom's right hand. There was no blood on Tom's person; neither on Uli's.

- Gabriel.
- Tom, are you OK? Tom.

Uli tapped his sibling's right shoulder. The two carcasses in front of Tom's eyes disappeared and so did their bloodied, disembodied parts.

- He touched it. Don't do the same Uli. I'll explain later.

The blacksmith released the ax from Tom's grasp and wrapped it in a burlap bag. Tom removed a two dollar bill from his wallet and gave it to the trader. Securing the package with some shipping twine, he handed it back to Tom.

Both men exchanged uncomfortable smiles.

...

Making a b-line for their favorite spot, they settled in a rear car cubicle. Uli placing his duffel bag atop the storage rack, above the cubicle. Their package of fresh Chinese provisions on the forward facing seat next to him, and away from the train's heaters.

Tom, seated on the rear-facing bench, his burlap bag, discarded to his left.

- Can I touch it now?
- No, not yet.

- Who is Gabriel?
- Presnec. Gabriel Presnec.

- The Sarajevo Hacker.
- I was watching a moment in the past. Through his eyes. As I touched the ax, I touched his soul.

- The ax you purchased wasn't the ax he used.
- No. It was a similar ax. He touched them both. It was the time and space that changed.

- At the moment of impact, outside the Chinese market, he was heading back from the Bonsecours Market.
- Exactly.

- Now can I touch it?
- Yes.

Uli picked up the burlap bag. He carefully untied the shipping twine. Unrolling the ax from the bag, he grasped the Hickory handle with his left hand. Tom disappeared.

- What do yo see, Uli?
- You've been replaced by the big fat Roman Catholic priest.

- The one the gray-headed Scot-Irish was running after?
- The same. I can hear you. I just can't see you. Very creepy.

- Creepy but insightful.

Uli repackaged the ax, and placed it back where he found it. The big fat Roman Catholic priest disappeared.

- You're back. Say something. You're scaring me.
- Gabriel was coming back from the Viger Train Station. He detoured through the market.

- The past I observed was a recent past.
- Mine was less so but not by much.

- Did you see?.. oh.
- The Hacking.

- With a capital h.
- Absolutely.

In the northern provinces of Serbia, November is the month of owls.

- This is even better than the last time I had owl. And that says a lot about this excellent dinner. Do you agree Tom?
- Absolutely. Let me explain. It was three years ago. Almost to the day. We were in Szeged, about two hundred kilometers southeast of Budapest. How and why Uli and me ended up in Hungary, would easily fill the pages of a novel. So please accept my apologies if I skip a few details. Though our adventure in Hungary had begun only a few days earlier, we had unexpectedly run out of travel money.

- Now that's an understatement! Sorry, Tom. Continue. You have always been better at this than me.
- We were planning to stay a fortnight in Sveged. Luckily, we had paid for our stay in advance. It would take a week before our uncle could reach us from Imatra and extricate us from our predicament. Only breakfast was included with the room. The innkeeper was as generous as he was resourceful. Being well aware we were both construction workers as well as amateur hunters, he made us an offer. He had recently built a pub as an annex to the inn, but the interior had yet to be finished. He was willing to refund our stay at the inn, in exchange for helping him complete the pub's interior. As for dinner, he offered to have us hunt for it. Lunch was on the house. We got up before the break of dawn, and hunted on the crown lands behind the inn. After breakfast, we worked on the pub's interior till the early evening. On the first day, no ungulates to be found, but there were long-eared owls everywhere.

- Six, the first time out!
- Uli was twice as effective as me.

- Things evened out by the end of our stay. But we are getting ahead of ourselves.
- A long-eared owl is a smaller beast compared to the owl Louis captured yesterday. There wasn't enough meat for the innkeeper to offer owl on that night's dining room menu, so he decided to have the cook prepare the birds for the employee's dinner.

- Having dinner around a back-of-the-house kitchen table, with nine full time employees, all Portuguese nationals, and no bosses nearby was very, um...
- Enlightening?

- No.
- Insightful?

- Yes! Insightful would be a better word, Tom. The stories these people recounted after a day's work made for very colorful and adventurous storytelling. Observing a mostly Prussian clientèle through the eyes of foreigners, hailing from a dying empire, made it possible to see the forest for the trees... It was like listening to the present global conflict, three years before it started.
- You are getting better at this than you want to admit, Uli. Please, continue.

- One of the offshoots of looking at things from a different perspective resulted in a similar and different feast as the one first suggested by Mr Morgan. The Portuguese cook, not bound by the traditions of his local consorts, decided to make Hungarian Goulash, replacing the stewing beef with owl and strips of pork lard.
- Calling that dinner, a feast is a bit of an understatement.

- Your right. That was by far the best goulash we ate during the entire length of our stay in the Prussian Empire. However, as I mentioned earlier, Josée-Anne and Henry's Asian interpretation beats its Hungarian and Portuguese counterpart.

- Though neither of you are either Prussian or Portuguese... I will take that as a compliment.
- Nor are they Scottish or Asian, Josée-Anne.
- Nor French, Henry. The wonders of observing things from a different realm.

- I say hacking away at owl carcasses far more productive than hacking away at Prussian royals.
- Oh ik.
- And far more delicious. The owls, not the royals.
- Oh ik.

- Do you think Gabriel ate... oh, never mind...
- I wouldn't be surprised, Josée-Anne.
- Oh ik.

Louis didn't have any qualms about hunting, skinning and cleaning any number of edible beasts. Neither did he have trouble hunting pests. He drew the line, however, when it came to bipeds. For some reason he could not consciously explain, even bears were off limits... And ~~were~~wolves.

- What makes you think that, Henry?
- I was there when he bumped into you this morning.

- I didn't see you on Craig... Nor on the train.
- Discretion is my forte.

- We can't say as much for Gabriel. Do you think he is a ghost?
- It depends on who you believe. Don't loose the ax. It will help you triage observation from propaganda.

- Wise words.
- Wise ax.

Tom smiled. So did Uli.

Ghosts that may not be, bumping into Tom. Deadly axes and those that are wise. Observation verses propaganda. Josée-Anne and Louis were getting confused. Alexander was briefed earlier. He volunteered to do the same for his two hosts.

- What about Albert?
- Brosseau aka Lesage?

- You know Albert, Henry? Of course you know Albert. Silly me.
- You're starting to catch on, Louis.

- Let me see how well... He introduced himself under a false name and purchased a pistol. Discrete but of adequate caliber. Superior craftsmanship. Austrian rather than Russian.
- Correct on all five counts. Continue.

- Gabriel is a ghost to the eyes of the living. The living that have yet to befriend a ghost to the eyes of the dead.
- The dead only see the dead, once they become aware of their own demise.

- Albert can see. Gabriel cannot.
- Gabriel is dead but to those that wish to believe so. Demise has several definitions.

- Albert is dead. He told me so. He chose to be honest with me, but not with Antoine.
- It is a question of honor.

- There is no honor amongst thieves.
- But there is amongst noblemen.

- I will take that as a compliment.
- You would be wise to do so, Louis. It will serve you throughout this adventure.

- I have a question, Henry.
- Questions are a sign of intelligence, Josée-Anne.

- Are you strong enough to push Tom to the ground?
- No... And neither is Albert.

Josée-Anne added:

- I'm beginning to understand.

- You are strong enough to pull the trigger of a gun.
- And so is Albert, Uli.

Louis added:

- I'm beginning to understand.

☠☭☮

Gabriel is dead.
Long live Gabriel.

8 million souls in the Dominion.
66000 dead.

November is a month of remembrance.
Following the night of the dead.

Gabriel is dead.
Long live Gabriel.

8 Billion dollar debt to the Dominion.
A decade to pay it off.

Death and taxes: lest we forget.
Income tax introduced in the Dominion.

Gabriel is dead.
Long live Gabriel.

The Weimar Document propels Germany in an endless spiral of social-democracy; one forced upon a nation not ready for peace.

The Weimar Republic is a state of revolution and reform; one forced upon a nation not ready for change.

The German Revolution is seen as revolutionary but to the victors; one forced upon a nation not ready to accept defeat.

Four decades of turmoil propels the globe into an endless spiral of depression. One forced upon it by perpetual taxes and the doctrine of an expanding economy.

Perpetual as the swaying movement of a pendulum.

☭☠☪

"You are listening to the Northern Mariana Islands Broadcasting Cooperative at 106.9 FM and on the Internet at 1069nmibc.com. At the sound of the tone, following ten seconds of silence it will be precisely one o'clock, Saturday, June 28th, 2004. Blip, blip, blip, blip, blip, blip, blip, blip, blip, beeeeeeeeeeep...

... Saddam Husayn, the former dictator of Iraq, was hung today by the new interim government, according to the governing procedures of The Transitional Administrative Law for Iraq..."

For four decades, Saddam artfully balanced greed and fundamentalism, as well as public relations and hidden intent, keeping the pendulum from swinging too abruptly between war and peace.

As one reaches the age of retirement, the pendulum inside one's internal clock speeds up as one begins to realize the fragility of the time span allocated to us by our genetic heritage.

The fleeting moments of our youth have long passed as we face a bucket list that has yet to be fulfilled. Greed overtakes fundamentalism in a futile attempt to regain the drive of a waning sexual fortitude.

Switching petro-dollars from greenbacks to euros was too much to ask. Saddam's pendulum flew off its bearings, bringing his bucket filled with greed, sex, and fundamentalism, to a crashing halt.

...

"You are listening to the Northern Mariana Islands Broadcasting Cooperative at 106.9 FM and on the internet at 1069nmibc.com. At the sound of the tone, following ten seconds of silence it will be precisely one o'clock, Saturday, April 18th, 2015. Blip, blip, blip, blip, blip, blip, blip, blip, blip, beeeeeeeeeeep...

... Mohamed Aldori, Saddam Husayn's, high level military adviser, is killed, during confrontations in Sunni controlled Iraq..."

...

There is an advantage to working the graveyard shift for an EMS company: making the same products you used to make next door; now for one third the salary; next to a Persian alcoholic heroin junkie with an aversion to any form of work ethic and dreams of becoming an RCMP officer; dreaming being the operative word.

You learn a couple of things, in hindsight, about heroin junkies and the relevant drug trade you hadn't already learned from the school-of-hard-knocks and a childhood growing up in Bedalini controlled Upper Chanticleer.

One is that heroin junkies tend to be dreamers. Dreams they use as doors to hide behind the realities of a failed existence. Heroin they use as a door to hide from the nightmares of a distant past they are desperately trying to transform into unwritten dream visions.

The other is that in a world where the global village is collapsing upon itself, succumbing to the forces of a virtual society, the Bedalinis are no longer the only game in town. If ever they have been.

The opium of the people has long been used to conquer the latter, as a burgeoning empire builds upon the ruins formerly belonging to those they have conquered.

Vladimir has learned to use a collapsing global village to his advantage. Lessons he had learned without ever attending a school-of-hard-knocks, nor ever having traveled upon Chemin Chanterelle.

He dœs know a thing or two about Persian fundamentalism and the greed of Mexican Zeta cartels.

☭☪✝

In Baltimore, Maryland
The opium of the people,
Young, illiterate and destitute.

In Charlotte, North Carolina
The opium of the people,
Young, educated and well-heeled.

In Baltimore, Maryland,
The gated protest,
Black lives matter.

In Charlotte, North Carolina
The gated text,
White lives don't.

In Baltimore, Maryland
The opium of the people,
A gentle breeze from the Gulf of Mexico.

In Charlotte, North Carolina
The opium of the people,
A gentle breeze from the Black Sea.

The Feminine

"Oh no – what possessed me."...

With those words, Anna Maria ended up head first in the-not-so-raging-rapids of the Red River. Having lost control, moments before, of her wooden-ribbed canœ, the latter capsized and quickly drifted to the end of the rapids 50 meters away.

Control was the first of three things Anna Maria lost during that adventurous summertime canœ trip to Mont-Tremblant Park. The second, were her white canvas running shœs, purchased a few months earlier at K.D. Pennyworth's. Its Newton-Center branch just across the street from the Clayman Brothers', where she worked as a teller.

As a biophysical example of conservation of momentum, the forcible thrust of her head into the rapids resulted in the forcible thrust of her feet towards the smog-less blue sky of the Northern Laurentian Mountains. Resulting in the forcible transformation of her K.D. Pennyworth sneakers into footless projectiles, the latter eventually finding their way to the bottom of the Red River.

At 36 years of age, Louis was just at the doorstep of his mid-life crisis.

Not to be outdone, Louis lost four things during his first summer as a wilderness adventure guide and founding owner of Chanticleer's first specialty sports shop. Unlike Anna Maria's physical loss of control, Louis' was more pecuniary, which in turn took the form of an irrational decision. An emotional loss of control in the form of a brand new 1950 Indian motorcycle. Already in debt following the launch of two new businesses in one summer, the last purchase he could justify at the time was of a motorcycle that would serve little to no purpose as a company vehicle for either his wilderness guide or retail entrepreneurial endeavors.

Alas, his midlife hormonal imbalances got the better of him.

Not-to-mention, the sinking self-awareness of an adolescence and early adulthood lost preparing himself for an abruptly-aborted attempt at a clerical life serving a monotheistical doctrine imposed on him at birth.

ii

"Oh no – what possessed me." ...

Those were last words Louis uttered that evening, on his way to Mont Tremblant Lodge with a new pair of Swiss-made Tyrol hiking shœs in his backpack. As a more-than-adequate replacement for Anna Maria's lost footwear, these were the best alternatives he could find in his sports shop.

Consciousness was the second thing Louis lost that summer, following his airborne flight over a full-sized adult cow, which staggered in front of his Indian's path on the outskirts of Mont Tremblant Village.

...

- Where's my moose?

Those were the first words Louis uttered when he awoke in his room on the orthopedic ward of St-Agathe's Hôtel Dieu Hospital. Being an avid hunter, Louis knew that if he inadvertently hit a moose on a public road, he could claim ownership of the subsequent roadkill, even if the moose was downed out of season.

- I don't know. We will have to ask the police when they come by to fill out the accident report. You gave us a scare Monsieur de Ville-Amois. You have been unconscious for over 8 hours now. That must have been a big moose.

The professional tone of voice emanating from the nurse's scripted answer, reeked of dispassionate intent. A typical response from a nunnery care giver of a certain age.

- She was huge and for the little time I got to see her, she seamed to be in good health. There was enough meat on her to feed a good sized family for 6 months and her hide would be big enough to make a beautiful motorcycle jacket. I hope the game warden had the foresight to keep the carcass for me.
- Unfortunately it's 3 o'clock in the morning. We will have to wait a few hours before your inquiries are adequately answered. The ambulance driver told me they found you sprawled feet first in a bog next to the road. He figured the soft peat moss of the bog cushioned your landing. We took an x-ray of your lower left leg, as it was the only part of your body that was inflamed when you arrived at the hospital. You have a

hairline fracture of the lower left leg, so that explains the cast. Apart from your head and your left leg, are there other parts of your body where you feel pain?

- No, not that I can tell.
- While keeping your left leg and head still, move each of your other extremities, one at a time. Do you feel any pain in these extremities now?

- No, not that I can tell.
- That's good. Thank-you. The doctor will examine you more thoroughly later this morning. It is best you try not to go back to sleep for at least the next three hours. There are some magazines for you to read on your left and a urine pan on your right. Please do not try to stand up until the doctor has a chance to see you... Are you thirsty?

- A little.
- I will go and get you some cold water to drink and update your file. I will be back in a few minutes.

ØØ

Captain Lapointe's response wasn't the one Louis wanted to hear.

- When I returned to the crash scene with the game warden in tow, it was too late. Someone had already salvaged your moose. I had even went to the trouble of tagging the carcass before leaving the scene. I'm sorry.
- No need to be sorry. I'm not sure if I'm more disappointed with loosing the cow or with the unscrupulous people who stole the carcass after ownership had already been clearly claimed and identified. Since the end of the war, honor and respect have slowly been replaced by tribalism and egotism. When those too young, go to war, and taste the blood of their fellow man, all of society suffers the consequences.

- Your observations are nearly identical to those of one of my colleagues from Ville St-Léonard, on the Island of Montreal. His accounts of what gœs on there would make the hairs on the back of your spine stand strait. It was just a matter of time before such degenerate behavior began to show itself in a small weekend resort town like Mont Tremblant Village.

With a justifiably mischievous smirk on his face, Captain Lapointe changed the subject.

- On a more cheerful note, I received a call from a Miss Anna Maria Diele this morning. She explained to me that she was a canœ-expedition client of yours and that you were supposed to meet Miss Diele at Mont Tremblant Lodge yesterday evening. When you failed to show up, she grew concerned for your well being and decided to phone the police. I took the personal initiative to tell her that you were OK, but that you would not be canœing for at least a few weeks due to your broken leg. I hope I wasn't being too forthcoming with the details of your condition.

With an equally mischievous blushing red tinge rolling down his face, Louis suddenly shaved twenty years off the latter, making himself look more like an embarrassed adolescent rather than a middle aged adult.

- Oh, Good Grief. I totally forgot about Anna Maria. Thank-you for the information, Captain. Nurse... Nurse Bécancours. Excuse-me, can you tell me if there was a backpack with my personal items when I was admitted to the hospital yesterday.
- I am almost finished with this patient. I will be with you in a few minutes. Your valuables are in a safe at the front desk, and personal clothing and other items are in closet "D" next to the entrance of this room.
- I remember placing your rucksack in the ambulance before your trip to the hospital. If you permit me, I will go check in the closet for you.

Captain Lapointe retrieved Louis' bog-soiled but none-the-less dry backpack from the closet, dusted it off, and gingerly placed it next to Louis' lap. Opening the top flap of the backpack, Louis removed Anna Maria's new hiking shœs.

- Well at least they weren't damaged during my flight over that wandering quadruped. This is the reason why I was to meet Miss Diele yesterday. Her canœ capsized going down the rapids yesterday and she lost her sneakers during all the commotion. I went back to my sports shop and got a pair of hiking shœs as replacement for her lost footwear.

By now everyone in the room had strikingly similar smirks on their faces, except for Nurse Bécancours.

- Well, that explains things. I am sure Miss Diele will find these very adequate replacements for the ones she lost. As for me, I just about have all the information necessary to write your preliminary accident report. Oh, I almost forgot. Your motorcycle was taken to Ferguson & Sons Maintenance & Repair on Route 11 in St-Jovite.
- Do you have an idea of what shape it is in?

- Not to be alarming or anything, but I believe the moose got the better of it. The motorcycle was found several feet from both yourself and the moose. And judging by the trail of oil left behind, I think the engine case was damaged. The front wheel and forks are barely recognizable.
- That sounds like a write-off to me. Thanks for letting me know.

- It's time for me to go. Take care of yourself, Monsieur de Ville-Amois. If you have any further questions, you can reach me at the St-Jovite Police Headquarters.
- Good day, Captain Lapointe, and thanks again for all your help.

With those courtesies, Louis' rebellious motorbike riding days came abruptly to an end.

xoxo

With an operatic exuberance tinged with honest concern that can only be fully understood when observed with non-Bostonian eyes and ears, Anna Maria entered the room Louis was sharing with three other patients.

- Oh Looouis! Daaarling! You should know that a motorcycle is no match for a moose. Poor daaarling.
- Well, I did kill it.

- And she almost killed you! Poor daarling.
- I only have a broken leg. I was lucky enough to dive over her and land in the soft bog instead of on the hard asphalt. I figure the Lord guided me in my misfortune.

- And what about your head, daaarling. You were unconscious for several hours. How do you feel now?
- I'm a stubborn and persevering man. I think that's where the term hardheaded comes from!

- Mr. Ferguson, the manager of Mont-Tremblant Lodge told me he is a good friend of yours, and he knows you like roast beef. So he made you a roast beef sandwich on sourdough bread with hot mustard. And the cook prepared you a special rice salad with home made mayo and fresh chives from the forest. Mr. Ferguson told me you have a sweet tooth, so I bought you some chocolates from the Trappist monks in Oka that were on sale at the lodge's gift shop. I hope you like them.
- I did my agricultural studies on the seignory of the Oka Monastery. Their chocolates are my favorite sweets. Now, I'm more hungry than ever.

Anna Maria carefully placed the contents of her small picnic basket on the bed table, and slowly moved it over Louis' lap. As he took the first bite from his afternoon lunch, a tear rolled down his cheek. She took out a paper hankie from her purse and softly wiped the tear from his cheek, and proceeded to give an equally soft *snog* on the latter.

Preservation

He was ice fishing, off the southern shore of La Rivière des Milles-Îles, on the outskirts of Ste-Rose-de-Lima, on the Island of Laval. With the help of Montreal, these two islands separate the Saint-Laurence into three interlinked parts. The Mille-îles to the north, La Rivière des Prairies slicing Laval from its bigger sister to the south, and what remains of the Saint-Laurence separating the south shore of Ville-Marie from the north shore of Longueil.

Why was The Governor of the Independent State of Texas ice fishing, three thousand kilometers northeast of Houston, his namesake state capital?

He was escaping the heat:

The military heat from the gringos fighting for territory on his southern border; the political heat from the American Union forming around him, and the physical heat resulting from a prolonged and unexpected heatwave stretching from the Gulf of Mexico westward to the foothills of the Colorado Rockies.

Having skipped the Yuletide holidays to tend to these three events, it was time for a respite, one that would help him generate more permanent solutions to the turmoil inside his burgeoning state.

He remembered the date. For several reasons.

It was February 24th, 1833. He simply wanted some time alone. In cooler climes. He got more than he bargained for.

Her name was Angelica Meier. The immigrant daughter of a Presbyterian cobbler from Dresden and the fiancee of Antoine Lacloche: Antoine *Sr.* A generational title yet to be bestowed on the principle concerned. Antoine is the owner of several fishing shacks including the one presently occupied by Sam. Angeica was helping out her enterprising ~~pimp~~ partner by tending to the shacks... And their clients inside.

She too was an entrepreneur. One made possible by the hypocrisy of her newly adopted faith.

Angelica looked nothing like the French Lower Canadian women of her entourage. Her Prussian heritage made her eerily reminiscent of Sam's own wife. A past memory thirty years in the making.

Hey, the plumbing still worked. A little breath of nostalgia was just what The President ordered. Just enough to bring the frigid temperatures inside the shack to a comfortable cool. Like a long forgotten Chinook furiously wafting through the foothills of the Northern Rockies and dissipating to a gentle breeze over the parched streets of an overheated Houston presidential estate.

Antoine and Angelica got married in a Roman Catholic Church. Well before she began to show.

They had a son and a daughter. Not necessarily in that order.

They called him Junior.

☞☠☟

Though in moth balls for the past twelve decades, Rosepierre's razors weren't the worse for wear. They were rounded up from warehouses in Bordeaux, Lyon, Paris and Rennes; crated, and placed inside the hull of a French coaster for the short jaunt from the Port of Nantes to the Port of Lisbon.

You know what they say about repeating the same thing over and over, while always getting the same result...

I think I can hear Maximilien cracking a left leaning grin as he awakes from his graveside slumber.

The monarchs' newborn son is spared; smuggled out of Portugal before his parents' rendezvous with the recycled National Blade.

The orphan is raised by the Trappistine nuns of Macau's "Our Lady Star of Hope" Monastery. They name their new son Ihsahn.

ΔΣ∇

- I'm guilty.
- Based on the Laws of Nature or the Magna Carta?

- Nature.
- Time to fess up.

- I've been focused on the Who, What, Where When, and Why of the Resistance.
- Instead of the How of the Resistance?

- Exactly. I've been focused on the W5 of the Conflict instead of the Logistics.
- A procedural error.

- Yes. I was observing the Actors to the detriment of the Instigators. The conflict is not between two Actors.
- The Sino-Russians and the Anglo-Americans?

- No, the Eurasians and the Mediterraneans.
- It's probably something in the water.

- The Black Sea dœs eventually flow into the Mediterranean.
- So it's not between a Queen and a Marxist Consortium?

- No, the conflict is between a Tzar and a Prince.
- The conflict is therefore between an Actor and an Instigator.

- The Actor is both.
- That would make the Portuguese Revolution, "La Deuxième Terreur".

- I may be going to far back in the past with my observations of the present.
- Probably not. In interesting times, history has a tendency to repeat itself.

- The probabilistic nature of the future is muddying the waters.
- Keep focusing on the How, not the What. Remember the most important of French truisms.

- Jamais deux sans trois?
- Exactly!

...

Ihsahn is named the captain of a major Portuguese transport ship whose regular route starts at the port of Göteborg, Sweden, with stops at the Port of Lisbon, Algiers, Suez Canal, Kuala Lumpur, and ending its journey at the Port of Aoumen, Macau...

At around the same time as Louis' male-biased adventures had (finally) exited the exploratory stages of his gig at the Grand Seminary as he started a new, active one, just south of Algiers.

Gofer ~~will~~ would be proud...

Louis' first Algerian exploratory encounter was not in the numerous seaman's bars of Algiers, but rather in between two of the latter's warehouse hangers constructed on the pier furthest east of the downtown core.

The narrow alleyways separating the series of identical, corrugated-steel constructions created a nocturnal maze of nooks and crannies nestled amongst the temporarily deserted entrances and exit doorways of these pier-side storehouses. Their arced design making the roof the integral third wall of each building. The gentle curvature of the roof, reaching all the way to the footing of the storehouse, doubled as an ideal abutment for the occasional humping or two, depending on one's level of testosterone at the time of the latter.

The Maze as this transitory neighborhood was notoriously and affectionately known by, was most popular with the Waffen sailors manning the German U-boats discretely docked at the pier just west of the Maze...

- How did you figure this out already, Gofer. We both settled in the monastery only two days ago.
- Hey, if I'm going to tag along, all the way to Algiers, I'm going to make the most of it. The Maze is one of the most infamous latent homosexual landmarks of the Capital.

- One of the most?.. Figures. This is Algiers after all.
- You're catching on, Louis.

The Masculine

The Laurentian mountain range is the oldest on the planet and as such has been withered away by millenniums of northern winds, rain, snow, and the occasional retreat of an ice age glacier.

This natural regression has turned these mountains into hills and the impervious bedrock of the Laurentian Highlands have dotted their valleys with several lakes inter-connected by streams and rivers flowing south to the Saint-Laurence and north to James and Hudson's bays.

While I was attending the Chanticleer Elementary School, Donna Summers was starting her musical career and *Le Petit Train du Nord* was at the end of its life cycle, the latter being replaced by the Laurentian Auto-route. The wealthy replaced their train tickets for keys to luxurious automotive status symbols from Germany, Italy, and America.

The twenty-somethings speeding up the Laurentian Auto-route to their parents weekend retreats, were about to come of age as they fashioned what had yet to be coined the postwar Baby-Boomer generation. They would pass the winter time alpine skiing in German, French, and Austrian designer sportswear. In the summertime they would water ski behind jet boats, orders of magnitude larger and more powerful than necessary for the aquatic surfaces they were navigating upon. No matter the season, these well-dressed and well-heeled Baby-Boomers would spend their nights in rural – but no less upscale – versions of discotheques found in Montreal and New-York.

These tragic followers of Narkissos were reared to indulge in the finer things of life, favoring the addictive consumption of annual Eurasian poppies and bitter crystalline alkaloids of the $C_{17}H_{21}NO_4$ variety. *Buvard*[4] and Woodstock era organic weed would simply not do for the Bourbon Street crowd.

Too poor and cerebral to partake in such extravagances, my presence was relegated to simple observer status. One aggravated by the temporal consequences of my delayed arrival. The latter due not only by my father's exploratory tardiness, but also by his obsession in having at least one gestation-capable male offspring to carry on the family name. Following six consecutive misfires.

---

4 *Buvard* is Quebecois slang for 1 cm^2 blotter paper imbued with a solution-based drug of dubious quality and origin and sold in At Risk neighborhoods such as Quebec City's *Quartier St-Sauveur.*

Capable being an operative word. One not yet, or ever, appropriate or functionally plausible.

Another significant consequence of my tardy arrival into the physical realm of Midgard, was its timing with that of the process hysteresis spanning the end of the Baby-Boomer generation and the start of the X generation. A span – or bridge – forcing those traveling upon it to be forgotten characters in the annals of mainstream 20th century anthropological and historical literature.

I guess you could say such a consequence would partially explain my penchant for being more a narrator than an actor.

I digress.

It was no surprise that Frank Bedalini, the enforcer of Montreal's Sicilian Mafia cell would choose a secluded upscale cottage on Chemin Chanterelle as the primary residence for two of his three sons, Michæl and Jimmy, and as a secondary residence for his eldest son Frank Jr.

Both of Frank Sr's two youngest sons also attended the Chanticleer Elementary School.

Micheal Bedalini choose not to follow in his father's footsteps for two reasons. The first, the result of being a first-hand witness to the consequences of his father catching Mrs. Bedalini in the starfish position on the kitchen table, at the same time as Mr. Maillet of Maillet Landscape Maintenance Services Inc. in the doggy position on the same kitchen table.

Though Michæl was at school at the porn-film-inspiring moment, and Mr Bedalini didn't do or say anything immediately after he had entered and subsequently exited the family kitchen, it was how Frank Sr chose to deal with the awkward situation, a few weeks later, that helped push his second eldest son away from a career in organized crime.

La Taverne du Village was conveniently located on the corner of Route 11 and the same street as Chanticleer Elementary School. Both institutions were close enough to each other that you could see the school playground from the tavern parking lot. The tavern was a tad seedier an institution than the educational one situated a hop, skip and a jump away. The former doubling as a combination strip-joint and whore-house.

I jest.

...

To be brutally honest, calling *La Taverne du Village* seedy would actually be a compliment. Mentioning Chanticleer Elementary School and *Taverne du Village* in the same sentence would not.

The owner of Maillet Landscape Maintenance Services Inc. was a happy-hour regular of the tavern and could regularly be found there, on a late Friday afternoon, wolfing down a Boston-baked beans and wiener special while sipping on a *Grosse Tablette*[5] before heading out on a last check of his Portuguese immigrant employees, hastily finishing their grass-cutting chores at the weekend residences of his Upper Chanticleer clientèle.

Coincidentally, Frank Sr would make a point of always picking-up his two sons from school on Friday afternoons, as *business* obligations forced him to stay in and around the vicinity of his Ville St-Léonard, Jarry Street headquarters for most of the *work* week.

Exceptionally, on this particular Friday afternoon, two and half weeks after his unexpected kitchen-party encounter with Mr Maillet and Mrs Bedalini, he had Frank Jr pick-up Jimmy in his Black Camaro SS and Michæl would join his father in his Metallic Champagne Town Car. Frank Jr headed east towards Chemin Chanterelle and Frank Sr headed west towards *La Taverne du Village.*

- Son, you are going to be a teenager in a few months and it is time for you to learn about traditional Sicilian honor and respect.

Frank Sr's violence-infused, greed-inspired concepts of honor and respect were, to say the least, particularly distorted, even by Sicilian standards. In 1972, you don't become the head enforcer of the leading Montreal-based Sicilian crime family without passing on these traditional Sicilian concepts to your offspring as soon as appropriately possible.

- ...

---

5 *Grosse Tablette* can be loosely translated as "Big One Off the Shelf". In other words a *Grosse Tablette* is a super-sized bottle of industrial Canadian beer, served at room temperature. Attempting to down the equivalent of two and half regular, lukewarm servings of lowest grade Canadian beer in one sitting is a near life-changing experience, rarely, if ever promoted in French-Canadian tourism brochures.

- No matter what your mother says, Serge Maillet is an out of control animal. An animal that took advantage of a virtuous, caring home-maker and treated her like a street whore instead of the loving mother she deserves to be regarded as. What Maillet did to your mother a few weeks ago is tantamount to rape and he will now be dealt with accordingly.
- ...

By now Frank Sr's Town Car was parked on the left side of *La Taverne du Village* in sight of Serge Maillet's company pick-up. Three Armani-suit wearing Sicilian blow-up dolls were escorting him out the tavern. Two of the dolls headed for a black Crown Victoria and placed Mr Maillet in the back seat. The third doll headed for the company pick-up. The pick-up headed north on Route 11, towards Mr. Maillet's home. The black unmarked cop-cruiser look-a-like headed south, followed relatively closely by Frank Sr's Champagne Limousine.

"At 96.9 FM here is the news for Wednesday, June 25th, 1975 ...

... Frederico Fauchesco, the leader of Spain's fascist dictatorship for nearly two generations, died today in his mountain-top villa, just south of the Spanish-Andorran border.

... in other news..."

Micheal Bedalini's second reason for avoiding a life of Sicilian crime was less traumatic for him than the first but none-the-less influential on his final decision. He had a far more introspective character than his farther and he quickly understood that his father's violent demonstrations of Sicilian honor and respect were simply psychotic attempts at concealing a failed passage into manhood. If Michæl was ever to enter manhood in a proper and balanced fashion, he instinctively understood the necessity to avoid the distorted examples of masculine behavior bestowed to him by his father and the latter's business associates.

Frank Jr, on the other hand, was as obnoxious and arrogant as his younger sibling was discreet and insular. And it was precisely this obnoxious arrogance that would lead to his ultimate demise.

Jr's eagerness to emulate his father's psychotic mindset was essential in propelling himself to the highest ranks of Sr's Canadian-based Sicilian Service Organization.

No matter if the cell was located in Buenos Aires, Città del Vaticano or Chanticleer, the trademark characteristic of all authentic enforcer divisions of the Sicilian Mafia was their discretion. If you didn't deal in any of the Mafia's spheres of influence, the leaders of this organization, their enforcer subordinates and most importantly their business associates would have no need to approach you. Two simple rules to remember. You mind your business, they mind theirs. Out of site, out of mind.

Oh how times have changed in the post-millennium information age of Facebook, Twitter and Blackberry Messenger Services.

In a small town like Chanticleer, where the main and virtually only industry is four-season tourism for the rich and fashionably-heeled, those two simple rules resonate equally for the tourists as they do for the local population. When I was growing up, there was on average one murder per decade in this town. Everyone, including the local police force, knew the who-what-where-and-why of the crime. When the *who* was up to his armpits in Italian-by-tradition mozzarella, defining his ultimate demise as an anticlimax, wasn't much of a stretch for the imagination.

Arrogance, showmanship and trigger-happy paranoia were forcibly absent in any and all Sicilian Mafia enforcers. The fact that these two undesirable character traits were conspicuously present in Jr's behavior were written off by his father as an over-abundance of twenty-something testosterone. By the time he had reached thirty, Jr's cocaine addiction had brought the third undesirable character trait to the forefront of his increasingly unpredictable behavior.

At the doorstep of his post-andropausal golden years, Frank Sr faced a twofold dilemma. The first was how to deal with the enforcer franchise destroying behavior of his eldest son. He had spent the last twenty years of his life carefully grooming his son to become the undeniable successor to the family service organization. And what did he have to show for it? A worthlessly-arrogant cocaine-addicted pompous jerk.

Great.

How do you deal with a worthlessly arrogant cocaine-addicted pompous jerk when the latter happens to be your son. You do a *Frank Jr.*

The Dominion is a protectorate where corruption has become a national institution ever since the Bronfbergs[6] began building a spirits, real estate and financial wealth-management empire from the proceeds of cross-border booze running. Following Prohibition, that flaming torch of corruption was passed on to the Slopulos, who built a dairy, wood and industrial cupcake processing empire from their pizzeria-owner-knee-breaking proceeds obtained during the Duplessis era. Consequently, doing a *firstling Frank Jr* was a piece of Jœ Luigi[7] cupcake for Frank Sr.

₱

---

6 Bronfberg is a civil lawsuit avoiding fictional family name for an (in)famous family that recently emigrated from the Dominion with the *conveniently* capital-gains-tax free proceeds from the sale of their spirits empire to start a media empire south of the border.

7 Jœ Luigi is a copyright-and-trademark-infringement-avoiding fictional brand of petroleum-byproduct-imbued artificial-chocolate-flavored-icing-covered, simulated-vanilla cupcakes, with a petroleum-byproduct imbued-simulated-creme filling, manufactured by the civil-lawsuit-and-broken-knee-cap-avoiding fictional enterprise named after the equally fictional Slopulo Familia.

For Jr, Colombia was, on the surface, just another wintertime tourist destination. Underneath that winter sun hid passions even stronger than his insatiable greed. A passion for greed never quite equaled by that of his father's. Jr's status-defining passion was an addiction. His hidden passion was an obsession.

Jr's multiple cocaine-smuggling, cocaine-snorting excursions soon became difficult to justify as vacation time to the Colombian, American and Canadian authorities.

Including Frank Sr.

Sr's legitimate concern for his son's safety became a near-perfect opportunity to deal with his offspring's addiction and overbearing failure as a traditionally discreet Sicilian mobster.

Lit

Sr's main headquarters, nestled appropriately just left-of-center[8], in a standard issue late-sixties era strip mall, is a storefront Italian-Canadian social club, conveniently located a couple of blocks away from Ville St-Léonard City Hall. The almost-comically bogus social club's name, obligatorily referencing the Virgin Mary, is plastered on a nondescript black-on-white neon sign. The only distinguishing characteristic of this sign is that it is written in Italian.

Speaking both figuratively and literally, these neighboring establishments constitute an ideal *corporate toolbox* of interconnected businesses at the service of Sr's *social* organization.

A local branch of NBN Financial Services[9] is a must for Sr's toolbox. Placed as an anchor store on the left side of the strip mall, NBN Financial

---

8 Left-of-center is a relatively bad pun referencing the significantly more than cozy relationship between Sr's corporate and para-corporate endeavors, and the provincial and federal wings of Canada's traditionally liberal-minded, pot-headed, and fist-fighting political party.

9 NBN Financial Services is a copyright-and-trademark-infringement-civil-lawsuit-broken-kneecap-avoiding fictional name for one of the province of Quebec's most popular pseudo-private-provincial-government-sanctioned-and-approved, Montreal-based chartered banks. If you are curious about the significance of NBN in NBN Financial Services, here's a hint: it's a reference to the banks now infamous corporate slogan which happened to still appear following the Quebec Premier's, Grosse Tablette imbued, 1990s version, post-referendum speech.

Services' dedicated wealth management offerings, custom tailored to the needs of Sr's superior and subordinate business associates, gives a fresh-from-the-laundromat look, scent, and feel to all of Sr's related business transactions.

Anchored to the right side is an Italian-Canadian supermarket, part of a chain of stores popular in the north end of Montreal. These stores are renowned for predominately featuring the traditionally Italian cheeses produced by the Slopulo Family and the delectable deli creations of unsurpassed quality and freshness, produced by the Canada Packers Corporation.

I jest.

The offices on the second floor of this strip mall are leased out to two service organizations. To the right, an insurance company whose presageful specialty is offering coverage to owners of custom American motorcycles.

To the left, houses the main offices and classrooms of the Canadian National Union of Electricians. The union president's office is conveniently located just above the Vatican-certified social club with the virgin-sounding name.

And it's in that office that Sr hatched his latest parental endeavor.

- I have two people that need their basic lineman's certification but only have three months to obtain it. How do you make this possible?
- As you know, Mr. Bedalini, if they plan on working for a private firm, the standards are not as high as if they are working for Dominion Hydro. If you are here, I deduce you want them to work for Hydro.

- Yes. Go on.
- Under normal circumstances, a lineman working for a private firm, that has no technical college degree, must obtain 3000 hours of practical experience before being able to work as an apprentice-lineman for Hydro. They will have to work under the direct supervision of a certified Hydro lineman for another 5000 hours before obtaining their basic lineman's certification. Getting the construction commission to recognize the first 3000 hours is not too difficult as I am sure you know of several reputable electrical contractors that can vouch for their initial work experience.

- What about the next 5000 hours? I don't want them to work under direct supervision.
- There are two exceptions to the rule. Emergency situations, such as a natural disaster. And contractual work where Hydro would do work in a jurisdiction that is not bound by certification requirements as stringent as those here.

- Like for instance, Central and South America?
- Yes. The only exception being Argentina, where certification is required due to the extensive development of their network of nuclear power generating plants. Apart from these two exceptional circumstances, the apprentice-lineman can work independently and only has to report back to his supervisor when asked to by the latter.

- Anything else?
- They will need to complete a three-week workplace safety course. The upcoming course starts next Monday in the classrooms next door. If they are going to be working together, at least one of them should have his double-axle driver's license. Though to be honest, the driver's license requirements are rather loose south of Mexico.

- That leaves them nine weeks for a crash course in lineman work. Here's a list of electrical contractors that I would like to use as teachers. Which one do you consider to be the best for this job?
- Um, no, no, no, oh. Calibri Electrical Services Inc. Guido has the patience of a Buddhist monk. He's been in the business for over 30 years.

Sr reached forward, took one of the union president's business cards from the front of his desk, and began writing on the back of the card with his white gold Mont Blanc fountain pen.

- Here's the names of the two safety class students. Could you please add them to next week's course roster.
- Consider it done.

- Thank-you Mr. Dupuis. I'll have a word with Guido this afternoon.

For over a decade now, Gino and his trusted assistant Miguel have been manning the neighborhood garbage truck. Every Monday and Thursday their run takes them through the rear of the strip mall. At the request of Mr. Bedalini, they always make a point of paying particular attention to the dumpster shared by the social club and the mall's very own Sicilian butcher and sandwich shop.

On this particular Thursday, Miguel was kind enough to finish the strip mall's garbage removal by himself, as Gino was summoned to the social club for a private chat with Mr. Bedalini.

- My apologies Gino for disturbing you during your work hours, but I have a business opportunity that may be of interest to you.
- If it's anything like the business opportunity you offered me last month, I'm all ears.

- It's similar in nature but more time consuming. I remember you telling me that your younger brother Dino was looking for a summer job. Is that still the case?
- Yes it is.

- Excellent. I was hoping you could have him take over your garbage run for the summer holidays while you take an extended vacation. Your vacation will however be short lived as you will be spending most of your time learning to be an electrical lineman. You're not afraid of heights are you?
- No sir, I'm not afraid of heights. And yes, I'm sure Dino will find it quite profitable doing my garbage run for the summer. But may I ask you what an electrical lineman has to do with the work I completed for you last month?

- You will eventually be doing contractual work for Dominion Hydro. In Colombia. Your main task will be to head to Colombia with a new Hydro lineman truck, spend two weeks working in Colombia, then, return to Canada with another lineman truck that is due for scheduled maintenance at Hydro's logistics repair facility in Montreal.
- And I figure there will be a lot of empty space in the truck heading back to Montreal as I won't be bringing along tools in a truck that is temporarily decommissioned.

- Exactly. You catch on quick. That's why I like doing business with you. Is this of interest to you?
- Yes, Sir! I will let Dino know he has a job for the summer.

- You start a three-week workplace safety course on Monday morning at eight o'clock in the union offices on the second floor. Once you have your safety certification, you will begin a crash course in high-voltage electricity by working for Guido Calibri. I will have you meet Mr. Calibri at the appropriate time. I will let you get back to work. Miguel must be waiting for you by now.
- Thank-you Mr. Bedalini. Have a good weekend.

And with both men smiling, Gino headed out the social club's rear door to finish his garbage run.

Convincing Jr would be more difficult than it was with Gino. While the latter was as greedy, apathetic, and criminally minded as anyone in the Sicilian Mafia's sphere of influence, he was no less-willing to accept salaried wages when necessary or appropriate.

The former was born in a world of luxury and grew up with a silver spoon down his throat, and more recently up his nose. His sense of entitlement was way beyond that of his egocentric boomer-generation compatriots, and nearly the equal of today's Millennial generation. He was a true pioneer in the field of instant gratification, decades before it became a standardized global phenomenon in today's age of 7-second video bites, 0.99₵ mp3s, and 140 character tweets.

Alas this father-and-son duo's mutual admiration for the evil-eye glaring god of lust and greed, was the trump card in Sr's calculated and risky endeavor to salvage his failed attempt to functionally rear the eldest offspring of the Bedalini family.

- You don't work for the money you make. Why should I?
- If I were your age, you would have a point. Alas you weren't even a twinkle in your mother's virgin eyes back then. It's precisely because I had to work when I was younger that I found the drive to Sicily for the Dominion. And it is through the recognition of that drive that I was given authority to start a cell in Montreal. Given, I had the privilege and opportunity to start business in a colony that was bathing in corruption and political collusion decades before it even was granted the symbolic and token status of a Dominion. It took me and my Old World superiors years to make the Sicilian way of running business, government, the

justice system and even the police, the norm in the Dominion. Just like our colleagues the Bronfbergs, we are now a well established and permanent institution that has been carefully woven into all aspects of Canadian society. It is that drive I want to instill in you, my son.

- You make a good argument. I can see how you have become such a good *negotiator*. But an electrical lineman? I know nothing about electricity.
- For reasons of union certification, you will be a Dominion Hydro employee. But in truth, you are a sub-contractor working on a temporary and occasional basis. Your main job will be to deliver a newly-built truck to the work site in Colombia and return with an older truck to Montreal for repair and maintenance. During your two weeks in Colombia, you and Gino will have the status of a back-up crew. You will never touch an electrical line. Think of it as having a job similar to the one your cousin Alphonso has.

- Alphonso? The city sewage repair worker? He hasn't been inside a manhole, or even near the handle-end of a shovel in over twenty years. Now that's what I call a worthwhile punch-clock job.
- Even better. Since Gino is the only one with a dual-axis license, he'll be doing most of the driving. And as for a punch clock, this job dœsn't have one so you don't have to worry about that. All I ask is for you to pass your safety course and to pay attention to Mr Calibri's teachings during your nine weeks of training. He is a good and patient man. It should not be too hard for you.

- That sounds reasonable. I've had a few beers with Gino. He's not hard to get along with.
- That's what I want to hear. You start your safety course with Gino on Monday morning. The next three months will go by faster than you think.

♚♜♟

Jr's uncharacteristic attention in class was a surprise to his garbage removing classmate despite the insomnia-curing subject matter of this workplace safety course. Granted, Sr's presence, a mere ten feet under Jr's classroom chair, may have had an influence on the latter's exemplary academic behavior.

The following nine week crash course on electrical power transmission, infrastructure, maintenance and logistics was another ball of wax. If it weren't for Gino's breaking-dawn work routine, and Mr. Calibri's perseverance and patience, both men would have given up on Jr after the first week of on-the-job training. Sr be damned.

The reasons for Jr's total absence of enthusiasm and personal discipline were primarily due to his chronic cocaine addiction and his night-owl drug-dealing lifestyle. Five nights a week, Gino made it a point to park his car halfway between the Jarry Street Metro and the Bedalini's St-Léonard residence, take the 45 minute subway ride to Lucien-L'Allier Station, walk up Mountain Street to the Limelight night club, and drag Jr out of the club before one AM. Then, he would commandeer the mafiosi prince's late-model jet black Ferrari and drive him across town back to his consort's home, where Jr would get the semblance of a few hours sleep. Walking back to his car Gino would head back home to do the same.

In the morning Gino would head back to the Bedalini residence in his early-model Chevy Nova, shake Jr out of his cocaine and margarita stupor, and drive him to Calibri Electrical Services Inc. headquarters so both could start their lineman work shift on time.

Despite of Jr's occasionally violent, cocaine-induced outbursts of narcissistic posturing, Gino's 6'5" garbage-man physique and Sr's promise of fast money made it possible for the sanitation engineer to keep up this routine on a consistent basis. An offshoot of Gino's adult baby-sitting was the formation of a begrudging friendship between the two men. For better or for worse, they both were working towards the same objective of completing their condensed trades education.

♜♟

- Well Junior, we made it. It's our last day of this Campbell Soup Lineman course and not only did we not get electrocuted, but Mr. Calibri is satisfied that we can pass for a basic linemen under most circumstances.
- Well Grouch, we didn't get electrocuted... yet, and hopefully we don't cross to many hurricanes during our gig because what we didn't learn during this course is going to get us in a whole heap of trouble, if Hydro asks us to do some emergency repair work while we are on the road.

- You have a point Junior, but we are not due for our first gig before November and hurricane season will be almost over by then. That gives us almost two months to prepare ourselves for unexpected events.
- You have that evil grin on your face again. You're not suggesting we continue doing this lineman work for another two months, are you?

- Me?! No... not at all. Dino's summer holidays are almost over, and I'm heading back to garbage duties on Monday. But since I do the industrial garbage runs on the weekends, I get Tuesdays and Wednesdays off. And even the Limelight is dead on Tuesdays and Wednesdays during the off season. So...
- There's that evil grin again. You didn't.

- I did. Mr. Calibri also thinks it's a good idea. All his regular team of men are back from vacation, and now there is a backlog of work to complete. Having an extra couple of men helping out with secondary duties will be a welcomed addition for even the most experienced workers. And that will give us the chance to observe and participate in work events we haven't had the chance to experience yet.
- You are even more Machiavellian than my father. I figure that is one of the main reasons why we get along. Since you have gone to all the trouble of making this a done deal, the least I can do is tag along. Those experienced workers better be Italian. If I have to work with a bunch of local, unionized old-farts, I don't think I'll make it through another two months of training.
- That's the spirit! Since most of Mr. Calibri's staff is anglophone, he makes a point of not hiring anyone from the *Fédération Coopérative Indépendante des Travailleurs Socio-democratiques du Québec Solidaire et Nationale.* All his lineman employees are members of the Canadian National Union of Electricians. So under normal circumstances, Italian coworkers are almost always a certainty.
- All Right, all right. I'm in. Now let's get out of these work clothes and head to *La Sauteuse Parisienne.* I'm paying.

- The pictures in the travel brochure do not convey how spectacular this hotel is. I can see why so many heads of state are housed here when they visit the Dominion.
- It's once you enter Montebello's lobby that you realize you are in a special place. As for heads of state, I am but an enforcer. My superiors insisted you stay here when I invited you to come and visit. Though you are not an elected official, in the eyes of my masters, you are the most powerful and influential man in Colombia. It is a privilege to speak to you in person again.

- Canada has become an essential gateway for the movement of product to the lucrative American market, and it is your intimate ties to the Port of Montreal, that have made it possible for the logistics of that gateway to become a reality. And for that I thank you, Mr. Bedalini.
- It is precisely because of the success of that gateway, that any logistical adjustments I undertake, must not be linked in any way to the Port of Montreal.

- Speaking of logistical adjustments...
- I love my son dearly, but as a successor to the family business he has been a failure up till now. Cocaine is meant to be used by the goyim, not by their masters. Alas, it is not only my son's addiction that is causing me sleepless nights. His obnoxious arrogance and his lack of discretion are truly uncharacteristic of even the most low level of juvenile street dealers, let alone someone of his age and stature in the organization.

- You need not be so harsh on yourself, Mr. Bedalini. However if you permit me I will agree with you on one point. I have seen and read often about situations very similar to your own. In the corporate and feudal worlds, it is not uncommon to see sons and daughters languish in the shadows of very successful and powerful men like yourself. It is not for me to suggest a cause or solution to such events. That said, I commend you for taking action before the situation gets out of hand.
- Your comprehension and support are very important to me. It is the reason why I have asked to meet you face-to-face. I am well aware that by undertaking this endeavor, I am putting at risk a new and potentially very profitable land-based distribution network. And for that I take full responsibility for any loss of revenue the failure of such a network may entail. However the future integrity of the family business is at stake and as such draconian measures must be taken.

- You have several aces in your hand, not the least of which is your favorable relationship to the local and national police forces. Under those circumstances your chances of success are quite good.
- Thanks for the vote of confidence! It's almost supper-time. I have made reservations at an excellent Italian restaurant in the village. It is a bit out-of-the-way but the food is excellent. They source their produce and meat from the Oka Trappists down the road. I think you will enjoy.

♟♟

Our two graduates' first task landed them in the Morgan, Tennessee production-facility parking lot of Meier-Tec Corporation. The Meier family have been engineering and building specialized trucks for the telecommunication and electrical distribution industries for over forty years, and was a major supplier of rolling equipment for Montreal-based Dominion Hydro.

The two would detour through Mexico and Central America to break-in the new vehicle and return with the decommissioned truck, via the Dominican Republic, Bahamas, and Florida.

November rolled around and no major hurricanes had yet to hit the Tennessee Coast. Mexico, Guatemala, Belize, Honduras, Nicaragua, and the Northern tip of Colombia were another story altogether. Of the latter countries, only Colombia had signed a post-disaster services agreement with Dominion Hydro due to its ongoing commitment to help build most of Colombia's new hydro dams in conjunction with a large Montreal-based engineering firm. The same firm who was also managing hydro-electric mega projects in Northern Quebec at the time.

This engineering firm and Sr's international business division were a perfect fit for each other. This cozy relationship was primarily due to the firm's involvement in such varied fields ranging from the construction and development of agribusinesses in Central and South America to the design, engineering and construction of penitentiaries and physical interrogation chambers for the Libyan government.

A more than intimate relationship between these two organizations was essential in the development of a land-and-sea-based logistical network for the smuggling of large quantities of cocaine between Medellin and Montreal.

No matter what the outcome would be of putting Jr in charge of smuggling drugs using Hydro Lineman trucks, Sr knew he could always depend on this engineering firm's varied international dealings to help him find a proper route for the transportation of his illicit produce from South to North America. When one door closes, another one will inevitably open.

"And on San Antonio's number one station playing Latin America's greatest hits WLAT 92.5 on your FM dial, here is the mid afternoon news...

...Hurricane Veronica made landfall on the Central Cayman Islands about five hours ago and was downgraded to a tropical storm by the time it left George Town during the lunch hour. Veronica is now headed north-northeast and should reach the Gulf of Mexico by tomorrow night."

- See Junior, it's all a question of timing. Once Veronica reaches the Gulf we will already have reached Monterrey and will be quietly drinking a regionally brewed alcoholic beverage while being entertained, hopefully by one of Monterrey's finest erotic dancers.
- And what if Veronica takes a quick left turn tomorrow night and heads for the east coast of Mexico. If we stay too long in Monterrey we won't be in Mexico City before the next couple of days and risk being in the eye of the storm. Especially if it gains strength while heading across the Gulf.

- You do have a point. All right. We'll stay over in Monterrey just long enough for supper and a good night's sleep and head out for Mexico City before dawn tomorrow morning.

☾ ☟

"At 107.1 on your FM dial you are listening to Monterrey's only English language music station. And here is the 6:00 AM news...

Huricaine Veronica has picked up while entering the Gulf of Mexico and is now heading due East and will make landfall in Corpus Christi, Texas by late this afternoon."

- See. See! I told you so, Grouch.
- I've got to give it to you. My former girlfriend Shirley has excellent intuition but not as good as yours.

- Are you insinuating that I'm effeminate because my intuition is better than yours? And why are you calling me Shirley?
- No, and No. No I don't think you're effeminate. We all have intuition. And just because it's considered by many as being a feminine characteristic dœsn't mean a man can't put his to good use. And no I'm not calling you Shirley. My former girlfriend was Shirley. Shirley Bergstein.

- Bergstein? From the Bergstein supermarket empire? How long did that last?
- Only a few months. That was several years ago. Even back then, all three of Mr. Bergstein's daughters were heavily into using coke. I wasn't able to keep up with her lifestyle. I had the bod but not the riches.

- Wasn't she a bit old for you?
- Cougars have the experience and the knowledge to be excellent partners in bed. In those few months, she taught me a lot on how to treat a woman inside and outside the bedroom. With that experience came a refined sense of intuition. She would always know if and when I cheated on her. I wasn't able to go out on a night with the boys without getting caught doing the Hanky Panky. Her words not mine.

- Hanky Panky! My mom dœsn't even use that expression anymore. I can see why the relationship only lasted a few months!
- You got that right. But the experience was worth it. You know what they say. You learn from your mistakes. That's too is an old expression, but one worth remembering.

❧❧

It was just about Noon when the Hydro truck crossed Cludad Valles' city limits. It was time for a pit stop on several fronts. For Gino that meant a leak, lunch and a walk around the restaurant-bar parking lot on the outskirts of town. For Jr that meant a B-line to the bar's restroom for a nose job.

- This blow is cut! If I wanted to snort Robin Hood, I'd go to the supermarket.
- You purchased the best product offered in Cludad Valles. As for your other comment, I don't understand English very well. Do you speak Mexican?

- Never mind. I guess it's time for me to take Spanish lessons.
- That is an excellent idea. If you need more service you know where to find me.

Fortunately for both of them, Gino was in the loo at the same time this latest altercation took place. Jr's awareness of his baby-sitting partner's presence made it unnecessary for the latter to intervene.

Sr had taken the time to warn both men not to have any illicit drugs on their person while they were transiting to or from Medellin. Getting busted for simple possession was simply not a risk worth taking. In the US, getting good quality coke wasn't a problem for Jr, his father's name being well established along the I-95. But it was another story altogether in Mexico and the Central American countries they were transiting through. These were foreign territories, literally and organizationally. For Jr, being at the mercy of local vendors was an unsavory experience – to say the least – especially for a man used to having the best of everything back home in Canada.

Of more importance was the necessity of passing incognito through these same Latin American countries. Needless to say, the discussion of their criminally-predominant organizational tasks in public was also verboten.

1/3

It was hard to tell which of the two were happier to cross the entrance of the Mexico City Hilton. Gino, for successfully squirting the consequences of an angry mob of rural Mexican drug dealers on his tail from Culad Valles to Mexico City. Or Jr, for having finally entered a city where he could easily find some quality snort.

- This is incredible. I was able to take a shower, have dinner, and a nap. Not a cockroach in site.
- That dœsn't count, Gino. You haven't walked around Mexico City... yet... The one memorable observation my father ever told me about Mexico City was not in relation to the cockroaches. It was about the sewer rats. They were big enough to entertain Thanksgiving Dinner with.

- If you were a Chinese Christian.
- I'd rather eat a table...

- How long ago was that?
- He last passed through Mexico City almost fifteen years ago. But I'm pretty sure the comment still holds true today.

2/3

The duo exited the Hilton parking garage only after having taken one last shower and a late-morning trip to the Hilton breakfast buffet.

By the time they had reached Escárcega, it was well past supper time. The ideal time, and place for these two professional tourists to discretely settle-in for the night. To call Escárcega a dump would be like calling Jérômeville, north of Montreal, a major tourist destination for the jet-set elite. With one of the highest unemployment levels in Canada, Jérômeville is only under-rated by Lisatichi, New Brunswick as one of the worst places to live in the Dominion. Alas, I am getting ahead of myself.

Like Jérômeville – and to a greater extent, Lisatichi – it's not the employment statistics, nor the geography that makes Escárcega such a dump. It's the people, and how they have molded the space-time continuum they call home, into a nightmarish oasis of mediocrity.

- What do rednecks call themselves in Mexico?
- EEEEIIIII...KA!!! Mama Vergas!!

Please accept my apologies. As our team of linemen traveled through Southern Mexico, it simply would be inappropriate of me not to reference at least two stereotypical observations relating to radioactive-mutant-sized cockroaches. In this case, hiding underneath Gino's accent pillows placed atop his highway-motel room bedspread; as he was about to take a load off his feet with a can of lukewarm industrial lager, before heading out with Jr for a late supper.

- I don't think that's what they call themselves, Gino... Oh... Now I understand. You haven't got used to them yet?
- There not spiders. Spiders are gentle beasts that tend to be more scared of you, than you are of them. These are brutally aggressive. I don't think they would make very good pets. As for your first question, I'm not sure what they call themselves.

- I guess we will have to ask one of the locals. On second thought, that's probably not a good idea. Chances are, whœver we ask around here will probably take it the wrong way. And, if we're lucky we will both exit town with no more than a couple of broken jaws. I will wait till we get to the relative security of Belize City before attempting such inquisitions.
- Now, that is the wisest commentary I have heard you articulate since the first day I met you, Jr.

- All that diplomacy of yours must be starting to rub-off on me, Grouch!
- Thanks for the compliment. Okay, let get going before all the restaurants close for the night. *À la soupe*!

Placing a pink Canadian bill underneath the pile of paperwork, Gino handed over the file folder to the Belize border guard.

- I am more used to seeing Americans pass through here. But on occasion, it is a sufficient change to have a Canadian on hand.
- Thank-you for your generous understanding. If ever we meet again, I will try to be more American in my... demeanor.

...

- I told you giving Canadian currency would be risky.
- He let us through, and don't forget, Mr Calibri gave me 85 cents on the dollar. For a dirty-pink bill, that's better than what NBN Financial gives me for having my heavily-soiled laundry go through a wash-and-rinse cycle.

- If we're not careful, this will come back and bite us in the derrière.
- Bite?! You're making me hungry!

- We should be in Orange Walk in less than hour.
- With your help, I just made a windfall, Grouch. We'll find a restaurant whose fare is beyond our daily allowance. My treat.

"At 96.9 FM, the Belize Broadcasting Network presents you the news for Friday, July 10th, 1976 ...

...The Belize Seaway Commission celebrates today, the fifth anniversary of HMS Black Prince's christening. The ferry between Belize City and Puerto Cortez, was inaugurated in response to the continued military tensions pitting Guatemala and the Motherland; making it prohibitory to travel on land between Belize and British Honduras. The Governor-General was on hand this morning, as well as the president of the seaway commission to officiate the celebrations. As is customary during this annual event, ferry crossings will be free of charge today, for all British subjects."

- Drats. Had we left a day earlier, we would have made it to the ferry in time for a free crossing.
- For a high roller, you're quite frugal, Jr.

- A frugal high-roller?
- Oxymoron aside, that's my point. You won't bat an eye at the price of an Alpha Romeo. But to save a few dollars you will have me risk both our butts at a critical border crossing, three thousand miles from home. I don't get it.

- My mama grew up in the small town of Bronte, during the Great Depression. On a clear day, she could see Mount Etna from her back porch. I don't know if it was the fear of disaster or the fear of doing without, but frugality became a traumatic part of her daily life. I promised myself, I would never follow such a desperate lifestyle. Somehow the frugality rubbed off... a bit.
- You bring a whole new meaning to the expression "A penny saved is a penny earned".

- As long as it dœsn't get in the way of me and the keys to a new banana-yellow Spider 2+2.

The contrast between the sex-tourism decadence of Orange Walk and the abject poverty of rural South Mexico, less than twenty kilometers away, is almost discretely humorous. In a Hitchcockian sort of way. The majority of prostitutes populating Orange Walk coming from these same aboriginal villages on the west side of the Belize border.

As such, finding a half-descent eatery was easier for Jr than first expected, given the number of British perverts vacationing in Belize City, less than 90 kilometers from Orange City's coveted main strip. To Jr's utter contentment, good eats and good head weren't the only delights one could find on the strip. Some of the best Colombian coke was as easy to find as a hissing cockroach under an Escárcega motel pillow.

With two Aston Martins and twice as many Jaguars patently parked in front of the multilevel, creme-white building, Jr. knew exactly where to invite Gino for a travel-expense busting dinner.

To call this a building was a bit misleading. It was more of a complex to be exact. Composed of nine perpendicularly imbricated, 60x30 foot rectangular concrete boxes, each 10 feet high, the boxes were strategically stacked in such a manner that the resultant architectural sculpture had a total height of between one and three stories, depending on your location relative to the structure. The streamlined and classic lines of the exterior, combined with modern construction techniques gave a unique style to the complex. Somewhere between an art-deco design exercise and a miniature Habitat 67'.

The complex had a multipurpose vocation. Three of the concrete boxes were reserved for a multilevel discotheque, four housed an upscale boutique hotel, and the remaining two served to house the visitor inside a Michelin *quatre-fourchettes* restaurant disparately-sandwiched between the hotel and its discotheque.

The one-hectare estate the establishment stood upon, was landscaped in traditional English style, and surrounded by a sprawling orange grove to the east, a tropical botanical garden to the west, and the remnants of an ancient Mayan temple to the north.

- Wow. I never ate fresh swordfish before, but if ever I do again, it probably won't be as good as this.
- I'm not sure what is more spectacular, the view of the Mayan pyramids from our dinning table or this tuna steak and curried linguine. Even my Mama dœsn't cook this well. Don't tell her I said that.

- If the hotel is half as good as the food they serve, I'm staying here for the weekend. I don't care how much it costs.
- Throwing out my Mama's frugal ways for a couple of nights sounds like a good idea. Don't tell her I said that.

☕♥

On Friday nights, the discotheque did not come alive till well after midnight as it awaited the beating tempo of Doc and Gripfast healed contingents of orange pickers, streaming through the discotheque's entrance doors, as well as a few exits, after their last dawn-to dusk shift for the week.

At the request of the Complex management, and with the financial help of its owners, a roman-styled bathhouse was built on the grove's estate to permit the local workers, on both sides of the border, to rest and prepare themselves for their recreational night-shift. Or not.

- I know we specifically agreed upon mutually avoiding to stick our noses into the others' business and private life during our time off ...
- Don't ask, I won't tell.

- By the look of your *nuit blanche* demeanor ...
- Ask me no questions, I'll tell you no lies.

- Okay, the plural form of *nuit blanche* ...
- I'll pack-up. It shouldn't take more than a few minutes.

- I took advantage of the going-rate station-to-station calling service offered by the hotel and called Mr. Calibri to give him an update. As agreed upon during dinner on Friday night, I told him everything was just fine, and that we would be taking the first ferry crossing from Belize City, on Monday morning. I think your Mama's frugality is starting to rub-off on me ...
- What time is it?

- It's five... AM.
- That dœsn't give us much time.

- I'll go to the check-out desk, while you finish packing. If we are on the road before 5:30, we should make it to the ferry ticket booth with time to spare. We'll eat breakfast on the ferry. The hotel manager told me it's the best morning fare in all Belize. Coming from him that is no small feat.
- Good idea. It'll give me time to nap before we get there...

☼☕

Jr. having napped twice in the quite comfort of the over-sized lineman-truck passenger seat, our electrodynamic duo debarked, hitch-less, from the HMS Black Prince and onto the chaotic noontime streets of Puerto Cortez.

...

The Honduran sun had turned the Juticalpa golden arches from yellow to white. Having reached the store's parking lot half an hour before the supper time rush, oddly the only other vehicles in this space were three military junta *Humvees,* whose occupants were escaping the hottest moment of the day in typical policemen-at-the-doughnut-shop style.

What dœs one do when you are wielding a tray-full of America's finest processed saturated fat while the biggest of nine M-16 touting military police officers stands up, and in his best broken English, invites you over to their makeshift officers mess? Why, you put on your best I'm-from-Canada smile, and graciously accept the offer.

- I see by your truck, you must be heading to the new Colombian Hydro project.
- Yes, sir. We are from Montreal. We will be working on the electrical distribution network connecting the new dam to Medellin. Please excuse me, but I am curious. I haven't listened to the radio for a few hours. This morning the latest forecast said the weather would be beautiful for the next five to seven days, with no signs of hurricane activity in sight. However as I was driving along the main strip, I got stuck in a traffic jam just before passing in front of the Safeway, all three motels I passed were each putting up No Vacancy signs, and it is almost supper time but the restaurant is almost empty. I don't understand.

- You will have to stop listening to cassettes and open the radio more often! The Marxist rebels in Nicaragua are up to their old tricks again. At around lunch, an anti-government protest in Matagalpa, took a turn for the worst when a high ranking government official who was trying to give a speech at the time, was shot in his um... private parts by one of the protesters. He died in hospital two hours later. To try and find the criminal, the Nicaraguans, have closed the border crossings at Jalapa and Somotillo at least until tomorrow morning.

- I think I am starting to understand. If It is not hurricanes, it is civil unrest.

- That is the best... and shortest um...
- Explanation? Summary?...

- Yes! Exactly. The best summary of life in Central America I have heard in long time. Getting the comment from someone that can see – how do you say?...
- The forest for the trees?...

- Yes! Exactly. The forest for the trees. Sometimes speaking to someone that dœs not live here is um...
- Enlightening?

- Yes! Exactly. I can tell you now, if you have not a hotel room, you are not lucky.
- I guess we will just have to sleep in the lineman truck tonight.

- Um... Not a good idea. The *banditos* will be busy tonight between Juticalpa and the Jalapa border. Foreigners are always first targets. If you sleep on the side of the road, you will wake up on ground with no more truck in the morning. If you are lucky. If you are not, um...
- ...

- I have better idea. We will be patrolling all night but we have only three Hummers for 50 kilometers of road. We have secured two motel rooms, and will take turns resting during the night. We are allowed a maximum of three people in each room. If you and your partner take one room each, we will be okay. You will always have at least one soldier in the room all night. You and your truck will be safe and we will have one less target to worry about. Deal?
- Deal!

- You know what Gino? I think I'll drive the truck this morning. OK?
- Don't ask, I won't tell.

- Not like I'm asking or anything, but I slept like a baby last night. I didn't even hear the patrolmen swapping nap duty. They were as quite as a cockroach under a motel room pillow.
- Ask me no questions, I'll tell you no lies.

- Okay, the singular form of *nuit blanche* ...
- What time is it?

- It's five... AM.
- You know what, Jr.? I think I'll let you drive the truck this morning. OK?

- Yes! Exactly.

Before conking-out in the lineman truck's passenger seat, Gino had just enough time to warn Jr not to give Canadian currency as tokens of appreciation at the Jalapa border crossing. By the look on Gino's face, he well understood that American currency was *de rigueur*. And with the latter's emphasis on the plural form of token, Jr. also understood that crossing this particular border, at this particular time, would be an expensive endeavor.

...

- Mr. Calibri will not be amused.
- Turn left here.

- OK. But why?
- We will be taking the tourist ferry between Bluefields and San Andrés. And one more between San Andrés and Cartagena, Colombia. It's a bit of detour but we will avoid the civil turmoil around Managua. Not to mention the two most expensive Noriega-esque border crossings in Central America.

- Bonus!
- Wake me up when we reach Siuna.

- Okay, Grouch. Grouch is my hero, 'cause he's so big and strong.
- ...

With the majority of the border-crossing backlog heading to Managua, the road to Sinua was far more quiet. Ironically, having traveled nearly 6ooo kilometers so far, Jr had yet to use his brand new Pentax K-1000. With all the paranoia-laden drug dealers Jr. had to interact with to keep up with his own addiction, the last first-impression he wanted to convey to the former, was one of a nosy camera-touting tourist from the Dominion. As such, his hobby tool was kept at the bottom of his knapsack.

Gino, who was now in a semi-comatose state of profound slumber, Jr figured it was high time to indulge in a little nature photography. Though too far away from the Pacific lowlands to witness any active volcanœs, the Nicaraguan highlands between Jalapa and Siuna resembled the tropical version of a Laurentian drive between Chanticleer and St-Jovite.

While keeping his eye on the road, several of the fowl he observed that morning, including jays, hummingbirds, and goldfinches, bore a striking family resemblance to their Laurentian counterparts. Except one. He was having breakfast in the median branches of a fruit-bearing tree, the latter just off the left side of the road. His plumage was bright green and of Monty-Pythonesque beauty. In an Emerald Toucan sort of way.

Slowly coming to a stop, he parked the International on the right shoulder. Making sure not to startle both the toucan and his dozing partner, Jr quietly opened the driver side door, jarring the latter behind him. Crossing the asphalt path, he was now far enough away from the bird to approach it amongst the underbrush on the side of the road. He was able to get close enough to the toucan, with only a 50mm focal-length lens, as the bird was way too preoccupied with dinning than to worry about any impending bipedal ogre in the vicinity of his perch.

Focusing on the tip of the bird's banana-shaped beak, he snapped three successive shots, each at a different aperture setting, before the bird's instinct kicked in, as it became aware of an intruder inside its safety zone.

...

- Gino? Are you awake? We're in Siuna.
- Thanks. Now look for a white, two-story, concrete building with black-out windows. There will be a green and white neon sign with a red star on the white side. Underneath the star, you will read *La Sauteuse Coquette*.

- The Cute Stripper? Why in French?
- The club is owned by an expatriate Algerian, who grew up in Laval.

- How did he end up here? Oh, never mind. Ask no questions, I'll get no lies.
- Yes! Exactly.

- I'm hungry... Look! There it is.
- The best breakfast tortillas in town. My treat.

↴⇘

- Now what?
- We're taking the road less traveled to Rama. It is a gold-mining road and only graveled, but in good condition. Halfway to Rama, you will come to a fork in the road. Keep to your left. If you go right we will end up in Río Blanco. We detoured through Siuna to get away from Río Blanco. Stick to your left.

- Stick to the left. Got it.
- I ate too much. Wake me up when we get to Rama.

Gino's tortilla-filled somnolence, was Jr's opportunity for further discovery. The three-hour drive between Siuna and Rama was taken at a leisurely 70 kilometers per hour; not because of the road's unfinished condition: it was all the beasts, birds, and creatures that paid no mind to these civil intrusions to their natural habitat.

The oak and pine covered escarpments of the sinuous mountain road between Jalapa and Siuna, had given way to a road almost as straight as an arrow, with but a slight kink at its midpoint, to make room for the bifurcation to Río Blanco. This stretch of gravel-top cut through the heart of the Nicaraguan rain forest like the blade of an old-style bucksaw through a fallen poplar branch.

The second time Jr. unexpectedly slowed to a stop, was not of his own fruition. The beast stalled in the center of the road was too big to swerve around. Jr. took the opportunity to leverage the obstinacy of this otherwise fast moving cross between a pony and a rhinoceros, inside the relative safety of the truck's cabin.

- Flap-Click! Flap-Click!
- Mm. What are you doing stopping in the mid... Oh. It's just an ungulate. Most are but harmless herbivores. And this one dœsn't even have any horns. Put the flashers on and go outside to take a closer look. You'll get a better framing.

- You think so. Okay, I'll take your word for it.

The tapir being orders of magnitude larger than the toucan, Jr was able to keep a relatively safe distance from the former, while still being able to fill the lens image circle with the subject's presence. And crouching down, took a further three shots while focusing first on his snout, second on his eyes and thirdly, just as he sped away into the jungle, on his behind.

If you thought Jr's first photographic pit stop was reminiscent of a Monty Python moment, his third was even more so. Only time and space separated the two virtually identical parrots in question. The one perched on the sign post indicating the fork between Rama and Río Blanco, was well inside its living time-frame and nowhere near having ceased to be. Though not precisely in its natural habitat, the living parrot was much closer to its habitual ecosystem than his stuffed consort, the latter nailed to a perch, inside the realm of an English pet shop.

Stopping five meters before the fork, on the Río Blanco side of the gravel road, and having kept the motor running to assure that Gino's air conditioned slumber would stay intact, Jr was able to exit the cabin and close the door without disturbing his partner, who had unconsciously grown accustomed to the combined whirring of the running engine and of the compressor's Freon-flowing pump.

Unsurprisingly, the macaw was as curious about his new found intruder as Jr. was of his new found photographic subject. His first shot was a waist-high composition of the parrot-accented road sign.

Slowly walking around the engine compartment of the lineman truck, Jr. crawled to the bottom of the road's ditch. Using the crest of the ditch as a makeshift camera support, he reduced the speed of the camera's shutter from 1/500th to 1/250th of a second as the afternoon sun was casting long shadows on the huge tropical trees lining both sides of the road. The parrot was having nothing of it. Just before snapping the shutter, the male macaw jettisoned from his road-sign launching pad, and flew three feet above Jr's head, diva style, landing on the lowest branch of a road side tree just behind the amateur paparazzi.

As the fowl diva squawked in his general direction, Jr turned around to observe the parrot only six feet from his head. Sitting on the side of the ditch, the photog clicked off several more shots, to the delight of the winged, tropical drama queen.

One shooting session having finished, a new one was about to begin.

Getting up and turning around to head towards the International, Jr stopped in his tracks. No less curious and photogenic than Jr's last subject, the one quietly sitting on the passenger side of the engine hood was an even better opportunity. Looking straight into Gino's unconscious gaze, the adolescent-sized arboreal monkey was obviously trying to figure out what all the snoring was about. Placing his lens for a full-on monkey level view of the truck's passenger side, Jr. took several shots in full manual mode, using the optimum aperture and speed settings for this particular composition. Once finished, Jr was about to head back to the lineman truck, when Gino suddenly awoke. Seeing the tiny primate, the latter figured a polite but terse discussion with the little fellow would be sufficient to have it head back to the relative security of the surrounding rain forest. Stepping down from the passenger side of the cabin, Gino approached the little beast, still quietly being massaged by the rumbling beats of the engine under his buttocks.

Now granted, the fact the Zelaya Department they were driving through, was a former British Protectorate as far back as the mid 17th century, did not in any way insure the tiny ex-Brit would understand English. Or Garifuna. Or Miskito. Or Sumo. Or even Rama for that matter.

Figuring the big and friendly two-legged beast just wanted to socialize, the little guy, stood up and gently jumped onto Gino's right shoulder, so the latter could more easily continue the discussion without hurting the primate's sensitive ears.

In a whispered tone, Gino gently explained to his new friend that it was time for him to continue on his way to Rama. Carefully taking the monkey off his shoulder and placing him across his upper chest, as you would a baby needing a burp-inducing tap after a feeding, both of them headed to the limit of the rain forest. Silently taking the primate in his arms, he gently gave the tiny tot a *snog* on the nose and crouching down, set him off his way into the tropical jungle.

That's what nice about *snogs.* They are a universal way to say hello. And goodbye.

?¿

- Gino? Are you awake?
- Now I am.

- We're in Rama.
- Do you have enough gas to get to Bluefields?

- Yes.
- Wake me up when we get there. Again.

The ferry connecting Bluefields and the Colombian Island city of San Andrés is owned by the same British company that owns the one between Bluefields and Puerto Cortez.

Gino still wearing his nickname with style, and having not yet finished compensating for yesterday's sleep-deprived adventure, it was mutually agreed upon by both men to abort any activities in Bluefields other than boarding the afternoon ferry; the latter scheduled to depart half an hour after they had reached the port's ticket booth.

Jr ate lunch alone.

And yes, the food was just as good on the HMS José Santos Zelaya as it was on the HMS Black Prince.

Like a slumbering Pavarotti crescendo, in an endless sound-design loop, cycling to the rhythm of his cerebellum-dictated oxygenation, Gino's sleeping opera reverberated with Windsor-Hotel-concert-hall-filling intensity, inside the confines of the International's cabin. Making it possible for Jr. to transfer from the José Santos Zelaya and onto the deck of the waiting Cartagena-bound ferry, without ever forcibly exiting Gino from his self-induced state of unconscious bliss.

Jr ate supper alone.

With all the decorum and panache of a Northern-Laurentian bear preparing to extricate himself from his hibernation den, Gino snorted, grunted and yawned his way into consciousness.

Alone. In the parking lot of the Cartagena Hilton.

- Good evening Mr. Alaric. Welcome to Cartagena. Your workmate has transferred your luggage to room 486. Here is your key. The supper time buffet ended about an hour ago, but the *a la carte* menu is still available till 11:00 PM. Your partner is in room 484. Is there anything I can help you with?
- No. That will be fine. Thank-you for your help and patience.

When Gino got to the entrance door of room 484, there was a Do-Not-Disturb sign on the handle. Entering room 486, he quickly took a shower, and slipped into his last set of clean clothing.

After dinner and a few nightcaps at the hotel bar, Gino did the only viable thing one who had spent most of the day asleep would do, under the circumstances.

He headed for the in-house laundromat.

☕☣

Jr knocked on the door of room 486. No answer. He knocked again. No answer. And a third time. No answer. It was 7:30 AM. He headed to the dining room for breakfast.

Alone.

Jr knocked once more on the door of room 486. No answer. So dœs one occupy oneself, at 8:30 on a weekday morning, in an isolated hotel complex off the main highway? In the middle of nowhere. In a foreign country.

You take your duffel bag full of dirty clothing and head for the in-house laundromat.

Alone.

When he got back to the front door of room 484, he noticed the door next him was ajar. Peeking inside he noticed Gino, sitting quietly in a far-side corner of the room, reading what looked like a copy of some type of glossy 4-color, web-offset, dead-wood printed sports magazine.

It was 10:30 AM.

- Be careful, Jr. Curiosity will kill you.
- I'm not a cat.

Jr closed the door behind him.

- And neither are you an engineer. Curiosity is the lifeblood of the latter. It is the fatal toxin that flows through the veins of the dealer.
- If this gig dœsn't work out, you could start a new career as a fortune-cookie writer.

- And you, a shock jock.
- We would have to part ways.

- Why?
- There are no shock jocks in China.
- You are starting to get the hang of this, Jr.
- I have a good teacher, Grouch.

Despite Gino's latest adventure, he was now more than in fine form to take back the wheel of the Meier-Tec mastodon. Negotiating the virtually desolate gold-miner roads between Jalapa and Bluefields was good practice for Jr's novice-level aptitudes as a lineman truck driver. For the hot-blooded son of a mafia kingpin, tackling the equally hot-blooded chaos of a mid-morning downtown Cartagena traffic jam would be a bit of a stretch.

Sticking to the main highway between Cartagena and Montería, via the state capital of Sincelejo, made it possible for the two men to avoid any unwanted confrontations with the ever growing presence of anti-government gorillas controlling much of the Colombian countryside.

The sweet taste of discretion turned sour, once they reached Yarumal.

- Whèl. What is this?

The makeshift road blockade masquerading as a protest by the local insurgents, was set-up on the outskirts of Yarumal, minutes before the expensive, shiny-new government-sponsored utility vehicle – with foreign license plates – was about to exit the small rural town north of Medellin.

- Your wallets please. We wish to verify your identification.

The two pairs of camouflage-fatigue suited twenty-somethings, each sporting a shiny-new anti-government-militia-sponsored Kalashnikov, were strategically standing on each side of the truck, blocking both cabin doors. The insurgents closest to the latter, had their utility persuaders, pointed in the general direction of each Italian-Canadian's respective cranial temple.

Each of the wallet-wielding persons-of-interest, carefully removed their rear-pocket-sized leather briefcases from their seated seat, making sure not to tussle with the delicate muzzles on the Russian-made advanced-interrogation-technique mobile assemblies, held daintily in-hand by the local Nicaraguan xenophiles closest to the vehicle.

The latter's accompanying consorts, were handed the suspicious hide-covered receptacles and headed back to one of two Lada Nivas, parked over the median line of the two-lane highway. The freedom-fighter-four-wheeler contained a foursome of equally xenophilous members of the regional insurgency. The one old enough to be the grandfather of any of the twenty-somethings, exited the Niva holding the two miniature briefcases, and headed towards the passenger side of the lineman truck.

- Your last name is Bedalini.
- Yes.

- Your first name is Frank.
- Yes.

- You are from Canada.
- Yes.

- Close to Montreal?
- Less than an hour away.

- I have heard of a Frank Sr, who is a well regarded business associate of our revolutionary army.
- I am Frank Jr. Frank Sr is my father.

- Oh. I think the term in English is oops?
- Oops will do.

- I will make a point of limiting the repetition of such an unfortunate event. Here are your wallets back. I have added compensation to each.
- Thank-you for your understanding and generosity.

The xenophile-stuffed Nivas headed back to the center of Yarumal. Gino and Frank, set out to finish their last 100 kilometer stretch of road to Medellin.

- Wow. It's a little late for Halloween and a little early for Christmas, but the old fart left me enough treats and Yuletide cheer to cover all the border-crossing insurance-premiums we paid out since we started our trip. And in American currency to boot. What about you, Grouch? What did the Warlocks and Santa-Clauses leave you?
- Hold on. I want to keep my eyes on the road. Here's my wallet. I never keep much cash on me at one time, in anticipation of just such

encounters. I think there was a hundred American dollars and about two hundred pesos inside.

- They weren't as generous with you as they were with me, but you should have enough for that lawn tractor you were eying back home.
- With or without the snow-blower attachment?

- Um. With.
- Yikes! And this is the first time you were cœrced into name-dropping.

- And I hope it will be the last. I still have the *heebie-jeebies,* and they're sloshing around in my stomach.
- Well. You definitely didn't act like a flibbertigibbet during your chat with the old fart.

- Flibbertigibbet?
- I'll explain after we had a few beers. We're almost in Medellin.

With a population three times that of Cartagena, you would think one would be greeted by a bustling metropolis, once one had crossed the city limits of Medellin. At the tail end of 1976's hurricane season, this wasn't the case.

The ideological and criminal mutualism, fueling the multiple paramilitary insurgents warring amongst each other in the jungle heat of the country's rural *tierra caliente*, has forced the majority of Colombia's Amazonian peasantry to find refuge in the cooler geopolitical climate of the nation's urban centers.

The shantytowns lining both sides of the highway entering Medellin, were but an introductory tribute to this forced exodus. An exodus, the original city planners did not foresee when the first structures of this town were erected in the shadows of the Andes mountains.

The municipal authorities were now painfully overwhelmed by the logistical, criminal, and traumatic aftermath of these rural conflicts, imported from the Amazon rain forests east of the *Cordillera Oriental*, and from the Pacific Lowlands west of the *Cordillera Central.*

Amongst this chaos, Donna Summers was on the verge of being officially crowned the Queen of Disco, at around the same time that Colombia was being crowned the King of Cocaine.

Oh, the humanity of irony.

Guess what was blaring out of the JBL speaker enclosures, bolted to the walls of the downtown discotheque Jr had chosen as the hops-and-coca temple, where he would exorcise the *heebie-jeebies* from his stomach and soul.

At least for a moment.

- It's not the Limelight, but it'll do.
- I'm just tagging along for the free beer.

- Consider it my contribution to your four-season yard tractor.
- Cheers to your generosity and cheers to Timothy Eaton! May both live on in infamy.

When Sr got word of Jr's first and last digression, coke and beer were not on the formers immediate list of priorities. Knowing full well that discretion and reserve were not his son's forte, keeping his mouth shut when tested, was the least the elder Frank could expect. And the only promise the latter had asked Jr to keep as he prepared for his journey to Colombia.

☎♬

As Hugin flies, La Dorada, on the border of the Magdalena river, is almost exactly halfway between Medellin and Bogotá. Making it the logistical choice for the MGI hydrœlectric dam's location. MGI, having been built years earlier, La Dorada would be where our electrodynamic duo would exchange their new International for an old one. And head north to the construction site of MG2, about 35 kilometers north of Puerto Boyacá.

The first half of their circumvented jaunt from Medellin took less than two hours to complete. Despite being of the same length, the second half, bordering the raging Magdalena River, took twice as long as the first, due to the verging treachery of this rural Colombian pathway's condition.

- It's not that raging.
- We're well into the dry season. Most of the runoff has flowed out of the region by now.

- So no more hurricanes?
- I hope not. We're at least 300 kilometers away from either the Pacific or the Caribbean. No more hurricanes. No more monsoons. For now.

- It makes me think of the Red River in springtime. But bigger. I went on a canœ expedition in Mont Tremblant Park last year. I brought one of my younger brothers along. Now that was an adventure.
- That sounds like fun. But I find canœs too tipsy for the rapids.

- You got that right. When they extricated me, Michæl, and the canœ after our first attempt, there was nothing left inside the canœ except a lot of water and an old pair of canvas running shœs. And they weren't even mine. Nor Micheal's. By the look of them, the tour guide figured they must have been at the bottom of the river for at least twenty-five years.
- Ha. Speak of the devil. Look.

- What? Oh. Now that's an idea.
- The sign says the camp is only 500m away. Let's take a break for a few minutes and find out what they have to offer.

The sign was more like a billboard. A hand-painted depiction of half a dozen adventurers negotiating as best they could, a stretch of Magdalena River rapids in what looked like a bright yellow Zodiac raft, made a lot more sense to both of them than attempting the same in a canœ.

When they got to the entrance of the parking lot, the owner of *Aventuras de Propulsión*, and three of his employees were doing some preventative maintenance on a deflated raft. Sensing a potential customer, Marco stopped what he was doing and headed towards the parked Lineman truck.

- Hello Sir. We are heading for the first time to the MG2 construction site and saw your billboard. It says you speak English.
- Yes, sir. My name is Marco. Marco Maçón. I am the owner of *Aventuras de Propulsión.* My English is not perfect, but we should get by.

- I am sure your English is better than my Spanish. My name is Gino and my friend is Frank. We have rapids back home but most ride them with canœs or kayaks. This looks less dangerous and more fun.
- Yes the rafts are much more stable than canœ. If you fall over we have kayakers to get you out of trouble. Kayaks not like Eskimos. They are made of fiberglass not sealskin. You use kayak?

- Only once. At the Chanterelle Hotel in Chanticleer, Québec. On *Lac Rond.* Small lake. No rapids!
- We teach you how to kayak on rapids. More fun than on flat lake. But first you try rafting.

- Exactly. How much for a ride?
- Fifty pesos for half a day, Mr. Gino. Forty with a group. That includes lunch or supper. Miguel, the Cook. Makes best *arepas* west of Bogatá!

- We haven't tried *arepas* yet. This sounds like fun!
- You in for treat, Mr. Frank. Good rafting. Good food. There are two groups from MG2 reserved for Saturday. Linemen in the morning. Construction workers in afternoon. Room in both for two more.

- This will be a good way to get to know the lineman. What do you think Jr?
- Rafting in the morning. *Arepas* at noon. Nap in the afternoon. Sounds good to me. Do you wish for us to pay you now?

- No. No. Not necessary, Mr. Frank. You pay on Saturday. If you happy, pay after ride and lunch is finished. If unhappy, pay nothing.
- Fantastic! We will see you on Saturday. We won't eat *arepas* until we try yours.

- Sleep well before Saturday morning. Keep room in stomach.
- Promise! Nice to meet you, Mr. Maçón.

For Gino and Jr, as well as all the other unionized MG2 workers about to embark on Mr. Maçón's adventure, keeping the first part of that promise intact, was as easy as the second was hard.

Despite the country, the local workforce, and the social conditions of the former being vastly different, the mafia-controlled union and its accompanying collective agreement were virtual carbon copies of the ones found at the work sites of hydrœlectric dams being built in Northern Quebec.

As a consequence, overextended, nap-inducing union coffee-breaks and eating all the food one could ram down ones equally unionized throat, were strictly-enforced, unwritten workplace health-and-safety rules at the MG2 construction site.

One promise Jr was able to keep was not eating any *arepas* until he tasted Marco's first. The workforce was divided along national lines, as was the canteen. Though all the fare on the site was offered to anyone willing to be gastronomically adventurous, those that were more finicky by nature or by upbringing were able to stick to a traditional diet, on their respective side of the construction site's cultural divide.

Arepas notwithstanding, Gino was one of the most adventurous of all the workers at MG2. Seeing that several of the local fast food delicacies had a French-Canadian equivalent, he would regularly ask the cooks to crossbreed his lunchtime fare. His first gastronomic experiment ended up being his favorite. Replacing the French fries with *papas criollas al horno*, and the curd cheese with *aborrajados*, he would have the two covered with a generous dollop of *Napolitana* pasta sauce. He christened his creation Colombian–Italian *poutine*.

- What are you doing, Gino?
- I'm eating. It's the law, around here.

- I know. But what are you eating?
- It's a hybrid. *Poutine*. Try some.

- Okay... Wow. That's really good.
- Sweet, but not too sweet. Spicy but not too spicy.

- Nairo. Try this.
- Okay... Hmm. That is better than Quebecois *poutine*. Tomás. Try this.
- Fantastic!
- Hey. That's enough. Go ask the cook for a Colombian-Italian p*outine*. He will make you the same thing. Now let me finish my lunch.

Before lunchtime was over, a substantial majority of the gourmand workforce had polished off their own serving of Gino's hybrid dish. And were looking forward to his next creative endeavor. They didn't have to wait long. Afternoon break was only two hours away.

By the end of the week the cooks had written up three menus. One Colombian. One French-Canadian. And one for the Gino-turned-*Cordon-Bleu* aficionados. By far, the third menu became the most popular, resulting in the crumbling of the gastronomic divide at MG2.

If only geopolitics were that easy to resolve.

☕⚓☟☝☞

Saturday finally rolled around, and never having slept as mush as they had in the last three days, Gino and his consorts were more than ready for their weekend adventure. The former wasn't sure what he most anticipated. The taste of white-water rafting. Or the taste of his first *arepas.*

- So Mr. Gino, was your rafting adventure worth the forty pesos?
- No. Mr. Marco. At eighty, it would still be a bargain!

- That is the best compliment I could ask for. Thank-you. And what about the *arepas*?
- I kept my promise, Mr. Marco. This was my first time eating these cakes. And they were delicious, to say the least. I ate nine of them.

- And I ate twelve! No more room for another bite. And the rafting. Much better than canœing the rapids. Safer and much more spectacular. Like a Belmont Park roller-coaster ride with lots of water and beautiful scenery.
- I will have to start an *arepas* eating contest. I will place bets on you Mr. Frank!

- Be careful Mr. Marco, when placing bets. Looks can be deceiving. Tomás is almost half my size but he ate fourteen!
- Fourteen?! You will put me into bankruptcy, Tomás. Just kidding. Now what about trying kayak? More dangerous than rafting but, what-you-say?, more…

- Thrilling?
- Yes. Thrilling.

- Count me in. And what about you Gino? Do you still want to try the rapids in a kayak?
- Yes. But with lessons on a calm river first.

- I give lessons with maximum three people at a time. Still room for you Mr. Tomás.
- Yes! I'm in. On one condition. *Arepas* after lesson.

- That is a deal! I give lessons during the week, after MG2 work day. From six to eight PM. *Arepas* till ten PM. Around warm camp fire. One lesson and supper, thirty pesos. Four lessons and four suppers. One hundred pesos. With four lessons, cook make special meals. *Arepas* with *sancocho, arroz de lisa,* and for dessert, the best *tres leches* cake east of Medellin. And that is only on Monday. Next three suppers are surprise. Always pleasant surprise. Even for me!
- Four lessons for me.
- Me too!
- Count me in for four lessons.

- Beeheheheh!
- Who is this, Mr. Marco? She is beautiful, and friendly to boot.
- This is Dilma. Dilma the goat. She is our mascot. She is not a mean goat. She supplies the milk for the *tres leches* cake. And keeps everyone company.

- Much more useful than a dog or cat, Mr. Marco.
- And more intelligent than both, Mr Gino.

✝↘

With their tummies full, and union-backed, nap-inducing *cocadas* fairies dancing in their heads, our electrodynamic duo's ~~Yuletide Holiday~~ two-week MG2 work-site gig had to come to an end. It was now time for them to head off in their newly-exchanged, battered-but-functional lineman truck, where they would have the latter filled with apothecaries' cheer from the enchanted coca fields, east of the Andes Mountains.

A relatively short detour to the major border town of Cúcuta was in order. There the mechanics of the closest International-Harvester dealership to the MG2 work-site, would complete one final, quick verification and oil change on the old vehicle, before the two Sicilian-Canadians would return to Cartagena, for their Caribbean-Island journey back to North American Continent.

It was also the most critical of all stopovers for our processed coca, double duty, exporter-importers.

They weren't the only ones doing double duty that night. The graveyard-shift mechanics working on the vehicle were not only responsible for changing the oil, they were also responsible for carefully taking apart sections of the lineman truck and stuffing every available exposed orifice with Saran-wrapped inserts from the cash-crop fields of Eastern Colombia. And then just as carefully, putting the partially disassembled vehicle back together. Ready for Gino and Jr to pick up in the early hours of the following morning.

☟☠☦

Now, how two makeshift electrodynamic technicians ended up as Trappist monks at Monasterio Nuestra Señora de los Andes in El Vigía, barely 100 kilometers northeast of Cúcuta on the Venezuelan side of the border, will have to wait.

My apologies. I'm getting a little bit ahead of my narrative duties. Again.

Suffice to say, the alternative would have been orders of magnitude worse than the ørlög finally chosen by the two coca-smuggling lineman turned reformed Cistercian Order contemplatives.

♛↘

In a psychotic moment of difference, Sr was in an equally contemplative mood, as he meditated over what was more threatening to his waning criminal career. The strategic but none-the-less significant loss of a major cocaine shipment and its accompanying profitable and recently-instituted smuggling network, or the disappearance of both Gino and his failed son, who both have vanished from his end of the organized-crime radar screen.

Without knowing if both members of this electrodynamic duo were either dead or alive, they now became more of a threat to Sr than they were when the former unwittingly began their crossing of this Latin American asses' bridge. A bridge they had ironically driven over with success. A successful crossing Sr had yet to be aware of.

The only outcome of this risky endeavor Sr could be assured of was the one he dreaded the most: the dread of the unknown.

Official word of Frank Sr's failure swept quickly across the Atlantic, through the Strait of Gibraltar, detouring at the tiny Maltese Capital of Valletta, to finally anchor at the small town of Pozzallo. The latter but fifteen kilometers northeast of the nearly as small town of Scicli.

- It is for the better. I had written off Jr well before his father's latest attempt at rectification. Such endeavors rarely, if ever work out.
- And what about Micheal?

- Too young. And he already expressed his ambivalence.
- That eliminates Jimmy.

- Yes. And he is too desperate to show he is the boss.
- Latent frustrations?

- Probably violent trauma before his puberty.
- Frank Sr?

- Senior has shown erratic behavior ever since he emigrated from Scicli.
- His last trip to Colombia was bizarre to say the least.

- The monkeys?
- Yes. You can contract simian syphilis if you get too close, too long. And Frank Sr definitely got too close.

- Too long. I asked Dr. Ciao. He says simian syphilis, when crossed into humans can have unexpected repercussions.
- That might explain why he is always under the weather.

- Most probably. Such erotic deviancy is rare. We know little of the medical consequences.
- But syphilis is as old as time itself. We have extensive historical records of this chameleon pathogen.

- You would have made a good doctor. If not an anthropologist!
- Ha!

Principle

With the Bedalini family establishing themselves as the main enforcers of the Sicilian Mafia in Canada, it became not only unnecessary, but also undesirable for the Slapulo Family to partake in such hand-soiling activities on their own.

For years, the Slapulo's unspoken corporate motto was "Buy my cheese or I'll break your legs!"[10]

With their family business rapidly transforming and expanding into a multinational corporation spanning across the Americas and Europe it, was time for them to scrub up their corporate image and give it a sparkling clean shine. At least on the surface.

The Slapulo's sanitized new corporate image makes it possible for them to infuse an Alpine fresh scent to their political transactions as well. What better to compliment a glass of Slapulo milk? Why a freshly-baked Qly-Nord cupcake, of course. Alas this industrial bakery was "nationalized" years ago to insure its financial viability in the politically sensitive Beauce region of Quebec.

No problem. With the swirl of Guido's platinum-plated fountain pen on a NBN Financial branded certified cheque, Mr. Slapulo can now purchase this provincial crown corporation with no need of discrete brown paper bags filled with unmarked currency imbued with the pungent smell of his famous Parmesan cheese. And the Price? The equivalent of a handful of Italian-by-tradition bread crumbs.

---

10 With thanks to Right Honorable member of Parliament Mr. André Arthur.

Light

You would think that our Sicilian Gran Khan would have known better.

And he did.

At least the timing was right. We were after all, well into the post-Woodstock era. It was high time for the rural conservative Sicilian hierarchy to let its hair down, or at least grow a bit. What better research station than the Dominion of Canada. It could learn how to embrace and subsequently exploit the burgeoning Global Village, far away from its shores, in a huge space, the latter being neither a nation, nor a country. All the advantages of Malta with none of its disadvantages.

If things got out of hand, what better place to screw up, than one burdened with snow in the winter and mosquitœs in the summer. And with a total population barely that of California, the losses would be insignificant.

Little did the Khan know how enlightened his thoughts were at the time. You should always plan to learn from your mistakes. After all, that's what experiments are for.

♂⚑♂

"At 99.6 on your FM dial, here is a 90 second WFIM news update, for Friday, June 13th, 1980 ...

... In a brazen daytime attack, reminiscent of the Capone Era endeavors of old school South Chicago, two local mafia kingpins, and their accompanying bodyguards, were blown to indistinguishable bits, as they attempted to drive away, following lunch at the gangsters' well established haunt of *haute cuisine.* This time it wasn't a Chicago pizzeria, but none other than Guido's Sicilian Seafood Emporium on New York's Lower East Side..."

Not only was this latest event located in a different space-time continuum as the ones of Chicago past, the perpetrator wasn't even from the same country.

But for our Mediterranean-Island Khan, the second generation Sicilian-Canadian tripping the remote-controlled detonator was exactly the replacement he was looking for. Right down to the psychotic, drama-queen psychiatric profile.

♂✝♂

Though nowhere near as mind blowing as the events going on at the same time on New York's Lower East Side, my own mid-June, afternoon adventure was none-the-less a pivotal one, as I slowly exited the authoritative rigidity of pubescence, and entered the plastic no-man's-land every prospective male explorer roams through, as he searches to define his future manhood.

As both the grounds keeper and the alter boy for Sainte-Margurite Station's Roman Catholic Chapel, I got my fair share of post-pubescent molding and influence peddling from Monsignor Bifett: despite the fact that most of the time, he wasn't even near the chapel, nor the station.

I don't ever recall asking him. I didn't have to.

Just about every time, okay, every time he would happen to ride by as I was cutting the chapel's expansive lawn, I would slow the progression of my work to a crawl pace, and with the anticipative gaze of a teenager sporting a vividly overwrought imagination, watch as Monsignor Bifett would complete his parking ritual.

On this particular afternoon, I had finished a little earlier than usual, and was in the process of partially disassembling my magnesium-bodied, two-stroke Lawn-Boy in preparation for the latter's transfer into the trunk of my mother's Mercury Zephyr, when Monsignor Bifett rode up beside me and began the process of extricating himself from his fiber-reinforced-polymer-bodied, four-stroke Honda Gold-Wing.

- Buuzzzzz-Toc... buuzzzzz-Toc...
- Hello?

- Hi, Mom? It's Sylvain.
- Is there something wrong, Sylvain?

- No, no. I just want to know if you need the car for anything this afternoon.
- No, no. Why?

- Monsignor Bifett, is here, and he offered me to go on a small ride on the back of his motorcycle. We're only going to L'Eaubonne and back. I'll be home before supper. Is that okay?
- If it's Moan-seen-your Bye-fett, that should be okay. Be careful. Wear a helmet. And wear a coat. And boots.

- I have my work boots. And Monsignor Bifett has an extra coat and helmet for me. Thanks. See you later.
- Bye-bye, Sylvain. Be careful.

- Bye-Bye.
- Clic!

A customary "*C'est correct*", addressed to the Monsignor was in order.

But useless.

By the look of the irreplaceable, cheek-spanning grin on my face, Big Bertha Bifett knew the comment was expressively redundant.

Now to be precise, Eaubonne is the town. *L'Eaubonne* is the hotel complex, on the shores of Eaubonne Bay. Eaubonne is to Ste-Margeurite proper, what Upper Chanticleer is to Chanticleer Valley. A rural refuge for the wealthy and well-heeled weekender of Montreal.

One may ask, what's the difference, between the wealthy and well-heeled?

Credit.

The wealthy don't need it. The well-heeled live by it.

Being the youngest of six children, I guess you could say my initiatory ride on the back seat of a Roman Catholic priest's over-sized motorcycle was a fitting tenth anniversary celebration of my father's death.

His third, and an even more fitting thirtieth anniversary celebration of his first.

Isn't synchrony neat. Sometimes.

That afternoon, as I began the simultaneous crossings of several of the most treacherous asses' bridges I was about to embark on, my father's past losses would be beacons, lighting each span as I struggled to reach their other sides.

Beacons, I would learn to use to better advantage as I embarked on future bridges, leaving the old ones far behind in the memories of a distant past.

✐✒

When the original, wealthy, urban owners of *L'Eaubonne* are replaced by recently well-heeled, rural residents, an architectural-design tornado can be seen on the horizon.

The complex, one of the Dominion's original art-deco masterpieces, could have been restored, renovated and expanded to rival the visual and structural beauty of its Orange City counterpart, had it not been for the unfortunate transfer of the formers title to a gaggle of rural rednecks with copious amounts of questionable cash.

It was not to be. Boy, was it not to be.

The resultant disparate mishmash of pseudo-log-cabin and faceless-seventies-style, government-building architectural styles used in the construction of *L'Eaubonne*'s numerous patchwork additions, made the final product a weekend-resort disaster, as forgetful and unappealing as an over-sized suburban strip mall.

The only other disgraceful aspect rivaling the visual soreness of this waterfront resort, was the waterfront itself. Or more precisely, the water bordering the waterfront. The bay, having no rivers entering nor exiting its shore and only a narrow opening between itself and the neighboring bay of the lake, Eaubonne Bay has become a natural storage tank for the discarded effluent spewing from the over-sized, look-at-me jet boats crisscrossing its surface on any given seasonal holiday.

As a result, Eaubonnel Bay is both a visual and olfactory disgrace. The spent mixture of two-stroke oil and petroleum, covering the murky, stale waters of the bay with a slick multicolor-hued sheen, is accompanied by the constant stench of internal combustion gases emanating from the water's surface.

Even the soft-frozen, commodity-indexed, Brazilian-milk-ingredient treats both of us indulged in at the royally-named dispensary across the street from the complex were, as expected, unmistakably lousy.

No matter.

The first half of my ride on the back seat of Big Bertha Bifett's Honda, virtually etched that irreplaceable grin, like a full-face tattoo, on those sun-dried, wind-swept cheeks of mine.

The second half of our ride back to the chapel's refectory parking lot was just as pleasant as the first, cementing my resolve to, one day, ride my own Honda to the shores of Eaubonne Bay for the useless indulgence of a crappy soft-ice-milk cone.

+

Though well over two years had passed since Big Bertha Bifett's initial recruitment ~~ride~~ drive, my resolve to one day acquire my first Honda had only increased, instep with Bifett's resolve to promote me to Prospect status, inside the secret confines of his cult.

No, no. Not that cult.

His religious cult.

It was the Fall, and I was well into the last year of my Applied Sciences college degree at the *CEGEP de Jérômeville.* I was at one of the pivotal moments in my life, where I had to decide for the first time, how, where, and more importantly in what direction should my initial career path take me.

It had been several years now that I had my heart set on becoming an engineer.

Or so I thought.

Big Bertha had other plans.

I was removing my alter-boy robe, following Sunday service, when he popped the question. Actually it was more of an influential suggestion than a question. Monsignor Bifett thought I had what it took to become a Roman Catholic priest. Flattered, I accepted his offer to visit one of his contemporaries. A theology intern stationed in Jérômeville.

Be it a former convent, seminary or monastery, the majority of government owned-and-operated post secondary colleges known as *CEGEPs*, were constructed around the core of such Roman Catholic institutions, the latter having been virtually abandoned in the early seventies. A casualty of Quebec's Quiet Revolution.

Jérômeville's contribution to Quebec's *CEGEP* network was no exception.

As such, my rendezvous with Big Bertha's protégé was less than a dead-city bloc away from the *CEGEP*'s Applied Science department.

To call my encounter with this theology intern bizarre would be unfair. It was more enlightening than it was bizarre.

Our conversation was rather unambiguous to begin with. Your standard inconsequential banter. One you would likely have with a stranger seated next to you during an extended intercity bus trip. Things turned bizarre when I asked what motivated him to choose a career as a Roman Catholic priest.

By the time he had finished explaining to me that his decision was not his own, but the result of a divine apparition, things turned uncomfortably bizarre.

I could sense myself squirming in my seat. It was time to leave.

Apparitions, be they physically or metaphysically induced, were not amongst the causative events contributing to the engrams of my observational legacy.

A legacy that would evolve with time.

✢⚠

In the autumn of 1983, when you entered the city of Kitchener for the first time, the only two industrial icons that would suggest you were now driving through what used to be called Berlin, were the Schneider's Sausage and Kaufman Boot factories.

The Second World War hysteria that demonized everything German at that time, pushed city council to give the municipality a more Dominion-like nomenclature. Hopefully, Horatio Herbert was a fan of bangers and mash, or the chosen name change wouldn't of made much sense to the disgruntled local Teutons. On second thought, as a field Marshall, it wouldn't be a stretch if it was disclosed the Earl had a boot fetish.

Oh, the humanity of rationalizing the irrational.

As a temporary student resident, the only way I knew I was about to exit the twin city of Waterloo, and had finally entered ~~Berlin~~ Kitchener, was when I would walk in front of the very Dominion-like Sir Wilfred Laurier University campus.

A Polish-sausage ring-toss away from Sir Wilfred Laurier on University Avenue, stands the Waterloo Campus. At the time, if you wanted to be an engineer, the University of Waterloo was the place to be. As close as you could get to a MIT degree, north of the border.

As one of the first asses' bridges I have crossed during my lifetime, its teachings were revealed to me only decades after having crossed its span.

That lesson was the importance of taking risks and, more importantly, how to calculate them before choosing such undertakings.

Ironically, choosing to move to Waterloo, Ontario to undertake my graduate studies was a significant risk worth taking. Playing it safe and moving back to Quebec to finish my engineering degree in Sherbrooke turned out to be an even riskier endeavor than staying in Ontario. It resulted in more grief and missed opportunities than I could have ever anticipated at the time.

Alas, they don't call them asses' bridges for nothing.

☾ ☼ ☽

"In the heart of London's Financial District, on Blüteberg TV and on The Blüteberg Radio Network throughout America, you are listening to The London Breakfast...

...Good morning. My name is Marc Barstone. And on this Friday, May 8th, 2015, our top story is twofold, and spans as many continents. In Edmonton, Alberta, The Dominion of Canada, Heather Fisterslutvale, the former CEO of The Dominion's largest chain of cultural trinket emporiums, is celebrating one of The Dominion's greatest political C changes in its short history, as she settles into her new career as Alberta's first female NDP Premier, after over two generations of continuous Progressive Conservative Rule.

While Albertans were splitting the Right, Heather's Left leaning NDP cruised into a parliamentary majority. Her Majesty's British subjects on the other side of The Pond, have split the Left, permitting Nicholas Mac Avalon, to continue his career as UK's Prime Minister, with an even larger Conservative majority in Parliament, than the one he had a month earlier.

UK voters abandoned the very Right leaning United Kingdom Independence Party, and chose stability over confrontation..."

...

Vladimir, is playing Stephanie, Heather, and Nicholas like strings on a fiddle, as he serenades the zombie remains of Joseph (the Soviet despot not the presumed father the Ancient Hasid) and Mao on history's merry-go-round. At least they are feeling better than they did a few moons ago.

Darkness

Two years had passed.

The darkness had begun.

My first encounter was synced with my driver's license morphing into a pass to most of the bars I desired to enter. As long as I had the credit. That credit was made possible following my first cooperative education work-term during my stay at the University of Sherbrooke.

Ironically, the encounter was not in the dark recesses of a downtown bar, but rather in the starlit recesses of Jeanne-Mance Park, bordering, what else, Park Avenue and on the opposite side of the Avenue bordering, what else, Mount Royal Park.

He wasn't the most handsome. Neither was I.

I don't know if he believed me or not when I told him it was my first time. We exited Jeanne-Mance Park, and headed to his apartment on, oh, never mind, Jeanne-Mance Boulevard.

His was but a few three-story wrote-iron exterior staircases north of the one I was renting a room from during the duration of my work-term. A room no more than a large glorified storage locker with a single bed, barely passing the lowest of Ikea Standards. The bed, not the locker.

Since this was the first intimate encounter of my late-blooming life, you would be hard pressed to add homosexual as a modifier. The encounter, not the life.

Homœrotic? Barely. To paraphrase an infamous radio-phonic comedian who was overheard saying, not long before this initial encounter...

"When you're 21, someone shouts out Hippopotamus!.. and you come."

Though I was old enough to no longer be on the fence, I chalked this one up to a preliminary exploration.

As I entered onto the campus of the University of Sherbrooke, to begin my third autumn semester as a mechanical engineering student, I would walk up to two of the darkest and most challenging bridges encountered during my short fortnights in Midgard.

One conscious. One instinctive.

The first was scouted by the second oldest of my sisters, Suzanne. And the second by the ghosts of my unfulfilled desires.

There are many ways to measure intelligence. One of the best is defined by our creative ability to adapt. Using the latter as a yardstick, Suzanne is undoubtedly the brainchild-ruler of the family.

She was born too early to repair the gap. She grew to adapt to her deformity. So did her heart. Where there were no arteries, veins expanded to replace their absence. The muscle that remained worked twice as hard, and grew to fill the emptiness of a failed gestation.

The knowledgeable said she would not see her tenth birthday.

Little did they know.

When pneumonia struck her, she was at the doorstep of her thirtieth birthday.

She would alpine ski during the winter. Explore her natural surroundings during the summer. Her childhood was filled with the beauty of classical music. Legacies handed over from her father.

She would sing in the choir, accompanying the Montreal Symphony Orchestra. Following her studies at Vincent d'Indy, she taught classical guitar, one student at a time, in her bedroom of the family homestead. She would practice every day. The structured melodies of the chords emanating from her guitar, would fill the wood-panel cathedral ceilings of her second-story lair.

Like the morning tunes of a backyard sparrow.

She had a second deformity. A hunched back, forcing her to never be taller than 4 feet 11. And a half. Unlike her Notre-Dame consort, her back only served to emphasize the delicate nature of her body. And soul.

Like an over-sized porcelain doll, she never tipped the scales much past 100 pounds. A porcelain doll filled with life and energy.

The knowledgeable said she would not make it through the winter, if they did not intervene. A decade of financial abuse at the hands of my mother's second husband reduced the family estate to a shriveled pittance of its former self. Neither the estate, nor the modest revenue of her teaching practice would ever give Suzanne the pecuniary power and influence to push her name to the top of any heart-transplant list.

She would counter with the power and influence of her personal will.

An alternative was presented to her. A series of surgical procedures would need to be undertaken. Some traditional and proven. The others experimental and not. They would be subsequently completed in one marathon intervention. One never before performed on a human. Making Suzanne a two-legged guinea-pig and the subject of a lengthy article published in an appropriate medical journal.

♫⚕

Entering the operative theater at the Montreal Children Hospital, Suzanne's face and extremities were a morbid shade of blue, the result of pneumonia-weakened heart and lungs.

A fourteen-hour surgical performance was presented, including five six-minute bursts of death, where Suzanne's heart would be stopped, and her delicate, momentary cadaver would be plunged into a pool of ice water to preserve her muscle tissue and vital organs.

During these short-lived moments of death, several reconstruction procedures were conducted, including but not limited to, the removal of Suzanne's self-morphed heart valves and replaced with those donated by an unsuspecting pig; born, bread and raised for just such an untimely medical blot...

When Suzanne awoke from her white-water rafting excursion through the numerous rapids of death's river, she had but her defining willpower to help her get to shore.

The piezœlectric sensors and fluid tubes covering her former cadaver, were more of a hindrance. They would be only of help to the helpless. The knowledgeable that would interpret their data, and man the responses of their twentieth-century process control mechanisms.

It was time for that defining willpower to begin healing her wounds.

You already know what they say about time.

❥♬

The second bridge I would encounter that autumn was manned more by infatuation than by any love of an animated mechanical device. One that would take the form of a 1985 CX650. Black with silver-gray and Honda-red accents.

The bridgehead on the first side of this ass-roaming span took the form of the service-garage doors shared by both the Lennoxville UJM dealer and the Lennoxville chapter of a two-wheeled porcine dispensary.

The owner of this two-sided establishment was known by his self-imposed and deceivingly-inappropriate surname of Mr. Friendly. He was sort of like a Guy Smiley with latent psychotic tendencies. Just the right psychiatric profile for a motorcycle peddler.

I would have to wait till the spring equinox had come, and passed, before I could exit this first bridgehead atop of the three-shaded apple of my infatuate eyes.

Having disposed more than my fair share of the past summer's work-term income on this audacious frivolity, I was relegated to hitchhiking between Sherbrooke and Montreal in order to bring a little love to my sister's silent rehabilitation.

Oh, the humanity of blinded hindsight.

♂☠♂

- Oh no ...

For me, the nighties started on a *memorably* sour note. Allow me to elaborate.

- So what do the x-rays tell you, Doctor?
- Let me put it this way. You will be needing more than today's May Day holiday to recuperate from this latest misfortune, Mr. de Ville-Amois. You have suffered an inter-trochaic fracture of your left femur. In other words, you have a hairline fracture of your left hip bone just under the joint connecting the femur to your basin. We will have to proceed with surgery in a few hours to stabilize the fracture. As you are relatively young and in good health, you will have the choice in about a year, to stick with the status quo or to have the stabilizing hardware surgically removed, once the hip bone has completely healed.

An adult male moose can rival the volume and weight of a single-cab Ford Ranger pick-up. A light blue 1987 single-cab Ford Ranger pick-up.

Despite having similar dead-weight linear momentum, the living inertia of an adult male moose will result in a more forgiving impact target than a rigid-body Ford pick-up truck, should either collide with a 1950 Indian motorcycle or a white-red-and-blue 1987 Yamaha FZ750 motorcycle.

- Your records show you were conscious when admitted to the emergency room. Do you recall loosing consciousness at any moment before that?
- I closed my eyes just before impact. I recall hitting something with my helmet and when I opened my eyes, I was on the asphalt, sitting up, about two to three meters southwest of the intersection's center. I figure I must have been catapulted over the pick-up truck and landed there, as the pick-up and what was left of my motorcycle, were about ten meters away. I don't recall falling on the asphalt. The event felt like it took place inside the span of a heartbeat.

That's when the adrenaline kicked in.

Adrenaline is a curious trauma-induced secretion. From the first months of our fetal life, till the moment we take our last breath, we condition ourselves to recognize the time between two at-rest heartbeats as a constant that varies only slightly as we travel through the subsequent phases of our life journey. Our sinoatrial node serves as a real-time internal clock.

When adrenaline is suddenly secreted in copious amounts, responding to stress or trauma, it has the effect of shifting our perception of reality from the conscious to the instinctive hemisphere of our realm of self-awareness. As a consequence, we become hyper-aware of the surroundings outside our immediate self to the detriment of the awareness of our inner-self. The latter having been severely compromised following millenia of neglect and the atrophic devolution of our instinctive capacities.

The calming effects of the endorphins produced as a response to the pain of trauma, combined with the awareness-shifting properties of our increased adrenaline levels, trick our atrophic instinct to believe we are at rest. While in realty, our heart rate is orders of magnitude higher than normal. As a result, our sense of time compresses, and what is actually but a few moments in time will now seem to be an eternity for the traumatized observer.

⊛✪

Love and hate.
Rain and tears.
Water under the bridge.

War and peace.
Toil and sufferance.
Blood under the bridge.

Crime and justice.
The rot of social decay.
Rats under the bridge.

The hypocrisy of democracy.
Draco's logic.
Empires crumble under the bridge.

Mind and memory.
Hugin and Munin.
Ravens over the bridge.

Quebec City's Place d'Youville is a different place today than it was at the height of the biker wars.

Economically, we were over a decade away from the Great Recession of 2008.

Les Punks de Fin de Semaine, Weekend Punks, were a revolving mainstay around the walled entrance to St-Jean Boulevard. The average lifespan of a Weekend Punk's career was three weeks during the summer months, and two weeks if this high-maintenance beggar chose this career path during the wintertime. About half of these designer-punks were the sons and daughters of career deputy ministers from the provincial government. The other half were for the most part, the sons and daughters of CEOs at the head of overwhelmingly-subsidized, quasi crown-corporations, all members of a cartel of make-work projects known today as Quebec Inc.

Socially, we were nearly two decades away from the National-Socialist inspired, White-Supremacist leaning policies of Quebec's 2013 vintage, Charter of Values.

Ironically, the white-laced skinheads from Levis and surrounding suburbs were being forcibly segregated from Place d'Youville by plain-clothed Quebec Municipal and Provincial police officers in a move to discreetly protect the Global-Village inspired, Left-Wing leaning high-priced Punks, who twenty years later, are now the champions of this Quebecois Charter of Values. To paraphrase a famous politician of the second world war: a teenager that is not a socialist, has no heart; an adult that is not a conservative, has no brains.

Sexually, Place d'Youville was a hotbed of gay public and corporate activity. As a center and starting point for tourists visiting Quebec City's heritage *Haute-Ville,* this public square also served as one of the main terminal hubs of Quebec City's Public Transit Authority and most importantly, was only a five block limo drive away from the provincial legislature.

Politically, this latter observation parallels a phenomenon seen in many small-city legislative centers of the Dominion. As is also the case in Ottawa, Quebec City's gay per capita quotient is orders of magnitude higher than its non-legislative urban counterparts, making it possible to plant a relatively large and profitable gay ghetto onto a small urban landscape.

Statistically speaking, the single most important profession chosen by those starting a career in politics is that of a lawyer. The following commutative conclusion arises: where lawyers abound, life is gay. Interestingly enough, the same commutative conclusion arises when criminal biker gangs abound.

Combining, profits, gay ghettos, lawyers and criminal biker gangs all in the same space-time continuum, it comes as no surprise that the vast majority of Quebec City's gay enterprises, were in the 1990's, and are to this day, owned or controlled by Kopfschmuck bikers and their close legal and business associates.

The closest of Quebec City's three gay male bathhouses to the provincial legislature was non-descriptively nestled on the upper floors of an aging commercial low-rise office tower, on the corner of St-Jean Boulevard and the Duffrin-Montmonrency highway.

In a tragically humorous twist of horrendous engineering design and nearly as horrendous urban planning, the office tower was erected amazingly close to the corner of this multiple-lane highway and historic St-Jean Boulevard. When an unsuspecting tourist, would stand waiting on St-Jean Boulevard for her turn to start the harrowing journey across the Dufferin-Montmonrency highway, she stood a statistically significant chance of being virtually decapitated by the over-sized driver side rear-view mirror of the record-breaking-extra-wide public transit buses, *Qualité Québec* engineered and manufactured by one of the most infamous commercial ventures of Quebec Inc.

I digress.

Though this office tower was discretely acclaimed as an urban planning disaster, its equally discrete claim to fame in the local gay community was the result of being Quebec City's most important meeting place, servicing the in-the-closet, legislative, legal, and corporate elite.

Sauna D'Youville was a near perfect fit for John. Though only a few hours past his 19th birthday, he was already over 6 feet tall and a respectable 205 lbs, butt naked. His stereotypical, V-shaped, Adonis physique was courtesy of his equally stereotypical farm boy childhood which in turn was courtesy of the less-than-stereotypical consequence of his mother being the wife of a Northern New Brunswick potato farmer.

The potato farming part needs some explaining. So bare with me.

John wasn't born a Thébeau. His original birth certificate was penned in as John Josef Überstehen, son of Ted Überstehen and Mary-Lou Houston. To this day, Mary-Lou insists on preserving her maiden name as a badge of defiance, having long ran away from her famous rural Tennessee parents. The reasons for this escape, now hidden in the electronic pages of her daily diary. A diary that is now preserved inside the recess of a solid gold, heart-shaped locket she has worn as a pendant around her neck for well over half a century. A pendant of significant personal value as it is the only family heirloom she owns. An heirloom given to her by her grandmother on her 8th birthday.

An antique locket she uses to hide the mysteries of her past. A past one must unlock to unveil the logic behind her ørlög. One pushing Mary-Lou to become a street whore on the borders of Mengen's Victoria Park. That is where Ted met her for the first time.

As the go-to defense lawyer for the local cell of the Sicilian Mafia, Ted is no stranger to prostitutes. Contrary to the low-priced street-level sex workers of Victoria Park, Ted's high-priced services tend, more often than not, to be used by the equally high-priced call-girls performing in and around Mengen's popular gambling and hotel complex. At first glance you would think Ted, with his Teutonic heritage physique, finely manicured presentation, and credit-limit-less American Express Cards, would have no trouble what so ever starting a long-term relationship with any of these top-level ladies of the evening. But, alas you would have to ignore the unavoidable. Ted is a successful criminal defense lawyer.

As such, Ted's greed-ravaged absence of social ethics, honor, and morality, not to mention his perversely corrupted social skills, makes him a complete and total turn-off to all but the most equally greed-ravaged escorts.

Male or female.

For the moment, Ted's legal practice is situated in New Brunswick, the most chronically have-not of the Dominion's have-not provinces. If he wants to marry a high-priced, high-maintenance whore with a similar psychiatric profile as his own, he's going to have to move to a geopolitical region such as Nevada or California, where greed is a universally accepted and deified institution.

Having taken well over a month to travel from Southern Tennessee to Southern New Brunswick, and with only a few hundred dollars left over from a weekly allowance that she was conditioned to spend in a few days, Mary-Lou was well aware that she urgently needed an alternative form of income to satisfy not only her heroine addiction but also her shopaholic dependency. Her genetic mixture of Scot-Irish, Tennessee Redneck, Middle Eastern, and Amerindian heritage, combined with a traditional, Golden-Arches dietary regimen quickly negated any possibilities for a career as a luxury female escort. All that was left was Victoria Park.

♂£♀

Mars, Venus and the corporate headquarters of HSBC must have been all aligned at just the right time when Ted drove up to Mary-Lou and rolled down the passenger-side window of his black BMW 740i. After nearly two months on the street, Ted was her first client to drive up in something other than a rusted-out pick-up truck or an equally rusted-out late-model Datsun B-210. For both of them, it was greed-lust at first sight. The ink was barely dry on their prenuptial agreement, when they were both on a private charted jet to the Cayman Islands for a customary civil marriage followed by a perversely romantic and memorable sex, cocaine, and heroine smörgåsbord which conveniently doubled as their official honeymoon.

Greed-lust fueled both sides of this relationship. Infatuation fueled only one. By the time their first and only baby was two years old, Mary-Lou's infatuation and Ted's patience was wearing thin. Well before any marriage contract was signed, a thorough background check, combined with Ted's operatic but none-the-less brutal cross-examination skills, revealed much of Mary-Lou's short past. Most importantly was her relationship to Sandy, her great-grandmother. Not only was Mary-Lou the most cherished of Sandy's eleven great-grandchildren, she was also the only human beneficiary of Sandy's will. Two secrets shared only by Sandy, Mary-Lou and now Ted. And what a will. As one of the founding members of the family business, qualifying the total value of Sandy's will as a fortune would be, to say the least, an understatement.

All those super-sized, *quarter-pounder* cheeseburger combos were bound to get to her sooner or later. Sandy was diagnosed with diabetes-accelerated chronic heart disease, barely a year before Ted and Mary-Lou headed off to the Cayman Islands. The doctor gave her five years at most. Making sure to sign and seal her final will while still of sound mind, was the pivotal, motivating factor that triggered Ted's marriage proposal.

As Sandy was the only family member Mary-Lou kept in contact with after her first marriage, she made sure to be at her great-grandmother's deathbed. Sandy died on the same day her great-great-grandson turned four years old.

The near totality of the will was comprised of stock options wholly owned by a newly created, arms-length foundation whose board of directors would be chosen, every 5 years, by a vote of all the corporation's employees. Each employee would have one vote and be able to suggest one director on the ballot following the successful petition of at least 5% of all the corporation's employees.

All corporate dividends owed to the foundation would be kept in the form of capital liquidity, and not reinvested in any third-party corporations. Mary-Lou would only own and be able to redeem a time-lapsed portion of the foundation's capital liquidity, on or after her 65th birthday.

In the advent of Mary-Lou's untimely death before her 65th birthday, the foundation's capital liquidity would be used to buyback the original corporation's voting and non-voting shares, not already owned by the foundation, until the complete transfer of the corporation's ownership to that of the foundation.

Ha-Ha. Ted got screwed.

He'd be a post-andropausal, Viagra-popping, coffin-tire-kicking, old geezer before he could ever touch a cent of Mary-Lou's inheritance.

With a one-way business-class ticket to in one hand, and a hastily-crafted copy of his divorce papers in the other, Ted was off to Los Angeles to start a new criminal legal practice and, if possible, to find true lust.

He agreed to minimal alimony payments in return to forfeiting his right to any part of Mary-Lou's inheritable and would take custody of his son two months a year during the summer holidays.

Not wanting to return to Tennessee under any circumstances, Mary-Lou chose to stay in New Brunswick. With an adequate alimony check coming in every month, she was able to fend for herself and her son. A humane intervention clause included in her great-grandmother's will, made it possible for her to enroll in an effective private detox clinic and to obtain continuous addiction counseling for the rest of her life. By the time John was eight years old, she had married a Northern New Brunswick potato farmer whose farmstead was situated just on the northern outskirts of Kedgwick, a small village about 60 kilometers southwest of Cambellton.

Stephan Thébeau was only half Acadian, his mother being a Lebanese refugee who immigrated to Mengen during one of several mid-20th century armed conflicts between Lebanon and several of its neighbors.

At first glance, you would think that an obese, Eastern Tennessee, spoiled brat redneck, single mom with a severe opiate addiction was a tough sell as a potential marriage candidate. But not for Stephan.

Being part Lebanese, part Acadian, he was no stranger to the presence of obese women. As for courting a Tennessee redneck, the only significant difference between Tennessee and New Brunswick is that New Brunswick has more snow during the wintertime. Mary-Lou's status as a single mom was more a blessing than a hindrance. Suffering from a rare congenital disease, Stephan was diagnosed at birth as being impotent. Adopting John would mean one less temporary foreign worker to hire during harvest season.

Stephan and Mary-Lou met each other during a group addiction counseling session, transforming the last obstacle into a common interest.

Though it has been a decade since he was adopted by his potato farming stepfather, his biological father was still able to retain custody of his one and only son two months out of the year. John would spend a month and a half, between planting and harvest season, and two weeks during spring break at Ted's Hollywood Hills mansion. And it's during those two months of the year that John learned everything he'd need to know about organized crime, including the drug trade, the entertainment industry, prostitution, politics and the law.

Two of John's defining character traits, greed and his closeted bisexuality, were more inherited than learned from his biological father.

These were also the prime motivating factors that propelled John into trying his hand at three careers undoubtedly more profitable than the one resulting from the running of a rural potato farming franchise.

The first two were hockey and prostitution. From a relatively young age, his talent for hockey was observed by both his fathers. The popular and generously-funded junior hockey programs fostered by the two successful Southern California professional hockey franchises, made it possible for John to attend hockey training camps year-round, even during his Hollywood-bound holidays.

One of the advantages of attending top-level hockey training camps in Los Angeles during the summertime, is the opportunity to get coached by local professional players that have time on their hands during the off season. That's when John met the equally-closeted Great One for the first time. The latter soon becoming John's first john. Before you could say body check, John was the talk of the local, regional, and former, closeted professional hockey player's boy-toy circuit.

♂♂♀♀

For John, it was now time for a long overdue Birds and the Bees discussion with his father.

- So, how was hockey practice today?
- Dad, I'm gay.

- What a coincidence. So am I. So when did you figure that one out?
- The first time I overheard you ass-fucking the Mexican drug cartel leader in the basement wine cellar.

- Which one?
- The short fat one. Just listening to the scene gave me a hard-on. It's the first time I ever came.

- How old were you?
- Ten. A week later I overheard you do it with the tall muscular one. You were both speaking Mexican. I barely had the time to pull my pants down. I creamed the outside of my jeans. Since then, I never looked back.

- Now you're giving me a... Never mind. Those cartel leaders are like EverReady Bunnies. They make excellent legal and erotic clients.
- That's what I want to talk to you about.

- What do you want to talk to me about?
- The erotic client part.

For the first time since the beginning of this conversation, Ted took his eyes off the road and flashed John a congratulatory smile.

- My first client was the Great One. He introduced me to Robinson Sr. Then Sr introduced me to ...
- Wow, you've been around and you don't even have a car... yet. You've only been on summer holidays for two weeks. When did you start?

- Last week. I made more money in a week than I do in two months playing hockey for the Edmundston Border-men. I'm doing okay in the junior leagues back home, but breaking into the big league is another story. I'm trying to figure out if it's not better for me to quit my hockey career while I'm still ahead to concentrate on an escort career here in L.A.
- Why don't you do both?

- The junior league is nowhere near as developed in California as it is in Eastern Canada. I don't think I'd make much money playing junior hockey in L.A.
- Not L.A., Quebec City. There are more wealthy gay politicians per square foot in Quebec City than there are unemployed porn stars in West Hollywood. And that's my point. You may be popular now, John, but once you've done the rounds a couple of times you'll soon find out how ferocious the competition is in the local male escort industry. In other words, you are better off being a big fish in small waters than a minnow in a pool of sharks. With your handsome, athletic bod, the connections you are making in the hockey industry, and my connections to the legal and organized crime industries, it won't be long before you become one of the most profitable, if not top player in the Quebec City escort business. For its size, Quebec City is more gay-friendly than Montreal. And Quebec City is one of the Commonwealth's major high-priced tourist destinations. Now that you finished high school, didn't you say you wanted to enroll in the Nicolet Police Academy?

- Nicolet is only ninety minutes away from Quebec City and just across the river from Trois-Rivières. If I buy a house halfway between Quebec and Trois-Rivières, I can play hockey for either team and will be only 45 minutes away from school or my male escort duties.

- Not to mention the fact that Nicolet has an excellent athletics program developed in conjunction with the junior hockey league which will permit you to attend school part-time while you play hockey in the juniors. When you are playing hockey in places like Montreal, Laval or St-John's, you'll have more than enough time to service a few local johns during off hours to compensate your time away from Quebec City.

- Great idea. I'm sold!
- Now lets start by finding you a house. Somewhere between Quebec-City and Trois-Rivières.

- I'll get right on it once we reach home. Let us see how fast your Beemer can handle traffic. Extra points for pedestrians!

- Grondines! Your road map places it almost exactly between Quebec-City and Trois-Rivières on the 138. Is that a nice area?
- Yes. I would take the 138 often when visiting clients in Eastern Quebec. The 138 is a heritage road that borders the Saint-Lawrence River. When they built Highway 40, the 138 became the milk run. But in terms of real estate there is a lot of prime river front properties at attractive prices. Well attractive compared to southern California. Good investment opportunities. I'll talk to my real estate agent tomorrow. He has connections all over North America. Grondines is a small town, but I think you will like it.

- This makes sense. I'm going to be busy enough like it is for the next few years. When it's possible, I want to be able to go home to a quiet place.
- And you can always bring home tricks when discretion is of importance. Sort of like The Little *Whore* House on the Prairie! Ha! Ha!

- What?
- Oh, never mind. I am dating myself. Little House on The Prairie was a popular sitcom when I was a kid. I'll get you a couple of season-box-sets before the end of the week. We can watch an episode or two during the weekend. You grew up on a farm, so you should at least relate to the storyline.

Munin

- Oh...

Memory is a faculty that forgets.
Desire trumps memory.

Power and discretion make good bedfellows.
A lesson I learned at a young age.

I should have known better.
The consequences of a sheltered adolescence.

Urban liberalism is a sign of youth. And ignorance.
Urban conservatism is a sign of maturity. And wisdom.

They were entering the terminal.
About to take the last ferry to Lévis.

Rural liberalism is a sign of youth. Crushed.
Rural conservatism is a sign of youth. Ignored.

I was about to exit the terminal.
I had taken the last ferry from Lévis.

I should have known better.
Expressing your conservatism only instigates the rage of an ignorant youth.

I had only taken two pints.
One too many.

An unprepared instinct,
Will make you lose your consciousness.

"At News-Talk 99.9 FM and on your smart-phone at newstalk999.com here is a 99 second news update for Thursday, March 4th, 2004...

...Northern Telephony's financial wœs are far from over. If recent events are any indication, things are only getting worse. On Wall Street this morning, the Security and Exchange Commission, warned the corporation to post their revised financial reports, dating back to 2001. If not, they risk penalties, not to mention the possibility of delisting their ticket on the New-York Stock Exchange. As of today, Northern Telephony stock has lost over 99% of its value from its record high, back in the spring of 2000...

♚♟

To say the writing was on the wall, would be an overwhelming understatement.

When the dust settled after the dot-com crash, in the Montreal area alone, over 32 000 Northern Telephony and direct third-party employees had lost their job.

Many were replaced by temporary foreign workers from southeast Asia and Northern Africa. They were hired at EMS (Electronic Manufacturing Service) plants, set up an airport parking lot away from the now-defunct Northern Telephony plant, where I had received my lay-off papers three years earlier.

Several of these foreign workers came from the Philippines. Some were from the clothing industry. Some were from the electronics industry. Many were from the streets.

Depending on how you define lucky, an opening was available at one of these subcontractors looking for former Northern Telephony post-production test technicians to help them improve quality and more importantly, reduce reject rates on products I used to make at STL-1.

At one-third the salary: when you factor in the loss of all Northern Telephony social benefits.

When the production managers would give a monthly manufacturing and strategy session in the cafeteria, they would do so with two separate presentations. One in French. One in Filipino.

The Filipino session was standing room only. During the French session, one could move the cafeteria tables to one side, and arrange an impromptu regulatory game of basketball. The only problem being the lack of enough employees to make up the two opposing teams.

The only thing funnier than the failure of being able to play a game of basketball with the members of the local workforce during a strategy session, was getting updates on the number of temporary foreign workers on one single-person work visa.

The record was 14.

Working the graveyard shift, one meets the most colorful of characters. From the Chinese national with the uncanny ability to always ask the most intricate questions about certain product lines, when the latter were the result of the latest cutting-edge patented technologies, exclusive to Northern Telephony. To the Moroccan Sunni fundamentalist, preaching the evils of consuming pork.

The funniest and most annoyingly entertaining of these characters, was the Persian national sharing the same post production department I was working at. Part heroin addict, part alcoholic, he dreamed of being, one day, an RCMP officer. Dreaming was the most activity he would get done during a typical work shift.

Sixteen months of this graveyard-shift circus, was enough for me. Time for a better gig. It was a post-production coworker, who I had worked with both at Northern Telephony and at this latest job, that convinced me of a possible alternative.

He was in the process of getting his apprentice-electrician certification. After doing a bit of research, I found out my past education would permit me to do the same. With the housing bubble having yet to burst, the local construction commission was at a loss of certified electricians. They were accepting applications from outside the normally-accepted fields of education. A college degree in electrical engineering would do fine.

All I needed was to complete my workplace safety course certification.

At the local electrician's union headquarters.

On Jarry Street. Just above...

There are a lot of Mr Bigs in the world. Some strive to be Mr. Big, but are yet to be recognized as such. Some pretend to be. Some think they are, but never will be. Some of them are on their way out, as they scurry into a state of not being at all.

The first lesson I learned was the most import of all, and would most likely never be used in the context of a construction-site workday scenario. With the possible exception of a work shift during which one would encounter cement pouring contractors in the vicinity.

The lesson in question was presented to us in the form of a veiled warning, wrapped up in an irony-scented disclaimer from the heavily-syndicated former construction worker at the front of the classroom.

A few weeks earlier, at around the same time I had run away from the EMS circus to join the union, a commotion was overheard in the union corridors outside the classroom. The local Mr Big had a very- ong espresso break cut short by the muffled *rat-ta-ta-tap-tap* of a briefly-encased-MP5 touting temporary foreign worker from mainland Italy.

During Mr. Bedalini's tenure, such public displays of Latin-blooded latent-homosexual-rage would have been unheard of.

What a difference thirty years make...

- I don't know what was more satisfying, the expression on his face when he was being dispensed the disclaimer, or the event described inside the disclaimer itself.
- It won't be long before he exits the raging waters of his adolescence, and crosses over into the uncharted ones of his preparatory years before adulthood.

- He'll only pass through adolescence once.
- A generation late.

- They will be the most difficult years, and the most formative.
- They don't call them asses' bridges for nothing.

- Finally, a springtime breeze from the bay.
- The leaves will soon begin to rustle.

Symbiosis

It has been over a decade now since the center of power began moving from Toronto, Ontario to Calgary, Alberta. At the turn of the century, the power brokers traded in their Gucci loafers for Boulet Boots and started heading west.

The western conservative momentum of the W. Bush era to the south and the merger of the Progressive Conservatives with the Reform Party to the north were infused with timing that an Olympian synchronized swimmer would die for. The divide and conquer tactics of the Liberal Party jousting match, between the right-wing leaning Paul Martin and the left-wing leaning Jean Chrétien, were also orchestrated with the help of a conductor tuned to this same tempo beat.

The spit shines on those power broker Boulets were barley dry when you could start reading about the demise of the federal Liberal Party on the bathroom walls of parliament hill.

The advantage of cowboy boots over loafers is that you can conveniently attach a pair of spurs on the heels of the former. Those western spurs have been popping bubbles left, right, and center since the turn of the century. The first to burst was the tech industry. A quarter century of building the information superhighway went down the loo in less than a year.

The next to burst was the American housing bubble. Which in turn burst the mortgage derivative bubble, which in turn burst the financial bond market bubble, bursting the commercial banking services bubble, which in turn imploded the North American and European economies and plunged both into the greatest depression since the 1930's.

When it came to saving the industrial casualties of this latest economic depression, those Boulet wearing power brokers knew exactly what industries to salvage. The oil burning, North American auto industry was spared from total collapse with billions of dollars worth of make-work-project subsidies, while Canada's jewel of the global tech industry, which at its height was the single most important contributor to the Toronto Stock Exchange's value, was given an unceremonious death sentence.

In this multiple dip depression economy, the further east you go, the worst it gets. Once you reach the Kouchibouguac National Park, you're scrapping the bottom of the barrel. As the raven flies, Cambelton is about a dozen^2 kilometers northwest of Kouchibouguac. The line that this raven draws, as he flies from Campbellton to the park delimits what is known as the geopolitical Acadia Peninsula.

Once that raven has reached three quarters of his journey to Kouchibouguac, he will be flying over the northern skies of Lisatichi.

This area of northern New Brunswick is one of the most economically and socially depressed areas of all the Americas. To be fair, you can't put all the blame for the Acadia Peninsula's predicament on the heels of those western power brokers, as several of Acadia's wœs are of its own making. The western power shift has been more an accelerator than an instigator of Acadia's demise.

£$

"At 99.9 FM and at 999solfm.com, here is the latest news on this Monday, May 24th, 2004 ...

Prime Minister Stephanie Herumtreiber's first order of international business after having recently appointing her newly elected Conservative cabinet, was to head off to war-torn Afghanistan accompanied by the Minister of Defense, Peter MacNine:

- As your new Minister of Defense, I consider it an honor and privilege to share this moment with our Canadian contingent in Afghanistan. Though it is the previous government that have sent you here following the attacks of 911, may I speak on behalf of your new government in expressing our continued and unwavering support for all our troops fighting terrorism not only in this hotbed of Afghanistan, but also in other territories where we have a presence.

The Prime Minister segued by pronouncing a short speech of her own followed by both officials handing out fresh Dominion-made treats... Jœ Luigis, graciously offered by the Slopulo family.

... And in other news ...

... The UNESCO World Heritage site of Bam, in South-Central Iran was literally flattened by an earthquake of unprecedented intensity, which left a swath of devastation encompassing all of this city. Prior to this day, Bam was the planet's oldest city still actively being used in its original state of construction..."

£$

Stephanie is an excellent strategist. Her agenda seems to be a simple one. Her core support base is fundamentally concentrated in the oil, tar-sand, and ~~mad~~-cow fields of Alberta. This support amounts to 30% of the country's voting population.

To stay in power she must maintain a five party state and polarize public policy forcing the opposition parties to concentrate on countering the polarization instead of developing there own political and social agenda. Once the opposition parties' political platforms are rendered indistinguishable, split the opposition vote. Repeat as needed.

Despite her perpetual minority status in relation to the popular vote, building her economic, financial, and social agendas to satisfy her core base, can now safely become the first and only priority.

An economic agenda based on a resource export economy, and a give-and-take political philosophy.

Give those Boulet wearing power brokers as many financial, fiscal, political, and diplomatic resources as necessary to build western-based resource-extraction capacity, and the corresponding distribution and export infrastructure.

Take as much tax dollars from the eastern automotive and technology sectors as possible. If the latter gœs bankrupt, let them eat ~~cup~~cake~~s~~. If the former suffers the same ørlög, prop it up as best you can until it is bought out by ~~cupcake-making~~ close-knit business associates.

A social agenda based on fiscal responsibility and a tough-on-crime policy. In other words, when it comes to the welfare state, strikeout social and replace its modifier with corporate. When it comes to being tough on crime, make sure it's of the disorganized variety. Don't bite the hand that feeds you. If you're hungry eat a cupcake.

As for a financial agenda, see above, and make sure the Canadian banking system benefits the most from the verbiage emanating from the federal finance minister's voice box.

$$

"At News-Talk 99.9 FM and on your smart-phone at newstalk999.com here is a 99 second news update for Saturday, July 13th, 2013...

...Yesterday, a train pulling several tanker cars filled with refined shale crude, raced, engineer-less through Jackman, Maine's downtown core, jumped the tracks, and burst into flames in front of a popular show bar and pub in this small town straddling the Maine-Quebec border. The explosion occurred just a few minutes before midnight, a time when the pub was filled to capacity with revelers from both sides of the border. The train was parked just outside the Jackman city limits and somehow freed itself from its braking system. By the time it jumped the tracks, witnesses of the event estimated its speed at between 80 and 100 kilometers per hour..."

♺⚠☣

Stephanie's symbiotic relationship to the Anglo-American Empire is at odds with her predominately libertarian core voting base, forcing her into running the Dominion's slice of the empire's geopolitical pie under a motherland-inspired parliamentary democracy.

Consequently, she is reduced to paying lip service to the motherland's feudal origins. At best, she grants symbolic importance to the British Monarchy, despite the underlining reality of the Dominion being just that. A colonial satellite on the Anglo side of the Anglo-American Empire.

If the feudal intentions on both sides of the Sino-Russain Empire were ever in doubt, they became as clear as a crystal vase when Vladimir Artëm brought his KGB know-how to the Russian Federation's governing infrastructure.

Ironically, it's his former covert mindset that has given him the insight to forge a balance between the deep-rooted, strategic operations outside his governing borders and the transparent clarity of his internal politics.

If you are a citizen of the Russian Federation, you know who is in the driver's seat. If your own deep-rooted intentions are to take over the steering wheel, you may or may not know what to expect next. One thing is for sure. Be you a carpet sweeper or a robber-baron billionaire, your ørlög will be severely defined, at least in part, by Vladimir's steely grip on that same wheel.

It's the strength of that grip which, at best, is at the core of his populous appeal, and at worst, the source of every Russian citizen's begrudging acceptance.

When that governing transparency is packaged around Vladimir's signature Russian discretion and reserve, his populous appeal is only bolstered by the nation's federal consorts. South Chicago, drug dealer trash talk is not his style. Neither is South Calgary, fundamentalist redneck saber rattling.

Like a Karl Marx zombie riding a time-warped merry-go-round, what gœs around comes around. Karl must be rolling in his grave.

Sitting next to Karl on that same merry-go-round, is an equally out-of-sorts Mao Tse-Tung.

As Vladimir methodically distances himself from the fundamentalist rigidity of Karl's teachings, so have the post-Maoist leaders on the sinological end of the Sino-Russian coming-of-minds.

As this emerging empire slowly shifts away from a five-year Gosplan economy and gradually adopts capitalism in its original, true republican form, both the sinological and Russian governing philosophies are in turn, shifting back to a modern version of their monarchist past.

… ♲ …

Whenever a major shift to a process variable is applied, upheaval occurs. That's the Proportional part of a process loop. To avoid the disturbed system entering harmonics, a modulating event on the process is applied. That's the Integral part of a process loop. To flatten-out the integrated waveform of the original upheaval, a stabilizing event is applied to bring the newly shifted process value to its intended state. That's the Derivative part of a process loop.

For a given timescale, a moment is the formers shortest defined span of time.

The Proportional, Integral, and Derivative responses of a process-loop system are all time dependent. For these responses to be effective, their common moment – their shortest span of time or Δt – must be long enough for the process-loop to recognize Δt as a defined entity.

If your process-loop is a global empire: your Proportional upheaval is war; your Integrated modulator is occupation, and your Derived stabilizer is transfer; be it technological, social, economic, spiritual or political in nature.

Global empires come and go. Case in point. Mongolia. If one was to choose a neutral geopolitical epicenter for the emerging Sino-Russian Empire, Ulaanbaatar wouldn't be a bad choice for a likely candidate. The former Mongolian Empire, including the Chinese and Russian sides of the one emerging from its ashes, all share a common denominator. Time. Or if you prefer, their common perception of a moment in time.

That common denominator is orders of magnitude longer than the one perceived by the millennial, smartphone-texting, Facebook-liking, Twitter-tweeting subjects of the Anglo-American Empire.

After having been divided up in the 13th century and conquered in the 14th, Mongolia has swayed since the 15th century, between the spheres of influence centered in Beijing and Moscow. Finally coming to rest, at the turn of the millennium, under the simultaneous influence of both. Eight centuries of geopolitical Ping-Pong between these three former kingdoms, teaches you a thing or two about the timescales necessary, to effectively dissolve superpowers and to transfer dominant control from one dying global empire to a newly emerging one.

Russia and China have been excellent students of Mongolia's historical teachings. The UK and the US both skipped class.

"At News-Talk 99.9 FM and on your smart-phone at newstalk999.com here is the midday news for Saturday, March 12th, 2011...

...And now breaking news from our national news desk. Live from Toronto, here is Mœ Levine...

- About 45 minutes ago, a major earthquake hit just off the northeastern coast of Japan's main island, with its epicenter closest to the city of Fukushima. On the line, I have Akita Nagaoka from our sister station at NTN News. Akita, where are you now?
- I am just outside the broadcast studios of NTN News, in the state capital of Sendai, about 90 kilometers northeast of Fukushima. As you can hear in the background it is pretty chaotic out here, as the severity of the quake has forced everyone out of their respective buildings and into the security of the open spaces. Several heritage buildings in the downtown core have suffered extensive damage, while most modern structures are still standing. However, the structural integrity of all major office towers, bridges and multistory industrial complexes will have to be verified in the days to come.

- And what about aftershocks, Akita?
- I witnessed a smaller tremor about 15 minutes ago. Our immediate concern is for the possibility of a major Tsunami that could hit at any momen... *Ohh, Bonzai!!...*

- Akita? Akita!... We seem to have lost contact with Nagaoka-San. We will pause for a short commercial break as we try to reestablish communication with Sendai.

♛↘↘

"You are listening to the Central Broadcasting Cooperative at 106.9 FM and on your smart-phone at 1069cbcftqsq.com. At the sound of the tone, following ten seconds of silence it will be precisely one o'clock, Friday, June 21st, 2013. Blip, blip, blip, blip, blip, blip, blip, blip, blip, beeeeeeeeeeep...

... Pope Francis was in the mainland, port city of Reggio di Calabria to denounce and condemn the violence and criminal terror introduced on the global stage, by Italy's most powerful organized-crime syndicate. Unique to his speech, was for the first time in recorded history, a Pope has declared as automatically ex-communicated from the Roman Catholic Church, all such mobsters engaging in this destructive and sinister behavior. He went as far as stating that such forcibly ex-communicated souls will be barred from crossing the gates of Heaven...

... And in other news...

... Prime minister Stephanie Herumtreiber's South-Calgary riding constituency was hard hit today by some of the worst flooding in the city's history. The trauma in the pour souls of the wealthiest city in the Dominion could be seen in the tear-filled eyes and heard in the emotionally-cracked voices of the residents of this Albertan metropolis."

Alberta's Premier, Anita Bluechev, invited her federal consort to equal the one billion dollars in aide her government had already pledged to the suffering Central Alberta victims of this devastating flood. As the two most influential women in the Dominion's political landscape boarded a military aircraft to view the devastation for the first time, Ms. Herumtreiber turned to the crowd attending the departure, and proudly stated that she had already accepted her provincial partner's invitation for federal disaster aide. At present, no casualties, missing persons, or critically injured victims of the flood had been reported by the RCMP, nor the Calgary Municipal Police.

Damage so far, has been limited to personal property and corporate infrastructure, both critical to the expansion of this bustling resource economy.

... And in other news ..."

...

When our species transferred from being scavengers to being predators, greed replaced symbiosis as our prime motivator of survival.

Power

The early spring snow that had fallen the night prior had already begun to melt with the morning sun, in the Swiss Alps valley of Saas Fee Village.

The flurry of goose feathers and down bursting from the overstuffed pillow Vladimir had torn apart at the height of their sexual *ebats*, had finally begun to settle, when the two alpha males took a breather, as they swallowed their first sips of Irish coffee, atop the Swiss cotton bedsheets of their top floor chalet flat bedroom.

- Oh Vladimir, you are such a frisky Russian Czar.
- And you, a voluptuous Prussian Queen, Angelica.

Even out of drag, Vladimir would address Angers by his female persona. Once a drag queen, always a drag queen.

After all, it was now close to forty years since Angers had caught Vladimir's eye when the former began to work as a KGB operative in the former East Germany.

☘☭⚖

"You are listening to the Central Broadcasting Cooperative at 106.9 FM and on your smart-phone at 1069cbcftqsq.com. At the sound of the tone, following ten seconds of silence it will be precisely one o'clock, Thursday, November 13th, 2014. Blip, blip, blip, blip, blip, blip, blip, blip, blip, beeeeeeeeeeep…

...Bill C1519080506 entered final debate before parliamentary commission hearings begin. According to the Prime Minister, the recent terrorist attacks in Quebec and on Parliament Hill, in addition to terrorist threats in Alberta, have forced the federal government to reduce the length of the hearings from two months to two weeks.

The bill will permit the linking of databases from 17 government agencies giving the RCMP and CISSIES access to the unified data following a court ordered warrant. The Judge signing the warrant will be the ultimate and only third party authorized to provide oversight as to the justification of the warrant. For reasons of national security, what is done with the data following the signing off of the warrant will be kept confidential, including the reasoning behind the preventative arrest and indefinite detention of the citizen referenced in the warrant.

Richard Richardson, the Chief Commissioner of the RCMP, was asked to comment on Bill C1519080506 following the recent release of a video taken by the Ottawa shooter's smart phone...

... following the elimination of 500 RCMP administrative positions including our internal investigation department, this new legislation will permit us to focus on the priority of keeping the Canadian citizenry from apparent future large scale terrorist threats. This new priority will be instituted by devolving 321 current small scale federal investigations perpetuated by organized crime. This will free the 681 RCMP officers who had currently been working on these investigations and permit them to focus on possible future terrorist threats from suspect citizens based on human and computer instigated psychiatric profiles using the Unified Database or Udb and from anonymous sources such as Crime-Stoppers. For reasons of national security, and to encourage the citizenry to continuously enhance the Udb, this legislation will permit the use of unverifiable information provided by unknown human resources, whose anonymity will be protected by Bill C1519080506.

...in other news..."

...

What do the Kopfschmucks call those who are not part of their cult?

Citizens.

Sacrifice

I was at the doorstep of the great recession of 2008 when I first started clearing my acreage and began to renovate the inside and outside of this vintage mobile home. The latter built when John Travolta was the poster child for Du Pont de Nemours' fashion conscious innovations.

Stephanie's west-leaning agenda has transformed the already decrepit maritime economic ecosystem into a veritable wasteland. The tar sands of Northern Alberta have unleashed a demand for unskilled cheap labor harking back to the mass migrations triggered by the Dominion's original Klondike and Trans-Continental railway mega-projects. Morphing the Atlantic menhaden-force into modern day Chinese migrants of a bygone era.

As a result the bursting international housing bubble which helped trigger the great recession had little effect on the Maritime real estate landscape. It had already hit barrel bottom years earlier.

This was my first real estate purchase.

The house had recently been winterized with a sloping insulated roof added to the existing flat roof common to mobile homes designed for Tennessee winters. The electrics, plumbing and water had also been upgraded or replaced to foundation home standards. That left only interior finishing and outside cosmetic improvements to complete. This would transform my small cottage into a livable four season home. A wood stove and proper chimney would have to wait until I felled enough trees around my newly purchased acreage.

Though barely more than an acre in size, my property was thick with vegetation. Hidden amongst seedlings and thick underbrush, one could find trees of all sizes and species native to the region. You could hardly see the house from the main road.

Judging by the standard disregard for the posted 90 km/h speed limit by the local pick-up truck and intercity eighteen-wheeler drivers alike, calling Route 237 a road is a bit of a misnomer. You might as well call this main road an expressway.

The hard-packed dirt and flat stone driveway, overgrowing with dandelions, split the front of the property in two. Its north side was covered in birch saplings suggesting this section of the property had been cleared several decades earlier and subsequently left to seed. Its south side was populated by thick underbrush, poplar and maple trees.

The property behind the house was dominated by a dense covering of trees far more mature than those in front. In the center was a small marsh overgrown with aquatic vegetation and moss encrusted dead timber. The grading of the marsh at its borders seemed too pronounced to be crafted by the hands of Ymir.

The marsh seemed to have been dug up with the help of a mechanical hœ, and used as a drainage pond for the surrounding land. The north side of the property was graded with a gentle slope towards its northern limits, and at one time served to drain the water from the marsh towards the main road's ditch in front of the house. Decades of neglect had rendered the drainage process virtually useless resulting in the partial flooding of the surrounding property even several months after the spring runoff.

This would explain the numerous, otherwise-healthy trees toppling over dead into the marsh, having had their root system rotted away by flooding water. Some of the trees on the borders of the flooded drainage ditch were on the verge of becoming standing dead timber.

A few of the pine trees looked like wind-swept specimens taken from a Group of Seven sub-arctic canvas. One side of the tree was devoid of branches; the result of a competing poplar tree serving as a widow maker. The other side was covered in branch moss, giving this still majestic pine the look of a Salvador Dali creation, frozen in the throws of an agonizing death that refuses to end.

Suffice to say, months of landscape work would be necessary before this worthless drainage system returned to a functional state of affairs.

But first things first. On the south side of this artificial marsh lay the carcasses of two tire-less cars from an era when Nissans were Datsuns and Chrysler was still decades away from becoming an American government token-of-appreciation in recognition of the Sicilian Mafia's invaluable contribution towards the nationalization of the Anglo-American banking system.

In other words, there was a rusted out B-210 and a similarly rusted out vintage Dodge Charger that I needed to have removed before I could properly start clearing the back of my property.

☎☏

The slave morality expounded by Bellstadt's trinity of Vatican-controlled Judeo-Christian institutions of indoctrinated salvation, heavily influenced the choice of a *cooperative business* model during the creation of the preeminent general store by the local masters of communal planning.

Consequently, the mantra "think local" trumps all other forms of ~~ethical~~ established business practice, whenever an ~~unsuspecting~~ client asks one of the store's unionized masters of customer care for advice on the choice of an appropriate product or service outside their cooperative sphere of influence.

With a trademark Acadian smile, the hardware department clerk eagerly applied this advisory mantra, following my inquiry about obtaining landscaping and auto-salvage services.

What luck, I thought to myself, when the counselor of cooperative corporate culture, responded by giving me the personal cellphone numbers belonging to the owners of the two ~~respectable~~ respective businesses.

Little did I know.

☢☣

As I hung up the land line, I figured my offer to give away the two vehicles in return for getting them off my property, increased my chances of receiving some form of result-oriented service from the local auto-salvage proprietor.

As to be expected, even the junkyard owner recognized the advantage of such a lopsided barter.

In more ways than one.

First, I had to clear a rudimentary pathway amongst the overgrown underbrush and standing deadwood blocking the extrication of said vehicles from my property.

What must have been an old backyard garage, replete with piles of discarded car parts from the 70's would also have to be cleared and the triage of parts offered to the recycling dealer.

As I simultaneously worked on clearing both a pathway and the long-collapsed ruins of the backyard structure, I slowly discovered the foraging potential of the plants and fungi growing all over the acreage. Not to mention the sap-extracting potential of the numerous mature sugar maples to be found both in front and behind my home.

⊡⊡

With the vast majority of the polymer, glass, and metal based automotive ruins having been removed from the acreage, it was now time to prepare the topics of discussion to address with the owner of the landscaping company. Two were chosen.

The first would be drainage. The second would be on the necessity of adding landfill over what used to be the railway-sleeper foundation of the ruined structure.

...

The person at the other end of the line wasn't the owner of the landscape company. It was the Director of Landscaping and Preparatory Construction Services.

When your title is longer than the name on your birth certificate, you know you are in for a challenging discussion.

The patchwork of partially-flooded sectors surrounding both the man-made marsh and the moderately elevated clearing of the former foundation made it difficult for the uninitiated to determine if the floodplain waters were flowing into or out of the marsh.

With shrugged shoulders and a trademark Acadian smile, the Director of Landscaping and Preparatory Construction Services was not able to tell me the direction of the floodwater's flow.

At least, he didn't want to.

He was no more willing to give me a cost estimate on depositing a three foot layer of landfill on the 36 foot by 36 foot square area of land where I would set the foundations of my new structure.

I would have to wait for the expert calculations from the landscaping corporation's CEO, as he would ponder the complex intricacies of determining the exact number of bucket truck-loads of landfill necessary for the transport of 144 yards of earth from the CEO's backyard quarry.

Wow. I guess you don't become the Director of Landscaping and Preparatory Construction Services on smarts alone. Or not.

The resultant estimate was as overinflated as it was overdue.

It would take me longer, but borrowing a bit of my sister's willpower, I would clear and landscape the totality of the property by hand, and preserve the edible underbrush to make a foraging garden. If it was good for the Neanderthals, it will be good for me. They were, after all, the original masters of a simple life.

...

Frugality is sacrifice. Be it at work or play, for pleasure or survival, when a frugal will is properly applied, unforeseen benefits often arise.

Sacrifice has different meaning depending on the perspective

When instigated by an outside source, sacrifice is an expression of that source's dominant power over the one subject to the sacrifice.

When instigated by one's self, sacrifice is an expression of self-discipline.

Creation

Though the original Acadians were shipped on the same Royal French vessels as the rest of the Bourgeoisie-defined peasant-undesirables that colonized 17th century New France, most of the former ended up being physically isolated from the rest of French-speaking Lower Canada.

The Acadians' decision to settle across the gulf of St-Lawrence, resulted in them being sandwiched between the privileged land owners bordering the St-Laurence to the north and the British colonialists to the south and west.

The French monarchists weren't the only ones that found them to be undesirable. Those same British colonialists proceeded to instigate their partial expulsion to New Orleans, during the later half of the 18th century, resulting in many of the remaining Acadians who avoided expulsion, hiding and interbreeding amongst the aboriginals of the surrounding uncharted forestland.

The purebred fundamentalist aboriginals were the third heritage group to propagandize the undesirable nature of the Acadian colonialists, as they proceeded in turn to expunge these mestizos from their native tribes. These geopolitical refugees and their half-breed offspring, returning to what was left of their forcibly abandoned fishing settlements, further exasperated the sociocultural and sociopolitical isolation of Acadia from the eventual federally-united, francophone centers of influence.

There are at least two major consequences of this geographic, social, political, and cultural isolation.

The first is the degenerate creation of a unique and dysfunctional linguistic dialect. When a dialect is created in a vacuum, that is, when the creators of this dialect have little or no interactions with the rest of the general population using the original language that the dialect is derived from, the latter becomes progressively incomprehensible to the original language users. This comprehensibility schism is further exacerbated the more the original language evolves outside the social ecosystem of the dialect's creators.

The Acadians' historic disdain of both education and their educated Bourgeois counterparts from the now former French aristocracy, has forced the only officially-sanctioned form of the French language, promulgated by *L'Académie Française, to* further distance itself from the linguistic deviancy of the Acadian dialect.

To this day, in rural Acadia, this socially acceptable and encouraged repulsion of both education, and outsiders more educated than themselves, can at times take on quasi-psychotic undertones.

Under the influence of the more traditionalist segments of the Acadian population, the combined effects of this hyper-insular dialect and a cultural tradition of sub-standard education, have accelerated the demise of Acadia during the colonial era, and have brought it to the brink of oblivious irrelevancy during the information age.

Cultural institutions are living entities that build on the traditions of the past and evolve with the creative innovations of those members whose aptitudes of inspiration, observation, comprehension, synthesis, and technical prowess make it possible for a particular component of this culture to progress into the future while being embraced by a critical mass of the society the cultural institution belongs to.

When culture is overwhelmed by tradition, the former stagnates, and like the muscles of an inactive body, suffer the consequences of atrophy.

When innovation and creativity are frowned upon by overtly conservative religious doctrine, the cultural institutions under their control, are relegated to being faith-based promotional tools for the religious and political agendas of the doctrine's creators.

Comprehension is the result of a well exercised brain. When properly applied, education is an excellent cognitive exercise. In religious circles, an uneducated flock is a properly controlled and subservient one. In the overwhelmingly insular and poverty stricken context of a family unit consisting of two dozen siblings, these overpowering factors of poor education and strict social traditions espoused by the oldest members of the family on their younger brethren, have a stifling effect on the slowing progression of a dying culture, such as the one encountered in Acadia.

To this day, the social, cultural, political and educational agendas of rural Acadia are still heavily influenced by those of the Vatican. Unlike their *Quebecois* counterparts, who, at least partially freed themselves from the grip of the Vatican's influence as a result of the Quiet Revolution, rural Acadia's sociocultural integrity and by consequence its relevancy, has devolved to a point where it is now relegated to a quaint side show for RV-driving urban rednecks from Nova Scotia and New England.

☦☠☭

A virtual generation's worth of post-Duplessi era social ~~engineering~~ democracy staged by the *Nous-Les-Québecois* movement, combined with the late 80's global economic collapse, has pushed the traditional gay ghetto from Lord Stanley's old stomping grounds to the decidedly more *Québecois-de-souche* friendly Beaudry Street, well east of Montreal's *main* linguistic buffer zone.

Consequently the accompanying urban fauna slowly slithered, crawled, and squirted along the city's underground subway tunnel, transporting the heart of Montreal's Night-Zoo from a St-Laurent to a Berri rolling metro stop.

It was still a little too early for him to suffix his name.

It was on the taffy-encrusted and canonized sidewalks of La Catherine, that he began his demonic graveyard shift. The sexual assaults at the fists and Prince-Albert-pierced genitals of his psychotic elder, had long forced him into a dual-state of male-pedophilia and heterosexual impotence.

Having stalked most of the alcohol-serving enclosures of the zoo's gay-themed grounds, Mr P was at a loss for alternatives. He didn't want to set-up shop in one of the numerous bathhouses of the ghetto. Too many redneck tourists from Northern New Brunswick.

Neither did he want to negotiate the seedier, opiate-addict-roaming alleyways and *cul-de-sacs* around the ghetto's Beaudry-Station epicenter. Too many redneck tourists from Northern New Brunswick.

So where dœs a redneck tourist from Northern New Brunswick, desperately trying to avoid his hygienically-challenged and closeted consorts, find prepubescent openings to fill on a hot construction-holiday Tuesday night?

Only the hairdressers know.

Thank the gods for staff-night at Madeleine's Cabaret.

- So sister, where dœs one find young flesh around here?
- Fresh out of pampers, or Indigo-blue?

- Diapers are too messy. Indigo will do.
- *La Sureté* and the vice-squad invited everyone to a major take-down party on the whole length of La Catherine's village stretch last week.

- During the construction holidays? So where did they move for the time being?
- On Dorchester, between the Propaganda Cathedral and Jacques Cartier bridge.

- The Propaganda Cathedral?
- The Central Broadcasting Cooperative Tower.

- Oh... okay. Thanks sister. Cuddles.
- Cuddles.

...

Snogs and snuggles.
Kisses and cuddles.
They can be as beautiful, as they are ugly.

He was heading east, on the corner of Papineau and Dorchester when he crossed her path.

- Got a light, sailor?
- Yikes. The Old Port is for tourists and the new one is miles away. The last time I heard that line, I was watching a Bogart era B-film on the Classics Cable Network. You can do better than that.

- You smell like you haven't taken a shower in a month.
- *Geez.* I thought bathing once a week and a bit of Old Spice would have been more than sufficient to ward off my cousins from New Brunswick.

- Only an Acadian would have a grin like that. I figure you're from the Peninsula.
- Close. Santa-Anna.

- Tracadie-Shiela. I'm just about finished my shift for the night, and thought turning your crank would be good for a laugh. You're half a block away from Indigo Park, and your smile only emphasizes the hypocrisy of your true intentions. You can do better than that.
- *Touché*. With an attitude like that, I figure we both have more in common than either of us want to admit.

- *Touché*. Now that we got that out-of-the-way, I guess it's a good time to let you know I've overheard the Fagot-Police is going to clear the park before dawn.
- Thanks for the warning. If the token lesbian is up to date, the park must be empty by now. I think I'll call it a night. Let me at least pay you an early breakfast for your trouble. Is there good eats nearby at this time of night?

- The Village Deli is open. It's just a few blocks west on Wolfe. If you're not fussy, you might even get lucky.
- Ha! You're wiping the hypocrisy off my face.

The decimal probability of a given urban ghetto housing their own version of a Village Deli is as close to unity as one can fathom. Rural gay-ghettos are as rare and disparate as a Sasquatch sighting, and would only serve to skew the results.

The factors of size, prudishness, visibility and client demographics, of such a refuge catering to the late-night lonely and rejected, in no way correlate with those of the ghetto it is symbiotic to, nor with those of the urban center the ghetto is engulfed in.

Quebec-City has its *Village-des-Moumounes* where impromptu *Jeanne-Benoit-Parlons-Micro-Ondes* foodie seminars are setup inside the apartments of the local male nurses and hairdressers alike.

Toronto-the-Good has it's police-less, Church-Street Doughnut-shop, no bigger than Montreal's Wolfe-Street kitchen turned café.

The original Village Deli restaurateurs were merciful and frugal enough to preserve the interior's tin ceiling, old-school linoleum flooring, and ceder-strip paneling, giving as much a sense of comfort and solace to the establishment, as to the homemade food served to its clientèle.

Exceptionally, for a Tuesday night, the café was packed with refugees of the prophetic Indigo-Park take-down. The harsh lighting inside the café, only served to shine a light into the lifeless eyes of the johns and tricks, exposing the closeted monsters inside their tormented souls.

- I told you^2 would get lucky.

Mr P wrinkled-out a smile, making him look a generation older than his age.

- I'm hungry. But it's too early for a real breakfast and too late for a real supper. Time for some comfort food.
- The only shepherd's pie better than the one offered here, is the one served at a small diner about a block away from Laliberté Hotel. When I first ran away from home about five years ago, I worked as a prostitute for the local drunks inside the hotel's pub.

- Why did you leave?
- It burnt to the ground. If you spoke to the owners, it was arson. If you spoke to the police, it was an electrical fire.

- How did you end up here?
- The money was lousy. I barely got by with what I made on the weekends. Chanticleer is a tourist town about an hour's drive north of here. The rich and infamous would more often than not, bring along a call-girl from the city's escort services as entertainment. If he was wealthy, they would spend the weekend at his over-sized chalet. If he was well-healed, they would share a room in a pricey hotel. So I moved to south-central Montreal.

- Why didn't you join an escort service?
- I'm from the peninsula. I'm not a trophy girl. Call-girls have class. They know how to entertain. I know how to do the star-fish … and reproduce.

- Do you have a child now?
- He's in the oven. My first. I'll probably start showing in a few weeks.

- Do you have an idea who the father is?
- A prominent rabbi from Côte-St-Luc-Hampstead. He's the only regular that refused to wear a condom.

- Well. You won't be getting an alimony check any time soon! What happened to the pill?
- It was a choice between paying the pharmacist or the dealer. The dealer always wins out.

- What do you do now? Go back home?
- A cocaine-addicted, lesbian single mom living alone in Tracadie-Shiela? You got to be kidding.

- What if a lesbian junkie that hasn't started showing yet, marries a closet-gay, recently-graduated psychology intern, looking to rapidly advance his career, and starts her own career as a trophy-mom?
- Beats converting to Judaism.

- Where should we move?
- What's your major?

- Criminal psychosis.
- Walking distance from Pinel. I'll be able to use your pickup while you're at work.

- Ha! You're putting the hypocrisy back in my smile. Twice.
- Eat up. Your shepherd's pie will get cold. You can buy me an engagement ring in the morning. I'm not fussy ... yet.

iii

Her mongrel offspring wasn't hard to differentiate. Not counting the ones in the ICU, the newborn was Sainte-Justine's scrawniest baby.

A social consequence of her equally chronic heroine addiction, his mother's state of chronic malnutrition was inadequately compensated by her soon-to-be-chronic bouts of binge eating. The latter initiated once she had settled in to her new role as a freshly married mother-to-be.

The hospital pediatrician was soon able to project a probable diagnosis of Attention Deficit Syndrome for her newborn. A physical consequence of her cocaine addiction.

He wasn't sure what would predominate in the near future. The mongrel's potentially violent, psychotic behavior or his mental deficiency caused by an interbreeding predominant, genetic heritage. A conjecture he wisely kept to himself.

At least the offspring's biological father was well nourished and only suffered from a sexual addiction. Unfortunately, the pediatrician would not be able to postulate on the multiple consequences of the sperm donor's dependency, as neither he nor the street whore who provided the placenta during the fetus's gestation, had access to the rabbi's medical records.

They both wanted a boy, but not for the same reason. Not to jink it, she shunned echœncephalography during gestation. They didn't even attempt to find a girl's name.

They both were disappointed. When the nurse asked her what name to put on her daughter's identification bracelet, she told her to use the hospital's namesake.

Mr P didn't protest.

He didn't care.

In an ironic twist of Judeo-Christian faith, the second consequence of the Acadia Peninsula's isolation, was aggravated by an event even more degenerate than the isolation itself. An event arguably recognized as the most important and influential social engineering strategy instigated by the Roman Catholic Church, and subsequently used to counter the invading British colonialists on the territory of New France.

Following the colonial wars between New France and the territories controlled by the Hudson's Bay Trading Corporation and the British Monarchy, the Romish missionary priests in all areas of British North America, including Acadia, instigated the Vatican ordered doctrine of *La Revenche des Berceaux,* literally translated as the Revenge of the Cribs.

As the name suggests, the Revenge of the Cribs, was a doctrine which stipulated that all wedded, French colonialists of rearing age must be in a continuous state of gestation; otherwise may they be sent to a life of purgatory for the rest of eternity, following the end of their days as mortal souls. The basic premise of this doctrine was for the French Catholic colonists to out populate their English Protestant counterparts.

The first social institution a person encounters and interacts with, is family. His first encounters with authority are with his parents, and his first social interactions with those of his age, are with his siblings. For these social interactions to be constructive, relevant, and edifying for all siblings, the age difference between the oldest and youngest should be no more than half a generation. Taking into account health concerns, miscarriages, and politically-instigated logistical obstacles, a healthy, stable, mother will therefore go through, at most, four successful birthing sessions in her lifetime. Ignoring a set of twins or triplets along the way, the largest number of siblings in a functional and healthy family unit should be 6.

For the proponents of the Revenge of the Cribs doctrine, a normal sized family unit consisting on average, between 18 and 24 siblings would be three to six times the norm. When the youngest sibling is forced to relate to his oldest counterpart as a grandparent rather than a brother or sister, the social relevancy of this relationship and by consequence the social fabric of the family institution as a whole begins to fall apart. Combined with the insular nature of both the family unit and the rural collectivity they live in, the risk of dysfunctional relationships between siblings is increased by several orders of magnitude.

Though nearly four hundred kilometers away from the heart of the Acadia Peninsula, Quebec City diligently followed the social engineering practices of the Revenge of the Cribs doctrine prior to the Duplessis era. When combined with the south-shore suburbs of Lévis-Lauzon, Saint-Romuald and St-Nicolas, the Quebec City regional municipality has a total population rivaling that of New Brunswick.

Quebec City's geographical position makes it one of the most isolated metropolitan regions on the North American continent. With the possible exception of modern day Halifax, and based on a North American standard, let alone a global one, the Atlantic provinces taken as a whole have no urban municipalities large enough to be characterized as metropolitan.

Though not extensively covered by the local media outlets, for evident reasons of political correctness, Quebec City has long been a scientific destination for genetic pathologists studying the long-term, health corrupting effects of trans-generational interbreeding on isolated communities.

The number and severity of genetic defects, chronic diseases, and the devolving effects on mental capacity found in the Quebec City studies, pale in comparison to the devastating physical, psychiatric and social effects of interbreeding found in the general population of rural Acadia.

...

Bellstadt's local phone directory, which includes the neighboring villages of Acadia Crossing to the south and Little Collar to the north has a disproportionately large number of Arsenaults as land-line phone users. Other overwhelmingly popular family names found in this directory are Caissie, Leblanc, Richard, Gallant, and Robichaud. As is the case for nearly all the towns and villages of Acadia, a significant proportion of Bellstadt's collectivity is intimately and genetically related.

My first encounter with the neighbor to the south was a few days after I brought home a used wood stove I had found on-line from that classified site with an African sounding name for a village. The stove was of good quality and little used. The Riverview suburbanite was asking a Sally-Ann thrift-store price for it, so purchasing it before I needed it was a worthwhile transaction.

A coat of black motorcycle exhaust paint I had kept from a former life and new gaskets around the doors and the stove would make it good as new.

When I had got to Télésphore Arsenault's property, his front door was open. It was late afternoon. I hesitantly knocked on the open door. No response.

With a not too loud, not too authoritative voice I asked:

- *Y'a quelqu'un?* Is someone home?

Mr. Arsenault slowly walked into the accompanying living-room I was speaking into. I presented myself and explained I needed someone to carry in my wood stove the few steps up my front porch into my house.

With a smile that emanated irony, hesitation and contempt all at the same time, Mr. Arsenault responded with an

- I will try.

Once we got to my driveway, I strapped my wood stove to the refrigerator trolley purchased as a Crappy-Tire flier special when I was preparing my moving journey from Laval-des-Rapides, Quebec to Acadia Crossing, New Brunswick and we proceeded to lug the heating implement into my living-room.

- I remember this place as being much darker.
- You've been here before?

- Only Once.

The hesitation in his terse response and the fidgety body language that accompanied it made it clear he didn't want to get into any further details.

- I've been working hard to liven-up the place to my liking, frantically attempting to change the subject.

- I want to thank you for helping with this. I was hesitant to ask anyone to help me out with moving my stove, but I figure the neighbors are used to helping each other out.
- You will find out that this is not the case with the people around these parts.

The accompanying smile Mr. Arsenault flashed was the same as the first one he gave me a few minutes earlier, minus the hesitation.

♂?♂

Unbeknownst to me, the neighbor to the north soon became the unofficial Welcome Wagon Customer Care Representative for the neighboring "people around these parts".

Roland Caissie could easily be a poster child for the Revenge of the Cribs babies disproportionately common on the Caissie family tree. Somewhere between post-andropausal and *Vielle Sacoche* in temporal appearance, the post-spawn absence of an extending member on the right side of his upper torso was his most obvious physical attribute, tempered by his equally obvious lack of personal hygiene, short stature, and Torngat[11]-Lager-bonus-pack abusing obesity.

Attempting to visualize Roland Caissie in the raw would give even the most seasoned amputee-fetish aficionado a gag reflex.

When Raymond Caissie presented himself, uninvited, at my front door, he had in his remaining hand two bottles of cheap industrial beer. The latter popular in the province of Quebec. Though an immediate neighbor to the north, Mr. Caissie, was still obstinately a stranger. A generalization my immediate neighbor to the south warned me about, weeks earlier.

- Can I come In?

My lingering stereotypical notion that rural Atlantic Canadians were all neighborly, goodhearted folk got the better of me, and before I could properly assess the situation and muster a diplomatic excuse to convincingly disguise my urge to tell Mr. Caissie to take a hike, he had already successfully negotiated my doorstep, and was placing the two beers on my kitchen table.

- What's inside all those boxes?

As Mr. Caissie spoke, he was scanning the contents of his new surroundings. His movement and tone of voice made it hard to establish if he was a potential thief thinking aloud or if the question was a prologue to a more lengthy interrogation. A third possibility, being a mix of the two.

---

11 Torngat is a mountain range in Northeast Labrador, whose average mountain height is lesser than the *Alpine* mountain range of the European Alps. In the context of this novel, Torngat Lager is a copyright and trademark infringement avoiding fictional brand of industrial beer popular with the pseudo-redneck-social-welfare-dependent clientèle of the maritime provinces.

At this point in time, it was clear that explaining to him the boxes were filled with the contents of my home office, which was in the process of being renovated in the room at the other end of the house, would be a prudent waste of time. My response was silent acknowledgment.

- Are you looking for pot? Or maybe coke? Do you do drugs?
- No, I don't do drugs.

I held back a sigh.

- We think you're a cop. Last time an undercover cop moved to these parts, it didn't take too long before we got rid of him.

Mr. Caissie's threat was given with a nonchalant stand-up-comedian delivery and a Télésphore Arsenault smile.

- No, I'm not a cop.

I shook my head in disagreement and gestured for him to sit at the kitchen table. I took a couple of lager glasses from the top shelf of the hutch and took a seat opposite Mr. Caissie.

Time for a diplomatic change of subject.

- I purchased a mobile home because I wish to build a *pièce-sur-pièce* log home myself on the site of the old building that is in ruins in my back yard. I only have an acre of land and there is not enough mature trees on the lot. I'm looking for someone to sell me a trailer flat of raw cedar logs, 12 to 16 inches in diameter, 8 foot lengths. Do you know anyone that could sell me that?
- Most people, around these parts, don't bother with ceder logs. Too hard to find. Too expensive. When their building a hunting shack, they cut whatever trees they can find into 6 foot lengths and set em' up vertically on a homemade cement footing. That should be strong enough to hold a pitch roof and if the footing is tall enough you can pour a cement slab for the floor. Helps to keep the rodents out.

His reply was less than helpful. I wasn't looking to build a shack but a new permanent home, using the existing infrastructure on my property. Once completed, I would remove the mobile home and landscape the empty space. Explaining this to him would only get myself into an argument, so I chose to stick to my diplomatic agenda. At least now I know why there are no traditional notch-and-scribed log homes "around these parts".

- Thanks for the information. I never thought of building a cabin that way. A great idea.

It was the best, aversive reply I could think of at the time. This subject-changing conversational strategy seemed to have given the desired results. By now, my interrogator had already emptied his bottle of industrial beer.

- It's OK to use your bathroom?

Before I could determine if that was a statement of fact or a question, he was already heading towards the bathroom with no need for directions. I chose to follow him, and as he walked through the narrow corridor towards the loo, enumerating aloud my belongings of value observed in the adjoining rooms. I stopped before passing the bathroom door and waited.

Once he finished micturating, avoiding to wash his hands as he left, I escorted him to my front door. As he stepped on the front porch, he turned around and said:

- Welcome to Acadia Crossing. I'm known around here as the Maimed Marauder.

⚑

Though I have been working on my small business for several years, I've always considered it more of a hobby than a reliable form of self-employment. By the time I had moved to Acadia Crossing, this hobby had morphed into a specialized leather-wear design, tailoring, and manufacturing business. A decade of motorcycle riding and crashing taught me about well designed and manufactured leather motorcycle gear. My first full-time job as a product testing engineer for a hockey equipment manufacturer, at a time when such equipment was still made in the Dominion, taught me a little about the sportswear industry.

By choice and necessity, this small business endeavor was self-financed from the start. Alas, as anyone with the wisdom from having endeavored in such an enterprise will tell you, small businesses are money pits that take time before they become self-sustaining, let alone becoming profitable enough to earn the status of self-employment.

As my hobby progressed, it inevitably took more of my time and energy to sustain. It no longer was feasible for me to work a full-time job to support my hobby and my own urban lifestyle. One of the two would have to give. By moving into the most socially and economically depressed region in the Dominion, it was possible for me to purchase a small home and acreage for about the price of year's rent in Laval. Having squirreled enough money to purchase such a property outright and with an annual property tax bill equivalent to a month's worth of broadband Internet, I was able to eliminate the single most expensive overhead expense slowing the progression of this hobby into the self-employment enterprise I wanted it to become.

Years of investing into the company have made it possible for me to acquire all the design and production assets necessary with no accumulated corporate debt. All that was left to cover were electricity, Internet, and food bills. A simple part-time service industry Mac Job would cover that and then some.

That job took the form of a shelf clerk at the local supermarket. With one fell swoop, my employer-dominated and urban-oriented lifestyles were brought to a close.

Calling the supermarket local is a bit of a misnomer. Its actual location is inside the multipurpose complex of the BellStadt Cooperative, over 3 kilometers north by northwest of my newly acquired Acadia Crossing abode. The one and only four-wheeled vehicle I had ever owned at the time was an Iaccoca-era Ram Van purchased a year earlier for the sole purpose of moving myself and my corporate assets to Acadia Crossing. Purchased at a fraction of the cost of a moving-van service call, this past-due clunker equipped with a smoking V8, was guaranteed to put a smile on a Saudi prince's face.

Consequently, frugality dictated that my daily commute to the supermarket would be undertaken by foot. This 45 minute hike also doubled as my twice-daily exercise session. Pursuing a part-time Mac Career at a supermarket offers the possibility to combine several perks at the same time, including a pedestrian commute home, a food shopping excursion, a daily cardioid session and upper body workout.

☺...☹

Following Télésphore Arsenault's advice, I made it a point, whenever possible, to decline the locals' offers to give me a lift during my daily commute. I would politely tell them that walking was part of my daily exercise routine and continue on my way.

On this particular day, my homeward bound hike was accompanied with frugal bags full of weekly specials. My proverbial eyes being larger than my stomach made things worse, and I ended up entertaining an upper body workout more intense than first anticipated.

Halfway through my journey back home, a dark green and authentic-rust colored, middle-aged model GMC Jimmy slowed down with an older than middle-aged trademark local at the helm. A thirteen-day-shadow, salt-and-pepper face, was topped with a groundhog-bad-hair-day, 1960's-barber-shop coiffure. His bloated *Vielle-Sacoche* cheeks made it impossible to imagine him without an equally bloated Torngat-Lager belly.

You could almost visualize the industrial-grade alcoholic breath, wafting from his mouth like a stinky, emanating from the ass of one of the main characters in a Ren-and-Stimpy cartoon.

Ignoring the critical, aforementioned advice and my most basic of instincts, I crossed Route 237, placed my groceries in the back seat, and took one on the front passenger side of the Jimmy. Then, it dawned on me. His equally trademarked absence of personal hygiene combined with the mid-summer afternoon heat in the non-acclimatized vehicular interior, resulted in an odoriferous presence that would make that same Ren-and-Stimpy stinky Alpine-Floral-Fresh by comparison.

The Jimmy owner's sense of hygiene was only reinforced by his concept of order. Discarded items and garbage of all types and vintage were strewn everywhere. On the back seat, the back floor, the passenger seat and floor, dashboard, front visors, side-door compartments...

Everywhere.

The most memorably predominant items of refuse were the empty bottles and cans of industrial beer.

The most memorably toxic odor was a toss-up between the *Eau-de-Vielle-Sacoche* emanating from the driver and the acrid smell of stale urine emanating from the vehicle's turn-of-the-century upholstery.

By the time the vehicle was parked in my driveway, the small talk between the driver and myself had morphed into an interrogation between the driving inquisitor and the interrogated passenger. A scene strikingly similar to my Welcome-Wagon *tête-à-tête*, the previous year. All that was missing this time, were the death threats.

They weren't necessary a second time.

I gained two enlightening insights into the local Acadian mindset during that day's interrogation. One imposed, one deducted.

The first was imposed on me without an inkling of provocation on my part. In typical oh-wowas-me-remember-1755 Acadian fashion, my interrogator insisted on letting me know he was dying of prostate cancer.

The second was deduced from this latest fishing expedition on the part of my interrogator with the help of the two previous less-than-neighborly encounters.

When an Acadian approaches you with a smile, expect *questionably-pleasant* pleasantries to ensue.

⚢⚣⚤⚥⚠⚦⚧⚨⚩

The timing was right. The social media bubble was still waiting for the hot air generated by the latter's server farms to fill its casing.

They waited for the local media circus to pack up and leave Montreal. People have short memories; having been shrunk by the expanding popularity of Reaganomics followed by the equally expanding irrelevancy of designer drug inspired grunge rock.

By the turn of the millennium, they both yearned for the xenophobic serenity of their native backwoods. Once a redneck, always a redneck.

She may have not been raised where her backyard was a woodlot filled with THC annuals, but the basement was always filled with a rotating crop of the latter. By the time he had reached pubescence, he had been more than adequately programmed and equally ready to tag along.

The timing was right. The Federal government had just built a maximum security pen in nearby Schwarzdorf.

©☜®

"At News-Talk 99.9 FM and on your smart-phone at newstalk999.com here is a 99 second news update for Friday February 10th, 2012...

... In the small town of Bellstadt, the main municipal building including the RCMP detachment, burnt to the ground early this morning. According to Ronald Bourque, Bellstatd's fire chief, a preliminary investigation suggests faulty electrical wiring to be the official cause of the blaze. No foul play is suspected by the authorities.

We sent out our man-on-the-scene, Stew Santos, less than two hours after the first sitings of fire were observed at the site, and he was amazed to find but a smoldering pile of indistinguishable rubble where the municipal building used to stand.

Stew did get a firsthand account of the event from a Bellstadt resident who witnessed the blaze while exiting a local diner earlier this morning ...

- Ya, wehl you know, da flames were at leeest twantii feeet igh when I left Télésphore's dii-ner dis morning. I wasan't sure if it was the munecepal building or the clinique that was tor... I mean burrr-ning until I got into my trock to take a closser lok.

... And in other news ..."

Propaganda

"At 96.9 FM and at 969solfm.com here is the news for Thursday, June 25th, 2015 ...

... The Confederation of Cooperatives for the Coastal Provinces, Atlantic Division, entered into receivership by filing papers at the Court of Queen's Bench in Mengen, this morning. CCCP Atlantic placed itself under protection of its creditors, after years of declining membership and sales. Of the nine grocery stores communally owned by the distributor, five were sold to private interests, and four are in the process of being liquidated before closing permanently.

The remaining independently owned cooperative stores have alined themselves under cultural and linguistic lines and are in the process of negotiating supply management agreements with privately held distributors, in an attempt to stave off bankruptcy at the local level. Over 400 CCCP Atlantic employees will be terminated in the coming weeks.

The remaining CCCP Atlantic assets, including their home energy and agricultural supply distributors, will be sold or possibly liquidated to pay off creditors.

... In other news, MoneySmart Magazine has published its annual ranking of The Best Places to Live in The Dominion for 2015. Lisatichi fell twelve positions compared to the 2014 rankings, and is now placed 204th amongst the 209 largest towns and cities of The Dominion. The editors of the magazine mention the level of crime in the region as one of the contributing factors in the decline of Lisatichi's standing.

On a *positive* note, these same editors do mention that the Lisatichi region has some of the most affordable real estate in The Dominion.

... In national news, Dominion Statistics has just published data on migration trends for the first quarter of 2015. New Brunswick has the fastest shrinking population of all the provinces and territories inside the protectorate. An aging population, the exodus of young professionals, and the declining birthrate are mentioned as contributing factors to New Brunswick's demise..."

...

- That free fall, the Acadian Peninsula has found itself in for the last few centuries seems to have morphed into a death spiral...
- ... Headed for oblivion.

- I guess you could call it a *cooperative* effort.
- Birds of feather, flock together.

- Those birds have crossed the traditional cultural and linguistic divide of The Peninsula.
- The centuries-old, French ancestors of Maximilien Robespierre's wrath, the equally-old Irish ancestors of Lakagígar's wrath and the Mongolian exiles from the ice-covered Bering Strait, have all assembled their disparate offspring to form a cacophony of resistance and rejected opportunities.

- Turning this Atlantic corner of the Boreal forest they have adopted, into a desert of social, economic and cultural desolation.
- Desolation fosters isolation.

- Isolation fosters xenophobia.
- Pushing all to their mutual demise.

- Greed fosters greed.
- Greed fosters Resistance.

- Resistance brings change.
- From oblivion, a new cycle will inevitably begin.

Instinct

- *Arrête Mamy! S.V.P., Arrête....*

JP's beatings and subsequent sexual assaults always followed the same scenario. By the time she was of preschool age, she had coined a name for them. She would call them,"Love Beatings".

¿

JP's grandfather, a lobster fisherman from the small coastal town of Santa Anna – where corporal punishment is a socially acceptable and expected form of child rearing – instituted the same type of love beatings on his son as the latter would eventually institute on his grandson.

There is a running joke in psychology circles that is so common, it has become a virtual truism.

"Why would one be motivated to choose a career in psychology? ...

A degree in psychology is the best way to hide one's own hang-ups!"

As a victim and a perpetrator of the same abuse, Mr P's choice of criminal psychology as a career path was literally and figuratively a brainless endeavor.

The Schwarzdorf Institute is conveniently situated a short 55 kilometer pickup drive west of his hometown, and built in a regional municipality that is also home to the local chapter of the Kopfschmuck biker gang.

By now, you can see this coming. Literally and figuratively.

All those years of multiple-generation sexual, physical, and psychological violence both received and handed out by an established penitentiary psychologist, has created a near-perfect father-son dynamic drug-dealing duo.

...

As the raven flies, local mobster kingpin, Morry the-Junkyard-Dog Ziegenficker's vehicle-salvage business is less than 30 kilometers due east of Schwarzdorf, in the-less-than-picturesque one-saloon Acadian village of Bellstadt.

Unlike his dynamic drug-dealing associates from nearby Santa-Anna, Morry's latent homosexual tendencies didn't derive from any childhood physical abuse, but more from the lack of attention from his lumberjack father, during his critical prepubescent years of development. The fact that he was introduced to Monty Python's Flying Circus by his anglophone friends, likely contributed to his cross-dressing desire to emulate his father once he reached puberty.

Needless to say, Morry's tea-bag friendly, transvestite aptitudes were a determining factors in insuring his good standing *vis-à-vis* the Kopfschmuck bikers.

This Morry-Kopfschmuck-JP love triangle makes JP's father a critical link in what is now the most profitable illicit drug Autobahn in Acadia. Though the volume of sales transiting through the Schwarzdorf Institute psychology office is nowhere near the amount of opiates intentionally over-prescribed by the resident doctor at the Bellstadt Health and Wellness Center, the markup for illicit drugs of all types sold at the Schwarzdorf Institute is orders of magnitude higher than for those sold in the parking lot of the nearly abandoned Bellstadt train station.

The quantity of locally grown marijuana and over-prescribed opiates sold by the resident criminal psychologist was so appreciated by the local inmate population, that the latter affectionately coined the drug-Autobahn "the Skyway" and the psychology office "Crystal Sodden's[12]".

As is the case for the P in JP, the inmate-psychology clientèle address their therapist by the inside-the-Pen nickname of the-Shrinking-P.

However, the more the latter's penchant for prepubescent male flesh became evidently apparent amongst the youngest looking, well-toned and shaved inmates, the less the P in the-Shrinking-P stood for the therapist's namesake.

---

12 Sodden's is – to say the least – a long-winded visual and etymological pun with a dual purpose. On its' own it is a copyright and trademark infringement avoiding fictional brand of supermarket stores popular in Atlantic Canada. Used in the context of "Crystal Sodden's", the pun is self explanatory.

Once it became known that the only sure-fire way to obtain an in-store special at Crystal Sodden's was if you were "lucky" enough to have the physical profile to turn the-Shrinking-Ps crank, the third most smuggled items at the Schwarzdorf Institute, after drugs and cell-phones, were Yea-Yeas[13].

⚥⚦

When greed settles-in and becomes your latest addiction, dealing prescription low-grade weed and illicit anti-ADS drugs simply won't suffice. What is a penitentiary psychologist to do?

- This is going to be as hard for me to admit as it should be for you, but sooner or later both of us have to come to the realization. Your mother was right. You will never make it as hockey player. Apart from a few lost teeth and maybe a broken nose, it won't do you any harm to join the local garage league. But that's as far as you'll ever go in the hockey-entertainment industry.
- ...

- You definitely don't have the chops to be a fisherman, and if you ever graduate from high-school I will be surprisingly proud of you.
- ...

- I have a better idea. My clients at the penitentiary have been chomping at the bit, literally and figuratively ... he-he, to become more than just friends. They want me to become an associate. But I can't risk being seen socializing with the higher-ups. That's where you come in.
- Keep talking. You're on a role.

- One of my patients is the cousin of my weed supplier, a couple of kilometers south of Bellstadt right on the 237.
- Unless your a piece-of-s**t come-from-away[14], everybody's a cousin in Bellstadt.

---

13 Yea-Yea is a copyright and trademark infringement avoiding fictional brand of "cute little hair removal kits you can carry with you almost anywhere".

14 Now, of course, for the near totality of the heritage population from the Dominion's Atlantic provinces, calling someone a piece-of-s**t come-from-away would be considered redundant. But you get the message. If they think you don't, they'll beat it into you.

- He's also his father. And the boyfriend of the Maimed Marauder. The Marauder is camping out at the house of a trucker working in Fort Mac Money. Just to the south of his boyfriend.
- How convenient.

- You bet. I heard the Marauder has been eying you at the local coffee shop of late.
- Well he can't point and drink at the same time. So I guess that's his only alternative.

- A little head...
- And I'll get ahead.

- Got it?
- Got it.

- Good.

Consciousness

The Kopfschmucks had been grooming John Thébeau for this position ever since they decided he wouldn't make the cut for the starting line-up of the Quebec City Bridgeheads, in time for the 2004-2005 hockey season of the LTCLHJMQNSISS. His stick-handling was quite refined and he could fight as good as the rest of them, but he couldn't skate fast enough to be a forward and he wasn't big enough to be an enforcer. But as a discrete and high priced male escort for the influential Quebec-City politicians, John became well versed in manipulating the lawyers and government-subsidized businessmen at the local, provincial and national levels of power. All to the advantage of the Kopfschmucks' short and long-term agendas, including, but not limited to, those of collusion and corruption they now forcibly shared with the Sicilian Mafia.

Now that Sébastien Lapierre had been successfully transferred to the Schwarzdorf detachment, it was now time for the former male escort, turned semi-professional hockey player, turned RCMP Officer to take over the reins of the Kodiak RCMP.

"At News-Talk 99.9 FM and on your smart-phone at newstalk999.com here is a 99 second news update for Saturday September 10th, 2011...

... Several dignitaries were on hand today, including Mengen's mayor and the Premier of New Brunswick for a press conference announcing John Thébeau as Mengen's highest ranking police officer and the new head of the Kodiak RCMP...

... And now back to the weekend edition of Atlantic Morning with your host Scott Duftwasser. Here is your host Scott Duftwasser..."

- Well it's already the second weekend of September and frosh week has just finished at most of the universities across the Dominion. With it comes a fresh new batch of post-pubescent students at the height of their sexual performance curve. Unfortunately, in an age of social-media websites, these same students are more and more preoccupied with looking at the screens of their mobile phones and tablets than they are looking in the eyes of their friends and possibly future sexual partners.

With their lack of abilities interacting and socializing face-to-face with their passing acquaintances and old friends alike, these students' social maturity is lagging further and further behind their sexual performance and natural inclination for sexual exploration. As a consequence, a majority of these male students are turning to professional sex-trade workers for their initial, and for some, regular sexual encounters.

To talk to us about this phenomenon, I am pleased to have in studio, Collette Leblanc, President and founding member of the New Brunswick Coalition of Sex Trade Workers...

- Good Morning Ms. Leblanc and welcome.
- Yes. Good Morning and thank-you for this opportunity.

- First off, give us a bit of background on how you got involved in the New Brunswick Coalition of Sex Trade Workers.
- Yes. I started in the sex trade industry, many years ago now. Late 1970's, after running away from a Mengen juvenile halfway house. I was a far more slender and attractive women back then, and was able to land my first gig at a very popular strip bar on Boulevard Lacloche in Laval, Quebec. By the start of the '80s, I got married to my pi... um boyfriend who was also the owner of the strip club. Three years later, I moved back to Mengen and started my own business, after the untimely death of my husband.

- Rest his soul.
- Yes, thank-you. With the money from my late husband's estate, I was encouraged to start a business in Mengen. One which I already understood the inner workings very well.

- That would be what is now called the R & W Emporium. I have seen you have expanded your business from a strip-club and pub in the industrial section of town, to a veritable alternative lifestyle superstore including a hemp shop, a bring-your-own cigar and medical-marijuana room, an upscale by-the-hour hotel, a custom motorcycle store, a pawn and tattoo shop, a walk-in Cayman-Islands financial services company and even an extreme body modification clinic with their own resident, board-certified surgeons, anesthesiologists, geneticists, dentists, and hair implant specialists.
- Yes. We have been expanding since the turn of the century. In the next few weeks we will be opening up Mengen's first canine pet shop

specializing in the selling, breeding and training of bull dogs, Rottweilers and Doberman Pinchers.

- Now this brings us to the present and your decision to start the New Brunswick Coalition of Sex Trade Workers. Tell us your motivation behind founding the Coalition.
- Yes. "As you have eluded to in your introduction, in the last four years, we have been having ever-increasing issues with the SŒ[15] generation clientèle due to their lack of interpersonal social skills."[16] In other words, they don't have any.

- I figure this must lead to some embarrassing and difficult situations for sex trade workers having to deal with this new generation of clientèle.
- Yes. "As of late, this particular ever-growing sub-section of our regular clientèle have been causing a disproportionate amount of alleged incidents of libelous behavior including, but not limited to, verbal taunting, intimidation, disgraceful introductions, inappropriate *texting* and smart-phone camera use. Alleged incidents of assault including, but not limited to, assault, assault with a weapon, inappropriate touching and unwanted evacuation of bodily fluids have also been on the increase." In other words, these SŒeys[17] have been acting like a bunch of bleep-bleep-bleep-bleep overbearing, obnoxious, arrogant, uneducated, bleep-bleep jerks that learned manners from a brochure they printed off a bleep-bleep-bleep-bleep-bleep Internet website.

- So have sex trade workers begun to adopt strategies to deal with this issue?
- Yes. "In the favorable social-economic context of sex trade workers employed by reputable and well-established Escort Service Agencies, the readily available financial and logistics resources at the disposal of the former make it possible for these workers and their supervisors to access the latest generation of mobile risk assessment applications including, but not limited to, Preliminary Background Check Verification Software or PBCVs. These PBCVs leverage the multiple-database linking abilities developed by the major credit-card companies to determine if the potential client has a history of High Risk Behavioral Issues or HRBIs. If the severity and number of HRBIs is unacceptable to both the supervisor and the worker, the client is charged a Preliminary-Service Service

15 SŒ: Sense Of Entitlement.

16 This last passage was read out verbatim from a text prepared by Ms. Leblanc's civil and criminal defense lawyer Moishe Bergstein.

17 SŒeys: members of the SŒ generation.

Charge, which will discretely appear on the rejected client's upcoming credit bill summary, as a credit-card company initiated PSSC. In the less-than-favorable context of street-level sex trade work, these street-workers are faced with multiple issues. Not only dœs their service price point negate the possibility of using PBCVs, a significant proportion of the immediate supervisors tutoring these street-level workers exhibit the same HRBIs as those of the rejected clients of the well-established Escort Service Agencies. At this time, adequate solutions to these and other issues have yet to be established and implemented."[18] In other words the street worker is up sh-- creek without a paddle because chances are her pimp is a bleep-bleep-bleep-bleep overbearing, obnoxious, arrogant, bleep-bleep SŒey jerk just like that twenty-something *aggro-john* looking for a cheap blow job cause his mom is out-of-town for the weekend.

- Well I'm happy you got that off your chest. I want to thank you for your enlightened and invaluable insight into this delicate and controversial issue. We're just about out of time so in closing, is there anything else you would like to add Ms. Leblanc?
- Yes. All men are pigs, and I'm a dyke. There. I said it. Now that's one fu--ing-crapola-sh-- weight off my chest. Caroline, I know you are still in the closet, but if you're listening over the Internet like you promised this morning, will you marry me? Just tweet me yes or no. Please.

- And who's Caroline?
- Yes. She tweeted Yes! Mrs Caroline Caissie, Maintenance and Repair Manager, Canadian Dominion Rail, Northern NB rail-line division, it's time to end the lie. It's time to divorce the man you have been using as a front to help advance your career all these years. It's time for you to become Mrs Caroline Leblanc.
- Wow. Two over-the-air outings and a successful social-media gay marriage proposal in less than a minute. That's a record for this broadcaster. Back after the break.

18 This last passage was read out verbatim from a text prepared by Ms. Leblanc's civil and criminal defense lawyer Moishe Bergstein.

"$$$ … ♀♀⚢

- Is it true you can earn *Cruise Miles* Reward Miles when I purchase auto insurance with you?
- Yes you always earn *Cruise Miles* Reward Miles when you purchase insurance and financial products at *Mac Dougal's* Insurance.

- That's great! I'll be able to save on that second honeymoon cruise I've been planning.
- And you can earn double your *Cruise Miles* Reward Miles when you combine your auto and home insurance with *Mac Dougal's* Insurance.

- Even Better! Now I'll be able to bring my husband!
- Value and personalized service are the hallmarks of everything we do at *Mac Dougal's* Insurance.

⚢♀♀… $$$"

- We're back, and opening up the phone lines. Ms Leblanc has been kind enough to stay in studio to help us answer your calls on this controversial topic. Our first caller is Sophia from Mengen.
- Yes, Hello. My name is Sophia Arsenault and I'm the Maintenance and Repair Manager, CD Rail, Southern New Brunswick rail-line division. I would like to thank Collette Leblanc for her courage and in a gesture of solidarity I would also like to declare over the air that I too am a Lesbian. There. I did it. Thank-you Collette.

- Thank-you Sophia for your comment and gesture. Our next caller is Lise Caissie from Fredericton. Go ahead Lise.
- Yes, Hello. My name is Lise Caissie and I'm the Regional President of the Railway Workers Union of Canada, Local 238. I would like to thank Collette Leblanc for her courage, and in a gesture of solidarity I would also like to declare over the air that I too am a Lesbian. There. It's done. Thanks again Collette.

- Thank-you sister!
- Well that's quite the declaration! Our next caller is Rebecca Mac Dougal, President and CEO of CD Rail, listening to us on the net at newstalk999.com.

- Thank you Scott. May I speak for all the employees of CD Rail and in the context of this special moment for all the LGBT employees of CD Rail, let's give a shout out to Collette, Lise, and Sophia for their invaluable contributions to our inclusive and diverse workforce. As CD Rail's first female and first openly gay CEO, I invite my compatriots flourishing in the Dominion's burgeoning corporate landscape, to celebrate the innovative talent, diversity and forward thinking mindset of all Canadian Workers.
- If I base myself on what's going on in our little corner of the twitter-verse, Collette's and Rebecca's comments are going viral. In our studio, I can safely say Colette is simply overwhelmed and literally speechless with emotion. Congratulations Colette. We are just about out of time, but I encourage you to follow this incredible event on Twitter. This is Scott Duftwasser and you're listening to the weekend edition of Atlantic Morning...

♜♜

"At News-Talk 99.9 FM and on your smart-phone at newstalk999.com here is a 99 second news update for Friday, May 10th, 2013...

... In the small town of Bellstadt, the newly-built main municipal building including the RCMP detachment, nearly burnt to the ground early this morning. According to Ronald Bourque, Bellstatd's fire chief, a preliminary investigation suggests an incendiary device was thrown on the roof of the building. Foul play is suspected by the authorities.

We sent out our man-on-the-scene, Stew Santos, and he was amazed to find significant, but not disastrous damage to the front northern section of the municipal building's roof. No municipal employees were present, nor any RCMP officers, as the interior of the new building had yet to be finished. Stew did get a firsthand account of the event from a Bellstadt resident who witnessed the blaze while exiting a local diner earlier this morning ...

- Ya, wehl you know, da flames were at leeest forrr feeet igh when I left Choux de Bruxelles dii-ner dis morning. I wasan't sure if it was the local dru ... I mean the Caissie Depanneur and Gas Baaarrr or the munecepal building that was tor... I mean burrr-ning until I got into my trock to take a closser lok.

... And in other news ..."

©®

- The best instigators are those that are not conscious of their instigation to begin with.
- It takes longer.

- Like cognac.
- Even cognac gœs sour after a millennium of aging.

- The vinegar from a well-aged cognac, helps in the preparation of the best of dishes.
- A millennium and a bit, if you include its hysteresis.

- Thank the gods … and giants for the tempering effects of cascading.
- It has kept us on our "tœs" for the last thousand years.

- And a bit.
- Ha! … What do you think of the latest response to our most recent intervention?

- Like adoptive father, like bastard son.
- Narcissistic psychotics are so predictable.

- In their unpredictability.
- Not to change the subject, do you think she will age like her mother-in-law?

- The democratization of social-media has applied pressures of perceived attractiveness and appearance on even the most rural of redneck lesbians.
- I say social-media is a fad.

- Do you want to bet on it?
- The loser sends his first and only tweet.

- Woof. That would be quite an exercise in irrelevancy.
- Consider it a form of fundamental cogitation.

Objectivity

To differentiate his public relationship from his private one, Laurence would call her Lucy. The rest of the world just called her Mabel.

Their son, J.D., was well into his late twenties, when he finally gathered enough courage to make the steam ship journey from Liverpool to Rimouski and pay homage to his parents, who had perished off the shores of *Pointe-au-Père*, two decades earlier.

J.D. was the black sheep of the family. A character trait he would bestow to his offspring. One that would become a family tradition. Money came easily to J.D., thanks to the success of his father and grandfather alike. If he wanted to rise in the corporate world, his predecessors' fame would not suffice.

Like his father and his grandfather before him, he would have to mask his latent homosexual tendencies by finding a wife. Preferably a lesbian.

Geraldine did the same.

Yes, that Geraldine. What was a lesbian telephone operator from Montreal doing in the middle of a maritime disaster memorial, on the outskirts of Rimouski, a good two months ahead of the tourist season?

The answer to this question gœs well beyond the scope of this present edition. I will attempt to satisfy your plausible curiosity at a later time. And space.

J.D. and Geraldine got married in an Anglican Church. Well before she began to show.

They had a son and a daughter. Not necessarily in that order.

They called him Junior.

Junior's apathy mirrored his parents'. An apathy that would seep throughout the empire he would inherit from his father's greed. An empire whose legacy would come to define "corporate welfare" throughout his domain of influence spanning the Dominion's Atlantic Commonwealth.

...

"You are listening to the Central Broadcasting Cooperative at 106.9 FM and on the Internet at 1069cbc.com. At the sound of the tone, following ten seconds of silence it will be precisely one o'clock, Friday, May 1st, 2015. Blip, blip, blip, blip, blip, blip, blip, blip, blip, beeeeeeeeeeep...

...A new chapter in The Mengen Bobcats scheduling scandal has just unfolded, with an additional $85 000.00 transferred to The Bobcats, on top of the original $100 000.00, transferred a month earlier, as compensation for scheduling errors committed by a top executive of the city-owned hockey arena. The errors were divulged to our news desk, following a PR leak, inside the walls of the mayor's administrative office.

We contacted the owners of The Bobcats, J.D. International, in an attempt to obtain a response from JDI's executive, about the subject of the leaked document. No one at JDI was available for comment...

...And now back to The Morning Wake-up Call with your host Rosanne Fisterslutvale..."

...

J.D. was having a field day. Almost as much as his two-wheeled, homœrotic business associates.

Homœrotic... At least in JD's eyes. For The Kopfschmucks, that's all that counted. Even though math wasn't their forte.

A $185 000.00 scheduling error pales in comparison to a 100 million dollar logistical error, intrinsically linked to the former, and in the shape of a new sports complex, that would have The Bobcats move to an expropriated piece of prime downtown real-estate.

Now, if only JD's voice box, Mengen's mayor, could convince the federal and provincial powers-at-be, to dish out their share of the development costs, JD, and his business associates would be in business... Again.

I wrote a short article -actually two- to the producer of Ms Fisterslutvale's morning show, to propose an alternative to the urban development project, promoted by the city's executive body.

I thought I would share them with you...

Doughnut Urbanism and The Mengen Center
People, Parcels, and Patients

I was listening to your debate on the Mengen Center this morning, and I couldn't help but observe the irony of the city counselor's argument for the building of such a center. He stated that approximately one percent of Mengen's population lives in the downtown core and contributes to 11% of the municipal tax base. That is the very definition of doughnut urbanism. Building a Colosseum that will be used by 99% of the population who live outside the doughnut hole, will only exacerbate the urban nightmare that the doughnut hole is instigating.

And that's where the irony lies. The oblivious nature of the hole. If Mengen refers to itself as a hub, it will have to act like one.

A hub is all about logistics. The 11 acre, 12.5 million dollar pile of rubble in the center of the downtown core has only one remaining asset, its inter-modal station. And it is that station that will become the heart of Mengen's downtown center.

Let me explain.

Logistics is about moving, interacting with, and servicing entities. A logistical hub for Mengen's downtown core will have to focus on three of them: People. parcels, and patients.

People will be attracted to the hub if they can effectively access, food, parcels, knowledge, health care, and other people.

I grew up in Chanticleer, a small town in the Laurentian mountains, north of Montreal. My first year of middle school was attended in one that was situated next to the main church. A few years latter they moved these first year students to the main high school in Mont-Rolland, a town that has since fused with Chanticleer.

Instead of tearing the school down after the transfer, the provincial government renovated the building and transformed the school into... a school. In other words it gave the school a new vocation. It became L'École d'Hôtelllerie du Québec. The liability that is Mengen's old and abandoned high school building, will become its greatest asset by giving it a similar vocation.

The difference between the two will be based on New Brunswick's greatest asset, its forest. More precisely the food one can forage and hunt amongst its trees. By placing a focus on the wild produce and game one can find amongst the Boreal forest's biodiversity, you will be able to give a unique flavor (pardon the pun) to this gastronomic, agricultural, fisheries and tourism institution.

As a younger man I had the opportunity to live live and work in both Montreal and Toronto. One of the common denominators of these two cities, is the proliferation of farmer's markets in the downtown core.

Where is the best place to build a farmer's market? In the center of a logistical hub where the farmers, the foragers, and the hunters can send their produce and meat "VIA" refrigerated rail car to the downtown core.

Who can best, process, cook and interact with the tourists and local population inside the food court and farmer's market at the center of the logistical hub? The students-in-training from the gastronomic, agricultural, fisheries and tourism institution.

I have covered the food and the people accessing the hub. What about the knowledge? In the age of information the most successful libraries have transformed themselves into logistical hubs of knowledge and innovation. They have recommissioned parts of their silent repositories of deadwood books into bustling incubators of innovation and creative thought.

That covers knowledge. What about health-care?

If you can move people, why can't you move patients? It's all about logistics. There are threes major advantages to moving people by rail car. The size, comfort and stability of the latter. Not to mention its ability to segregate one rail car from all others. In a world of instant real-time communications and remotely-controlled robotic interventions, transforming a traditional rail car into a mobile ambulance, iCU, and trauma center is now an economically and logistically viable reality. Not to mention the fact that such a rail car can be used as an effective biœnvironmental containment unit.

I'm not suggesting to build a full fledged hospital inside Mengen's new downtown hub. I am suggesting that the hub can house a series of specialized private clinics, easily accessed by the city dwellers and those using the inter-modal station. Those patients needing immediate care not offered by these specialized clinics will be a short ambulance or health shuttle-bus away from the city's major hospitals.

It's all about logistics.

I have covered the people and the patients, what about the parcels?

My first year of undergraduate studies, was in Mechanical Engineering at The University of Waterloo. At the time, the corporate world called it Northern Telephone & Telegraph, NTT for short. The politicians called it the builder of the information super highway. A decade after graduating from university, I had returned to college and obtained a technical degree in electrical engineering. The information super highway became the internet and I started working as a post-production test technician at Northern Telephony's Vile St-Laurent optical network equipment plant. The optical cables that run underneath and beside the rail lines of CN and CP's transportation network became the backbone of the Dominion's information superhighway. Why am I telling you this?

If you want to purchase, move, and deliver parcels in a safe and secure fashion you can no longer use the internet effectively. You can however use part of that transportation and information backbone to build your own separate physical and virtual logistical network. Mengen need not be the only hub. You can build smaller and if need be bigger hubs in Halifax, Amherst, Rogersville, Bathurst, Campbellton, Riviére-du-Loup, Lévis, Quebec-City, Saint-Hyacinthe, Longueuil, Montreal, Kingston, Belleville, Oshawa, and Toronto. Amongst others, on Via Rail's main corridors.

For sake of argument, If you limit yourself to the Atlantic provinces, creating several hubs along VIA's Ocean Line, Maritime Bus Service will no longer be an inter-provincial bus service but rather will be one that will move people as well as parcels to and from these hubs along the main transportation backbone. Granted, Via Rail will have to return to a daily or better yet twice-daily service schedule. You can't lose it if you can't use it. These hubs will become logistical nodes not just for VIA Rail and Maritime Bus, but also for the rural ambulance service, Canada Post, Amazon, and all other private logistics companies such as UPS, DHL, FEDEX, Purolator, and Walmart.

As the maritime population ages, the provincial governments will need to build new long-term senior care facilities. Why not build them as an integral part of these rural hubs. As rural communities become smaller and smaller, it no longer becomes economically viable to run a separate post office, mini mart, health clinic, pharmacy, train station, farmer's market and community center.

If you have to build new senior care facilities across the province, you might as well get private industry, crown corporations, and the local and regional municipalities involved.

Consolidate. It's all about logistics.

But I digress. Let's get back to The Mengen Center.

As mentioned I once lived in Montreal. One of the apartments I stayed in was less than a block away from the Pie-IX subway station. Right next to the Olympic Stadium. That was my first introduction to the concept of the White Elephant.

Why did The Big O become a white elephant and Toronto's Skydome didn't? It's all about logistics.

Though both were placed outside the downtown core, The Big O dœsn't have immediate access to a major metropolitan expressway. The Viau and Pie-IX subway stations were not designed to handle 60000 event attendees all at once. Making the event a logistical nightmare once it has come to an end.

Putting a Colosseum in the Mengen's downtown core will turn that logistical nightmare into a logistical disaster.

Mengen dœsn't have a subway system and dœsn't even have enough money to pay for a new bus route to move students from the downtown core to your new high school in The North End.

Like The Skydome, which has immediate access to The Gardener Expressway, The Mengen Colosseum has access to major expressways in and out of the Mengen region.

One of the debaters this morning said it would cost 42 million dollars to renovate the Colosseum. The other said it would cost 27 million dollars. For sake of argument let's take the best case scenario and double that to fifty-four million dollars.

That leaves you fifty-three million public dollars, an empty school, and 11 acres of prime downtown real estate to build and animate your downtown logistical hub.

If you are building a logistical hub in the shape of let's say, a horseshœ, you won't have enough public money. You will have more than enough private money.

Let's start with two anchor stores at the tips of the horseshœ, both facing Main Street.

Before Canada became a Dominion, much of the principality was known as Rupert's Land. Rupert's Land was the sole proprietorship of the Hudson's Bay Company. Kicking the principle forefathers of the Dominion of Canada out of the downtown core would be considered not too far from treasonous had the slight been committed in a civilized country.

It should be logical to place a Hudson's Bay Store as the first anchor. The second anchor should be more a compliment than a competitor to the first. In terms of Canadian retailers with a history of success, the only fashion retailer that can rival Hudson's Bay is Simons.

Now that you have two privately funded retail anchors at the ends of the horseshœ and a transportation hub at the bottom of the horseshœ, you need to populate a series of health condos above the latter. These health condos can include but not limited to a private multidisciplinary dental clinic an optometrist, a pharmacist, a private leading-edge technology diagnostics and medical imaging clinic, a non-invasive radio surgery cancer clinic, a physiotherapy clinic, a practicing nurse outpatient clinic, and maybe a chiropractor for good measure.

The food court and farmer's market will be on the left side of the horseshœ and the provincial library and innovation incubator on the right side. Canada Post and The DHL store will both connect the incubator to one end of the transportation hub. Amazon and The UPS Store will connect the farmer's market to the other end of the transportation hub. All these service and commercial retailers will either lease or purchase condos from the private developer of the horseshœ.

The fifty-three million dollars of public money will go to pay for the main world-class attraction at the center of horseshœ. Google will pay for the innovation incubator.

When I was a young boy, I visited Expo '67 with my parents. The most fascinating exhibit was the American one. As a young engineer the most fascinating engineering achievement I visited, other than Toronto's CN Tower was Montreal's Biodome. Both for different reasons.

Several years ago, the polymer exterior of the American Buckminster-Fuller geodesic dome went up in flames. The aluminum structure stayed perfectly intact.
Polymer technology has advanced quite a bit in the last half century. Buckminster-Fuller's creation needs no improvement. It is the most structurally stable and strong, integral, high surface area roofing system known to man. It will easily resist the most severe of Atlantic Northeasters.

Just such a geodesic structure will be built in the center of the horseshœ and cover a subtropical park where fir and maple trees will be replaced by olive and citrus trees. In the center of the park will be a slightly sunken performing arts theater surrounded be tables used by the clients of the food court.

There will be restricted access to the olive and citrus groves. However the clients of the food court will be served dishes and beverages made from the fresh produce grown in the Biodome. Small and relatively docile subtropical beasts will populate the groves and be tended to by some of the employees of Magnetic Hill Zoo.

Now you know how to fill a doughnut hole.

Salutations,

Sylvain de Ville-Amois

"You are listening to the Central Broadcasting Cooperative at 106.9 FM and on the internet at 1069cbc.com. At the sound of the tone, following ten seconds of silence it will be precisely one o'clock, Tuesday, May 5th, 2015. Blip, blip, blip, blip, blip, blip, blip, blip, blip, beeeeeeeeeeep...

... With the sudden, and yet to be explained permanent interruption in the renovation of the old, unoccupied, Lisatichi Long-term Care Facility, due to the equally permanent removal of Shades-of-Atkon Inc., the local contractor who was in charge of the renovation project, the feasibility study of a second yet to be built long-term care facility, which would have been located on the opposite side of town to the old now abandoned facility, has reached an impasse.

The municipal executives responsible for the feasibility study, are now forced to contemplate the cost overruns projected by building a single facility, twice the size as the one originally proposed, and demolishing the old facility whose renovations were in an advanced state of completion.

We contacted a private consulting firm, and based on the limited information provided to us by the municipal executives, the firm was able to give us a rough estimate of the cost overruns, according to their past experience analyzing similar logistical failures.

According to their best case scenarios, the total cost of building a new double-sized long-term care facility from scratch will now be at the very least three times the total cost of the original dual location proposal.

For his view on the situation, we also contacted The Right Honorable Jacques Shellack, the newly minted premier of New Brunswick...

- As the first premier of Haitian origin in the history of New Brunswick, I am used to witnessing cost overruns.
- And how would you describe the project now?

- Ah.. Um... Ahhh... Oh.. Ah.. Um..
- ... A mess?

- Ah.. Um... Ahhh... Oh.. Ah.. Um.. not in so many words.
- Thank you for this opportunity, Premier.

... And in other news..."

Here is the second article I wrote...

Selling a School for a Song
Transforming a Liability into an Asset

I'm in the process of preparing my corporate income taxes for the fiscal year that has has recently ended. Though I have been in business for over a decade, this will be the first fiscal exercise where I will have no liabilities to declare: either long term or short term; Only assets.

For the first time this year, I have added a new asset to the books, in the form of a copyrighted entity. One that has taken over a year to produce.

Time is money.

The copyrighted entity has yet to produce any income, so one would surmise that such an entity would be a liability. But it's not. No money was exchanged to add the entity to the ledger.

Only time.

It only has the potential to generate income, if someone pays the creative thought locked inside it. And that's why the entity is on the asset side of the ledger.

Years before I had started my own company, I was the employee of another. I was the product engineer for a medical geriatric mobility equipment manufacturer. One day, I was "chosen" to be half of a dynamic duo that would volunteer to transport a cube van filled with mobility equipment, from Quebec City to Atlanta, Georgia.

Atlanta is not only the home of CNN's flagship broadcast center, and The Coca Cola Museum (that's where I learned Santa-Claus was a but a marketing Hoax!), it's also the home of one of the largest convention centers in North America.

And that's where we were headed.

Somewhere between Richmond, Virginia, and Durham, North Carolina -I think-, the other half of the dynamic duo took an exit off the I-95. I think we were still on the I-95. I was lost. My partner wasn't.

The van stopped at the top of a roundabout, next to the front entrance of a modern and stately hotel. It was dark, but I could tell we were surrounded by a well tended-to forest. There were no other lights to be seen other than those of the hotel estate.

It was as eerie as it was welcoming. A welcome filled with reserve and distinction.

It was only when we had walked-up to the front desk, that I realized we were in The Hilton.

What dœs all this have to do with selling a school for a song?

It all depends to whom you are selling it to.

And what you are singing.

Late at night, well before dawn, and once the interference from the cellular towers has decreased, you can receive broadcast signals from as far away as Toronto's CN Tower. It's easier to receive those from New York. One of those signals broadcasts content from Blüteberg News 1310. Though it's 4 o'clock in the morning, in Acadia Corner, Londoners are already well into their breakfast routine. I was lost. In the Realm of Time.

And Blüteberg is broadcasting the morning show with Marc Barstone. Based on the off-the-cuff comments made by the shows co-hosts, I figure Mr Barstone is a dapper gent. Based on his own comments he is definitely well informed, if not well read.

A while back, I remember listening to him interview one of the top executives at Hilton International. What was striking about the interview was that the executive didn't define the corporation he was working for as a hotel chain, but rather a hospitality logistics company.

One is not a guest of *a* Hilton. You are the guest of *The* Hilton. The company dœsn't view itself as a set of distinct locations. It views itself as one hotel.

If you are a regular at The Hilton, and you reserve a room at a location you have never been to before, once you enter the suite for the first time, the room's temperature will be set at the one you prefer. The national newspaper you regularly read before going to bed will be on the coffee table, next to the former. If you routinely order a Cinzano on ice, with a twist of lemon, as a nightcap before going to bed, room service will contact you well before bedtime, and offer it to you. All without ever having to ask beforehand.

That's not a hotel chain. That's logistics.

To offer that level of service, all the employees, from the maid that has cleaned and prepared your room, to the hotel manager where you are a guest, have to be trained and educated to the same standards. A standard of excellence that can only be taught at an institution that will have at the very least, access to the wealth of knowledge and experience accumulated by a company such as Hilton International.

One of the products that I was working on at the mobility device manufacturer, was a modular patient hoist. Half of the system was a set of extruded aluminum rails -either curved or straight- that could be bolted to the joists just below an existing ceiling or sunken and integrated into a new ceiling installed during the final construction phase of a newly built long-term care facility.

The other half of the system was a portable hoist that one would hook to a small and discrete trolley integrated into the railing system. On the hoist was four hooks. The geriatric patient was placed on a fabric hammock, and the hammock attached to the four hooks. Now you can lift the patient out of bed and seamlessly transfer him to the bathroom or any other location the railing system will permit.

With the advancements in led lighting offered today you could easily install a multiple point lighting system inside the sunken rails of a newly constructed facility. The led lights would be similar to those used to light a Christmas tree but instead of being linked in series they would be linked in parallel.

What dœs all this have to do with selling a school for a song?

Patience. I'm getting there.

Remember. It's all about logistics.

The most conspicuous devices in a long term care facility, are those that are used to increase the mobility of a severely mobility depend patient. If one can design a patient room where all the mobility, monitoring, bathing and furniture are designed to be as functional and elegant to the eyes and needs of a long term care patient as they are to an able-bodied hotel guest, one will be able to serve the former one day and the latter the next. All from the same hotel suite.

In the first article I had written to you, I had suggested that if New Brunswick and Nova-Scotia are at a demographic point in their history where they will have to increase the construction of long-term care facilities, you might as well consolidate the small town product and service suppliers and these geriatric care facilities into a series of transportation, healthcare, and information logistical hubs along Via Rail's Ocean Line, from Halifax to the Northern Border of New Brunswick.

Now that you have an efficient transportation network, that can move people, parcels and patients, while housing and taking care of the geriatric patients located along the network, all that is left is the ability to temporarily house the doctors, logistics technicians, nurses, and their assistants, when they are away from home working along the network.

And what about the rural creatives that value their solitude, but still need to travel to the major urban centers along the network, when comes the time to promote and transfer their creative thought?

And all the urban extroverts that would like to take advantage of the recreational activities the rural regions along the network have to offer, but cannot afford a cottage in the country, let alone a car to get there? And all the international and transnational tourists that wish to do the same?

Now one can add a series of hotels to the hubs, where it would be logistically viable to do so. And let's go one step further and make as many or as few as necessary of those long term care patient rooms, high value-added hotel rooms at the same time. Simply by designing the rooms in an intelligent and logistically advanced fashion.

Now you can share all the cleaning, cooking, and back-of-the house management facilities that are both common to the hotel and the long-term care facility.

And you can hand over all the non-critical services of the long-term care facility, to a hospitality logistics company that has decades of experience doing just that. All the critical care will be offered on site -or remotely- by the advanced care clinics that have been integrated into the network.

Why would a hospitality network want to take on long-term care patients as guests of their hotel? To answer that question you will have to visit Wall Street, or at the very least listen to Blüteberg News at 4 o'clock in the morning.

The single most important parameter a Wall Street analyst looks at when he is planning on investing in a hotel chain, or better yet a hospitality logistics company, is occupancy rates. If such a company can demonstrate they can increase their occupancy rates by 20% to 50 %, simply by defining and serving a new clientèle, at a price point this specialized clientèle can afford, all the while offering them a level of non critical care orders of magnitude superior than one offered at a government run facility, the stock price of the hospitality logistics company will go through the roof in short order.

Now all the hospitality logistics company has to do is train and educate the employees that will be serving both the specialized clients and the regular guests of the newly built combined, multi-tasking hotels along the network.

And where will those employees be trained and educated? At the abandoned high school, in the heart of downtown Mengen that the global hospitality logistics company has purchased from the local school commission...

For a song.

Salutations,

Sylvain de Ville-Amois

...

- She knows her concepts will never come to fruition.
- When inertia is in a spiral of devolution, what should be rarely becomes reality.

- It made for an interesting read none-the-less.
- Interesting rarely translates to interest.

- Now, now, don't be such a knowledge seeker of noble negativism.
- Noble? Maybe. Negative? I would rather consider myself as objective.

Devolution

"At 96.9 FM and at 969solfm.com here is the news for Sunday, August 4th, 2013 ...

In Mengen today, a badly injured, mixed breed dog was left at the doorstep of the local SPCA. According to Nancy Belch, director of Mengen's SPCA, the dog was beaten and abused. According to Edgar Dreckskerl, the local veterinarian, it will cost at least $3000.00 to cover the necessary surgery to save the poor soul. Ms Belch has set up a Facebook page for the injured and abused dog in the hope of raising the necessary funds for the surgery that will save the dog from euthanasia.

An RFID implant has been located on the dog, making it possible for the Kodiak RCMP to launch an investigation to determine how the dog was injured and if necessary to lay charges of animal abuse on whomever is responsible for this tragic crime.

... And in other news ...

This is Darcy for 96.9 Fm Sol FM at the New Brunswick Day celebrations, this year, held in my hometown of Schwarzdorf. It's been raining most of the morning, so they have moved the activities to a huge white and red-striped tent where there is a barbecue, New Brunswick Day cake and lots of music from local artists and bands, amongst others, Philip Sobey, Claude Leblanc, the Docile Gorillas, the Heritage Rednecks, Joseph Jardine, Marie-Pierre Poirier, and local Italo-Canadian crooner and pizza chef supreme, Guido Rizotto. If your still in Schwarzdorf this evening, all of us at Sol FM highly recommend you head on over to Guido's Pizzeria for some of the best Sicilian pizza east of St-Léonard. Watching Guido flipping pizza dough while signing covers of Gino Vennelli, Frank Sinatra, and Sammy Davis Jr. is a sight to be seen, and heard.

On stage now is the Santa Anna sensations, Lapierre brothers. The threesome composed of Joseph on the fiddle, Joseph on vocals and Joseph on French horn have been composing and performing original music for over twenty years. They have coined there music post-modern Acadian opera. Though they have moved to Quebec City, ever since Joseph became a resident member of the Quebec Symphony horn section, they have never let go of their New Brunswick East-Coast roots. Joseph's fiddling bravado combined with Joseph's castrato vocals must be seen and heard live to be fully appreciated."

$

- Woo, woo, woo ... Are we there yet? Woo, woo, woo ... Are we there yet?
- Ms. Belch ... You are such a tease.

- ...
- ...

- The earth moved ... I'm sure the earth moved.
- Oh, stop it.

Of course she was a dike. And he knew it.

Of course he was gay. And she knew it.

They differed only in motivation.

His last all-male encounter was with an ICU nurse. That's when he finally clued in.

As a veterinarian, he spoke the language. The test was good for, at worst, three and at best, five mutations. At the time there was about three hundred of the latter. Today they have stopped counting; too many thousands.

He saw too many encounters die and too many side-effects of the toxic cocktails. The only way to find out if he was positive was to wait, and abstain.

As a veterinarian, he understood the cause. The real cause.

The politics wanted us to be all innocent.

The science. The real science and history said otherwise.

It took a decade to determine he was negative. And another to confirm his suspicions.

He had grown to know Ms. Belch well enough to be at ease with her prudish ways. A consequence of her former career as a Trappist nun at the Bellstadt Monastery. They both understood the cause. Neither had crossed the line. Neither wanted to.

She was up to her armpits in abandoned dogs. A consequence of the Tar-Sands migration. They both understood the Cause. Each had crossed the line. Each wanted to.

She needed the money. He needed the touch. Any touch. As long as it meant not having to spend the rest of his life at the cocktail lounge.

$$

"At 96.9 FM and at 969solfm.com here is the news for Sunday, August 4th, 2013 ...

The little mixed breed dog that was viciously abused and left at the Mengen SPCA is slowly recuperating from his injuries as he awaits for the generous donations of the public for the expensive surgery that will save his life.

Ms. Nancy Belch, director of Mengen's SPCA, gives us this update:

- The feedback from the Facebook page I set up this morning, has been outstanding and truly heartwarming. At this rate we should soon have enough funds to perform the life-saving surgery on this beautiful dog that was so brutally abused only a few days ago. I encourage all those that can spare a few dollars to go to facebook.com/savetheMengenmutt and donate what you can.

... And in other news...

A sense of tragedy and sadness has overshadowed New Brunswick Day celebrations with the deaths of two young boys by a 4 meter long African Rock python, during the overnight hours of Sunday to Monday.

The two boys aged 4 and 6 years old, were guests at their uncle's apartment in Campbellton, New Brunswick. Sedrick Thébeau, is the owner of Reservoir Reptiles, a pet store specializing in exotic reptiles, and situated just below the apartment where the two boys were sleeping when they were attacked by the python. According to Mr. Thébeau, the snake escaped from its glass-enclosed vivarium, the latter of which was situated next to the room where the two boys were sleeping.

Captain Roland Thébeau, of the Campbellton Detachment of the RCMP, gives us the latest details relevant to the investigation.

- The two victims of this tragic incident have been identified as Joseph Thébeau 4 years old and Sébastien Thébeau 6 years old of London, Ontario. The snake has been captured by members of the New Brunswick Department of Natural Resources. Euthanasia was performed, followed by a necropsy to determine the state of health and species of the snake.

Following Captain Thébeau's statement, Sedrick Thébeau took to the podium.

- On Sunday my two nephews Joseph and Sébastien spent a beautiful day at my hobby farm, just outside Howard. Joseph and Sébastien spent the day petting and learning about the goats, pigs and chickens on my farm. First thing in the morning, Sébastien tried his hand at milking a goat, and after breakfast, Joseph helped out in making some goat milk yogurt that we later ate for dessert after a wonderful barbecue on a sunny midsummer evening. After supper, we all headed back to Campbellton and I tucked Joseph and Sébastien in bed in the living room of my apartment. This day at the farm is how I hope, all of you listening will remember these two young inquisitive boys.

Antoine Thébeau, the mayor of Campbellton closed the press conference with his own statement. Here is an excerpt.

- May I speak on behalf of the all the people of Campbellton, as we grieve for the tragic deaths of these two young boys who came here this weekend to visit this beautiful region of Northern New Brunswick. A makeshift memorial has been established in front of Mr. Thébeau's pet store and I invite everyone to visit, as we all pull together and remember the short but wonderful lives of these two young boys. Already dozens of teddy bears have been left at the memorial and at the request of the family, will be donated to the NSK Children Hospital in Halifax Nova Scotia."

- What do you mean you need to change the script again?! I thought you told me you finished the final storyline last week. Morry's short-fused temper was getting shorter the further his addiction to *crystal-meth* took hold of his limited cognitive abilities.

Morry's short-fused temper was getting shorter the further his addiction to *crystal-meth* took hold of his limited cognitive abilities.

- There were some inconsistencies in the script relative to the time line of the final story. I've reread the whole story and corrected all the storyboards and corresponding scripts so that the plot dœsn't fall apart.

As he observed Morry's ho and ha body language, Dexter immediately understood that his unconvincing technical response went way over his boss's head.

- I knew I was going to have problems the minute I started recruiting a production crew on the Student Cinema Network. You New Yorkers are so cocky.
- Well look on the bright side Morry. You are paying a fraction of the price of a commercial production house and you have admitted that the results from our SLD[19] digital cameras adapted to old-school manual focus lenses give as good, if not better results than the high priced digital cine-cameras used by most professionals. As for being cocky, I bet you a month's pay that you wouldn't last a week with an LA production crew.

- Watch your mouth there, Dexter. With chapters spanning from Vancouver to Toronto and Montreal to French Village, the Kopfschmucks have more than enough members and intimate associates to help out with acting duties. And Vancouver as well as Montreal are established Canadian production hubs.
- Um... yes. You have a point. I will get back to work.

$⇧

19 SLD is an acronym for Single Lens Direct-view. SLD cameras are interchangeable lens cameras that lift the data from the digital image capture sensor to obtain a real-time streaming image on an electronic viewfinder for purposes of composition and parameter adjustment.

Snakes have been occasionally raised as pets for centuries, but have been relatively untouched in terms of breeding. In other words, snakes have been left alone to evolve on their own.

As cold-blooded, reptilian predators, snakes have never been known to have a natural symbiotic relationship with warm-blooded humans: be it mutual, parasitic, or absolute in nature.

Either as a consequence or a motivation, snakes' antisocial behavior towards humans tends to be mimicked by those who adopt them.

☮☠

"At 99.9 FM and at 999solfm.com here is the news for Wednesday, June 4th, 2014 ...

... And now breaking news.

From Mengen City Hall, we now bring you a live broadcast of the official update concerning the RCMP police shootings and the subsequent lock-down of the Mengen Northern Triangle. First at mike is John Thébeau, director of the RCMP Kodiak division...

- Please let me thank you all for attending this conference, during a most difficult and dark chapter in Mengen's history. Earlier this evening, at approximately 7:35pm, five officers of the RCMP Kodiak division, were shot on Crandall Street in the northeastern district of Mengen. Though we cannot release the names of the officers at this time, pending official communication with next of kin, we can tell you that three of the officers are confirmed dead and the two remaining officers are in critical but stable condition at a regional hospital. We are now able to give you the name of the prime suspect of these shootings, who is presently still at large and considered heavily armed and dangerous. His name is Pierre Elliot Gallant. A 24 year-old Caucasian resident of Mengen. As most residents are now aware, a lock-down perimeter was immediately established after the event and is still in place. This triangular perimeter borders Wheeler Boulevard to the west, Mountain Road to the east, and Killam Drive to the south. We ask all residents inside the perimeter to lock there doors and to stay inside their homes when possible during the duration of the lock-down. I will now hand-over the podium to the mayor of Mengen, Mr. Maurice Boucher-Faucher.

- Thank-you Director Thébeau. Let me reiterate, in the name of all residents of the city of Mengen, my most sincere condolences to the families of the fallen three RCMP officers and a speedy and complete recovery for the two injured members of the force. As mentioned by Director Thébeau, I exhort all residents of Mengen, inside as well as outside the lock-down perimeter, to cooperate fully with all authorities during this critical time in our city's history. Temporary shelters have been set-up at all schools outside the perimeter and the necessary emergency, lodging, counseling and logistical services will be available to all residents not able to reenter their homes during the duration of the lock-down...

... You have been listening to a live broadcast of the latest news conference from city hall updating the event s following the shooting of five Kodiak RCMP officers earlier this evening."

...

Tradition can often be the foundation of creativity. When overwhelmed by obsessive repetition, it can also be its assassin.

Thiazi

- CRACK!, PET!!, KABOOM!!!,KABOOM!!!, KABOOM!!!, KABOOM!!!, KABOOM!!!, KABOOM!!!

They both died. Almost on impact.

Leaving them to burn, the inferno above melting the asphalt below; the latter freshly laden days earlier.

The municipal workers, neighbors and passer-byes taking pickax, shovel, and bucket to hand, as they contained the spread of fire – both smoke-filed and invisible – from spreading to the dry underbrush on both sides of the village road. One shared by the outskirts of both Thomson Heights and Upper Chanticleer, not far from the Wulfilas' rural home.

He lost his mother. Just a baby.

Gofer gained a friend. They both had a lot of learning to do. Knowledge they would acquire from a distant past. The bear cub's astute instinct making him as much a teacher as an orphan.

His first weekend as a guest of the Wulfilas became his last. Taking up residence inside the second-floor flat of the newly built barn on Tom and Uli's acreage, turned hobby farm.

He would tend to the farm, during construction season. And work at The Grand Séminaire, during his friend's hibernation. The human threesome trading residence and chores, during the construction holidays. Giving a chance for Gofer to haunt his old stomping grounds during two weeks of the year's hot summer nights.

Once a trick. Always a trick.

☭☟☠

"You are listening to the American Broadcasting Cooperative at 98.6 FM and on your smart-phone at 986abc.com. At the sound of the tone, following ten seconds of silence it will be precisely one o'clock, Friday, June 26th, 2015. Blip, blip, blip, blip, blip, blip, blip, blip, blip, blip, beeeeeeeeeeep...

... As the Commander in Chief gave his eulogy to the survivors of the massacre that occurred a week prior, he made a point of stating what so many have stated before him, during this time of mourning:

- Let us pay tribute to these Christian souls, these American souls, ones darkened by the power of a black gun. Ones we will not forget, as our mortal wounds heal from this tragedy. If one can call this senseless act of hate, tragic. May we not forget. May we never forget the nation building contributions of these parishioners, and the contributions to come of those seated in the nave of this physically tiny but symbolically massive church in the heart of South Carolina's bible belt. The bedrock of our nation. We shall overcome. Weee shaaal OVERcome...

... Hailing the congregation to join him in joyous harmony and solidarity, the former began hesitantly, but soon broke out into a rallying choir of song. The latter to the tune of America's anthem of the civil rights movement...

...In other news, the Ukraine geopolitical crisis took a bizarre twist when the Russian Leader of the Kopfscmucks' Moscow cell lead anti-Kiev protests..."

...

- The wind smells of manure that has been freshly spread over the farmer's fields in the villages bellow.
- Spread with the help of a fan's whirling blades.

- Fields that have been sown with the seeds of war.
- Seeds both black and white.

Evolution

When Vladimir took the initiative to commence major renovations on Saint-Petersburg Isaac Cathedral, the endeavor wasn't meant to anchor the nation's spiritual beliefs in the past, but rather to springboard the latter into the future.

All governing process control systems have their advantages, and disadvantages. One, if not the most important, integral stabilizer of any system of governance is a common philosophical mindset. Extricating a system's philosophical sextant from its administrative infrastructure only serves to create a pair of competing leaderships. Eventually, the hilarity of civil unrest and upheaval almost always ensues.

Even the most zombie-inducing of monotheistic religious dogmas will have at its core, a set of guiding principles that, at the very least, will enhance and effectively mold the decision making process of your average subject residing in any system of governance. Be it by government decree, or a slow and sustained public relations media blitz, attempting to altogether liquidate the ethical leadership from these guiding principles, will only serve to deal a final blow to the subject's poor soul, the latter having already been severely battered and assaulted by the very monotheistic dogma he is trying desperately to follow.

In 20/20 hindsight, the vast majority of history's significant failures, all categories combined, share one common defining summation;"It seemed to be good idea at the time."

...

At the signing of the American constitution, in 1776, and following the subsequent inclusion of the constitution's defining amendments, the document, taken as a whole, was an excellent, structured framework for the newly founded republic.

Unfortunately, like most historic, structural failures, the founding fathers' decision to exclude from the constitutional framework, a set of guiding spiritual principles, and placing all their unwritten ethical regulatory eggs in one "God we trust" basket, lacked the foresight to project the eventual consequences of their inaction.

When one barters spiritual guidance in favor of freedom of religion, a Pandora's box is opened, preparing the groundwork for a future wrath of yet unknown shape and form.

Who would think, that less than two centuries after the signing of the original document, so many of the republic's members would lose sight of the spirit hidden amongst the constitution's unwritten paragraphs.

For the original authors, it was a self-evident presumption. The vast majority of the republic's members, from the simplest laborer to the most influential of corporate businessmen, would always apply to the new Republic's Constitution, the same spiritual and ethical principles that guided them in their daily lives as subjects of the British Monarchy.

Surprise!

It is in the context of a present day, economic, social order that this failure is most glaring. When symbiosis is replaced by greed, and the competitive spirit is replaced by the hunger for profit, the loss of these two founding tenets at the core of republican capitalism, that is capitalism of the founding republic, leaves our modern notion of this amputated and bastardized form of the latter with only its etymological leg to stand on.

If one thinks capitalism is all about fiat capital, one would be ascetically mistaken. When profit and greed become religion, one is left to drown in his own ørlög.

Be you on the stage of a theater of war, education or evolution, the only learning experience better than the one gleaned from our own mistakes, is the one deduced from the mistakes of our peers.

Vladimir has made a point of striving to master this very method of self-learning in a timely and efficient manner. He has applied this method to strategically and methodically evolve the social, geopolitical, and economic process-control systems under his sphere of influence. With every systematic process-control tweak, he has expanded the size and importance of his sphere of influence. More importantly than any successful expansion, he has demonstrated the ability to apply just the right amount of force, energy, and work to each individual process loop, so as to stabilize, and bring to rest his share of the newly-expanded Sino-Russian Empire.

Of interest, he has taught himself this control methodology, not only from the mistakes incurred by the peers outside his sphere of influence, but just as importantly, from those committed by his Leninist and Stalinist compatriots.

Despite, or more likely because of their envious discretion, Vladimir's sinological consorts are just as apt as he in the successful application of empire-building control methodology. They are responsible, after all, for authoring, "The Art of War".

...

"At News-Talk 99.9 FM and on your smart-phone at newstalk999.com here is a 99 second news update for Monday, July 21st, 2014...

... In the small town of Coudubonk, the main municipal building including the Fire Department, nearly burnt to the ground early this morning. According to Ronald Smith-Bourque, Coudubonk's fire chief, a preliminary investigation suggests an incendiary device crashed on the front doorstep of the building, the former possibly being a flaming Ford Ranger pickup truck located halfway inside what used to be the latter. Foul play may or may not be suspected by the authorities, as they have yet to receive the results of a breathalyser test performed on the suspected driver of the pickup truck who was seen exiting the driver side of said vehicle moments before said building went up in flames.

We sent out our man-on-the-scene, Stew Santos, and he was amazed to find significant and disastrous damage to the front northern section of the municipal building. Several municipal employees were present, including an RCMP officer. Stew did get a firsthand account of the event from a Coudubonk resident who witnessed the blaze while exiting a local diner earlier this morning ...

- Ya, wehl you know, da flames were at leeest forrr feeet igh when I left Border Biker Bistro dis morning. I wasan't sure if it was the local dru ... I mean Smith-Bourque Conveniaance and Gas Baaarrr or the munecepal building that was tor... I mean burrr-ning until I got into my trock to take a closser lok.

... And in other news ..."

♲

organ: from the Latin *organum, literally tool, instrument;* akin to the Greek *ergon* work ... a differentiated structure consisting of cells and tissues and performing some specific function in an organism... a subordinate group or organization that performs specialized functions.

organic: forming the integral element of a whole ... having systematic coordination of parts: organized < an organic whole >.

contrived: Artificial. Labored.

A process-control loop, or process, can be either organic or contrived. An organic process can be natural, artificial, or a hybrid of both. A contrived process is by definition meant to be formed or created in an artistic or ingenious manner.

An organic process is one that is not only whole, but has been created in a past time and space. As such it should be controlled from the outside in. Either by manipulation or infiltration.

A contrived process is one that is built from the ground up. As such it should be controlled from the inside out, either by remote or local intervention.

Ægir

"You are listening to the Eurasian Broadcasting Cooperative at 106.9 FM and on your smart-phone at 1069ebc.com. At the sound of the tone, following ten seconds of silence it will be precisely one o'clock, Saturday, April 4th, 2015. Blip, blip, blip, blip, blip, blip, blip, blip, blip, blip, beeeeeeeeeeep...

... The Russian consulate in Yemen successfully orchestrated the airlift of several British subjects of the Dominion of Canada, in this war torn region which has digressed into chaos, following the fall of the majority Zedi regime by minority Houtou rebels. The Houti militias are supported, recruited, and trained by their compatriots in Iran. The Zedi are a hybrid sect, mainly Shiite, with overtones of Sunni, borrowed from their Muslim consorts. The Houti are Shiite that adhere to a strict religious doctrine, similar to the orthodox Shiite of Iran.

The refugees were flown by Æroflot jetliners to the relative security of the Amman international airport in Jordan. The flights were paid for in their entirety by the Kremlin as a gesture of human empathy in the name of the Russian people. The British subjects were then transferred to a series of Air Canada transcontinental jets, where they were reunited with their loved ones at Pearson International Airport in Brampton, Ontario, the Dominion of Canada..."

...

As prewar propaganda gœs, it sure beats recruiting posters portraying caricatures of British babies skewered on the tips of bayonets, held by assault-rifle touting German troupes, at the start of regional conflicts that digressed into "The War to end All Wars".

You got to give it to Vladimir, Angela, and François, as they diffuse the particle physics splitting intentions of the Kremlin-backed Shiite puppet regime inside the fundamentalist wasp nest of Persia.

Last summer, there was a wasp nest growing on the trunk of a poplar tree, deep in my back yard. It started small enough, and slowly grew until it got to be huge: the size of large watermelon. I didn't have the money for an industrial quantity of pesticide to zap it into oblivion, so I had only two other possibilities left.

Whack it off the tree with the backside of a spade, or step back and leave it be.

Whacking it with a blunt instrument would only of gotten the flying colonists inside the nest, angry.

So, I stepped back and left the venomous critters alone.

I figure Vladimir has had to deal with his fair share of oversized wasp nests: be it in the back yard of his presidential palace on the outskirts of Moscow, or his palatial retreat on the shores of the Black Sea.

The last fourteen millenniums of observation have resulted in a simple truism. Evolution progresses with symbiosis, and sacrifice. It digresses with confrontation and greed.

The same applies to the top-of-the-food-chain predators in a forest, as it dœs to the top-of-the-food-chain predators in a global empire. Same process. Different ecosystem.

A viscous northeaster, strong enough to rip some lesser trees off their root system, shredded the wasp nest. The venomous critters abandoned their colony, and moved on.

All that Vladimir had to do was pull a little tight on the strings, and tell his puppets in Syria and Iran to step back. The tribal instincts of Arabia's border-less religious factions did the rest.

Like the gale-force winds unleashed by the pent-up fury of a Caribbean hurricane racing up the Atlantic coast, a thousand years of pent-up religious frustrations, were unleashed in the fury of an expanding caliphate, fueled by its power-broker's impulses of greed and confrontation.

All with a simple act of symbiosis and sacrifice.

Vladimir?.. Go Girl, you're on a roll.

Draco

"You are listening to the Central Broadcasting Cooperative at 106.9 FM and on your smart-phone at 1069cbcftqsq.com. At the sound of the tone, following ten seconds of silence it will be precisely one o'clock, Friday, July 25th, 2014. Blip, blip, blip, blip, blip, blip, blip, blip, blip, beeeeeeeeeeep...

For the first time in Spain's monarchist history, a member of the Spanish royal family was convicted of a criminal offense. Sonia Perez, the sister of Spain's senior royal monarch, was arrested for fraud and tax evasion, at her mountain-top villa just inside the Spanish-Andorran border of this feudal co-principality, the latter straddling the Spanish-French border in the northwest corner of Spain.

In a country economically devastated by the repercussions from the bursting of the 2008 global housing bubble and the continued political unrest fueled by decades of ETA terrorism, this latest spat of controversy will most certainly plunge the royal family's approval ratings to historic lows.

... In local news ...

The two bodies that were found dead in a house located in the Northern New Brunswick village of Howard, about 15 kilometers southeast of Schwarzdorf, have been positively identified as Nicole Poirier, 62 and her husband Raymond Poirier, 68 years of age. According to the neighbors, the couple had recently moved to Howard on a permanent basis following Raymond Poirier's retirement, where he worked for over three decades as a lobster fisherman in the small coastal town of Santa Anna. Autopsies will be practiced today to determine the exact cause of each death. Captain Sébastien Lapierre of the local detachment of the RCMP has yet to determine if foul play was involved and refuses to speculate on what Captain Lapierre refers to as premature speculation."

As Morry turned off the radio, the faintest of nostalgia-tinged crocodile tears rolled down his left cheek.

- Raymond was the best *fister* I've ever encountered: Ssall hands, impeccably manicured fingernails, and a slow-moving rhythmic penetration. He was one of the rare *fisters* that could thrust all the way to his elbow. Granted, his insistence of me being always bound, gagged and in full drag made things a little awkward. None-the-less, going through a fisting session with Raymond was always a memorable experience.

Without hesitation, JP wiped the tear off Morry's cheek.

- I thought Dr. Weiβer was your favorite.
- With all those collar-rectal cancer screenings he's performed at the Bellstadt Health and Wellness Center, he's had a lot of exploratory experience. He-he. Basil is excellent when starting a scene, but never gœs all the way to the elbow unless he is high on *crystal meth.* But enough about Basil, what about you?

- After all those cases of Jack Daniels Grand Papa downed over the years, I always thought it was his liver that would've done him in. He could polish off a whole bottle in one evening and be on his lobster boat at 4 o'clock the next morning. It's Grand Ma I'm not too sure about. She was acting funny as of late. I guess the autopsies will give an idea of what happened.
- Yes. Rest her soul.

¿?

If you want to take a living history class of what used to be known as Lower Canada, there are two routes you can borrow to do so. The 138 on the North Shore and the 132 on the South Shore of the Saint-Laurence river. Each, in turn, become the main street of the oldest villages, towns, and cities of what now has become the Dominion's Province of Quebec.

At the crossroads of Quebec-City's main street 138, and the Dominion's Old Capital east-west dividing line, Henri-Bourassa Boulevard, lies Hôpital Enfant-Jésus. What used to be a Vatican-controlled hospital, catering to the city's St-Pascal neighborhood residents, has now become one of the two main trauma centers in North America. The other being in Atlanta, Georgia, a stone's throw away from America's Centers for Disease Control.

Consequently, the concentric design philosophy used in the construction of the Atlanta trauma center, was the same one used to guide the planners of Quebec-City's sister center.

Its innermost ring, houses the trauma center's severe *bio-hazard* unit, and is located directly below the hospital's rooftop heliport. In the center of the ring, are a series of four hermetically-segregated pie-shaped elevator pods, the latter serving the ringed-complex, starting from the underground morgue all the way to the surface of the heliport. Each of the four elevator pods are capable of extending themselves into the belly of a purpose-built helicopter-ambulance, without ever having either the paramedics, the patients nor the pilots coming in contact with the out-side air wafting over the hospital's rooftop.

The subsequent outer-rings of the center, house progressively lower-level *bio-hazard* trauma units, each with their own triage, post-operative, and intensive-care units, in addition to their own operative theaters.

The fluid-mechanics management systems of each ring are independent and sealed from one another, to minimize cross-contamination. All air, water and bodily fluids coming in, and going out of each ringed trauma unit are independently regulated and processed.

Now you may be wondering why these two rural retirees were helicoptered to the severe *bio-hazard* morgue of Hôpital Enfant-Jésus's trauma unit, 600 kilometers away, in the middle of the night, and immediately following their untimely death. Unfortunately, to answer such an inquiry, one would have to ask Mary-Lou. Or better yet, consult her diary.

Fortunately, the heavily-censored proceedings of the final autopsy are now slowly becoming public knowledge...

- Which one do you wish to begin with?
- Let's start with the simplest case. The female.

- Female, Late sixties. Caucasian. 1702 cm. Obese.
- ...

- Clitoral piercing. White gold.
- Cling-clang-clang!

- 33 cm diameter inverse-pentagram, tattoœd to the left of the belly-button. Faded. Deformed. Probably due to stretch marks from earlier pregnancy.
- Shlick-Click! Shlick-Click!

- 10 mm diameter hole, 2mm above the bridge of the nose.
- Shlick-Click! Shlick-Click!

- 12 mm diameter hole at the rear skull. Just above the level of the cerebellum.
- Shlick-Click! Shlick-Click!

- Under the assumption both holes are caused by a single projectile, the latter likely belongs to a no larger than a 9mm bullet, shot at pointblank range. Entering just above the nose bridge and exiting at the rear of skull. Based on preliminary observations, shooter plausibly less than 10 cm taller than victim.
- Ummh… Thunk, thunk...

- Oouuuanhh-oooooooouuunhhhh … ... oooooooouuunhhhh-oouuuanhh.

- Initial full-body MRI scan indicate only one instance of internal trauma at the level of the skull. Linear definition of internal brain damage connecting both previously-observed external instances of head trauma, concurrent with assumption of bullet-wound, and its subsequent projectile trajectory...

- Click, click, clickity, tap, click, clickity, tap...

- One down, one to go.
- I'll go to the fridge.

- Need any help?
- No. That's okay. He's already on the trolley.

- Ooouph. Jigsaw has nothing to teach the perpetrator.
  - I couldn't of said it better.

- OK? Ready? One, two, three.
- Ummh… Thunk, thunk.

- There are simply too many instances of external trauma. Describing each one separately, will take several days. This calls for a picture-tells-a-thousand-words strategy. Do you have a wide angle lens for your SLD?
- Yeah. I have a 20/2.8.

- That will only give you a 30 mm equivalent on a APS-C sensor.
- No. This is a new camera. It's almost identical to the trauma unit's old camera, but there's a full-frame sensor inside instead of an APS-C sensor.

- How do they do that? It's tiny. The camera fits inside your coat pocket.
- I'll go change lenses. I'll be back in a minute ...

- That's a 20/2.8 full-frame lens? That can't be. It's way too small and short.
- Your half right. On a flat sensor this is an APS-C pancake lens. On a curved sensor this lens covers a full-frame surface area. By curving the sensor they were able to remove the lens elements that were used to correct the lens's barrel distortion. The correction is now done by the concave curvature of the sensor. The curvature also increases the light sensitivity of the lens-sensor combination.

- They must have had to optimize the barrel distortion to coincide with the curvature of the sensor.
- Exactly. That's why they changed the optical recipe of this lens. Both on a curved APS-C and a curved full-frame sensor, the lens's geometric distortion is physically corrected by the sensor. No software correction. The RAW files are no longer being manipulated by the sensor's image processor. What's neat is that the sensor's radius of curvature is the same as that of an average human eye.

- I think the Asian average is 22 mm.
- Actually, they used 24mm.

- If I'm not mistaken 24 mm would be based on American data.
- Exactly. It makes it easier for them to bend and set the sensor on the ceramic-matrix-composite sub-frame that's been wave-soldered to the camera's motherboard.

- That makes sense. This must have cost the hospital a fortune.
- Actually, the camera company is also a sensor manufacturer. They have recently invested heavily in expanded sensor production. Economies of scale have made it possible for them to sell a camera like this for less than a thousand dollars. And though not perfect in all instances, most of the old APS-C lenses purchased by the hospital still work fine on this new full-frame camera. The only lens that was really best to upgrade was the 20/2.8. And they packaged it as a kit lens.

- You mean the lens and the camera for under a grand? My old 21/2.8 alone, cost me nearly four times as much. I guess it's a good time for me to finally change from an SLR to a SLD.
- Oomph! Doctors are so conservative.

- Okay, okay. Enough tool-talk. Let's get back to business.
- I will get the step ladder ...

- Do you need any help?
- Just hold the ladder still while I get high enough for an adequate composition. Thanks... Shlick-Click! Shlick-Click! ...

- *Bon*, let's begin. We'll start with the most obvious... Crotch area has scorch marks that have permitted bleeding to stop. Forensic report states they have yet to find the body's genitals.
- Shlick-Click! Shlick-Click!

- Similar scorch marks all over front of body. Scorch marks actually appear to be slash marks burnt all the way through the incision.
- Shlick-Click! Shlick-Click!

- Tongue is also missing. Forensic report states they have yet to find it. Slash-and-scorch marks on inside of mouth. Several teeth have been recently pulled. All molars. Corroborates forensic report which states technicians have found five molars in the vicinity of the crime scene.
- Shlick-Click! Shlick-Click!

- Now for his back-side. OK? Ready? One, two, three.
- Ummh... Thunk. Thunk. ...
- Shlick-Click! Shlick-Click!

- Limited trauma to back side. Only three slash-and-scorch marks on back of neck and head. Corroborates forensic report which states technicians found body strapped to chair at crime scene.
- Want to transfer him now to the MRI?

- Yes, please. Ready? One, two, three.
- Ummh… Thunk. Thunk. …
- Weeeek-weeeek-weeeek-weeeek-weeeek-weeeek-weeeek …

- Ummh… Thunk. Thunk....
- Oouuuanhh-oooooooouuunhhhh … ... oooooooouuunhhhh-oouuuanhh.
- No internal trauma detected by initial MRI. Upper and lower intestines saturated. We best proceed with physical examination of abdominal cavity...
- Weeeek-weeeek-weeeek-weeeek-weeeek-weeeek-weeeek …

- Ready? One, two, three.

- Ummh… Thunk, thunk. …
- Vomit, pieces of tongue and pieces of male genitals found in intestinal cavity.
- Well that explains the dental dam.

¿?!

The autopsy report is sent to the National RCMP headquarters in Ottawa.

Captain Lapierre gets a censored copy.
Captain John Thébeau, dœsn't.

The-Shrinking-P is interviewed and released without being arrested.
JP is interviewed and released without being arrested.

Morry is interviewed and cracks a smile.
A trademark Acadian smile.

...

"At News-Talk 99.9 FM and on your smart-phone at newstalk999.com here is a 99 second news update for Monday, July 28th, 2014...

... In the small village of Millstadt, ten kilometers due north of Coudubonk, the main municipal building including the Fire Department and the municipal council chambers burnt to the ground early this morning. According to Ronald Bourque-Smith, Millstadt's fire chief, a preliminary investigation suggests an electrical fire could be the cause of the blaze. Foul play has yet to be ruled out by the authorities.

We sent out our man-on-the-scene, Stew Santos, and he was amazed to find but a smoldering pile of indistinguishable rubble where the municipal building used to stand, less than four hours after the first sitings of fire were observed at the site. Stew did get a firsthand account of the event from a Millstadt resident who witnessed the blaze while exiting a local diner earlier this morning ...

- Ya, wehl you know, da flames were at leeest twantii feeet igh when I left Gallant Dii-ner and Maple Sugar Shack dis morning. I wasan't sure if it was the local dru ... I mean Gallant Conveniaance and Gas Baaarrr or the munecepal building that was tor... I mean burrr-ning until I got into my trock to take a closser lok.

... The Dominion's highest court today, stuck down the controversial RCMP investigative technique known as the Mr. Big Sting. The operation is used to obtain confessions from recalcitrant criminals. A series of undercover RCMP officers pose as members of an organized crime gang and offer the suspect the possibility to meet Mr Big, the syndicate's kingpin. Once in contact with Mr Big, the latter pushes the criminal to confess his prior deed as a condition to entering the organization.

This tactic was used in the well publicized case of Moishe Leclerc, an unemployed former cod fisherman, from the coastal New Brunswick town of Santa Anna. Mr. Leclerc confessed to drowning his two daughters during the filming of a snuff film commissioned by an organized child pornography ring. The RCMP recuperated a copy of the film, in a separate investigation, but were unable to positively identify the two juvenile victims being murdered in the video.

The results of the sting operation were dismissed as inadmissible by the Supreme Court judges reviewing the former conviction of Mr. Leclerc. The judges' reasoning in overturning the conviction is based on their realization that the Mr Big technique is unconstitutional and contravenes the Dominion's charter of human rights.

In addition, the video was dismissed as credible evidence following the defense's presentation of a nearly identical video created using sophisticated – but readily available – CGI and post-processing imaging software. In the defense's version of the film, the juvenile actors were wearing full-body blue-suits and were never touched by any third party during the filming.

When both, the film used as evidence by the Crown, and the defense's version were played side-by-side, none of the judges were able to tell them apart...

... And in other news ...

... In the small village of Coudubonk, fifty kilometers east of the Maine[2] border, Jacob Van Brohken aka Marc Van Brohken, a dutch national originally from the large village of Den Haag, was arrested by the Ottawa RCMP's National detachment responsible for cross-border enforcement.

Mr Van Brohken, with the alleged collusion of members belonging to the Schwarzdorf cell of the Kopfschmuck criminal biker gang, was charged locally for orchestrating the export of prescription opiates, locally-grown medical marijuana, and treaty aboriginal and mestizo prostitutes, without a license.

Jacob aka Marc, 51, who has been hiding in New Brunswick for well over a decade, is now also in the process of being extradited to Den Haag, for a series of charges dating as far back as the early nighties.

These charges include, but are yet to be limited to, orchestrating the import of Dominion-made prescription opiates, New-Brunswick-grown medical marijuana, and treaty aboriginal and mestizo prostitutes, without a license.

Extradition papers, leaked to the national news desk of the Central Broadcasting Cooperative, stipulate that these alleged transnational crimes were orchestrated with the suspected collusion of members belonging to *Den*[2] Haag cell of the Kopfschmuck criminal biker gang.

In addition to these charges, Van Brohken is wanted on an Interpol arrest warrant, applied for by both the Netherlands' Den Haag police force, and France's Burgundy Regional Constabulary, to face charges including, but yet to be limited to, professional malpractice, fraud, and to at least two charges of first degree murder possibly related to those mentioned earlier.

The Interpol arrest warrant, leaked to the national news desk of the Central Broadcasting Cooperative, stipulate that these alleged Euro-zone crimes were perpetrated during a time when Van Brohken was masquerading as a Netherlands-based dentist serving clients in both *Den*[2] Haag and Burgundy countrysides."

...

- Things are getting coarser as we go along.
- Thank the Giants for Draco.

- One of the finest of instigators.
- To be expected.

- He has had nearly three millenniums of experience.
- The leaves are turning. I can feel the thunder.

nation: from the Latin *nation-, natio* birth, race, nation, from *natus,* past participle of *nasci* to be born...

The concept of nation is dynastic, and neither tribal, nor territorial in nature and origin. When defined as a tribe or a federation of tribes, history has shown that such entities are doomed to fossilize into archæological ruin. When defined as a territory, such entities are almost always subjected to the whims of technology, aggression, intimidation, provocation and greed, instigated from outside its borders.

A kingdom's time-span is measured in cycles of nations. A realm's time-span is measured in cycles of universal evolution.

There I go again. Getting ahead of myself.

The relationship between the Peanutbuttercup 13 – affectionately known as PB-13 – and the Kopfschmuck gangs, was a tenuous one at the best of times. PB-13's spheres of influence have always been contraband cigarettes, gun running and aboriginal pimping. The Kopchmucks criminal line-up was primarily, cocaine and *crystal-meth.* Both shared, intimidation, extortion and marijuana grow-op duties.

Things got complicated when MS-13 killer-heroin dealers started popping up on the American side of the Maine-New Brunswick border.

And were looking to divide and conquer, on both sides of the border.

☠⚕

- Got it?
- Got it.

- Good.

Though far from being a psychiatrist, or even a criminal psychologist, he could spot an ideal psychiatric profile when he saw one.

All that was left was to instigate at the right time... and place.

☠☠☠

"You are listening to the Central Broadcasting Cooperative at 106.9 FM and on your smart-phone at 1069cbcftqsq.com. At the sound of the tone, following ten seconds of silence it will be precisely one o'clock, Tuesday, July 29th, 2014. Blip, blip, blip, blip, blip, blip, blip, blip, blip, beeeeeeeeeeep...

...shale gas protests turned violent in Kent County today, as protesters clashed with Kent County RCMP officers at a blockade on route 245 near Rexton. The blockade was put in place two weeks ago by members of the Reesespeanutbuttercup first nation to prevent Boar Resources Ltd from accessing drilling equipment stored on land near the blockade.

Kent County officers had difficulty restoring order as the group of protesters threw Molotov cocktails and began shooting at the police with hunting rifles. Six RCMP police cars were set ablaze. Police retaliated with bean bags and rubber bullets. Several arrests were made but only after several hours of confrontation.
News of the violent protests spread with the speed of social media and before Kent County protesters were even booked, several other blockades in New Brunswick, Nova Scotia and as far away as Manitoba were set up by native groups in a sign of solidarity for their comrades in arms.

Our reporter on the scene, had an opportunity to record comments from Ethel Featherdress just before she was to be arrested by officers at the blockade.

- We are here today not only to protest the development of shale gas on our territory but also to reiterate our sovereignty over our ancestral land. As native people, we do not recognize the laws of the foreign British Imperialists who have always been considered unwelcome guests on our land. Just like the FLQ had to take up arms to defend Quebec's sovereignty, we the people of the Reesespeanutbuttercup first nation shall do the same.

... And in other news..."

Would it be an understatement to say that John's immediate criminal superiors were quite pleased by the outcome from the events of the past few hours?

Not only will this latest uprising tax the already limited judicial and law enforcement resources of the immediate region, but the failure of the Kent County RCMP to contain the uprising will finally result in undermining the credibility of the Kent detachment.

All to the professional, organizational and criminal benefit of the Kopfschmuck-controlled Kodiak detachment.

Or not.

...

Crime always flourishes in a flowerbed of chaos.

Future

"At News-Talk 99.9 FM and on your smart-phone at newstalk999.com, this is the weekend edition of Atlantic Morning with your host Scott Duftwasser. And now here is your host Scott Duftwasser.

- The controversy surrounding the development of shale fracking has heated up in the last week with the protests in Kent County meeting violent opposition by unwavering law enforcement and political regimes. In a sign of recognition for the courage and moral aptitude exhibited by the members of our first nations communities, solidarity protests have ignited all over North America. To speak to us about this evolving situation we have in studio Lisette Brummbär of the Maritime Coalition of Anti-Fracking Suporters...

- Good morning, Ms Brummbär, and welcome. To start, what is your opinion on the protests that turned violent last week.
- Based on what I have heard from representatives of the Reeesespeanutbuttercup first nation a climate of intimidation and provocation has been instigated by the law enforcement officials on site at the blockade.

- So are you suggesting that it's the police that started the violence and that the first nation people only retaliated in defense of their sovereign rights as founding people of the Americas. Not to put words in your mouth, but the unsubstantiated claims of the police saying that it's the protesters that started the violence shouldn't be taken at face value, especially with regard to the history of outstanding moral behavior of the first nation people.
- Though we do not condemn violence of any sort, the fact that the first nation people do not abide by the laws of the imperialist occupiers of this native land and has been substantiated by the support upwelling from social media and the *blogosphere*. Just like the Libyan rebels demonstrated their moral and ethical superiority by overthrowing the fascist Qadhafi regime with the help of social media, so shall the first natios overcome the obstacles set forth by the provincial and Herumtreiber regimes. We are open to negotiations with regards to shale fracking in New Brunswick as long as Boar Resources Ltd leave New Brunswick permanently and that all other gas companies never come back here to endeavor in shale gas exploration or exploitation of any sort.

- And it's precisely this willingness to negotiate, that in my opinion, has cemented your organization's credibility and that has brought on international support for your cause.
- Yes, support has been overwhelming. All over the Atlantic provinces and from New York to Boulder, Colorado, from Los Angeles to Vancouver, solidarity protests have ignited in support of our mission.

- I want to thank you, Ms Brummbär for stopping by our studios this morning. It has been a truly enlightening conversation. We'll be back for more of the weekend edition of Atlantic Morning after this 99 second news update."

"At News-Talk 99.9 FM and on your smart-phone at newstalk999.com here is news for Wednesday July 30th, 2014...

Early this morning, members of the native community confiscated all broadcasting equipment and media trucks from Earthsphere Communications and the Canadian Telecommunications and Vision network news teams at the site of the continuing blockade against shale gas exploration on route 245. Central Broadcasting Cooperative media trucks were not affected by this seizure. We would like to make sure to let the listening audience know that all equipment was returned unharmed after Earthsphere Communications and the CTV network agreed to unbiased and objective interviews on their local and regional radio and television stations...

... In international news, former Libyan rebels that now have formed a provisional government in this North African nation, have been accused of widespread torture against former Qadhafi government officials and against members of rival rebel groups that failed to take control of the government after the death of Colonel Muammar Abu Minyar al-Qadhafi. Though the claims are unsubstantiated, several members of Amnesty International have conducted interviews and have observed clear signs of physical abuse and post traumatic stress disorder amongst the alleged victims..."

⚡⚕

- I must be getting old. I was to mention the best instigators are those that don't know they are ones to begin with.
- Memory is a faculty that forgets.

- Thank the Gods for Fundamentalism.

·V

"You are listening to the Central Broadcasting Cooperative at 106.9 FM and on your smart-phone at 1069cbc.com. At the sound of the tone, following ten seconds of silence it will be precisely one o'clock, Thursday, July 31th, 2014. Blip, blip, blip, blip, blip, blip, blip, blip, blip, beeeeeeeeeeep...

... A court injunction banning protests at sites operated by Boar Resources Ltd has been lifted by Justice Ridein of Mengen Provincial Court today. The lifting of this injunction places in doubt the validity of several if not all the arrests made by the Kent County RCMP earlier in the week, after violence erupted at the Peanutbuttercup First Nation's blockade on route 245.

Chief Ted Featheronthewater of the Assembly of Buttercup First Nations, bolstered by the international recognition garnered by the recent Shale gas protests in Rexton, is expanding his demands beyond those concerning resource mining and exploitation:

- We are now going to the Court of Queen's Bench to claim all crown lands in New Brunswick including those being leased to Boar Resources Ltd.

... And in other news ...

... In the Mengen suburb of Salisbury, Arthur B. Goodyear, an officer with the RCMP Kent-South detachment, was arrested by members of the neighboring Kodiak Detachment, following a recent undercover investigation.

Constable Goodyear, an Innu from the Torngat mountains of Northern Labrador, was stationed at the Peanutbuttercup First Nation reserve, half an hour north of Salsbury. He has been charged with possession of cocaine for the purposes of trafficking. He is also suspected of sourcing cocaine from an unknown local supplier, and delivering it to his Native reserve in Labrador."

...

- One side instigates
- The Other Side instigates.

- One side retaliates.
- The Other Side retaliates.

- Thank the Giants for Sex.

ⓌD·

To better understand the plausible probabilities offered to us by the future, sometimes you have to look at the past from a different perspective than the one generally accepted.

Take a standard globe, and look at the planet from the North Pole instead of the standard equatorial perspective. Two affirmations become blatantly transparent. One well established, the other, less so.

We have been taught from our very first elementary-school geography class to recognize the preponderant bias of the northern hemisphere in terms of landmass. Now take that same globe, and look at the planet from the South Pole. This exercise demonstrates the established geographical and geopolitical insignificance of the southern hemisphere compared to it northern counterpart.

When we flip the globe back to a North-Pole perspective, and one looks at the planet from inside the 60°N latitudinal circle, you will notice just how much landmass from two of the largest countries on the planet fall inside that relatively small hemispherical slice of the marble.

That's when the second affirmation comes into focus. Russia and Northern Asia become much closer neighbors to Alaska and Canada than first perceived, when we look at the world from the North Pole rather than from the equator.

Stepping back less than eight hundred years, most of that hemispherical slice's landmass, west of the Bearing Strait was under the domination of the former Mongolian Empire.

The two affirmations described earlier, are the foundations of a theory stating that the majority of aboriginal tribes that now inhabit the disparate set of reserves across Canada and the United-States, originally exited Mongolia, in and around a relatively closed-spaced geopolitical time-frame in the Mongol's history.

The questions beg. If the Mongol tribes exited their homeland, never to return, why did they leave, and more importantly why did they not retain their Mongolian heritage and ties to the leaders who were in the process of building a North-Asian kingdom?

If they left voluntarily, or as subjects of this burgeoning kingdom, why weren't there any Mongolian principalities established on the shores of North America, when the Europeans first landed on the latter, half a millennium ago?

Now you could dismiss all three of these questions, simply by inferring that those who exiled themselves from their homeland into the civil desolation on the east side of the Bearing Strait, did so centuries before anyone even contemplated the strategies and processes necessary to conquer and build a globally-imposing Eurasian Empire. Your dismissive conclusions would plausibly be valid, if you frame time in a geopolitical envelop.

Less so, if that envelop is evolutionary in nature.

Even if we go back two or three millenniums, to a time when the idea of embarking on an empire-building adventure was barely a glimmer in the eyes of Chinggis Kahn's ancient ancestors, that conquering spirit would have already been mapped into the genetic heritage of those defined ancestors. Regardless of the structure the Mongolian nation took during those ancient times, it would be just that. A nation.

"At 99.9 FM and at 999solfm.com here is the news for Friday, August 1st, 2014 …

… Pierre Elliot Gallant, the suspect in the murders of three RCMP officers on June 4th, in Mengen, was found fit to stand trial, following a six-week psychiatric evaluation, at the Peanutbuttercup Healing Center. Sporting long, black hair and a patchy beard, he presented himself to Judge Ted Ridein of Mengen Provincial Court, where a trial by judge and jury was determined.

In unrelated news, Chief Ted Featheronthewater's tax-less, 1.3 million dollar annual salary was put into question today, by the New Brunswick Legislature's opposition finance critic. The most damning part of the finance critic's questioning, was when he commented on the fact that the Chief of the Peanutbuttercup First Nation has only 37 members inside the limits of its reserve...

... After months of investigation, spanning from Vancouver to Toronto, and Montreal to Saint-John, New Brunswick, a highly organized criminal organization was hit a major blow by the RCMP's child abuse division, as several suspected child pornographers were arrested and their computers confiscated, including one Mengen resident, taken into custody by members of the Fredericton RCMP. Five prepubescent boys were also rescued from the hands of there abusers."

...

- The time was right.
- It was worth the wait.

- The conquest will soon begin.
- Everywhere.

- Criminal gangs, drug dealers and mafia kingpins, don't build empires.
- Neither do SŒeys.

- In times of peace and war, you will find such undesirables, at worst in the heartlands of civil desolation.
- At best as the puppet-instigators of a future desolation.

- Desolation cleans the slate.
- And the puppet-instigators.

- A new empire can be built from the rubble left behind.
- By the puppeteers.

- Thank the Giants for Greed.

If you still have your globe close by, pick it up and look at the world from a standard equatorial perspective. Now lets try to figure out where the Mayans came from and why their civilization devolved into irrelevancy five hundred years before the Spanish Conquest.

To begin this exercise, may I suggest we adopt a focused science-and-technology mindset, rather than the more widely-used historical-and-archæological one. The Ancient Egyptians being a people of the Sahara Desert, traveling from east to west across the latter is not much of stretch for such a technologically advanced civilization.

But why bother.

With the Mediterranean Sea to the north, and their technological prowess guiding their innovations, Egyptians would be accomplished navigators, not to mention excellent ship builders. If you can travel over three thousand kilometers between Alexandria and the Strait of Gibraltar, your ship should be designed, engineered and built to be more than adequately seaworthy to travel between the shores of what are now Casablanca and Belize City, two or three Millenniums before Jesus of Nazareth's virgin birth.

Now that we have explained the advent of the Mayan temples, let us try to figure out why the Mayans act like Egyptians, but only look a little like the latter, a little like the Incas to south, and a little like the Amerindians to the north. If you are more into genetics than virgin births...

Now we just have to figure out the Mayans' devolution into irrelevancy. While keeping focused on an intuitive science mindset, let us add the study of etymology to the mix...

Inca: Spanish from Quechua *inka king, prince.*
Quechua: Spanish from Quechua *kkechúwa, plunderer, robber...*

...

- Well, that opened up a can of worms.
- I'm hungry.

- Worms are only good for robins.
- Robins, the most annoying of neighbors.

☟☣☩

"You are listening to the Central Broadcasting Cooperative at 96.9 FM and on your smart-phone at 969cbc.com. At the sound of the tone, following ten seconds of silence it will be precisely one o'clock, Monday, August 3rd, 2015. Blip, blip, blip, blip, blip, blip, blip, blip, blip, beeeeeeeeeeep...

...An icon of the Central Broadcasting Cooperative's Queen City Headquarters was found this morning without vital signs, in an alleyway next to his Eastern Ave. condo.

Abraham Lowman, the co-host of the popular lifestyle TV show Moishe & Abraham was dearly loved for his joyful and audacious demeanor.

His husband, Moishe Rabinavitch, was the other half of Moishe & Abraham. Together they started celebrating diversity on a number of similar shows and broadcasting networks, years before Ontario instituted its first openly lesbian Premier.

Abraham's mother, figured he fell from his penthouse patio. Her son told her that he was prone to daydreaming, and worse, night walking, ever since the couple moved into their Eastern Ave. home.

We will keep you posted as this tragic story unfolds..."

...

They felled the maple trees and tore down the brown brick townhouse to make way for a new condo development. The guests that once inhabited the former townhouse were as audacious as Abraham could ever be. But far more discrete.

Many were daydreamers, and night walkers. Creatives.

The living abandoned the townhouse. Their past, their pasts haunting its walls and its courtyard.

Equality for all. At all costs.

They moved to the walls of their new home. Built on the ruins of their formers foundations and its courtyard.

Greed, Sex, and Fundamentalism.
Processing the processed.
The condo and its occupants.
The townhouse and it's courtyard.

Time pushing them all to their penultimate ørlög.

Resistance

"From the heart of Milwaukee, Wisconsin this is The Fractionation Hour. Dr Gilles Johanson is the first in Wisconsin and the first in The Great Lakes Region, with fractionated radio surgery. Conveniently located next door to The Hog, Hondy-Johanson Owners Group's main headquarters, museum and Milwaukee's largest biker bar and pub...

- Hey Dr Johanson, we're baack.
- Yes, we're back. The Milwaukee Fractionation Center is a private cancer clinic specializing in non-invasive radio surgery precisely targeting cancerous growths of all shapes and sizes found anywhere on the client's body. Some of the most difficult cancers to treat with traditional methods, such as chemotherapy, are brain metastases (sarcomas). Our custom engineered PET-Scanner/Radio-Surgery-Carbon-Maiden not only effectively immobilizes the client during the duration of the treatment session, but also gives real-time, three dimensional imaging of the active brain and surrounding tissues.

The Proton Exchange Transfer Scanner is self-explanatory. The Radio-Surgery-Carbon-Maiden may need a bit of explaining. The Carbon-Maiden part of this device is, simply put, a short fiber, carbon reinforced thermoplastic matrix "Iron Maiden". The device is 3D printed where the inside surface is defined using a full body anthropomorphic PET scan of the patient, and the outer surface includes the support mechanism to the PET scanner and the precisely positioned tapped holes used to secure the radio-heads whose position is defined by the previous PET scan's imaging of the metastasized nodules. Each mobile radio-head is built on a spherical joint permitting the proper freedom of movement of each radio-head targeting a unique cancerous nodule during the treatment session".

?♚☭☦⚠⚑⚖♚¿

- Look!! To The Southwest. Over the horizon.
- Wow. Now that's dark.

- They called the last one Hurricane Claudette. She's now just a tropical storm skimming over the eastern tip of Newfoundland.
- What a coincidence. Newfoundland is the home protectorate of Louis de Ville-Amois's mother-in-law.

- An astute observation. If you're into mutual female homœrotic daydreams of a slightly distant past. Where do you think the epicenter is located?
- Somewhere over The Caribbean. It's hard to tell from here.

- I think it's over Juan Dolio.
- That's as good a segue as any.

- You read me like a book.
- You read me like a romance novel.

- Why do you think the National RCMP Director hasn't yet linked the killing of three Kodiak RCMP officers in Mengen by an aboriginal extremist, the killing of an RCMP officer in Edmonton by an aboriginal drug dealer, and the patently evident love triangle between the Kodiak RCMP, The Kopfschmucks Biker Gang, and the aboriginal drug-dealing-arms-running-anti-fossil-fuel-extremist-instigating tribal gangs?
- Not to mention the hate triangle forming between The Cree, Innu, and Mohawks of The Dominion's Province of Quebec.

- Over all things, the exploitation of natural resources!
- Ouf... The grotesque beauty of greed fermenting hypocrisy.

- You are such a hopeless romantic.
- You can't learn to love if you haven't learned to hate.

- And this is supposed to be the least romantic day of the year.
- Where did you find that tidbit?

- During my latest attempt over the Information Super Highway.
- Did you look both ways before crossing?

- Like a boyscout, I'm always prepared.
- If it comes from the Magical Web-net, it must be true.

- Ouf... We're both doing a Mulroney. You haven't answered the question yet.
- OK, OK. I think he's clueless.

- That is in the realm of possibilities. But what about, the link between the sudden uprising of rage against American police forces using long established standard operating procedures, the killing of nine parishioners in the Southern Bible Belt, and the silent condoning of this tinderbox rage by a self-proclaimed South-Chicago drug dealer turned El Presidente?
- Not to mention the sudden, knee-jerk demonetization of The Confederate Flag. I see a pattern forming.

- Or reforming. Like a process control loop.
- A process that will evolve with time.

∇Δ∇

- The waters are beginning to clear. I'm beginning to see the bottom.
- You are no longer looking into an undefined future. You are inside a present moment of observation.

- They would not have cleared had I not focused on the logistics of the conflict.
- So the resistance is not between the Eurasians and the Mediterraneans?

- No, its between the Ancient Hasidim and the Modern Hasidim.
- Exactly!

☭☪☩

From the forest of the Laurentian Mountains, they sowed the logs into 25 foot six-by-sixes for the main frame posts; three-by-sixes for the strapping benches and three inch thick, twenty-four inch wide slabs for the head gallows.

Nari and Victor-Louis would be proud.

From the northern forests of Finland, they sourced the blades. hammer struck from the finest tooling steel. Annealed and sharpened to a razor's edge. A National Razor.

Tom and Uli would be proud.

They put the lumber in containers that would be shipped across the Atlantic. They put the blades on rail cars that would be shipped across Northeastern Russia and Europe.

The cargo would be unloaded at the Port of Saint-Malo at the foot of Mont Saint-Michel Abbey. There, the New Ones would be assembled. The Old Ones long forgotten in nondescript warehouses on the outskirts of urban cities and rural villages of Portugal.

Laurent and Josée-Anne would be proud.

All six reveling in the pœtic justice of *La Troisième Terreur*: the Third Terror. French noblemen exchanging positions with Arab tribesmen.

They felled the maple trees.

...

Winter begins. Both sides lost.

Time discarded: hunting the hunters and the prep~~ar~~ers alike. Food for fodder, wolves and bears, lest we forget the tree monkeys.

All three at the top of the food chain: one that binds them to Greed, Sex and the Fundamentalism of survival. Motivations they will need to modulate, lest they forget the errors of their peers.

They know: better to inhabit the forest. Their ørlög can be seen on the horizon of its edges. A reminder to place Symbiosis over Confrontation, Evolution over Innovation and Cogitation over Faith.

Will their observations permit them to succeed? When it returns, Time will tell.

The Ravens will guide them.

⑤

Frederick was born in Normandy but moved to Sicily when he attained the judicial age of 21. That same year, he became the Holy Roman Emperor of the Kingdom of Sicily. Synchrony notwithstanding, back in Runnymede, King John's signature had yet to dry on the original manuscript of the Magna Carta.

Oh, the Magna Carta. What would modern society be without it?

All that was missing was a new university to give King John's Royal Assent credibility. It took nine years to build, on the eastern shore of the Tyrrhenian sea.

Officially, for the Neapolitan "Upper Crust", the opening ceremony was the most anticipated social event of the year, if not the decade. Unofficially, it was the second.

Latter that night, inside an ancient grotto on the outskirts of the capital, a secret ceremony would begin. There, Frederick would pledge allegiance to the tribal doctrine of Islam, making him the first Gran Kahuna of the Sicilian Mafia, and consequently, the original instigator of the concepts of *omerta* and common law.

...

- Well, that sums things up.
- In a nutshell.

- Mmm, nuts. You're making me hungry.
- You're always hungry. What's your favorite?

- Walnuts. But I prefer to scavenge for peanuts. The shells are easier to crack.
- I concur.

- We will have to settle for maple seeds for today.
- At least they're in season.

- CRACK!, PET!!, KABOOM!!!,KABOOM!!!, KABOOM!!!, KABOOM!!!, KABOOM!!!, KABOOM!!!

The explosions were caused by the rising magma forcing its way up the groundwater. Water serving the Kirkjubæjarklaustur villagers. The craters and fissures on both sides of Laki mountain redefined the surrounding landscape. So much so, that *Lakagígar,* craters of Laki, has become an integral part of the Icelandic lexicon.

200 years before Ozone Depletion, Acid Rain and Climate Change became buzz words of the modern era mass media, *Móðuharðindin,* Mist Hardships, had become a mythical reality for the people of Iceland.

Hardships felt from Reykjavik to Dublin, from the Laurentian mountains to Ville-Perdue, from Washington to Moscow.

Hardships harboring consequences that are not always what they seem to be. The Mist Hardships of 1783 caused far more than a change in global weather patterns lasting several years. Well before the industrial revolution, *Móðuharðindin* had profound repercussions on the empires of the era. Empires formed on the foundations of agrarian societies.

The Kirkjubæjarklaustur eruptions, spewing toxic emissions from the depths of Mother Earth, caused extreme weather events and famine throughout much of Europe.

Freya's morbid cloud of hydrogen fluoride brought death to thousands of subjects from as far away as Egypt to the east and Madagascar to the south, not to mention scores of agrarian quadrupeds, whose owners depended on for their own survival.

Hardships that brought poverty and famine to the *sans culottes* of France, less than half a decade from the closing of the 1780s. Yes, those *sans culottes.*

Death, pestilence, and an empty stomach almost always leads to revolution.

♚⚖☪

Six generations of *sans culottes* revolutionary metastasis has pushed the monarchies of Europe and Eurasia up against the wall. When one's power, influence and authority is at stake, how dœs one push back?

You start a war, of course.

The political and social instability prior to the First World War, bolstered by the domino effects of *La Grande Terreur,* were more than enough reasons for Laurent and Josée-Anne to emigrate to the Dominion.

A century before the establishment of the Age of Information, Laurent was unaware that the rise of Breton nationalism had also metastasized to *Curé Lacloche's* Chanticleer.

The grass is always greener over the septic tank.

- *Vous écoutez "Nos Découvertes d'Ici" sur" Ici Radio Cooperative"*[20], *et voici votre hôte Pierre Bedalini-Martin...*
- You are listening to "Our Discoveries" on "Our Cooperative Radio Network", and here is your host Peter Bedalini-Martin...

- *Aujourd'hui, sur ce plateau, nous avons invité le Docteur Charles Slapulo-Bronfberg. Dr Slapulo-Bronfberg est un chercheur à L'Université Laval, campus de L'Île Perrot. Son expertise est dans le domaine des modifications génétiques à partir d'une nouvelle procédure innovatrice connu suros le nom de Krisper. Pour commencer, docteur, explquez-nous cette nouvelle procédure Krisper...*
- Today, on this sound stage, we have invited Dr Charles Slapulo-Bronfberg. Dr Slapulo-Bronfberg is a research scientist at Laval University, Perrot Island Campus. His domain of expertise is focused on genetic modifications using a new innovative procedure known as Krisper. To start, doctor, explain to us this new procedure called Krisper...

- *La procédure Krisper est une forme de modification génétique active, c'est-à-dire, où la modification est entreprise sur les génes d'un organisme vivant et développé. La modification in vitro est possble mais pas nécessaire. Ma recerche se spécialize dans les thérapies par insertion virale. Les patogènes caractéristiques du virus sont désactivés pour les rendre inertes, pour ensuite être modifiés et ensuite réactivés pour qu'ils puissent attaquer les gènes patogènes d'un patient souffrant, par exemple, d'une maladie congénitale. Les patogènes sont donc désactivés par insertion virale en utilsant la procédure Krisper.*
- The Krisper procedure is an active form of genetic modification, one that is applied to the genes of a live and developed organism. In vitro modifications are possible but not necessary. My research specializes in therapies by viral insertion. The characteristic pathogens of the virus are deactivated to render them inert, then modified and reactivated to attack the pathological genes of a patient suffering, for example, from a congenital disease. The pathogens are deactivated by viral insertion using the Krisper procedure.

20 Ici Radio Coopérative is the french language network of the Central Broadcasting Cooperative.

- *J'ai lu que plusieurs défauts congénitaux communs aux Québecois de Souche pourront être traités par l'application de cette nouvelle technologie médicale.*
- I've read that several congenital defects common to the offspring of the original settlers from Quebec can be treated with this new medical technology.

- *Oui. Nous éudions en ce moment plusieurs maladies congénitales et dégéneratives du cervau qui affectent une proportion significative de la population Québecoise de souche.*
- Yes. We are now studying several congenital and degenerative diseases of the brain affecting a significant proportion of the offspring of the original settlers from Quebec.

- *Merci pour votre vulgarisation éclairante. Docteur. Vous écoutez 'Nos Découvertes d'Ici". Nous serons de retour après les nouvelles nationales et internationales...*
- Thank you, Doctor for your enlightening vulgarization. You are listening to "Our Discoveries". We will be back after the national and international news....

...

- The Propaganda Tower proletariat stuck their foot in it this time.
- The best screw-ups are those where the instigators are clueless.

- It's hard to see where your feet are when your head's up your a**.
- I concur.

- To their credit, or not, they did succeed to avoid mentioning "The Revenge of the Cribs".
- And interbreeding.

- Hey, look! Monseigneur has dropped something on the ground.
- Just before stuffing the same in his mouth.

- The wonders of gluttony.
- They look like walnuts!

- He didn't apply the five second rule.
- The coast is clear. Let's go!

☚∅☛

Curé Lacloche's psychosis was more planned than inherited from his mother.

Angelica Meier is an Enochian witch. Her true faith hidden behind doors of forced hypocrisy, having witnessed her fair share of burnings.

She made a point of leaving her first husband well before Antoine Jr's seventh birthday. The hatred for her son was only equaled for her love of greed and sex. She would find the latter in the same seed as of the former.

Angelica flees to Texas. As she fills out her application papers on a bench outside the border station, she contemplates what to call herself. The first inspiration that caches her evil eye was was wild and pink, on the side of the roadside ditch.

Busch is easier to pronounce in Texan than Meier. Busch it would be.

☘♆♞

Louis' explanation for leaving the priesthood was more an excuse than a reason. Cold feet? Not so sure.

Anymore.

When you have been living two thirds the way around the marble from home for well over a decade, one takes your word for it. He left the Port of Algiers on the second Sunday of May. By the first Friday of June, he was standing in the main hall of the *Île aux Coudres* Reception Center. For one who had just survived a bout of yellow fever, Louis was the healthiest looking man of those quarantined that day.

On the evening of the Summer Solstice, Louis had exited the Chanticleer train station, Laurent to his left, Marie-Josée to his right.

Laurent had mixed feelings.

So did Louis.

Laurent's Alpha male obsession with carrying on the family name, if not its dynasty, dominated over his fundamentalist christian obsession of having at least one son becoming a Roman Catholic priest.

Louis' alpha male obsession with proclaiming his masculinity through traditional sexual expression, dominated over his intuitive obsession to fully understand his own sexuality by having man-to-man encounters throughout his lifetime.

Tradition over intuition? Not so sure.

Anymore.

Now that Louis had abandoned his forcibly chosen profession of the priesthood, Laurent made sure Louis would marry and procreate until a healthy boy is born. If Laurent's son was no longer going to be a priest, he certainly wasn't going to be a *vieux garçon.*

Anymore.

✠☠⚑

It didn't take long for Louis to exorcize the ghosts of his celibate past. By the mid 50's, Anna-Maria had completed her third gestation, and a fourth offspring was already in the oven.

As Louis' family expanded, so did his sphere of influence. By then, Upper Chanticleer was well on its way to becoming prime cottage country for Westmount's wealthy weekenders and a choice tourist destination for the global elite. Having married a Bostonian whose father and mother were born in Wales and the protectorate of Newfoundland respectively, Louis had all the bases covered. With noble parents from Brittany and in-laws from Britain, Louis' strengthening reputation was already in good standing with both the oi-poloi of Lower Chanticleer and the corporate and social elite of Upper Chanticleer. Not to mention both the priests and followers of the Vatican and the Church of England's religious doctrines.

No wonder my family made a point of explaining to me at a relatively young age, that my father never paid protection to the Bedalini and Slapulo bullies. He was considered too respected by the community to have to endure such extortion tactics as a consequence of his entrepreneurial spirit.

◔☀◕

Back when Deep Purple was Deep Purple, I'm not sure If the band members would call a Ted, a Ted. Neither am I sure if the genre of music they were creating, had yet to be coined Metal. After all, I was only ten years old.

By today's standard, Ted was definitely a Ted.

As I was walking on the way home from school, Ted decided to taunt me, before ramming me in with his bike. A successful attempt to impress Jimmy Bedalini. Granted, the bike was only the peddling type.

A decade before the Dominion's Sicilian Mafia had begun transferring enforcer duties to the motorized bike riding Teds, Ted was just as much a bully as his future brethren. As thugs go, he would have made an excellent prospect, if it wasn't for the simple fact that he had received his comeuppance well before having begun the process.

Suffice to say, that to this day, Ted begins his digestive process with the help of a glass stomach rather than the traditional giblets type.

Che sarà, sarà.

...

- I say it will take a generation before Sylvain figures out that when it comes to extortion targets, the thug culture dœsn't give a rat's a** about ones reputation, and even less about their social standing.
- I say it will take two.

- Bet's on.
- A long one, but worth the wait.

- Speaking of giblets, I'm hungry.
- Time for some roadkill hunting. Let's go!

☹☼☺

Once you reach the age of six, your basic character is defined. From that moment on, one of the only events capable of affecting our basic character is a traumatic one.

As with all rules, there are exceptions.

The loss of a parent is not as traumatic as it is restrictive to an offspring's character development. The faster the mourning is successfully resolved, the faster the trauma dissipates.

The abandonment of a parent, either physically or perceived, is a whole other ball of wax. One far more difficult to find and extricate.

An offspring who cannot get over the loss of a parent is more than likely confusing perceived abandonment with physical loss.

Surt

Ironically, the peace of Basel was anything but for the Trappists of Mariawald Abbey. The left bank of the Rhine now occupied by the revolutionary *Sans Culottes* of 1795.

It didn't take long for Maximilien Rosepierre's thugs to expel the monks and shutter the priory. Some of the monks fled to Lower Austria and took refuge in the Cistercian "*of the Common Observance*" abbeys of Heiligenkreuz and Engelhartszell, others fled as far north as Alstadhaug, on the eastern shores of Trondheim's Fjord.

Laurentius de Place was the first of Mariawald's exiles to reach Alstadhaug Grange. At 20 years of age, Laurentius was also the youngest of the Trappist monks to be exiled from *Maria's Wood.* The Trappist monks of Mariawald had given him the nickname Brother Chanticleer to honor his affinity in raising *der gallische Hahn,* the French cockerel, during his relatively short stint at the foot of Eifel's Mount Kermeter.

How Brother Chanticleer ended-up glancing in the eyes of the Blessed Virgin's famous image would take up the pages of an entire novel. A challenge I have just endeavored to contemplate. Suffice to say, Brother Chanticleer's adventures that brought him inside the walls of Mariawald Abbey were a significant inspiration for Gofer finding himself inside the walls of Montreal's Grand Seminary.

♖✢♜

Fritz had issues.

Boy, did Fritz have issues.

He was 18 when he first visited Horten, Norway; a ~~Hare-~~hop, skip and a jump from the town of Notodden, the latter on the east side of Norway's Øst-Telemark District. Though he was still 38 years away from acquiring the throne, Frtz's father made it clear to his son, one must first explore his horizons if he wishes to expand them.

His first adventurous explorations were militaristic in nature. Again, a preference imposed on Fritz by his father's will rather than his own. Fritz's own decision to take on a *Sabbatjahr* once he had reached judicial adulthood was only grudgingly accepted by his father. A sabbatical that would extend well beyond two years in length. An extension that was mainly due to Fritz's second decision to attend the University of Bonn.

A reeducation that would transform his parentally imposed conservatism into an academically imposed liberalism.

Though the centuries' trends come to pass, some seem to always stay the same.

It was Midsummer, in the year of his Lord 1849, when he caught the eye of Jon's grandmother. Her name was Alice; an uncommon name for a Norwegian commoner. They were celebrating at the foot of a huge bonfire, a kilometer north of Horten's town square.

The bonfire had long replaced the traditional Norse Blot; a consequence of centuries of Christian conquest. Ironically, or not, the priest of the Heddal stave church was also in attendance that night, making sure nothing got out of hand.

Alice gave birth to Jon's father on June 5th, 1850. Fritz ~~wouldn't~~ couldn't marry Alice due to his future Royal obligations. A Norwegian commoner wouldn't do.

They named him Victor.

♂✝♀

One may question the plausibility of raising an orphaned child by exiled Trappists, ecclesiastic refugees of the Protestant Reformation and *La Grande Terreur.* And one's doubt would be an astute assumption.

Alas, Victor, like many of the other orphans presented to you up to this point, was no ordinary bastard.

Granted, using Trappist sign language to scold the only prepubescent boy inside the walls of this Norwegian grange would be a challenging endeavor for these monks of the Strict Observance. An endeavor which resulted in more than an occasional opportunity for guffaws and delayed laughter.

Alas, for the Trappists, laughter is evil and banned. At least, it's *supposed* to be. As French and Austrian exiles masquerading as Lutheran lay brothers, they were, at times, tempted to lift such restrictions in order to meld into their new surroundings, at others, they were forced to in order to be understood by their Norwegian masters.

Luckily for Victor, he was officially raised as a Lutheran parishioner with the help of a voluntary exile from Norwich, Norfolk. A Lutheran nun, brought up from the motherland by the Church of England to serve at the Alstadhung Church. In the shadows of the latter, she took up residence in the Alstadhung Grange with Victor and the exiled Trappists.

Her maiden name was Hélène de Chemillé, the consequence of a similar consummation as that of her newly adoptive son.

Che sarà, sarà.

At least Victor, would be fluent in Norwegian, French, English German, and Hungarian by the time he reached his sixth birthday.

♖✝♜

At 92 years of age, it had been two generations since Brother Chanticleer had undertaken the path to becoming a naturalized Scandinavian. The French cockerel wasn't the only entity Laurentius raised during his extended fortnight a stone's throw away from the Alvshaugen burial mound, the central attraction of Alstadhung's cemetery. He had become as much a grandfather as he was a father figure to the now post-pubescent Victor.

Laurentius' past would haunt both of them, pushing Victor to escape the deafening silence of the Trappists' Realm. It was time for Victor to take on the Mennonite equivalent of an adolescent sabbatical: a series of lonesome adventures that would both shape his adulthood and his ørlög.

Having grown up amongst the Mennonite of Germany, Brother Chanticleer's eyes lit up with agreement as Victor confided to his adoptive father. In the tradition of Trappist sign language, the latter's only response was "*Luceat lux vestra*".

They both held back the urge to grin. That was all that needed to be expressed, as they sat in the silent splendor of Alstadhaug's 12th century church.

☨☼☩

He left on foot that night. With a past taken away from him on the spur of the moment, Victor was not one to worry too much about the future. His first stop was a visit to the ghosts of Alvshaugen. They asked him to return. He couldn't promise them the future, but he did promise he would try.

By daybreak, the Trappists had begun preparations for Laurentius' burial. Victor had reached Trondheim.

- I'm headed to Amsterdam and am willing to barter my fare in exchange for working on a ship in need of a deckhand.
- You're a bit of an indigo for a sailor.

- We have all been indigœs at one time in our lives. One has to cross more than one Asses' Bridge to garner wisdom.
- You are wiser than your years. Who have been your mentors?

- The ghosts of Alvshaugen. I am learning from the mistakes of their pasts.
- One could do worse. What chores have you tried your hand at?

- I have been raised by the lay brothers of Alstadhung Grange. Rare are the farm chores I have yet to have undertaken.
- The chores found on a farmstead are not those of a ship's bridge. Though granted, they are equally as toilsome. We will have to find you work inside to begin with. The cook on the S/S Surt got sick from the mushrooms he foraged on Tautra Island last week. Captain Luftschiff is looking for some extra chef's helpers as he recuperates from his toxic adventure.

- Captain "Airship"? *Suum cuique.*
- Airship is his newly appointed nickname. Ever since he returned from a trip to the Persian Gulf, he has been high as kite. We thought of calling him "Highliner", but that would have been a bit vulgar on our part.

- He's been into the milk of *Papaver.* Once possessed by *thy jonke,* always possessed by *thy jonke.*
- *Lacrimæ rerum.* How many languages do you speak?

- If you include Pig Latin, six.
- That will come in handy as a deckhand. Come with me. I will introduce you to the captain.

...

I'm not sure what it is with the Dutch. When cogitative, they tend to be more open minded than the median. Be it the ingenuity of the Mennonite, or more recently, the unusual acceptability of the gay *joie de vivre,* the Dutch have been historically artful in their ability to adapt.

Maybe it has something to do with having successfully built a nation on and under the swamps of Northern Europe.

Victor's short jaunt from Trondheim to Amsterdam on the S/S Surt, was extended half way around the globe and back. For Victor, a working detour that was predictably unexpected.

He returned to the Port of Amsterdam the same day; one year later. It was the late Summer of 1868. His pockets were filled with the currencies of several kingdoms and his mind with the perspectives, the memories, and the languages of those he learnt to speak with on his most recent adventure; bringing his spoken fluency to nine.

⚒⚓⚔

- Ever been to sea, William[21]?
- That's Victor, and yes. I have just returned from a year's work on the S/S Surt.

21 At least he refrained from calling him Billy.

First and second rules of hunting for a john inside the walls of Amsterdam's most infamous gentlemen only sailor's bar: never correct your potential client, especially by giving your given first name.

Third rule of hunting for a john inside the walls of Amsterdam's most infamous gentlemen only sailor's bar: if you are an actual sailor, and only moonlighting as a potential trick, never mention the ship you are working on.

...

Victor's faux pas entered a process control loop whose hysteresis lasted well over a century: his ørlög affecting Mary-Lou's ~~mis~~fortunes from Tennessee to New Brunswick.

Mr Woolf defines fortune as "a hypothetical force or personified power that unpredictably determines events and issues favorably or unfavorably. From the Latin *fors* meaning chance or luck"[22]. With an an emphasis on the unpredictable, I couldn't of said it better myself. The future is unpredictable. It is our past that fleetingly influences our present.

Victor's first unconsummated client was far more a v*ielle sacoche* than Ted was when the latter first *laid* eyes on Mary-Lou. Pardon the pun.

Unfortunately for both tricks, their respective johns had one thing in common. They were both counsel to their respective monarch's court.

Victor's indiscretion had an immediate effect on the counsel's discretion. The *vielle sacoche* of high standing wasn't going to risk his reputation and possibly his job just because an indigo wasn't able to keep his mouth shut at the appropriate time, no matter how handsome the latter was. Even a lawyer can think with his *head* rather than his crotch when need be. Ok, I take that back. Lawyers always think with their crotch. It's just that they sometimes favor their survival instinct over their desire for instant gratification.

Verbum sat sapienti est. It was for Victor, regardless if it came from the mouth of an old purse. Learning discretion from the Trappists offered no room for modulation. Their is a time for silence, and a time to be heard. To find a balance between the two, Victor would rely on trial and error, and the past adventures belonging to the ghosts of Alvshaugen.

---

22 Woolf, Henry Bosley, Webster's New Collegiate Dictionary, eighth edition, 1981, page 449.

He may have spent a year traveling the seas, Victor had yet to cross the bridge of his own adulthood. And what better companions to guide him to the exiting bridgehead of such a crossing? Why, a pair of asses of course.

His first course of business, after advising Captain Luftschiff that he wouldn't be accompanying him back to Trondheim on the S/S Surt, was to head for the city of Hoofddorp. If he couldn't find a reputable ass breeder from a town with a name like that, one would be out of luck.

With less than twenty kilometers to cover as Hugin flies, Victor didn't hesitate to make the short trek by foot. He tidied up his cabin one last time, and gathered his worldly belongings into a well worn French Navy duffel bag he purchased earlier that day at the Amsterdam Armeeüberschuss.

- Captain Luftschiff, may I take a moment of your time?
- Hm. Yes, Victor. Come in, and take a seat.

- I want to thank you for the adventurous employ you have offered me on your ship. As I explained to you last year, it is time for me to continue on my travels.
- You left Amsterdam a child and returned a young man. Pretty good for a year's work.

- An asses' bridge I have much appreciated to cross in your company and that of your crew.
- Our crew, Victor. If ever you need, or desire, to take to the seas again, you are more than welcome to return to the deck of the S/S Surt. As I could sense you are a man of your word, I reserved a case of your favorite fermented molasses, in anticipation of this discussion. We will be in port for another two days, this will give our crew and I time to recuperate from the celebration of your hopefully temporary departure.

- Will you be searching for a new deckhand, Captain?
- A worry I will address once the S/S Surt reaches Trondheim. I better get to the kitchen, and advise the cook to prepare your favorite dish.

- Mm. Roast pork with chanterelles and fried apples.
- And mead from Abdij Maria-Tœvlucht.

- Fantastic! I will finish my afternoon chores, now. It will take my mind off my grumbling stomach.
- Be at the mess hall by six.

- Yes, Captain.

The celebrations lasted well into the night. The ship's crew began to head back to their cabins only an hour before daybreak. Victor was the last to return. As he entered his cabin, he made a last sweep of his surroundings; making sure not to forget any of his personal belongings.

The coast was clear. Without closing shut the door behind him, Victor headed to the bows deck. Having reached the bows head, he placed a snog on the latter. An unusual but appropriate gesture of thanks to the ship's spirit, for having given him the privilege of a safe adventure.

During days of r&r, Captain Luftschiff made a point of leaving the gangplank extended throughout the night. A gesture that was one of personal interest, rather than one of acknowledgment for each of the crew member's sense of self discipline.

Like clockwork, Victor waited. Once the captain had disembarked, and was out of sight, Victor did the same: Victor headed for Hoofddorp; the captain headed for Amsterdam's ghettos of disrepute.

⚒⚔⚓

Victor purposefully chose the road less traveled. One who had the most farmsteads fronting its borders. A wise choice on his part, as he was walking higgledy-piggledy: at times near the ditch; at others, near the center of the road. At least he was headed in the right direction.

By sunrise, the fog had dissipated. Figuratively and literally.

Fifteen years had passed since Haarlemmermeer became a polder. Under the auspices of William I[23], the lake's waterwolf was pushed back to make way for the village of Kruisdorp. By the time Victor had undertaken to visit this newly recommissioned peat bog, it had been freshly renamed Hoofddorp.

23 The Dutch monarch, not the Prussian one,

The farmsteads were impeccably maintained. Sort of like the Swiss countryside without the mountains. Some were discreet in their purpose and intent. Others had posted signs near their entrance welcoming passersby, and advising them of the produce on offer.

As *hamingja*[24] would have it, Victor was but five kilometers from the limits of Hoofddorp before he finally found what he was looking for. The deep blue engravings carved into the maple wood sign read, "Manes von Passau, Eselezüchter". With the number of mules, donkeys, and asses grazing and platonically frolicking on Herr von Passau's estate, the sign was rendered virtually redundant, though a welcoming addition nonetheless.

- Be careful, if you give him snogs on the nose like that, he'll fall in love with you.
- Eiee-aahh.

- Too late.
- I'm sorry. He's just monstrously adorable.

- I hope so. His name is Kampos.
- Why didn't you just call him Hippocampe? Granted, he's not a horse, but he is even less of a monster.

- It was my first intent. Alas, I am friends with the owner of an infamous Roman-styled bathhouse in Amsterdam. He asked me to refrain from using his establishment's namesake, when naming my asses. I obliged.
- Is Kampos a good swimmer?

- Rhetorical question.
- You must be Herr von Passau, I presume.

- Yes. And pardon my indiscretion. I should have introduced myself earlier.
- We are partners in crime. My name is Victor. I am traveling on foot, and am looking for a four-legged companion to help me along the way.

- I believe you just found him, Victor.
- I believe you are right. What do I owe you for the service?

---

24 *Hamingja* is an Old Norse expression often referred to as a form of '*luck*'. It is also referred to as an expression of a shape-shifting force.

- Not now. Let's get Kampos properly fitted with a comfortable harness and loin bags for the contents of the one you brought with you.
- You read my mind.

- It won't be the first time.

As Manes, Victor, and Kampos headed for the saddlery, Venery, a bodacious brown mare, strutted up to Manes' left side. Once Kampos was fitted and Victor's belongings were transferred to the latter, Manes did the same to Venery, including his own belongings.

With neither man saying a word, the foursome headed for the farmstead's entrance. Once all four had crossed the latter's culvert, the farmstead, its structures including the culvert, and all its remaining occupants disappeared.

- Are all three of you ghosts?
- Yes. However, as you can observe, we each have a very well developed *hamr.*[25]

- More so than the ghosts of Alvshaugen.
- Time is an excellent mentor. Gunnar will soon join us on our travels. He is not ready yet.

- You are Giuki, king of the Goths.
- Please refrain from using my real name, at least while we are in the presence of the living.

- *Discretion oblige.*
- You are learning, Victor.

♘ ♋ ♞

It took the sextet[26] as much time to cross the Netherlands and Germany as it took Victor to travel half way around the globe and back on the S/S Surt. Granted, there were stops along the way. They reached what was left of the Engelszell Grange, a week to the night before the Autumn equinox.

---

25 *Hamr* is an Old Norse expression, loosely translated as "aura". Using one's *hugr, one's* will, and with the help of one's *hamingja,* one's physical form takes shape.

26 Gunnar named his companion ass, Hapy.

The Engelszell Grange had been abandoned for the second time, eleven years prior. The first exodus was forced upon its occupants by the Holy Roman Emperor, Joseph II, 83 years prior. A consequence of the Emperor's dissolution of Engelszell Abbey.

The farmhouse and its accompanying buildings were none the worst for wear, mainly due to the generally accepted belief that the grange was haunted, following its most recent abandonment.

After a thorough sweep of the farmstead and its immediate surroundings by Victor and his ephemeral companions, the only ghosts that could be found were the latter.

- According to the local legend, I can see Giuki playing the murdered father, but his equally murdered wife, headless six year old son and three gruesomely slaughtered domesticated boars will be more of a challenge.

Victor barely had finished his sentence, when Gunnar had transformed into a convincing four foot high farm boy, holding his severed head in his left arm, and the three asses into equally convincing twelve hundred pound boars with their giblets and other bloodied parts hanging from their very aggressively active carcasses.

- Hm. Impressive. Now what about the wife?

Victor barely had finished his sentence, when Giuki transformed into a more than convincing fifty-something farm wife complete with a severely blood soaked Mennonite styled farmer's dress.

- And look Mommy, I can still speak!
- Why of course sonny boy, you can't go gallivanting around this haunted house carrying your severed head, if it's not a fully functioning specimen.

Giuki barely had finished his sentence, when Gunnar had transformed into the spitting image of Giuki's interpretation of the murdered father.

- Well that covers most of the plausible situations.
- The wonders of *Hamingja*, Victor.

- I heartily concur, Giuki.

As Victor spoke, Giuki ripped out his beating heart from his knife torn work dress.

- Oh. ik. Put that back.
- Eiee-aahh!, Eiee-aahh!

The Legend of the headless Engelhartszell farm boy has less to do with what took place than where it took place. The last Easter Sunday celebrations of the 17th century were memorable ones for the abbot and parishioners of the original Engelszell Abbey Church. Celebrations that got slightly out of hand.

Once the dust settled, and the smoldering embers had begun to cool, there wasn't much left of Engelhartszell's official home of Christian worship.

It would take several decades for a new church to be built. The abbey's hypogeum, dating back to the Roman era was virtually abandoned, and fell into a state of disrepair. The hypogeum was built on a large acreage just outside the limits of the village, a millennium prior to laying the foundations of the original Abbey church.

To help rebuild the abbey's finances following the devastating fire, a monastic grange was built atop the exposed ruins of the hypogeum. Fortunately for the venerated who were encrypted underground in the cavernous maze of burial chambers, the latter were kept relatively intact. Though they were unable to avoid the collapse of their own empire, the Romans knew how to build a few lasting structures when need be.

Mole ruit sua..

Several of the chambers had yet to receive the dead when the grange was built, and were left unoccupied. That was until our sextet of adventurous entrepreneurs took possession of the abandoned farmstead.

They named their new establishment, "Kampos, Venery and Hapy's Hypogeum", or KVH^2 for short. The opening celebrations were on the night before the Summer solstice of 1870. Though the celebrations definitely got out of hand, they were nowhere near as disastrous as those of Easter Sunday, 1699. Quite the contrary.

It was precisely those opening celebrations that sealed KVH^2's reputation. Word spread like wild fire. Pardon the pun. They came from as far west as Amsterdam and as far east as Vienna, bringing with them new explorers and the celebratory fervor of their past adventures inside walls of the hypogeum's maze.

The only other form of publicity, apart from word of mouth, was a matchbox[27] offered to the patrons: a seahorse engraved on its top face, and KVH^2 on its bottom side. Pardon the pun.

☭☠☩

It took four years, but Victor kept his promise. With his share of the fortune made from KVH^2, he headed back to Alstadhung Grange. Giuki did the same, though he hadn't made any oaths to the ghosts of Alvshaugen. He didn't need to. Those that remained behind knew he would return.

Giuki's journey was as much for Victor's benefit as it was for his son's. Victor had completed his own journey into manhood. Ironically, Gunnar's would take a bit more time and few more travels: a journey abruptly ended by his untimely death.

Victor celebrated May Day with his adoptive family, the living. The night prior, he celebrated the eve of May Day with his adoptive family, the dead. Laurentius was present in spirit, both figuratively and literally: his lifeless body having been buried a stone's throw away from the burial mound.

It was during these nocturnal festivities that the spirit of Laurentius would divulge the true family tree of his adoptive son. Four years of building and managing KVH^2 was more than enough proof that Victor was now capable of keeping a secret.

As June began, Victor officially acknowledged his manhood. It was time for him to place distance between himself and his adoptive families. He knew he would need their guidance, at least until the end of his own life.

He settled on Horten: a village to the south of Oslo. In the company of Kampos, it would take a day to reach the capital. Less so if they would take the ferry. It would take a fortnight to reach Alstadhung.

Far enough for Victor to breath. Close enough for them to visit on occasion.

---

27 With thanks to Robert Lepage, for his cinematographic ~~in~~discretion.

...

The secret Laurentius confided to Victor only gave a glimpse into the childhood the latter never had. If Victor wanted to experience such a childhood, it was up to him to create the experience for himself. A childhood built upon the memories of his father's past. One recalled by the ghosts of Alvshaugen and in the history books of academia.

Victor killed two birds[28] with one stone. He reported to Horten's Krigsskolen. It was there that Victor met Frigga: Victor studying to be a military engineer; Frigga a military nurse.

He made a point not to offer his seed until Winter Finding. They married on the third day of Yule, avoiding the obvious. Frigga broke her water on the graduation podium as she received her degree from the academy's headmaster.

Jon was born on June 5th, 1875. They would have 8 more before the start of the war to end all wars.

☚☼☛

Victor's twin brother was sent to a Lutheran orphanage in Braunau am Inn, Austria. He was the first out of his mother's womb. Of course it's his mother's womb: it's the late spring of 1850. Artificial insemination hadn't begun until 1884.

They named him Leopold.

Leopold was not cognitively preoccupied by the urge to follow in his father's footsteps. He did not have the opportunity to be raised in the shadows of Alstadhung Church's cemetery. He would have to rely on his atrophied instincts to guide him in his journeys to the realm of his unknown family's past.

By the time he was thirteen, that atrophied instinct began gnawing at his active cogitation. Like a snowbound cottager overwhelmed by an extended bout of cabin fever, it was time to escape the restrictive confines of the orphanage.

He scurried away well before the first snow had fallen on Braunau. That gnawing instinct pushing him towards Vienna. Why did Leopold chose the national capital to find work? For the same, oldest of reasons John Thébeau would choose the old capital of the Dominion, over a century later.

---

28 Any species other than the *Corvus.*

A decade of applying his chosen trade had given Leopold numerous[29] connections inside the governmental bureaucracy of the nation's capital. It was time for him to head back to Baunau to prove to the villagers who remained, that he was more than an orphaned bastard. It was not long before Leopold became one of the top bureaucrats inside the county's civil service.

The local population would christen him Leopold, the Servant.

Synchronously, on the outskirts Engelhartszell, Victor and his consorts decide to expand their burgeoning corporate empire. They begin construction of a new resort chalet just across the border in the Swiss Alps, nestled in the valley of the centuries old village of Saas Fee.

A further decade had passed, and Leopold had yet to marry. Freya hadn't either. She had begun her career at the same time, in the same building, and through similar connections as those of Leopold.

The villager's quiet gossip had begun to surface. To quell the rumors, Leopold and Freya began dating. They made a point of being seen and heard in all the appropriate establishments of the village.

Though, or rather because they were meant for each other, their relationship was a platonic one to say the least. By the Autumn of 1887, the rumors had begun to surface. Again.

By the Spring of 1888, they had finished sending out their wedding invitations. On April 21st of the following year, their first son was born. Of note, the priest that christened the new infant made an error on the newborn's birth certificate, replacing the "ü' of his truncated family name with an "i".

Together, the couple rose up along the rungs of the nation's bureaucratic ladder. On occasion, their work forced them to transfer to the neighboring centers of administration along the valley of the Inn. Their son would tag along.

29 Numerous being an understatement.

By the time Leopold had reached the age of 56, he and his wife chose to receive an early pension. The Engelszell Grange was for sale; at a bargain basement price.

Leopold would follow in his brother's footsteps, rather than his father's.

The former owners remained on the premises. In ephemeral body and spirit, they would guide the new owners in the management of the Hypogeum below.

☽☼☾

Militaristically speaking, Jon followed in his father's footsteps. He graduated from the same military academy as his elder; however, at the age of 19, Jon earned his commission as lieutenant a little earlier than Victor. That same year, the latter's eldest son entered the University of Berlin.

As the 19th century came to a close, he graduated as a mechanical engineer.

The construction of the hydrœlectric station on the nearby Tinnfoss waterfall having just been completed, there was no longer much work on offer for a recently graduated engineer from Horten.

After a year of fruitlessly searching for work in and around his hometown, Jon decided to take the plunge. He landed on the eastern shore of Ellis Island just before the hurricane season of 1901 had begun.

His first gig lasted half a decade. The Cleveland-based company offered him work on engineering projects in the Dominion's Northern Ontarian boreal forest. It is there that he met the Cree for the first time. They christened him Hare-Hop, for his abilities to negotiate the dense forests of Rupert's Land, faster and with more ease on his Norwegian cross-country skis than the Cree could on their Amerindian bear-gut snowshœs.

It didn't take Hare-Hop very long to begin a new adventure as a professional engineer once his first had come to an end. He figured he was now ready to begin "swimming with the sharks", both literally and figuratively speaking. Rather than applying for a job, he created one for himself, becoming an independent heavy equipment sales agent for a manufacturer with contacts in Cuba and Panama.

It's the quiet ones that tend to be the best under the sheets. Hare-Hop was no exception. Regardless of, or maybe because it was his first attempt at crawling under the linen with a female companion, Hare-Hop was able to take full advantage of his subdued demeanor.

So did Maria.

She would raise her daughter in a loft above the Havana café-bar, where she worked as a hostess. The building and the "establishment" below were owned by her father. At least she thought it was her father. The latter would serve as both a grandfather and surrogate father to the newborn bitch.

They named her Madeleine.

Like most mobster-thugs from Havana, Maria's father prospered during and following the Spanish-America war.

So did Jon.

Though granted, he was neither a mobster, nor a thug. The only link he would have to the mob would be in the form of a business loan from the Vatican Bank.

Why did Jon choose the Vatican Bank for a business loan? You will have to ask Gofer.

Like most mobster-thugs from Havana, Maria's father would become an influential member on both sides of the political establishment, decades before the yet to burgeon revolution. Even in 1907, his bar was a hotbed of Marxist-Leninist propaganda and logistical planning.

Back in Cleveland, where he was attending a heavy equipment training seminar, Hare-Hop was refining his subdued demeanor. What else are you going to do in Cleveland, on your spare time in 1907, in between two sessions of a heavy equipment training seminar?

It is their that he met Alice, the daughter of a wealthy Cleveland judge. They married at the Cleveland courthouse, Alice's father presiding over the ceremonies. She would have her first child in Havana.

♁♡♂

Having cut his teeth swimming with the sharks off the Caribbean Coast, it was time for Jon to swim with the sharks off the Jersey Shore.

By the Spring of 1928, the sharks had begun gnawing at his quiet demeanor. It was time to move himself and his family to the more placid waters of the Saint-Laurence River. The future looked bright. His only debt was with the Holy Vatican Pope.

Alas, the only certainty in the future is uncertainty.

His business foundered under the weight of the Great Depression.

Once more, Jon moved to the even quieter waters of the North River. There, Hare-Hop would introduce the Laurentian tourists to the benefits of Nordic skiing.

He would would have to wait till after Victor's passing before he could pay his debt to Eugenio, aka Pius XII.

Victor passed away on the eve of his centennial birthday. Jon inherited his father's Saas Fee Resort.

He would meet Gofer for the first time at the reception of Louis' wedding. Hare-Hop couldn't have chosen a more appropriate buyer than Gofer. Even if he had tried.

¿☠☣⚗?

It was during the Autumn of that same year, when Big Bertha Bifett entered the Grand Séminaire de Montréal. Big Bertha has more than a passing resemblance to Antoine's physical presence and social demeanor.

$♋♱

Five years had passed since my father had been silenced. It was the year of Hare-Hop's centennial birthday. As part of his celebrations, Jon was invited to meet the students of Chanticleer Elementary School.

As the principal introduced me to him, an aura of dread and disdain enveloped Jon's body, as well as his spirit. The aging man sat silent, as I stood speechless.

It took me two generations and the crossing of several asses' bridges to begin to understand the significance of that most enlightening moment.

A silent past is often far more telling than the one that has been spoken.

⚠☊☠

My first job as a freshly graduated mechanical engineer was in the Autumn of 1990, two generations after Big Bertha had started his own undergraduate studies. I worked for a large sports equipment manufacturer. I was still healing from my two-wheeled encounter with a lite blue 1987 Ford Ranger pickup truck.

It is there that I first encountered the underside of the hockey industry. I have never been a hockey player. Like my father before me, I was a skier. I went to a semi professional hockey game for the first time, thanks to an invitation by a longtime employee of the company.

It was hard to tell who were the most aggressively brutal of bullies: those on the ice, or those surrounding me in attendance.

By the spring, I was headed towards Europe on my first ski trip to the Swiss Alps. I stayed at a resort chalet, nestled in the valley of Saas Fee.

☀

Ishuma!

And what an intelligent idea it was. If Uli said so himself.

The construction, architectural, and artistic endeavors the Wulfila twins had undertaken in the last five decades resulted in a combined fortune for the two confirmed sexagenarian and confirmed bachelors.

The last of such endeavors were the preliminary design consultations commissioned by the main architect of Habitat 67' nearly a decade before its completion, coinciding with the start of Montreal's first universal exposition: Tom offering his expertise and experience in the construction of reinforced concrete structures; Uli offering his interior design expertise following the completion of a half century's worth of art deco projects.

They were both yearning to escape the unrelenting Laurentian winters for more temperate climes during the few retirement years they had left to contemplate.

They were trying to decide what to do with the virtually antique concrete casings they had preserved in the basement of their Thomson Heights abode when it dawned on him.

- Belize. It's a British colony. In Honduras if I'm not mistaken.
- We have both long become British subjects of the Dominion.

- We could build our own Tom and Uli.
- And our own tea room.

- And luxury restaurant.
- And luxury hotel.

- Art Deco architecture.
- Of course. And sculpted concrete walls for the interior walls of the discotheque.

- Now you're talking.
- Let's get started. Before all our active years are behind us.

☆♋☆

It was the last winter of the 20th century, when John Thébeau, Morris, the Butcher, and Patrick, the Unreliable would engage in a discreetly rousing threesome at the Place d'Youville Sauna: a latent homosexual bachelor's party, on the eve of the Unreliable's Kopfschmuck sanctified wedding.

Just for old time's sake.

Interestingly enough, that threesome became a foursome, when the ghost of Premier Bou-Bou joined the former hockey player and his brutal sidekicks at an equally infamous gentlemen-only sauna, just outside the limits of Youville Square.

Just for old time's sake.

☆♘♂♂♜★

I always wanted to be a garbage man: good exercise, good pay and a never ending scavenger hunt. One ogre's trash is an others treasure.

"You are listening to Blüteberg News 1310. And now from our London bureau here is Marc Barstone with 'Morning. Morning. Europe.'

- Morning, Marc.
- Morning, Ted. The top business story for this Wednesday April 15th, 2015 comes to us from Helsinki. Finland's largest network equipment company, Uli Telephony, just got a little bigger today. Uli has just purchased SNTSC[30] of France in a stock-swap valued at 15.6 Billion Euros. This is a 28% premium over SNTSC shares. The CEO of Uli Telephony, Fritz Wulfila is quoted as saying that this is best for the shareholders of both companies, as Uli only has 5.8 Billion Euros presently on hand.

... And now to our San-Francisco desk for today's top global stories..."

...

Speaking of trash, the collapse of the first Internet bubble, resulting in the brutal consolidation of the global network equipment industry, was but a precursor to the collapse of the real estate industry, resulting in the official start of the Great Recession.

Alas, as the *Sans Culottes* would say, *"Jamais deux sans trois."*

If the past is any indication, the stratospheric rise of the social media industry is but a precursor to the rapid expansion of a second Internet bubble.

How will things play out?

Not even the Giants know.

30 Société Nationale de Téléphonie Sans Culottes.

- CRACK!, PET!!, KABOOM!!!,KABOOM!!!, KABOOM!!!, KABOOM!!!, KABOOM!!!, KABOOM!!!

"You are listening to the Central Broadcasting Cooperative at 106.9 FM and on your smart-phone at 1069cbcftqsq.com. At the sound of the tone, following ten seconds of silence it will be precisely one o'clock, Saturday, July 16th, 2016. Blip, blip, blip, blip, blip, blip, blip, blip, blip, beeeeeeeeeeep...

... A major "biker" pileup was witnessed last night, just outside Legrand, New Brunswick, east of Edmunston.

One death, eight injured as a pickup truck pulling a fifth wheel was turning left into the Legrand Camping Ground. The lead "biker", Ted Rogers, newly minted Full Patch member of the Kopfschmucks, died on impact as he attempted to pass the pickup truck, the other "bikers" closely following suit, causing the pileup. Amongst the injured were one woman and eight members of the Burgandy Bangers, a "biker" school gang controlled by the Kopfschmucks..."

...

- First rule of "making it look like an accident": choose a plausible scenario.
- Second rule of "making it look like an accident": if the hit-man is inevitably identified, make sure he has no known ties to the accident's instigator.

☽☀☾

It was amateur night at the Stonewall Inn. The British Invasion had yet to begin. The participants and their audience had yet to be concerned.

Mario Gattiloni Sr had invited Frank Bedalini Sr for some ~~cross-dressing~~ cross-border trade and a bit of latent homosexual entertainment.

Peter was attending the same high school as Mario Jr.: a middle school of dubious, if not yet infamous reputation. Frank Sr was impressed: not necessarily by his singing abilities, although they were more than adequate. It was Peter's stage presence that caught his eye.

Frank Sr spent the night at the Inn.

So did Peter.

By morning, Peter had his first recording contract.

Less than a week after his graduation ceremony, Peter moved to Jérômeville. His family tagged along.

In between musical gigs, Frank Sr got Peter a job at the local radio station.

Peter would be the original member. Frank Sr would soon add Ginette and Jean-Pierre to his burgeoning rat pack. Mario Sr's already included Sammy, Dino and Frank.

♫♋♪

Peter first met Louis at Tom and Uli's: the underground bar on Stanley Street, not the two bedroom flat on the corner of Montcalm and Dorchester. Louis spent the night at Tom and Uli's: the flat, not the bar.

So did Peter.

Though Louis was twice Peter's age and a family man, Anna-Maria understood her husband needed a boys' night out, on occasion.

Those boys' nights out became boys' days out when Louis began inviting Peter on hunting trips in the mountains outside Upper Chanticleer. Anna-Maria had long since cease to tag along. The idea of shooting a moose, a deer, or heaven's forbid, a bear, once she had observed them alive in the wild, was now out of the question.

It was definitely not out of the question for Frank Sr. However, he was never invited.

☻☼

Not all thugs are created equal. Some are more sub-par than others. You already know about Frank Jr. For the Riceonos, it was Antonio Jr.

As Jr sat silent inside a Trappist monastery, the path was being cleared. The Bedalinis' journey would soon come to an end. The Riceonos' had already begun.

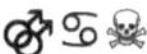

Birds of feather flock together.

Antonio Jr's social and sexual disorders mirrored those of the near totality of criminal biker gang members of his era.

It was the start of the 1980s, when Antonio Jr was ordered by the high ranking patriarchs back in Sicily to perform some out of town street cleaning on New-York's Lower East Side.

And it was towards those same biker gangs that Antonio gravitated towards when he returned to Montreal, and began sub-contracting enforcer duties inherited from the Bedalini family.

Louis definitely had enemies.

Be it a man, a tribe or a nation, empires come and go. The legacy of one's past is best measured, not by what remains, but rather by what has been erased.

Today, Upper Chanticleer is but a ghost of its former self.

Le Petit Train du Nord replaced by a multiple lane highway, more at home on the borders of metropolitan Toronto rather than splicing its way through the valleys of a world class tourist destination. The fine restaurants replaced with strip-mall burger joints and fresh-frozen-from-the-factory doughnut shops. The notch and scribed Scandinavian log structures and traditional French-Canadian styled rural wood frame homes replaced with concrete and fresh-from-the factory vinyl-clad pre-constructed monstrosities. The alpine and cross-country ski trails replaced with overzealous real estate development cul-de-sacs.

From one end to the other, the street that I grew up on defined my father's legacy: from his ski shop at the southern end, one of the very first specialty stores of its kind in North America; to the home at its center, where he raised six children, and to its northern end where one of the first alpine ski hills on the continent was built and preserved by the efforts of Louis B. de Ville-Amois and Charles Bronfberg, that street was a microcosm of Upper Chanticleer's history.

When Upper Chanticleer was forced to merge with a neighboring community, the street's name became redundant; replaced by that of friend of my father's, who had nothing to do with the immediate vicinity's heritage. The ski hill's infrastructure was demolished, and the property transformed into a useless city park, going against its vocation defined in the legal documents of the foundation set up to preserve the property's original mission.

Empires come and go. Chanterelles are timeless.

Open or closed,
Process is a loop.
One that gœs
Around and
Around.

Open or closed,
Process is a cycle.
One that starts
Where it first began.
A circle.

Open or closed,
Process is Procedure.
One that modulates
From the outside in.
A sphere.

Open or closed,
Process is Structure.
One that rotates
On an Axis.
A Planet.

Open or closed,
Process is Logistics.
One that spins
On another Axis.
An Empire.

Summer begins. Both sides won.

The mist blocking out the sun. The summer's heat not coming from the latter, but rather from the former. The mist's embrace trapping the heat of the hardships of war, social decay and civil unrest.

Time returns: the New freed from the shackles of the Old. Food for fodder, wolves and bears, lest we forget the tree monkeys.

All three at the top of the food chain: one that binds them to Greed, Sex and the Fundamentalism of survival. Motivations they now modulate with the help of Common Sense and Sacrifice.

They know: better to inhabit the forest. Their ørlög can be seen on the horizon of its edges. Its structure taking shape. A reminder to place Symbiosis over Confrontation, Evolution over Innovation and Cogitation over Faith.

Their observations permit them to acknowledge the reality of the past. Giving direction to the present. The uncertainty of the future maintained.

The Ravens guide them.

www.ingramcontent.com/pod-product-compliance
Lightning Source LLC
LaVergne TN
LVHW020526100826
845148LV00010B/1351

* 9 7 8 1 7 7 5 1 6 0 2 2 9 *